THE BLACK ROOM MANUSCRIPTS

VOLUME TWO

Further reading by the Sinister Horror Company:

THE BLACK ROOM MANUSCRIPTS VOL 1 – Various

CLASS THREE – Duncan P. Bradshaw
CLASS FOUR: THOSE WHO SURVIVE – Duncan P.
Bradshaw
CELEBRITY CULTURE – Duncan P. Bradshaw
PRIME DIRECTIVE – Duncan P. Bradshaw

BURNING HOUSE – Daniel Marc Chant
MALDICION – Daniel Marc Chant
MR. ROBESPIERRE – Daniel Marc Chant
INTO FEAR! – Daniel Marc Chant
AIMEE BANCROFT & THE SINGULARITY STORM –
Daniel Marc Chant

BITEY BACHMAN – Kayleigh Marie Edwards

THE BAD GAME – Adam Millard

TERROR BYTE – J. R. Park
PUNCH – J.R Park
UPON WAKING – J. R. Park
MAD DOG – J. R. Park

GODBOMB! – Kit Power
BREAKING POINT – Kit Power

MARKED – Stuart Park

*Visit SinisterHorrorCompany.com for further information on these and
other titles.*

The Black Room Manuscripts
Volume Two

First Published in 2016

Compiled by JR Park, Duncan P Bradshaw & Daniel Marc Chant

Edited by JR Park

Published by The Sinister Horror Company

Cover design by Vincent Hunt
www.jesterdiablo.blogsport.co.uk
Twitter: @jesterdiablo

ISBN: 978-0-9935926-0-7

This book is dedicated to all the doctors, scientists, charity workers and carers (both professional and voluntary) who work tirelessly to help those with dementia.

CONTENTS

DISSECTING LUCIFER'S SCRIPTS
FOREWORD BY CHRIS HALL
(DLS REVIEWS)

"I do not love men: I love what devours them."
André Gide, Prometheus III-Bound

"The charm of horror only tempts the strong"
Jean Lorrain

When I was approached by Justin Park – one third of the three headed beast that is the Sinister Horror Company – to pen a foreword for the second Black Room Manuscripts anthology, I must admit to being pretty damn shocked that anyone would ask probably the most painfully verbose reviewer to ramble on about horror for a handful of pages.

I then became increasingly concerned that I would just spend the whole time ranting (however enthusiastically) about how much I absolutely adore the genre. And if I'm honest – that's pretty much what I've done. Anyone who's spent more than thirty-seconds in my company knows how passionate I am about the subject, and what's incredibly heart-warming to see is that I'm increasingly not alone in this. There's a hell of a lot of us out there – devouring the books, pouring over the films – constantly delving into the darker side of things. It's like a thirst that can never be sated. And I for one would never want it to be.

Although the horror genre is such a big part of many of our lives, what can still sometimes be a tad ambiguous is exactly "what is horror"? Indeed, it's a question that's often debated at length. In fact, some authors try to step away from adopting the tag - seeing such pigeon-holing as unnecessary, counter-productive and potentially audience restrictive. After all – surely the term 'horror' is simply an emotion, a human response, and not necessarily a definable genre per se. Nevertheless, I personally stand by the application of such tags. I firmly believe that identifying horror as a genre is still an important task - if not damn essential for the survival of these twisted tales.

Okay, so pigeon-holing something that's creative, subjective, and free to explore limitless realms, is in itself somewhat restraining. Why do it? Why label and (by that very token) group together all these diverse and wonderfully exploratory tales? I see there being a number of reasons. Firstly – to make our lives easier! After all, how many of us have limitless time at our disposal in which we can browse bookshops, read blurb after blurb, and hunt through piles of books – just to find something that meets our particular taste? Genre labelling helps narrow down the field somewhat. It's a necessity of modern convenience. You like tales with a bite? You like stories that plunder the dark depths and far-reaches of the human psyche? Then you head to that gloomy corner of the bookshop where things are known to get a little bit sinister.

However, more importantly (for me at least) it gives the authors, the readers, and the books a collective identity which over the years has become something akin to an adoptive family. You devour your very first horror novel as an inquisitive youngster, and if the experience left a mark upon you, if it made an impact and reached out to you unlike any previous stories had, then there's a good chance you've taken your first step towards something that will become as much a part of your life as will your eventual career, your nationality, or your taste in music.

To this end horror is more than just a preference in books and films. Horror's a family. But more than that, it shapes you, moulds you, and (potentially) even strengthens you. In these tales of the macabre you get to embrace those things that would otherwise terrorise you, and through this face your own personal fears. You get to experience the dark regions of our world (and beyond) and gaze in awe at the horrors that are (worryingly) possibly lurking out there.

But why is it that so many of us are drawn towards such a genre? What is it in us that makes us want to seek out these horrors time and time again? For me at least there isn't one straight forward all-encompassing answer. First and foremost it really depends upon the type of horror. Your emotional response to a story will undoubtedly vary considerably depending on the style of horror novel you're reading. Take for example a 70's or 80's pulp horror – possibly involving some heavily-mutated creature that's gone on the rampage, slaughtering hapless bystanders as it goes about its bone-chomping business. For such a wildly exaggerated story it's simply a case of sitting back and enjoying the outlandishly over-the-top antics on offer. It's just pure entertainment. It does exactly what the author wanted it to do. And so we can't help but keep coming back for more.

However, the same could not be said for a gritty serial killer story (or the like). Here you'd expect to have a very different emotional response to the story. You want to feel terrorised, unsafe and on edge - expelling those lingering demons through a fictional experience of such traumatic events. Because of this, the draw is there once again. You want to experience that thrill of terror again. The buzz of the scare gets you clawing back for more over and over again.

Then of course you have all those novels that fall somewhere in between. Splatterpunk and Body Horror are designed to make you squirm in your seat. Their purpose is to make you feel sickened and repulsed – but at the same time, plastering a huge grin across your face in absolute delight at such grotesquely visceral imagery. It's more a test of how much of a messed-up imagination the author has than anything else. The more vividly repugnant, the more offensive and daring, the more the readers will lap up these distasteful delights.

Yet horror is still so much more than just a cheap thrill or the safe confrontation of our fears. The genre is incredibly complex and varied. Admittedly some authors do aim for the easy pickings – the simple fun of grossing out the reader with the most disgusting and outrageous atrocities that their worrying mind can conjure up. But then there's those horror novels that tiptoe with a lighter touch. Where it's the subtleties and atmosphere that make the story work. There's often a glimmer of poetry in the darkness; where death and despair are given a chance to sing us their bittersweet lullaby.

For those who dismiss horror as being in some way a lesser genre – more fool them. Let's be honest, you'll always encounter closed-minded ignorance and foolish snobbery in every form of art. I'm sure there's a veritable theatre's worth of classically trained musicians who would look down on the likes of Death Metal with an air of self-righteous condescension. Likewise in the world of fine art, I'm sure that you'll often have pompous art critics, with their paintbrushes shoved up their rear ends, instantly dismissing intricately created street art – no matter how wonderfully imaginative and talented the graffiti artist may be.

Nevertheless, for those that choose to venture into the dark depths of this complex and massively varied genre, they'll find themselves in a land of endless possibilities, rich with raw emotion and desperate personal struggles. Let's face it – horror is such fertile ground for exposing the raw stuff that's inside all of us. What's more honest than to be scared, shocked, disgusted or indeed horrified? It's our base human emotions, brought to the surface and then ripped raw.

I said at the very beginning of this rambling foreword that more often than not, if someone likes horror, then it will probably grow to become a big part of their life. Across the length and breadth of the many online social media sites you'll see evidence of this on a daily basis. And it's true. Those who have a taste for horror will often become very passionate about the genre. The fans are unquestionably some of the most dedicated out there. I said it before and I'll say it again – it's like one big (usually quite happy) family.

Another thing I've observed with dedicated horror fans is that they've often got a number of different hobbies and passions going on in their lives. Indeed, I'm an avid whisky enthusiast (unfortunately not exactly the cheapest of hobbies). At first glance horror and whisky might appear worlds apart - but I see horror being like a good whisky. As already mentioned, it can come in many different styles. But first and foremost, to be a notably good horror story, like with a good whisky, it's got to have its own distinct character and it's got to have its own unique flavour that distinguishes itself from the pack. Of course it's then got to have depth, as well as a good level of complexities lingering in its body - knitting together interwoven layers to pull you into its own little world. Indeed, good whiskies can send you on a journey, where the world around you disappears and you find yourself getting sucked into its variety of notes and carefully nurtured flavours. This is exactly what a good horror novel does.

There's something about horror, whether it's in fiction or films, that's inherently entertaining. When the shit hits the fan, when things get grim and the blood starts to splatter the walls, you'll inevitably find yourself sitting forward in your chair and basking in the blood red glow of it all! It gets the heart rate pounding away at a million miles a second. There's that irrepressible grin that unconsciously creeps across your face – probably sending worrying doubts flooding across your partners mind as you sit there smirking away. Your fingers tighten on the pages and you might as well be sitting on a faraway planet for all the awareness you suddenly have for the world around you.

Through horror fiction, authors have explored countless beasts and badasses, ghouls and grim reapers, mutants and maniacs, demons and the damned. Horror has allowed minds to be let loose; to plunder the darkest regions of a writer's mind, unearthing atrocities and abominations for us to stare in awe at.

We can use the first volume of The Black Room Manuscripts as an example of the mindboggling diversity of this crazy-ass genre. In it we had afternoon tea at a maniac's slaughterhouse, mermaid whores, a voodoo-risen zombie seeking vengeance on the racist creeps that murdered him, a haunted old beat-up van which makes its new owner rape and kill, a troll that happily resides at the bottom of a well, and a dimension-jumping wooden cabinet (to name but a few). The anthology showcased some spectacularly varied offerings of weird and wonderfully creative fiction – and at the heart of these incredibly imaginative slabs of strangeness is that all-encompassing genre tag – 'horror'.

As I sit here, sipping a wee dram of a particularly fine whisky whilst I finish penning this foreword, one final declaration still lingers in my excited mind...

All hail the horror genre! And all hail those that bring us these dark delights!

Forever your eager and willing servant.

Chris Hall

DLS Reviews

PROLOGUE

Entrails stained the plush carpet crimson as they lay strewn across the floor, soaking into the luxury shag pile. Their grisly lines stretched between torn pieces of ravaged flesh like a nightmarish dot to dot.

As the forensic team catalogued the remains of the party revellers, Officer Ridsdale tried to guess at the broken limbs, entangled within the shredded fabric of cocktail dresses and tuxedos.

"How many are there?" she asked.

"Hard to say at the moment," came the muffled voice of her colleague through protective clothing. "We're taking a guess around seven."

The smell assaulted her nose as the putrid remains festered in their own decaying filth. Today was Tuesday, and according to the invite card they found in the hallway, the party had been Saturday. It had been three days before anyone had raised the alarm, the postman noticing the red splashes that dried on the windows of Horsfield Manor.

Leaving the scene of the massacre, Officer Ridsdale ascended the great staircase, careful not to touch the bannister as she followed droplets of blood to the first floor.

The curtains remained closed, and not wanting to contaminate the scene with her own fingerprints, she chose to leave them drawn, shining her torch to the end of the corridor in an attempt to see through the gloom. Following the sound of a faint noise she tracked its location with the beam, stopping at a door that stood ominously dark. Its black presence seem to writhe within its frame, forcing the officer to rub her eyes in disbelief.

The large door looked heavy and thick, a key sat in its lock and ragged marks ran across the grain, as if monstrous claws had been dragged along its surface.

Officer Ridsdale stepped towards the door, trying to get a better sense of the damage that had befallen it.

She froze as she felt moisture hit her cheek. Shining the torch above her, she made out words, scrawled in red across the ceiling and dripping down onto her hat.

Was that blood? If it was, why was it fresh?

"Pasher tagoth imra," the policewoman repeated as she read the meaningless syllables.

Hinges creaked as the door gently swung open, pushed half ajar by an unfelt wind, inviting Officer Ridsdale to enter...

THE DRAWERS
TIM CLAYTON

Child One

Strangled with pale, trembling hands. Light slowly fading from the eyes, then a pump of blood across the right iris flooding it with colour. Panic set in, followed by a terrible satisfaction.

Child Two

Bludgeoned. A blunt chisel. A dark night. More blood than I knew could possibly be contained in one so small.

Child Three

Strangled. I watched my hands. They were not so pale this time, working on adrenalin rather than fear.

Child four

Suffocated. Asphyxiated. Deprived of oxygen. Cut off

from the elixir of life.

Morning check

All children

Temperature minus twenty. Ice on child two's eyelashes, just the same as it has always been. Frozen tears or rain from that night.

No failure in the new power supply. Drawer five still empty. Remove the build-up of frost that stops the mechanism from sliding open easily. Ready.

Evening check

Child one

Blue eyes, face blanched of colour. Tiny hands crossed over his stomach like a child behaving well at morning assembly.

Child two

Brown eyes and hair that was once fair but is now matted with blood and is dark brown with hints of red.

Child three

No eyes, an expression so horrific I sometimes find it hard to comprehend.

Child four

A faint smile, wry or silently amused. Always silent. Even at the time we met, there was no pleading, no screaming. I had to ask a hundred times before she whispered her name to me. Elizabeth.

I leave, turning the cellar light on and off seven times after ascending the steel steps, careful to miss every second one.

Morning check

Child one

David. 14 years old. Wrong place at the wrong time. A smart-cracking kid who spoke out of turn to a stranger on a deserted canal path after he had lost his friends.

Child two

Michael. Age unknown and difficult to ascertain with the face as it is. A people pleaser who didn't just want to give a stranger directions but also wanted to show the way through the alleyways of the town.

Child three

Luke. 12 years old. A fat child. A slow, lazy over-eater who it was a pleasure to work on.

Child four

Elizabeth. 8 years old. A little angel. Pangs of remorse in a corn field on a sunny day that made her hair shine the colour of the crops.

Afternoon check

All drawers at normal temperature. The freezer buzzes and hums in a comforting way that assures me of permanence and that these treasures will never leave.

I leave, forgetting to miss every second step. Awake to the sound of scratching in the cellar below. Go down to investigate. The scratching stops as I punch in the electronic code to the outer door. I enter. All drawers secure and temperature stable. I leave, remembering to miss every second step and to switch the light on and off seven times. I cannot sleep though the scratching does not return. I give up on the thought of rest and set out into the night.

Morning check

Child one

There was a brief moment of resistance. A toughness in the child that was obvious from the moment he back-chatted me in the tow path. He swung and kicked. He almost got away and gave the game up on me before it all even began.

Child two

Far too trusting to know that anything was ever going to happen. A face of dumb innocence, raised in a world where everyone is good. The first blow took him out. He never even saw it coming and was dead before he knew it.

Child three

Too slow to run. Too clumsy and heavy to twist away from the adult hands full of mal-intent and the rope around the neck. A short panic but to no avail.

Child four

She took it with good grace, allowed me to cut off the air supply as if it was lifting her to heaven and she would let me do it a thousand times over if it meant so much to me.

Child five

I couldn't sleep last night.

I awake in the night. I imagine scratching in the cellar. I put my head down and try to sleep it off. Thoughts are always confused like this around the time of a kill. A day before and a few days after, my mind starts imagining things that are not there.

I wake again. Scratching and the small but significant sound of metal hitting the floor. I go downstairs. All drawers secure. Temperature stable. Power supply normal. I leave and return to bed.

Morning check

Children one to four
Blueish-white skin, something like shrunken ivory.

Child five
Blotches and patches form on the skin. Blooms of dark roses, wild and wildly beautiful. Freezer burn on delicate skin. If I study carefully, I can find every colour of the rainbow from the green of the eyes through to the deep violet of the frozen bruises around the neck. Yellow hair, indigo and blue fingertips. And then there are the extremes: the white of the freezer and the ice that is enveloping him, and the black of his little soul. I could tell from the moment I saw him sleeping that he had a dark and dangerous nature. I was doing a favour to the future when I met Matthew sleeping in a doorway at night, covered in rags and cardboard. That is his name, Matthew. I write it in the notebook and then maintain to forever after call this child full of colours and darkness nothing more than Number Five.

I turn to leave. As I walk towards the stairs, I step on something sharp that almost cuts through my loafer shoes and injures my foot. I bend down. A screw. A shiny, aluminium screw with a tip like a razor. My breathing quickens. I want to rip open all the drawers but I have just checked and there is no sense. All the children are in a slumber from which there is no waking, no movement and no cry for help. I calmly put the screw in my pocket and walk upstairs.

Afternoon check

Child one

Reported missing. I have the cuttings from the newspaper and hours and hours of recorded newsreel of willing local volunteers forming chains to search the fields and canal where he was last seen. They found his bike not far from where we met. It was a long time ago now. The case is cold.

Child two

A sweet tale. A freak of circumstance; a father with a history of violence which had remained hidden from all until a boy went missing. He claimed to have been away on business but then the story changed. Within a week he was arrested and the vagaries of a broken legal system now have him sitting in a maximum security cell block a hundred miles away.

Child three

I knew him well before I did what I did. I was there to comfort his mother and take care of the funeral with no body.

Child four

A national uproar. A girl so young and so perfect, left alone to meet an untold ending at the hands of an uncatchable monster. The months of tabloid speculation with editorials and columns. The police chief who resigned and the one that took over had a breakdown from the pressure. Still they never got close.

Child five

    I check the news. Nothing. Not a word. Some street kid who nobody cared about any more. It was a spur of the moment thing but I knew at the time that he would not be missed—not a single soul would even notice that the cardboard and rags in that doorway no longer had anybody to own them.

I awake at night. The sound of scratching is more intense. I descend the stairs and unlock the door. My heart always jumps at this moment; it is coming home to where I feel safe, a hothouse full of orchidea that need my care.

    Suddenly it does not feel that safe. There is a vague unfamiliarity. Something is different but it is imperceptible. It may be the temperature; perhaps it is warmer than usual. I check the thermostat; it is steady, just as it always is. I sweep my eyes around the room, check the floor, behind the door and under the table. Nothing is unusual.

    The drawers slide open and closed with a satisfying crispness. The children are safe.

    I'm just leaving the room when the chill hits me on the back of my neck. A brief draft, almost unnoticeable on the still night. I turn and see that the tiny ventilation window in the corner of the cellar is open just a crack. The window is hidden from the outside by a bush and blacked out on the inside, so nobody can ever see in—not that any visitors ever make it out this far into the fields. It has never been open and there is no handle on the outside.

With a sense of confusion and unease, my legs weakened by the unfamiliarity of it all, I walk over to the window and pull it down. But I don't panic. I've learnt never to panic. I breathe in the cellar air slowly and calmly, check the children once more and leave the cellar by every second step with the right number of flicks of the light switch.

I return to bed but cannot sleep. My mind starts turning over possible reasons for the window being open. Had I opened it myself to get a little fresh air and forgotten about it? Am I going mad and acting in black outs or in a trance? Perhaps in the excitement of last night I did it whilst prepping Number Five and it escaped my mind. I'm sure nobody opened it from the outside; the security lights would have come on if someone had been on the grounds and I checked the cellar in minute detail.

Even with my mind slowly easing my fear and convincing myself that it was my own fault the window was open, I cannot sleep. I eventually get out of bed at 4 a.m. and go down to the cellar to padlock the window shut.

I return to bed but dawn is breaking and the birds keep me awake. I hate the sound of such vital joy of life; a dawn chorus to greet a new day. Angry and oppressed, I decide to make the best of it and face the world.

Afternoon check

I wander through the day deprived of sleep.

My alarm buzzes and it is time to make the afternoon check. My brain is tired and my focus is shifting all over the place. I inspect the children.

David – Cold. I hardly ever dare touch them but I feel an impulse to reach out and feel his skin, to check that it really is chilled. It is frozen to the touch but I leave my warm finger there for a second too long and the heat from my living flesh thaws some of the ice crystals on the skin of his arm. They melt like snow hitting a wet street. I become fascinated by this and do it several more times.

Michael – I'm so tempted to touch the ice crystals that have always fascinated me on his eye lashes; but something within me is aware that I would mourn them if they were gone. My hot fingers would melt them away in a moment. I close the drawer quickly to avoid temptation.

Luke – I've never felt this urge before but I reach out and touch him on the arm, just as I had with little David. Just once. I don't want to push my luck. I'm focused entirely on my finger and the skin, but from the corner of my eye I get a vague feeling that there was a tiny, momentary shift in his eyeless expression. I think I saw the mouth move a single degree towards a smile, as if human contact had awakened some long-held desire for touch and humanity. My finger springs back with shock. I'm tired, I haven't slept; my mind is clearly playing tricks on me. I lean over and study the face to see if it has changed from the way I have always known it. There is no discernible difference but a feeling in my gut tells me that there is now a faint smile where once the mouth was straight and taciturn. I stare for a long time until the vision starts to blur my thinking. Sometimes it is a smile, sometimes a frown—like looking at an ancient portrait painting. I close the drawer.

I dare not look at Elizabeth or Matthew. I feel things have gone too far.

I check the padlock on the window and leave the room.

Evening check

One to Five, all as I left them; I return to Luke's face but there is no way of knowing.

At night I try to sleep but there is a scraping, clawing sound keeping me awake. I stand by the window and look out into the garden for signs of life making noise. Living things make so much noise. They continually scratch and claw at life and refuse to just exist in silence.

My eyes grow accustomed to the dark and I see the sway of the trees in the breeze and the movement of the clouds across the moon. I concentrate on the movement and start to imagine that I can hear the creak and bow of the branches as they move and then the ethereal sound of the clouds moving across the sky. I hear animals crunching dry leaves with their light footsteps and the sound of the grass wilting in the darkness. At first each sound is so distant and hard to capture that it is easy to believe I am imagining it all; then my concentration grows and I can hear them more distinctly until the whole thing becomes a grotesque symphony of the sounds of living things. The volume continues to increase until each single noise is deafening in its intensity. I return to bed and cover my head with a pillow to block it all out but I can still hear everything. And, underneath it all, is the metallic scratching noise that persists and seems to increase in its urgency.

I hope to sleep but dawn comes again.

Morning check

My brain is fumbling the facts. I check the children and am on drawer one when I realise that I have already been here before and am making a second round.

Child five is frozen deep now. Like a fish that is all agility through the water, its fins would snap before they ever bent on being taken out of the freezer. I look at the child and am filled with mirth at the idea that he met the end he was always destined for. His lot in life was to be frozen to death in some doorway on a cold night—and now here he is frozen for all eternity in a tepid cellar. I cannot help thinking it is better for him this way. There he would have died alone and remained that way until somebody found him. He is never alone here; four little companions lay by his side and a child who had nothing in common with other children his age now has four friends who fully understand his position in life. Of the five of them, I imagine he would be happiest with his end.

Afternoon check

I panic for the first time in a long while. I don't remember losing control before. Child two is staring at me with those wonderful, dead, bludgeoned eyes and I am entranced by it. I look back at him, wondering if there is some flicker of recognition when he sees my face.

This thought delights me for some time until my consciousness is suddenly shaken by the realisation that those ice crystals I so adored on the eyelashes are there no longer. I have to look a dozen times to convince myself it is true. I finally pluck up the courage to touch him and the delicate eyelashes bend under the light touch of my finger. I remove my hand and they spring back to how they were. I run my fingers through the hair on his destroyed head. Ice builds up under my finger nails but there is also water and my hand is wet and covered in blood.

"What's happened, Michael?" I ask.

He does not reply.

I run to the control panel of the refrigeration unit and the temperature is above zero. When did I last check? How long has it been that way? I fumble around the back and find that the panel is hanging on by only one screw; the other three have come loose and fallen out, they are lying on the cellar floor in a dark corner where I would not have thought to look.

I struggle with the unit and turn it around so that the back is facing the light. Inside I can see that one of the wires is loose. Another has come out altogether. I quickly take my screwdriver and get to fixing the wiring and replacing the panel. By the time I have man-handled the unit back to the right way around, I am exhausted. The waves of sleep are finally coming to me.

I say goodbye to the children and wearily climb the stairs. Lights on and off seven times, I turn the door handle to leave the room. It does not open. I punch in the code. An error message flashes up on the screen. I am so tired I cannot get the numbers right. I try again but an error message appears one more time. I concentrate on the numbers and start repeating them in my mind; this goes on for some time until I realise that I have become confused and mixed them up in my mind.

I decide to give up and sit calmly in the corner to let my mind settle for a while. The answer will come.

Evening check

I cannot sleep but my thoughts settle down. The wiring and the screws threw me but now the unit is working again and the children are cold.

I decide to go through my normal routine.

Child one
> Cold

Child two
> Cold, his eyelashes now clean of the ice crystals

Child three
> Frozen solid but there is a new expression. The thaw must have loosened his facial muscles as the mouth now

droops down at one side. It is a slightly comical expression that doesn't look out of place on this obese frame.

Child four

Sweet Elizabeth. Her expression has changed a little too. I cannot explain how but it seems as though her features have become even more beautiful. Before there was an element of seriousness to her face, an almost pensive expression that seemed a little worried. The thaw has softened her; she looks younger and more at ease with the place she is.

Child five

He is cold, just like my feelings towards him. It is hard to feel deeply for them when they are new. For me familiarity does not breed contempt, it nurtures the bond. I like familiar things. Number Five is new. He is unfamiliar and seems to offer a foreign and almost dangerous element to the place. I tell him softly that we will get to know one another and it will come; there is no need to rush.

The thaw has given me new expressions and a softness on Elizabeth's face, as well as the absurd look on the fat one, but it has taken things away too. The crystals on the eyelashes are gone and there is a general change in all of them. I have grown so used to the way they all looked; even with tiny changes I feel like I will have to learn them all over again from scratch. It feels unfamiliar.

I try to leave the room but the code will not work again. I cannot remember when I ate or drank but I believe that I must have in all of the time I have been awake. How long that is I do not know; it is either a couple of short days or a very long time.

I resist the urge to leave the light on and decide to sleep on the floor in the dark.

I cannot sleep again. There is the scratching noise that has persisted in the darkness for so many nights now. It is close by; it sounds like it is in the cellar but I know it cannot be. I fear it is just the imaginings of my sleep-deprived mind. Or perhaps fear is not the right word; there is a cowardly piece of me that hopes it is the imaginings of a temporary mad man.

I try to block it out but it will not stop. There is a scratching and odd metallic squeaks and clanks. The relative quiet of the cellar is suddenly punctuated by the sound of what may be a tiny screw hitting the floor but it rings out loud like a gun shot. I jump up and turn on the light. I see nothing unusual and the cellar is plunged into a sudden silence except for the buzz of the electric light and the hum of the freezer unit.

I turn the light out again and go back to my place on the floor where I can close my eyes and dream of sleep. The scratching begins again. I jump up to turn on the light but there is nothing.

This continues most of the night; up and down the stairs, flicking the light on with the hope of catching a sight of I do not know what. And every time the light goes on, the sound stops dead. In the end, through resignation and exhaustion, I give up and listen to the scratching in peace. I begin to tolerate it and wonder if I would miss it if it were suddenly gone. It becomes hypnotic and almost comforting; something of a lullaby for a man trapped in the darkness.

I am just about to fall asleep when my watch alarm goes off. It is daylight. Life begins again.

Morning check

Child one – Gone.

Child two – Gone.

Child three – Gone.

Child four – Gone, a lock of her hair left in the drawer.

Child five – Gone.

I run up and down the line again, checking each drawer, convinced that each new attempt will reveal one of them to me. I check a dozen times but they are gone. I pick up the lock of Elizabeth's hair and smell it. I hold it close to my face and fall down on the floor crying. I am not sure if it is a sense of betrayal, a feeling of profound loss or just the sadness at being alone again in this world but I cry for the first time in maybe my whole life.

This lasts only a few minutes and then I reason that I must be dreaming. I put the lock of hair in my pocket and try to wake myself up. Nothing happens. I am awake but my mind is playing tricks on me because I am sitting on the floor opposite the drawers and there are six of them.

I jump up and try to disprove this hallucination by touching them. Drawers one to five are as cold as they ever were but as empty as I never remember them being. Even Matthew, who had only been there such a short time, seems like a gaping void when I open his drawer and he is gone, as if he had always been a part of my life. Maybe he was; is it not possible that it was always our destiny to end up together here and I knew of that long before I met him? Could I not have sensed his presence in my life even when he was not a part of me? I realise in that moment that my promise to him has already come true and that he already means as much to me as the others ever did: young David, poor bludgeoned Michael, fat Luke, sweet Elizabeth and lonely Matthew. I say his name over and again.

I come to the sixth drawer. It is open. I am so tired from the physical lack of sleep and the emotional pull of my abandonment. I want to lie down in a safe place and rest. I climb in and feel a release as it is pushed shut behind me.

It is almost sound-proof but I hear the noise of childish whispering and giggling. I listen, almost beyond audible reach, as five little sets of feet ascend every second step to the top of the cellar stairs. A light switch is flicked on and off seven times. From inside the drawer I feel no change in the light. There is only darkness in here. The cellar door is closed and the code is punched in. It is locked tight. I drift into sleep, wondering if I will wake up in the cold of the night. If I wake up, will I be able to open the drawer? Did I hear the sound of the heavy cellar table being pushed in front of the drawer to keep it closed? Such things seem of little concern right now as the waves of long sleep envelop me. My eyes close one last time and before I drift off I hear the sound of children running across the lawn, shouting gaily to one another as they enjoy the freedom of a moonlight night for the first time in a long while. I wonder if I will dream.

Afternoon check

Footsteps in the hall. The door opens. From the muffled confines of a metal drawer I hear the light flick on and off several times. There are heavy, adult footsteps coming down the stairs in an odd way. I would panic but my body is frozen solid. Perhaps deep inside, right down in the gut, there is still some part of me that is not petrified in ice yet; it matters not, I cannot move even an eyelash to give some sign.

I hear the table being shoved from in front of the sixth drawer. My drawer. The grunting sound of effort is familiar but my frozen brain is so slow that I cannot work out where I know it from. I give up on trying to find answers and wait for the drawer to slide open and the light to flood in. I am ready for inspection.

SPORES
JACK ROLLINS

Sheila stood up as the credits rolled on the property programme. She wished she had known how much value would have been added to the first home she and Bill had taken on when they were young. If they had perhaps rented out some of the homes they had lived in over the years, they could have been worth a fortune by now, she thought.

On the television stand, two photographs stood guard at either side of the screen – the youngest grand-children. Their little smiling faces caught Sheila's eye as they always did when she either sat down to or got up from, watching television. This action in turn always made her glance at a larger family photograph, mounted above the fireplace, taken before those little ones were born. On the picture were she and Bill, dressed up for their Silver Wedding Anniversary party, their three sons and their daughter, with all seventeen (as it was back then) grandchildren arranged around them.

Could have had a lot of money to split among you lot when we're gone, she thought.

With the property programme finished, she padded across the passageway and into the kitchen. She filled the kettle and stared out of the window, taking in the garden's decline into wet and muddy autumn. Stray red petals clung to the *Blaze of Fire* salvia plant that was one of her favourites over the summer, imbuing the scene with a hint of sadness – *the plant doesn't want summer to end*.

Switching on the black kettle, Sheila returned to the window and looked over at the greenhouse, in the corner of the upper garden, off to the left. She expected to see Bill's green flat-cap bobbing in and out of view as he worked, but there was no sign of him. The only place he could be, out of sight in this way, was the paddock.

The paddock was a small field to the rear of their garden, which Bill had purchased at the same time as he bought the house, to ensure that no housing developers could snap the land up and build a house that would spoil their view, overshadow their garden in the afternoons, and generally encroach on their space. The corner of the paddock was devoted to Bill's huge compost heap and Sheila guessed that her husband was there, throwing on all of the dead plants to keep the cycle of deterioration and growth going in their garden.

Sheila prepared two ham sandwiches and poured the tea, arranging lunch at the kitchen table rather than the dining room, so that Bill wouldn't make a mess of the good dining chairs with his gardening clothes. She peered out of the window, expecting to see Bill trudging up the garden path, whistling a tune she couldn't hear through the double-glazing. There was no sign of him.

It wasn't like him, Sheila thought. Since his army days, he was a real stickler for time and lunch was at 12 noon every day. Never before had she needed to go and seek him out – she always joked that she could set the house clocks by Bill's appetite.

The stillness of the garden brought about a stirring in the pit of her stomach, like that feeling of butterflies as her nerves seemed almost to stand on end. She opened the back door and stepped out into the garden, feeling the chilly air and the cold of the paving slabs cut through her flimsy slippers in an instant.

She glanced at the salvia just in time to catch another tiny red petal fall loose. For a second a silly notion played across Sheila's mind; she wondered if the petal had waited for her to look before it chose to let go of the stem, or had the movement simply caught the corner of her eye and drawn her full attention?

She passed the pond and noted a ripple playing across the surface, a disturbance, caused no doubt by something unseen, hidden within the murky water. A crow let his presence be known with a throaty call from the stark branches of an oak at the bottom of the paddock.

Tall leylandii formed a natural, green border between the garden proper and the field beyond, the arched opening at the centre forming a portal between order and the wild, unpredictable land beyond.

Sheila's footsteps slowed as she reached the gap, as the enormity of these final steps took prominence in her mind. The vision remained fixed in her imagination: Bill, lying face down in the grass by the compost heap. *Becoming compost himself,* she thought. Her hands raised to her mouth in shock at this careless, callous, unspoken joke.

She took one more step and jumped with fright as a burly figure burst through the opening, half of his face obscured with dirt, clothes streaked with wet mud. Dirty hands grasped her upper arms.

"Sheila," Bill gasped, "you almost gave me a heart-attack!"

Sheila pressed her hands to her bony chest and raised her eyebrows, waiting for the shock to subside and her heartbeat to settle into its ordinary rhythm. "Heart attack?" she cried. "I thought you'd bloody-well had one already!"

"Don't be daft! A specimen of health like me won't die of a heart-attack! I almost set my neck, though. I slipped and went right over."

"Why didn't you just come back in then?"

"Well… I think I may have been unconscious for a few minutes."

"We need to take you through to the hospital," Sheila suggested.

"Nonsense! I'm fine." He wrapped his arms around his wife and planted a kiss in the centre of her forehead. "I'm ready for a spot of lunch now, I must say."

Sat at the table enjoying their sandwiches, Sheila asked, "So, how did you manage to fall over?"

"I slipped on the damp grass. I found some toadstools growing, a real cluster of them. I don't know, I was just in a playful mood and couldn't resist giving them a kick! Next thing I knew, I woke up, flat on my back."

"Silly old sod. Children do that sort of thing," Sheila chided, chuckling.

"You know when you see something and you just can't resist?"

"Like bubble-wrap?"

"Exactly… I'm the same with ice on the pond, I can't help myself, I have to crack the surface as I go past."

"Well," Sheila said, lifting her steaming mug of tea to her lips, "they say men never really do grow up, don't they?"

"Ah, but I was a boy soldier," Bill replied, smiling, sticking his chest out with shoulders back in a jovial demonstration of pride. "I was made to grow up fast."

"Perhaps you're having your childhood now, then."

Bill scratched behind his right ear for a few seconds, then took a draught of tea.

"You still with us, Bill?" Sheila asked.

Bill shook his head for a second, as though suddenly roused from a deep daydream. "Sorry, what was that?" He rubbed his hand behind his right ear again.

Sheila frowned. "Are you sure you're all right, Bill? I think I should drive you down to A and E, get that head checked over."

Bill shoved his chair back from the table and almost leapt to his feet. "I told you I'm all right!" he snapped, then stormed out of the room.

Sheila stared at the kitchen door long after Bill had vanished through it to stomp off up the stairs. His temper had shocked her – he hadn't been so short with her, so *angry* with her in years. Age certainly had mellowed him. She had always hoped it would stay that way.

Bill stood at the guest room window, breathing in the soothing smell of the lavender and chamomile reed diffuser positioned on the window sill above the radiator. The pleasant scent could not take away the envy he harboured, staring out over the box hedge that separated his garden from that of his neighbours, the McKies.

Fred McKie, twenty years Bill's junior, worked his garden from morning until night every weekend. He was some sort of business law hotshot for a German manufacturing company with offices in North Tyneside. The McKies had no children and Fred threw a lot of his money into plants and beautiful wooden furniture for the garden.

Bill watched as Fred scarified the lush green lawn on the second of three terraces that formed a colourful cascade of lawn and blooms year-round.

"He works that grass too hard," Bill muttered to himself. "I've told him before. It'll all die off over the winter."

Once more, his fingertips returned to the spot behind his right ear, and he scratched again, but this time, something caught his attention, breaking the unconscious nature of the movement. He traced tiny circles with his fingertip, trying to locate the thing he had felt moments before. After a few seconds, he found it. The bump felt like a large pimple, but he knew from experience that pimples, moles, warts and wounds always felt larger than they really were when you couldn't see them. He hurried into the bathroom, listening for a moment at the top of the stairs to make sure Sheila wasn't heading in his direction. Her worry was the last thing he needed.

He flicked on the strip lamp above the main mirror and twisted his head aside, eyes strained to the right extent as he bent his ear forwards, trying to reveal the abnormality. He couldn't see it, so he grabbed his shaving mirror from the shelf and placed it on the windowsill. He had to change the mirror's angle twice before he got a view, and even then, the reflected reflection revealed only a tiny spot behind his ear. He dismissed it as a skin-tag or some other similar unwanted, benign growth related to his age.

It was when he replaced the shaving mirror that he noticed a cluster of bumps in the webbing between his right thumb and forefinger. Stretching the skin as far as he could, he probed the tiny growths with his fingernail. He tugged at his flesh and a tiny gap appeared between his skin and the lumps. These things were embedded in his skin, but not part of it – not the epidermis, at least.

He glanced about the bathroom, paused at his Gillette razor, dismissed it, then opened a drawer. He produced a pair of nail scissors, opening them so that the blades sat wide apart. Using the tip of one of the blades, he pressed down against one of the fleshy bumps. The structure gave way and he brushed it aside. He then pressed the blade tip down alongside one of the other bumps, opening that gap between his skin and the growth once more. Shifting the blade's angle, he applied pressure and lifted, popping the tiny sphere of matter out onto the rim of the wash basin.

He found the process most satisfying and began to dig again.

Sheila left Bill alone, feeling it was better to let him sulk alone upstairs than to force the issue. She settled on her favourite lounge chair with the latest Jo Nesbo thriller and determined to wait the afternoon out and see if Bill's humour improved later on.

The grandfather clock in the hall chimed the arrival of three O' clock. Sheila finished the paragraph she was reading, set her bookmark in place and put the book aside. She put the kettle on and decided that a nice cup of tea and a Kit-Kat were the most effective peace offering she knew of, where Bill was concerned. She carried the drink and biscuit upstairs, surprised by the stillness and quiet she found there. She wondered if Bill had fallen asleep and suddenly she found her heart pounding away at the thoughts of delayed shock, and for the second time that day, the possibility of her husband lying dead.

She burst into the bedroom, spilling dribbles of hot tea onto the cream carpet, and to her relief she found the bed empty and no sign of Bill there.

A cough startled her and drew her back to the bathroom. "Bill," she called. "Bill, I have a cuppa for you."

"I'll be down in a second," Bill replied.

"Is everything all right?" she asked, wondering what he was up to. She hadn't heard the bath running, and no movements had indicated his heeding the call of nature within a reasonable timeframe. She reasoned then, that something must be wrong. "Have you fallen again?"

Another cough broke the silence of the bathroom. Sheila pressed down the door handle and entered the room. Dark red splatter marks punctuated the brown cork tiles across the length and breadth of the room. The white of the washbasin was spoiled by brownish-red marks as blood broke down against drops of water.

The teacup and saucer smashed off the floor sending

fragments of china skittering across the room as tea splashed and splattered across the tiles. The Kit-Kat landed at Bill's bloody foot as he stood naked before his wife, his hands, stained red, clutching the open nail scissors.

"What have you done to yourself, Bill?" Sheila cried, taking in the series of punctures her husband had apparently dug into himself. His hands and arms had borne the brunt of the self-harm, but she noted a dozen or so wounds in his chest, a half dozen across his tummy and several on his legs, more prominently around the ankles.

"I couldn't stop myself, Sheila. There are just so many of them."

"So many of what, Bill?"

"There's something growing in me! It's all over my body. I need to cut it all out."

Bill turned and Sheila could then see the horrific work he had carried out on his back, with skin roughly hacked and torn where he couldn't reach and see what he was doing effectively.

"I need to call an ambulance! Put those scissors down, would you?"

"No ambulance, Sheila! I'll be fine. I just need to clean these cuts up."

Against her better judgment Sheila agreed to help Bill clean his wounds with surgical spirit, sticking plasters and dressings. The sting of the spirit elicited sharp intakes of breath from Bill, some of which in turn triggered a deep, hacking cough.

"Bill, at least let me make an appointment for the doctor. For the cough alone, if not the rest of this mess," she suggested.

Bill pondered the idea and, knowing that it would be at least a couple of days before he would actually have to attend the appointment, he agreed. By then, no doubt, the cough would have cleared up and he would be able to cancel the visit.

Every now and then, Sheila inspected a scabby patch at the back of Bill's head, where his hair was sparse and the relentless march of balding had taken its toll. It was impossible for her to determine if his head had been injured in the fall he described, as the self-inflicted wounds masked anything sustained earlier.

At dinner, Sheila managed only a few forkfuls of food. Bill ate voraciously, but his swallows were punctuated by phlegmy coughs and deep, grunting inhalations through his nose, snorting back globs of snot.

"Sounds like you caught quite a cold while you were lying on the damp ground."

"Must have," Bill agreed, barely looking up from his plate.

Sheila raised her eyebrows, disgusted at the sight and sounds presented before her. Revulsion at her husband was an entirely new experience for her; she had always found him loveable, but there was something about this odd behaviour, and the frustration of not being able to help him, that made her resent him.

She carried her plate into the kitchen and scraped her barely touched dinner into the bin. As she filled the kitchen sink to wash up the dinner plates, shallow, rasping breaths sounded above the noise of the pouring water. Sheila turned to see Bill leaning against the pantry door.

"Sheila, I need to get myself to bed," Bill groaned.

"Sorry, love. I don't think I can help with the dishes."

Sheila slipped an arm over his back and led him out of the room. "Bill, you look terrible! I don't care what you say, but if you're still ill tomorrow morning, I am calling a doctor out and that's the end of it!"

Bill leaned against the bannister, letting it take the bulk of his weight as Sheila assisted him up the stairs. His feet dragged over the carpet and every step seemed to draw a noticeable chunk of vitality from his muscles. When he reached the bed, he simply flopped onto the quilt and wriggled upwards so that his head eventually settled on the pillow.

Sheila watched her beloved husband for a moment as he descended rapidly into sleep. She felt guilty for the resentful thoughts she had engaged in at the dinner table. He was poorly, more poorly than she had ever seen him. It wasn't his fault that he was all snotty.

With the kitchen tidy, Sheila settled in her comfy chair once more and picked up her book. *Just an hour*, she thought, *then I'll check on him.*

The warm house, and the stresses of the day made Sheila's eyelids feel like lead weights. Her eyes seemed unable to focus on the words in the paperback and in minutes, sleep claimed her.

A noise somewhere between a slap and a thud shocked Sheila awake once more. The shadows of the room, beyond the pools of light offered by the twin lamps, lay deep and dark. Sheila realised that she had slept past sunset. She glanced at the clock and saw that it was a little after seven O' clock. As she stood, she noticed the Jo Nesbo by her slippered feet and realised that the book, having slipped from her hand, had served as her alarm.

She collected the paperback, slipped her bookmark

back into place and set it aside. Wondering if Bill fancied some supper, she walked up the stairs at a slow pace, feeling the tingle of increased blood flow into her legs. Upon entering the bedroom, she flipped the thin, brass switch and the wall-mounted lamps cast their comforting, soft glow over the room.

Bill seemed not to have moved a muscle in all the time on the bed. He lay exactly as she left him, naked, on top of the quilt. At first, Sheila thought that some of the sticking plasters had become dislodged by the blood collected beneath them, but as she stepped closer, she realised this was not the case.

Wanting to call his name to try to wake her husband, Sheila found the words caught within her chest. She tried to clear her throat, but the air she forced seemed to have no purchase, no power to it. Both the sensation in her throat and the sight before her eyes initiated a panic within her. She crossed the room in a sort of staggering lunge and collapsed on the bed alongside her prone husband.

With shaking hands she extended her fingertips towards his back, which had erupted in clusters of mushroom-like growths in white and red varieties. Of these growths, half of them bore heads the size of a thumbnail or smaller, and the other half had spread open to the size of a milk bottle top.

Thin, inch-long stems of orange and yellow held the red mushrooms above her husband's flesh, and white stems held the white caps in place. She touched one of the red growths first, just above Bill's right buttock. The cap had a waxy feel to it and as she enclosed it between her thumb and forefinger, with a mind to pluck it, she had the strange feeling that the mushroom had a pulse.

She stared at the clusters across Bill's back, positioning herself low, with her chin resting on the bed, she held as still as possible. It took a few seconds to really notice it, but the white and yellow gills under each of the caps certainly did seem to pulse – to *breathe*.

Sheila gasped and in that same instant, her finger and thumb increased pressure and she snatched the red cap up from its stem. The instant she did so, she looked into the thin black tube of the hollow stem and could not fail to notice that it was full of a dark red liquid. She knew the liquid was Bill's blood immediately, as it oozed down the outside of the stem as though she had opened up a wound.

This discovery forced her to take note of the cap in her hand, which she squeezed. The plump, saucer-like growth split open under only a little pressure, and blood trickled out into her palm, running between her fingers as though she had wrung out a sponge.

She turned her attention to one of the white growths, which seemed to occur in the centre of the clusters, surrounded by a dozen or so red caps. Reaching for the white cap, she unleashed a deep, hacking barrage of coughs and heard the phlegm loosen in her chest and throat. She tried to encourage further coughs to bring the uncomfortable mass up into her mouth, but it seemed to settle in place again, restricting her breathing to a thin wheeze.

Sheila's fingers inspected the white cap. It felt completely different to the red variety. Gone was the waxy, gelatinous feel; in its place was a rigid structure, with a surface which, although it appeared to be a single colour, was in actual fact two different textures. Some parts of the surface felt rough, grainy, while other areas felt smooth, almost glazed.

A desperation built up within her. Curiosity bubbled at the surface of her consciousness. She considered the fact that this was her husband lying before her, no more than Bill had considered the grass when he kicked apart the mushrooms earlier that day. She pulled the white mushroom, but it didn't break away. She tugged again and noticed that Bill's flesh rose around it with each exertion, as though the mushroom was somehow anchored into place. Adjusting her grip, she twisted the white cap and observed the flesh pulling as she did so. Eventually, she was treated to a sharp snap, like a wishbone breaking, and the white cap came loose in her hand. Rubbing her fingers over the upper surface, she realised that the glossy surface reminded her of tooth enamel. Staring at Bill's back, she noticed that a porous, pinkish matter filled the broken white stem.

Rubbing her finger tips over the underside of the white cap, she discovered that the gills were flexible, but somewhat delicate, almost brittle like fine china.

Another fit of coughing forced a lump into her windpipe which triggered her gag reflex. She raced to the bathroom and hung her head over the toilet bowl. She retched and coughed until her mouth filled with solid lumps which she promptly spat into the toilet.

The toilet water immediately darkened as bloody clouds curled and dissipated before her eyes. Lumps of deep red and purple bobbed on the surface and clung to the porcelain.

Sheila clasped a hand over her mouth, then inspected her palm to see thick, dark blood smeared over the pebbled surface of her flesh. She inspected both of her palms to find that both were rough with growths the size of pin heads. She screamed and plunged her hands into the toilet, her fingers frantically breaking apart the lumps she had coughed up and vomited.

Holding the glistening fragments in the light, Sheila could see pieces of red caps, just as she had found on Bill's back, and a purple, gelatinous variety, very similar to the red caps.

Her legs felt as though they could no longer support her weight and she staggered to the bedroom once more, where she fell upon the bed, collapsing partially onto her husband, squashing, tearing and breaking the fungal eruptions as she did so. The tang of fresh warm blood met her nostrils as she clawed at the bedding and wriggled until her head was next to Bill's.

Crying his name, pushing against him, Sheila tried desperately to wake her husband. Her arms seemed to have no power in them as she raised her hands to the back of Bill's head, rocking him. "Please, Bill! Wake up!"

Bill's thinning hair jutted out of his head at odd angles, where growths had burst through his flesh between follicles. Red caps even sported some of his brown and grey strands as they had become entangled in the rapid fungal growth.

Sheila's body shuddered as she was overcome with tears and dread. She could feel that Bill was warm, but his lack of response left her with no alternative but to assume the worst.

Then he breathed. The breath was a shallow, liquid wheeze, but it was definitely a breath. He twitched as consciousness began to fire inside his brain once more. He pressed his palms down on the bed and pushed, arching his back.

Sheila heard a sickening crunch from Bill's hands, which were spotted with clusters of red caps, punctuated with the white variety. Bill moaned in pain, but his voice was strained, *weak*. He raised his head and slowly turned to face her.

She gasped as torn stems leaked blood from his cheek and lips, and bony white caps encircled Bill's left eye which was blinded, itself ruptured by a cluster of red caps bursting from blood vessels.

Another garbled moan escaped Bill's lips as the inability to focus properly created panic.

Adrenalin burst into Sheila's bloodstream and she sat bolt upright immediately. Bill shifted his weight, trying to turn to face his wife properly. All of his upper body weight shifted to his left shoulder and he rolled his hips. Another crunch emerged and Bill's left arm collapsed. Rolling onto his back, Bill unleashed a gurgling scream. Speckles of blood sprayed into the air, peppering his face, Sheila's face, and the white and floral bedding around them.

Bill's right hand lashed at his left shoulder and he tore at the growths he found there, snapping the white caps which seemed to hold the strength and substance that his own skeleton now lacked. Red caps burst, leaking blood across the bedding. He tore at his left eye, snapping away the white caps, then pulling at the tough, spine-like stems, before plunging his fingers into the shell of red caps protruding from his eyeball.

He howled again, tearing at the growths on his lips, scratching at tiny white nodules on his teeth. At length, his fingers reached his neck, where red and purple mushrooms grew beyond his vision.

Sheila cried out, begging her husband to stop, but he either could not hear her, or would not take note. He tore away a handful of the fungi, unleashing a hot jet of bright arterial blood across the bedroom. Sheila screamed, pressing her fingers against the broken stems. Bloody bubbles, like red spittle, burped from the stems which had born purple caps, as his windpipe released air.

Sheila bucked and lurched as another fit of coughs broke loose. She took her hands away from Bill's neck instinctively, raising her hands to her face, where the fact that the swellings on her palms had grown became evident. Not only that, but she felt a strange sensation as though someone else's hands touched her face, and her hands touched someone else's face. She knew that if she looked in the mirror, that her cheeks would be stippled with spores.

Bill ceased to move, his eyes rolling back in his head as his blood pressure dipped dangerously low.

Turning towards the bedside cabinet, Sheila reached for the telephone. Her fingers felt swollen, *transformed*, and she cried in frustration when the telephone thudded on the bedroom carpet. Scrambling onto the floor, Sheila grasped the telephone and stabbed at the keys to reach the emergency services.

Sheila rasped and coughed into the receiver and the operator was unable to take any useful information from her.

"If you require emergency assistance, please press any of the keys," the operator instructed.

Sheila complied, squashing several keys down at once. The operator, hearing the tone, recognised that the person at the end of the line, *Sheila*, was in danger and that this probably wasn't an accidental or prank call.

Gurgling, liquid breaths built up in Sheila's chest and again she descended into a fit of coughing. More solid pieces broke free and burst from her lips.

The operator called out, asking questions, trying to get to the bottom of the problem, believing Sheila to be choking on perhaps a piece of food.

Unable to explain or give any indication at all what was going on, and afraid that the emergency services would not arrive and diagnose her correctly in time, an idea flashed in her mind. Sheila clawed across the floor and out onto the landing. She reached and grasped the newel post at the head of the stairs, hauling her body up off the thick olive carpet.

Her vision became grainy – she prayed it was from lack of oxygen and not a series of mushrooms preparing to erupt from her eyes. Clinging to the banister, she managed to make it to the foot of the stairs. She staggered to the front door, coughing and wheezing. Her thighs burned as the oxygen in her blood ran low, starving her straining muscles.

She tumbled on the stone paving by the pond and her forehead thumped down hard. She closed her eyes as her vision filled red and faded to black. Her ears seemed to fill with the sound of static as she battled to stay conscious. Blood cooled in the night air, dribbling down her brow and into her eyes as she rose to her feet and grabbed the wooden trellis to her right.

Her flesh seared with white-hot pinpricks of pain and she clawed at the backs of her hands, where the pain was most intense. The topography of her flesh had changed, as had the texture. She felt waxy pebbles coating her skin and her fingers curled into fists involuntarily as the growths dictated the behaviour of her tendons.

Barely able to flex her fingers, Sheila knew that her plan was running out of time as she arrived at Bill's garden shed. Her knotted hands slid over the damp brass door handle again and again as her coughing intensified. She pressed down with her elbow and the handle gave way, allowing her to access the interior. In the darkness she was unsure that she would recognise the fungicide bottle, but she squeezed her hands together, trying to break her fists open once more.

Knocking spray bottles of weed killer aside, Sheila fought against her closing fingers. She grabbed a tub of slug pellets and threw them to the floor, breaking open several of the growths on her palms, sending a fresh cascade of blood over her hands. She turned and yanked the pull-cord to turn on the single bulb and tried to ignore the sickening sight of the parasitic growths colonising the flesh on the back of her hands, and the bleeding stumps on her palms.

She scooped up a grey plastic bottle with a ridged grip at the sides and tried to grasp the black bottle cap. Her slick, bloody hands could gain no purchase on the plastic and so she looked about for anything that she could use. Her eyes fell upon a garden trowel hanging from a hook by the door.

Her hands faltered as she reached for the trowel when a fresh bout of coughing carried her off-balance and blinded her as her eyelids clasped shut and teared up. She spat a ball of matter from her mouth that was more solid than liquid, but which left the metal tang of blood on her tongue.

She wiped her eyes with her sleeve and grabbed for the trowel once more as the growths tugged at her tendons, forcing the fingers of her right hand to lock closed again. She picked up the tool with her left hand and felt her fingers tighten involuntarily around the rubber handgrip, with no little satisfaction - she finally had what she needed within her grasp.

Sheila returned to the bottle of fungicide and plunged the trowel down as close to the bottle cap as she could, two of the teeth biting into the plastic. As she pulled the trowel back, the fungicide bottle came with it, slipping off the teeth to fall to the floor, spilling the contents, with heavy *glugs* providing a countdown to her doom.

The siren of an approaching ambulance met her ears from a distance. She dropped to the ground and squeezed the bottle clumsily between her two knotted hands, the left of which was still locked around the handle of the trowel, ever more fungicide spilling out of the rents she had created. She opened her mouth and held the container up, feeling the chemicals splash across her face, pooling against her closed eyelids, burning inside her nostrils.

Sheila hoped the paramedics would check the shed soon, and she hoped that they could treat her for poisoning quicker than they would have removed the fungi from her compromised airway.

Fred McKie sighed deeply on his way to the kitchen. "Can't you just get into this? You've seen all those programs about having a forage and getting it into your home cooking."

His wife, Laura stared at the sizzling pan of mince, garlic and onions, then glanced at the red mushrooms she had chopped and set aside on the wooden chopping board. "They just look nothing like the button ones you get at the supermarket. I mean *nothing* like them."

"That's because these ones have some flavour to them! Probably, anyway." Fred raised his tablet and pointed at the picture of the red mushroom on the screen. "Look, it says here it's edible. Scarlet Hood, edible. See? There are some down here it can be confused with, but they are black when you cut into them."

"Yeah, that they know about," Laura protested.

"Oh, so you think that growing in our garden would be a brand new, never-before-seen type of mushroom. Come on!"

"Well, you never know."

"Living off the land, Laura! What could be better for you than that which nature provides in your very own garden?"

The idea did appeal to Laura, she had to admit it.

Fred flipped the leather cover back over his tablet emphatically. "Look, if you don't want to use them, chuck 'em in the bin. I just thought it would be nice to use what we have around us, that's all."

"I know, and it's a nice idea, but mushrooms are just one of those things I was always nervous about. Dad said never pick them and never eat them unless they're bought from a shop. He was always on about poisonous toadstools."

"Every dad goes on about them, but not one of them knew how to describe them, I bet. They didn't have the information we have at our fingertips! Christ, they didn't eat mushrooms unless it was in a fry-up, let's be fair."

Laura chuckled and slid the contents of the chopping board into the frying pan.

WHAT THE DARK DOES

GRAHAM MASTERTON

"Mummy -- please don't close the door."

His mother smiled at him, her face half lit by the landing light, the other half in shadow, so that she looked as if she were wearing a Venetian carnival mask.

"All right. But I can't leave the light on all night. Honestly, David, there's nothing to be scared of. You remember what granpa used to say -- dark is only the same stuff that's behind your eyelids, only more of it."

David shivered. He remembered his granpa lying in his open coffin at the undertakers, his face gray and half-collapsed. He had thought then that granpa would never see anything else, ever again, but the darkness behind his eyelids, and that *was* scary.

Darkness is only benign if you know that you can open your eyes whenever you want to, and it will have fled away.

He snuggled down under his patchwork quilt and closed *his* eyes. Almost immediately he opened them again. The door was still open and the landing light was still shining. On the back of his chair he could see his black school blazer, ready for tomorrow, and his neatly-folded shorts.

In the corner of his room, lying sprawled on the floor, he could see Sticky Man, which was a puppet that his granpa had made for him. Sticky Man was nearly two feet tall, made of double-jointed sticks painted gray. His spine and his head were a long wooden spoon, with staring eyes and a gappy grin painted onto it. Granpa used to tell him that during the war, when he and his fellow soldiers were pinned down for days on end under enemy fire at Monte Cassino, they had made Sticky Men to entertain themselves, as many as ten or twelve of them. Granpa said that the Sticky Men all came to life at night and did little dances for them. Sometimes, when the enemy shelling was particularly heavy, they used to send Sticky Men to carry messages to other units, because it was too dangerous to do it themselves.

David didn't like Sticky Man at all, and twice he had tried to throw him away. But his father had always rescued him – once from the dustbin and once from a shallow leaf-covered grave at the end of the garden -- because his father thought that granpa's story about Sticky Men was so amusing, and part of family history. "Granpa used to tell me that story when I was your age, but he never made *me* a Sticky Man. So you should count yourself privileged."

David had never actually seen Sticky Man come to life, but he was sure that he had heard him dancing in the darkness on the wooden floorboards at the edge of his bedside mat: *clickety, clackety, clickety, clackety*. When he had heard that sound, he had buried himself even deeper under the covers, until he was almost suffocating.

What really frightened David, though, was the brown dressing-gown hanging on the back of his bedroom door. Even during the day, it looked like a monk's habit, but when his father switched off the landing light at night, and David's bedroom was filled up with darkness, the dressing-gown changed, and began to fill out, as if somebody were rising up from the floor to slide inside it.

He was sure that when the house was very quiet, and there was no traffic in the street outside, he could hear the dressing-gown *breathing*, in and out, with just the faintest hint of harshness in its lungs. It was infinitely patient. It wasn't going to drop down from its hook immediately and go for him. It was going to wait until he was so paralyzed with terror that he was incapable of defending himself, or of crying out for help.

He had tried to hide the dressing-gown by stuffing it into his wardrobe, but that had been even more frightening. He could still hear it breathing but he had no longer been able to see it, so that he had never known when it might ease open the wardrobe door and then rush across the bedroom and clamber up onto his bed.

Next he had tried hanging the dressing-gown behind the curtains, but that had been worse still, because he was sure that he could hear the curtain rings scraping back along the brass curtain-pole. Once and once only he had tried cramming it under the bed. When he had done that, however, he had been able to lie there for less than ten minutes, because he had been straining to hear the dressing-gown dragging itself out from underneath him, so that it could come rearing up beside him and drag his blankets off.

His school blazer was almost as frightening. When it was dark, it sat hunched on his chair, headless but malevolent, like the stories that early Spanish explorers had brought back from South America of natives with no heads but their faces on their chests. David had seen pictures of them in his schoolbooks, and even though he knew they were only stories, like Sticky Men were only stories, he also knew that things were very different in the dark.

In the dark, stories come to life, just like puppets, and dressing-gowns.

He didn't hear the clock in the hallway downstairs chime eleven. He was asleep by then. His father came into his room and straightened his bedcover and affectionately scruffed up his hair. "Sleep well, trouble." He left his door open a little, but he switched off the landing light, so that his room was plunged into darkness.

Another hour went by. The clock chimed twelve, very slowly, as if it needed winding. David slept and dreamed that he was walking through a wood, and that something white was following him, keeping pace with him, but darting behind the trees whenever he turned around to see what it was.

He stopped, and waited for the white thing to come out into the open, but it remained hidden, even though he knew it was still there. He breathed deeply, and stirred, and said, out loud, "*Who are you?*"

Another hour passed, and then, without warning, his dressing-gown dropped off the back of his bedroom door.

He didn't hear it. He had stopped dreaming that he was walking through the wood, and now he was deeply unconscious. His door was already ajar, but now it opened a little more, and a hunched brown shape dragged its way out of his bedroom.

A few moments later, there was a soft click, as the door to his parents' bedroom was opened.

Five minutes passed. Ten. David was rising slowly out of his very deep sleep, as if he were gradually floating to the surface of a lake. He was almost awake when something suddenly jumped on top of him, something that clattered. He screamed and sprang upright, both arms flailing. The clattery thing fell to the floor. Moaning with fear, he fumbled around in the darkness until he found his bedside lamp, and switched it on.

Lying on the rug next to his bed was Sticky Man, staring up at him with those round, unblinking eyes.

Trembling, David pushed back the covers and crawled down to the end of the bed, so that he wouldn't have to step onto the rug next to Sticky Man. What if it sprang at him again, and clung to his ankle?

As he reached the end of the bed, and was about to climb off it, he saw that his dressing-gown had gone. The hook on the back of his bedroom door had nothing hanging on it except for his red-and-white football scarf.

His moaning became a soft, subdued mewling in the back of his throat. He was so frightened that he squirted a little warm pee into his pajama trousers. He looked over the end of the bed but his dressing-gown wasn't lying in a heap on the floor, as he would have expected.

Perhaps Mummy had at last understood that it scared him, hanging up on the back of the door like that, and she had taken it down when he was asleep. Perhaps she had taken it away to wash it. He had spilled a spoonful of tomato soup on it yesterday evening, when he was sitting on the sofa watching television – not that he had told her.

He didn't know what to do. He knelt on the end of the bed, biting at his thumbnail, not mewling now but breathing very quickly, as if he had been running. He turned around and looked down at Sticky Man but Sticky Man hadn't moved – he was still lying on his back on the rug, his arms and legs all splayed out, glaring balefully at nothing at all.

Whatever David did, he would have to change his wet pajama trousers, and that would mean going to the airing-cupboard on the landing. Mummy always liked to keep his clean pajamas warm.

Very cautiously, he climbed off the bed and went across to his bedroom door. He looked around it. The landing was in darkness, although the faintest of green lights was coming up the stairs from the hallway, from the illuminated timer on the burglar alarm, and that was enough for David to see that his parents' bedroom door was open, too.

He frowned. His parents *never* left their door open, not at night. He hesitated for a few long moments, but then he hurried as quietly as he could along the landing until he reached his parents' bedroom, and peered inside. It was completely dark in there, although he could just make out the luminous spots on the dial of his father's bedside alarm clock.

He listened. Very far away, he could hear a train squealing as it made its way to the nearest station, to be ready for the morning's commuters. But when that sound had faded away, he could hear nothing at all. He couldn't even hear his parents breathing, even though his father usually snored.

"Mummy?" he called, as quietly as he could.

No answer. He waited in the doorway, with his wet pants beginning to feel chilly.

"*Mummy?*" A little louder this time.

Still no answer.

He crept into his parents' bedroom, feeling his way round the end of the bed to his mother's side. He reached out and felt her bare arm lying on top of the quilted bedcover. He took hold of her hand and shook it and said, hoarsely, "Mummy, wake up! I've had an accident!"

But still she didn't answer. David groped for the dangly cord that switched on her bedside reading light, and tugged it.

"*Mummy! Daddy!*"

Both of them were lying on their backs, staring up at the ceiling with eyes so bloodshot that it looked as if somebody had taken out their eyeballs and replaced them with crimson grapes. Not only that, both of them had black moustaches of congealing blood on their upper lips, and their mouths were dragged grotesquely downward. Two dead clowns.

David stumbled backward. He heard somebody let out a piercing, high-pitched scream, which frightened him even more. He didn't realize that it was him.

He scrabbled his way back around the end of the bed, and as he did so he caught his foot and almost tripped over. His brown dressing-gown was lying tangled on the floor, with its cord coiled on top of it.

He didn't scream again, but he marched stiffly downstairs like a clockwork soldier, his arms and legs rigid with shock. He picked up the phone and dialled 999.

"Emergency, which service please?"

"Ambulance," he said, his lower lip juddering. "No, no, I don't need an ambulance. I don't know what I need. They're dead."

The red-haired woman detective brought him the mug of milky tea that he had asked for, with two sugars. She sat down at the table next to him and gave him a smile. She was young and quite pretty, with a scattering of freckles across the bridge of her nose.

"You didn't hear anything, then?" she asked him.

"No," David whispered.

"We're finding it very difficult to work out what happened," she said. "There was no sign that anybody broke into your house. The burglar alarm was on. And yet somebody attacked your daddy and mummy and whoever it was they were very strong."

"It wasn't me," said David. He was wearing the purple hooded top that his uncle and aunt had given him for his last birthday, and he looked very pale.

"Well, we know for certain that it wasn't you," said the detective. "We just need to know if you saw anything, or heard anything. Anything at all."

David looked down into his tea. He felt like bursting into tears but he swallowed and swallowed and tried very hard not to. He was too young to know that there was no shame in crying.

"I didn't hear anything," he said. "I don't know who did it. I just want them to be alive again."

The detective reached across the table and squeezed his hand. She couldn't think of anything to say to him, except, "I know you do, David. I know."

Rufus said, "Did they ever find out how your parents died?"

David shook his head. "The coroner returned a verdict of unlawful killing by person or persons unknown. That's all he could do."

"You must *wonder*, though, mate. You know – who could have done it, and why. And *how*, for Christ's sake!"

David took a swig from his bottle of Corona. The Woolpack was crowded, even for a Friday evening, and they were lucky to have found somewhere to sit, in the corner. An enormously fat man sitting next to them was laughing so loudly that they could hardly hear themselves speak.

Rufus and David had been friends ever since David had started work at Amberlight, selling IT equipment. He had been there seven months now, and last month he had been voted top salesman in his team. Rufus was easy-going, funny, with a shaven head to pre-empt the onset of pattern baldness and a sharp line in gray three-piece suits.

David heard himself saying, "Actually... I *do* know who did it."

"Really?" said Rufus. "You really *do* know? Like --

have you known all along, right from when it happened? Or did you find out later? Hang on, mate -- why didn't you tell the police? Why don't you tell them now? It's never too late!"

David thought: *shit, I wish I hadn't said anything now. Why did I say anything? I've kept this to myself for seventeen years, why did I have to come out with it now? It's going to sound just as insane now as it would have done then.*

"I didn't tell the police because they would never have believed me. Just like you won't believe me, either."

"Well, you could try me. I'm famous for my gullibility. Do you want another beer?"

"Yes, thanks."

Rufus went to the bar and came back with two more bottles. "Right, then," he said, smacking his hands together. "Who's the guilty party?"

"I told you, you wouldn't believe me. My dressing-gown."

Rufus had his bottle of beer poised in front of his mouth, his lips in an O shape ready to drink, but now he slowly put the bottle down.

"Did I hear that right? Your dressing-gown?"

Trying to sound as matter-of-fact as possible, David said, "My dressing-gown. I had a brown dressing-gown that used to hang on the back of my bedroom door and it looked like a monk. I always used to think that when it was dark it came alive. Well, one night it did, and it went into my parents' bedroom and it strangled them. In fact it garrotted them, according to the police report. It strangled them so hard it almost took off their heads."

"Your dressing-gown," Rufus repeated.

"That's right. Sounds bonkers, doesn't it? But there is

absolutely no other explanation. Unlawful killing by night attire. And there was something else, too. I had a puppet that my grandfather made for me, like it was all made out of gray sticks, with a wooden spoon for a head. Sticky Man, I used to call it. When my dressing-gown went to murder my parents, Sticky Man jumped on me and I think he was trying to warn me what was going to happen."

Rufus bent his head forward until his forehead was pressed against the table. He stayed like that for almost ten seconds. Then he sat up straight again and said, "Your puppet warned you that your dressing-gown was going to kill your mum and dad."

"There – I told you that you wouldn't believe me. Thanks for the beer, anyway."

"You know who you need to talk to, don't you?" said Rufus.

"A shrink, I suppose you're going to say."

"Unh-hunh. You need to talk to Alice in accounts."

"Alice? That freaky-looking woman with the white hair and all of those bracelets?"

"That's the one. Actually she's a very interesting lady. I had a long chat with her once at one of the firm's bonding weekends. It was down somewhere near Hailsham, I think. Anyway, Alice is great believer in crustaceous automation, I think she called it."

"What? Crustaceous? That's like crabs and lobsters, isn't it?"

"Well, I don't know, but it was something like that. What it meant was, things coming to life when it gets dark. She really, really believes in it. Like your dressing-gown, I suppose. One of the things she told me about was this armchair that came to life when anybody fell asleep in it, and it squeezed them so hard that it crushed their ribcage. It took forever before somebody worked out what was killing all these people.

"What she said was, it's the dark that does it. The actual darkness. It changes things."

David looked at Rufus narrowly. "You're not taking the piss, are you?"

"Why would I?"

"Well, I know you. Always playing tricks on people. I don't want to go up to this Alice and tell her about my dressing-gown if she's going to think that I'm some kind of loony."

"No, mate," said Rufus. "Cross my heart. I promise you. I'm not saying that *she's* not loony, but I don't think you're any loonier than she is, so I doubt if she'll notice."

They met in their lunchbreak, at their local Pizza Hut, which was almost empty except for two plump teenage mothers and their screaming children. David ordered a pepperoni pizza and a beer while Alice stayed with a green salad and a cup of black tea.

When he started talking to her, David realized that Alice was much less freaky than he had imagined. She had a short, severe, silvery-white bob, and he had assumed that she was middle-aged, but now he saw that her hair was bleached and highlighted and she couldn't have been older than thirty-one or thirty-two. She had a sharp, feline face, with green eyes to match, and she wore a tight black T-shirt and at least half-a-dozen elaborate silver bangles on each wrist.

"So, what did Rufus say when you told him?" she asked, lifting up her cup of tea with both hands and blowing on it.

"He was all right about it, actually, when you consider that he could have laughed his head off. Most of the rest of the team would have done."

"Rufus has his own story," said Alice. David raised an eyebrow, expecting her to tell him what it was, but she was obviously not going to be drawn any further.

"You know the word 'shoddy'?" she said.

"Of course."

"Most people think it means something that's been badly made. You know, something inferior. But it can also mean a woollen yarn made out of used clothes. They rip up old coats and sweaters to shreds and then they re-spin them, with just a bit of new wool included. Most new clothes are made out of that."

David said, "I didn't know that, no."

"In Victorian times, these guys used to go around the streets ringing a bell and collecting used clothes. They called them 'shoddy-men.' These days it's mainly Lithuanians who pinch all of those bags of clothes that people leave out for charities. They ship them all back to Lithuania, turn them into new clothes and then sell them back to us."

"I'm not too sure what you're getting at."

Alice sipped her tea, and then she said, "Sometimes, those second-hand clothes have belonged to some very violent people. Murderers, even. And clothes take on their owners' personalities. You know what it's like when you try on another man's jacket. It makes you feel as if you're *him*."

"So what are you trying to tell me? My dressing-gown might have had wool in it that once belonged in some murderer's clothes?"

Alice nodded. "Exactly."

"But it's not like *I* put it on, and *I* killed my parents. The dressing-gown came alive. The dressing-gown did it on its own!"

David suddenly realized that he was talking too loudly, and that the two teenage mothers were staring at him.

He lowered his voice and said, "How did it come alive on its own? I mean, how is that possible?"

Alice said, "The scientific name for it is 'crepuscular animation.' It means inanimate objects that come alive when it begins to get dark. Most people don't understand that darkness isn't just the absence of light. Darkness is an element in itself, and darkness goes looking for more darkness, to feed itself.

"That night, when your light was switched off, the darkness in your room found whatever darkness that was hidden in your dressing-gown, and filled it up with more of its own dark energy, and brought it to life."

"I'm sorry, Alice. I'm finding this really hard to follow."

Alice laid her cool, long-fingered hand on top of his. Her green eyes were unblinking. "What else could have happened, David? You said yourself that nobody broke into the house, and that you didn't do it. You *couldn't* have done it, you simply weren't strong enough. And your puppet man came alive, too, didn't he? How do you think that happened?"

David shrugged. "I haven't a clue. And why should

my dressing-gown have come to life *then*, on that particular night? It was hanging there for *months* before that. My mother bought it for me in October, so that I could wear it on fireworks night."

"Well, I don't know the answer to that. But it could have been some anniversary. Perhaps it was a year to the day that somebody was murdered, by whoever wore the wool that was woven into your dressing-gown. There's no way of telling for certain."

David sat for a long time saying nothing. Alice continued to fork up her salad and sip her tea but he didn't touch his pizza.

"How do you know all this?" he asked her. "All about this – what did you call it – screspusular stuff?"

"Crepuscular animation. 'Crepuscular' only means 'twilight.' My great-grandmother told me. Something happened to one of her sons, during the war. There was a lot of darkness, during the blackouts. So much darkness everywhere. She said there used to be a statue in their local park, a weeping woman, on a First World War memorial. Apparently her son and one his friends took a shortcut through the park at night, and the statue came to life and came after them. Her son's head was crushed against the metal railings and his neck was broken.

"Of course nobody believed the other little boy, but my great-grandmother did, because she knew him and she knew that he always told the truth. She made a study of inanimate objects coming to life when it begins to get dark, and she wrote it all down in an exercise book and that exercise book got passed down to me. Nobody else in the family wanted it. They thought it was all cuckoo."

To emphasize the point, she twirled her index finger

around at the side of her head.

"I don't know what to think," David told her.

"Just beware of the darkness," said Alice. "Treat it with respect. That's all I can say. And if you see a dressing-gown that looks as if it might come alive, then believe me, it probably will."

He returned home late that night. The bulb had gone in the hallway and he had to grope his way to the living-room.

The living-room was dimly lit from the nearby main road. He lived on the ground floor of what had once been a large family house, but which was now divided into eight different flats. His was one of the smallest, but he was very fastidious, and he always kept it tidy. Up until the end of last year, he had shared a large flat with two colleagues from work, and that had been horrendous, with dirty plates stacked in the kitchen sink and the coffee table crowded with overflowing ashtrays and empty Stella cans. Worst of all had been the clothes that were heaped on the floor, or draped over the backs of chairs, or hanging from hooks on the back of every door.

He switched on the two side lamps, and the television, too, although he pressed the mute button. On the left-hand wall stood a bookcase, with all of his books arranged in alphabetical order, according to author. In front of them stood two silver shields, for playing squash, and several framed photographs of his father and mother, smiling. And then, of course, there was Sticky Man, perched on the edge of the shelf, staring at him with those circular, slightly mad eyes.

When Sticky Man had jumped on David on the night that his parents had been murdered, he had terrified him, but David had come to believe that he had been trying to warn him, and that was why he had kept him all these years. Hadn't Sticky Men always been helpers, and facilitators – entertaining the troops in Italy during the war, and carrying messages under shellfire? When David was little, Sticky Man may have frightened him by coming alive during the night, but he had only been dancing, after all.

"Hey, Sticks," he said, but Sticky Man continued to stare at him and said nothing.

Although he had eaten only one slice of his pizza at lunchtime, David didn't feel particularly hungry, so he opened a can of Heinz vegetable soup, heated it up in the microwave and ate it in front of the television, watching *Newsnight*.

Afterward he showered and brushed his teeth and climbed into bed. He tried to read *The Girl With The Dragon Tattoo* for a while, but he couldn't stop thinking about Alice, and what she had said about inanimate objects coming to life when darkness fell. He still couldn't remember exactly what it was called. Crispucular automation?

Just beware of the darkness. Treat it with respect. That's all I can say. And if you see a dressing-gown that looks as if might come alive, then believe me, it probably will.

After his parents' murder David had been brought up by his Aunt Joanie and his Uncle Ted. They had bought him a new dressing-gown, a tartan one, but on the day that he had left home he had thrown it in the dustbin and he had never bought himself another one since. He never hung any clothes from the hook on his bedroom door, not even a scarf. Even before he had talked to Alice, he had always kept his clothes shut up in closets and wardrobes, out of sight. No jackets were hunched over the back of his chair. No shirts hung drip-drying in the bathroom, like ghosts.

He switched off the light, and closed his eyes. He felt very tired for some reason. Alice had disturbed him quite a lot, even though he found it very hard to believe everything that she had told him. The statue of the weeping woman he found quite unsettling. And he wondered what Ray's story was? Ray was so pragmatic, and so straightforward. What on earth had appeared out of the dark to frighten Ray?

He slept, deeply, for over an hour, but then he abruptly woke. He was sure that he had heard a clicking noise. His bedroom was unusually dark, and when he lifted his head from the pillow he realized that the digital clock beside his bed was no longer glowing. There were no streetlights shining outside, either. There must have been a power-cut, which might explain the clicking noise that had woken him up: the sound of the central-heating pipes contracting as they cooled down.

As he laid his head back down on the pillow, he heard more clicking. More like clattering this time. He strained his ears and listened. There was a lengthy silence, and then a quick, sharp rattling sound. He thought he heard a door opening.

He sat up. Something was outside his bedroom, in the

hallway. Something that made a soft, dragging noise. It sounded as if it were coming closer and closer, and then it bumped into his bedroom door. Not loudly, but enough to give him the impression that it was big and bulky.

His heart was hammering against his ribcage. "Who's there?" he called out. "Is anybody out there?"

There was no answer. Nearly half a minute went by. Then suddenly there was another clatter, and he heard his door-handle pulled down. His door swung open with the faintest whisper, almost like a sigh of satisfaction.

He waited, listening, his fingers gripping the bedcovers. What had somebody once said about bedcovers? Why do we pull them up to protect ourselves when we're scared? Do you think a murderer with a ten-inch knife is going to be deterred by a quilt?

"Who's there?" he called out, hoarsely.

No answer.

"For God's sake, who's there?"

It was then that the power came back on again, and his digital bedside clock started flashing green, and the central heating began to tick into life again, and he saw what it was that was standing in his bedroom doorway.

It was his navy-blue duffel coat, with its hood up. It looked like a dead Antarctic explorer, somebody whose body had been found in the snow a hundred years after they had died.

Beside it, tilting this way and that, as if it couldn't get its balance right, was Sticky Man. Sticky Man must have opened the door to the closet, in the hallway, so that the duffel coat could shuffle out, and Sticky Man had opened his bedroom door, too. There was nobody else in the flat, so who else could it have been?

It was then that he realized that on the night his parents had been killed Sticky Man hadn't been trying to warn him. Sticky Man had been probably trying to wake him up, so that he too would go into parents' bedroom, to be garrotted along with them.

"*You traitor, Sticks,*" he whispered, but of course Sticky Man wasn't a traitor, because Sticky Man was a creature of the dark, just as much as his dressing-gown, and his duffel-coat. It wasn't *them*, in themselves. They were only inanimate objects.

David's duffel coat rushed across his bedroom floor toward him. He lunged sideways across to the other side of the bed, trying to reach his phone.

"Emergency, which service please?"

" – *dark* -- !"

Then a struggling sound, and a thin, reedy gasp, followed by a long continuous tone.

It was what the dark does.

SCREAMS IN THE NIGHT

J. R. PARK

All I want to do is sleep!

I'm so tired. So painfully tried.

Daryl rolls onto his side and squints at his alarm clock. The numbers on the digital display glow a hellish red, penetrating the blurry vision of his bloodshot eyes. He sighs as through the haze he makes out 02:25.

The darkened ceiling offers no further comfort as a ghostly image of the time, still imprinted on his retina, floats in greens and purples above him.

It's been two months and there's still no sign of let up.

The screaming continues, just as it has done every night. Every single night. For eight weeks.

It seems louder tonight. More shrill. More desperate.

Sitting up, he feels his head swim. His temples pound.

Pain sears from behind his bleary eyes.

I can't take this!

The bookcase pushed against the wall is a reminder of his many failed attempts to soften the sound. The walls aren't that thin, but the screams manage to find a frequency that burrows through any barricade.

Crumpled ear plugs lie discarded on the floor, their forms misshapen from frustrated gouges.

The bed feels hard underneath him, the duvet constrictive. All comfort has faded.

But where to go?

For the first time in his life his two-storey, maisonette seems small. The niggling gnaw of claustrophobia creeps in. The living room, the box room, the landing, even the bathroom had become temporary bedrooms since the screaming started all those weeks ago. But nowhere has proved to be a place of solace from the ear splitting shriek he is forced to endure.

The screaming stops as the baby splutters.

Maybe it'll settle down. Maybe it'll die.

No, that's a terrible thing to think.

Daryl chastises himself for such an evil idea. His mind is fractured, his thoughts are fragments washing together, confusing each other.

He reaches for a packet of pain killers. His head throbs in time with the beating of his heart. The packet is empty.

Shit!

A voice comes through the wall. He's heard it many times before. The baby's mother.

"Roman," she calls.

Daryl likes the sound of her voice. He's always found

the accent of Eastern Europeans a turn on. Hers is no exception.

Aneta, he recalls her name. Recalls them meeting outside their flats a few days ago. He was carrying food shopping. She was taking rubbish down to the ground floor dump. The bin bags were bulging, leaking congealing liquid. They smelt bad. Worse than the usual smell of stale piss from the lifts. This was rotten. Putrid. Dirty nappies and God-knows what else.

He tries a smile as he thinks on her beauty. Glasses, brunette, foreign. She ticks all his boxes.

Roman begins to cry again and tears flow down Daryl's cheeks, matching the baby's next door.

What is wrong with that child?!

The weight of his body causes his legs to shake as he gets out of bed. The sleepless nights have weakened him. Exhaustion plays tricks with his eyes. Colours dance in the dark, obscuring his vision. Seagulls shriek from the rooftops.

Daryl feels a shiver creep down his spine.

They sound like the screams of the dying.

The baby competes with the birds outside. Both reach a cacophonous peak. Their shrill chorus sets his teeth on edge.

He remembers the last tenant's meeting. Margaret Woods suggesting to poison the winged vermin.

Poison...

Pain shoots up his foot as Daryl stubs his toe.

Fuck!

With his hands outstretched he searches in the dark and finds the door. He needs more painkillers. Maybe a shot of whisky.

No, not more booze. That won't help.

The words of his boss's latest reprimand scatter through his mind.

You look like hell, Daryl.

You need to sharpen up your attitude, get focused on your work.

You haven't looked the least bit interested or engaged for weeks.

Christ, today you could hardly keep your eyes open.

It's starting to impact on your performance.

Is that alcohol I can smell?

Lizanne is a tough cookie. She is known for her hard line management. Dismissal meetings are a regular occurrence in her calendar. He doesn't need that.

The cries grow louder still, stirring the gulls to fever pitch.

Daryl's head spins. His blood runs cold.

He takes the stairs in the dark. The city lights shine onto his tower block and through the frosted panel of his front door. The amber glow illuminates his path, but he still makes each step with great care. His balance is awkward, his footing unsteady.

As he walks past the front door he remembers an image. A flash from yesterday. A memory. Without sleep the night stretches on forever; yesterday feels like a week ago.

That evening a priest had rung on the doorbell startling Daryl and pulling him from a half-conscious stupor; a nap he'd taken after dinner, chancing upon a rare moment of quiet. His anger with being woken had been replaced by confusion when he'd opened the door to a man of the cloth.

"A priest?" he'd stupidly said aloud.

Even now he felt a twinge of embarrassment at his idiocy.

The visit had not been for him of course. Why would the world's most belligerent atheist have a priest come calling?

"Is Miss Buchwald in? Aneta Buchwald?" the priest had asked.

Daryl had directed him next door.

Maybe he'd come to bless the child.

Catholicism was still big in Eastern Europe.

Roman finds a new octave. It brings Daryl from his thoughts and back to the pulsating pain in his cranium.

He squints as he turns the kitchen light on. The fluorescent tube blinks a few times then fills the room with an unforgiving glow. Daryl's stomach turns as he sips on a glass of water. He ignores the dirty plates that litter the sides as he opens the cupboards and finds a new packet of pain killers. The food encrusted crockery makes him feel sick. Flies buzz between plates, capturing his gaze for a few moments. Insomnia has ushered lethargy into his life. His flat is disgusting; a testament to the exhaustion that plagues his days.

I can't live like this.

The pills slide down his throat easily, but they are not working quickly enough. He slumps to the floor as Roman's screams pull at his sanity. They won't stop. More tears fall down his cheeks. Daryl holds his head in an attempt to keep himself together.

A picture falls from its hook as a loud bang thumps from behind the walls. He hears the frame smash in the living room. Glass shards spread like dew across the carpet. The thumping continues, pounding with enough intensity to shake books from their shelves. The baby has not stopped. Roman cries with an unsettling ferocity. The seagulls shriek in a crazed and frenzied chorus, like men in their most awful dying moments.

"I hope we're not any bother."

He remembers the conversation he had with Aneta as he blubs into his own open palms.

"He can be such a little monster at times. And it's so hard now his father isn't around anymore. But if we're making too much noise, please let me know."

His heart is in his mouth. It beats with a power that almost stops him breathing.

I've had enough of this!

Daryl rises to his feet and wipes his tears. Anger swells inside him. It knots his stomach and twists his face. He opens his front door.

She wants me to let her know. I'll let her know. I'll wring that fucking baby's neck in front of her if I have to.

He steps outside and tightens the belt on his dressing gown to protect himself from the cold. Even so, his breath is stolen by the chill of the night air. It should clear his head but it makes him feel faint, a symptom of his exhaustion. Not even the adrenalin rush of confrontation can shift the deep set fatigue from Daryl's crumbling consciousness.

He balls his fists in fury.

Then stops.

Freezes for a moment.

The sight before him instantly defuses his temper, replacing his rage with fear and concern.

His neighbour's lock is smashed from its fitting. The panel is twisted, broken in its frame. The door sits ajar, buckled on its hinges; broken and forced.

Oh my God! All this time I've been cursing them and…

Daryl pushes the scenarios out of his head. Guilt drives him forward, makes him the hero.

With trepidation he enters the flat. The baby is still crying. The sound is raw to his ears. Unfiltered. Sick rises in his throat. A forced swallow pushes it back down, but not before the bile stings his taste buds. He coughs to clear the coating of stomach acid, but it has little effect.

Hello, he thinks about calling out, but fear keeps him mute.

Following the sound of the child in distress, Daryl slowly walks up the stairs. He pauses to flick the light switch, but it has no effect. On. Off. On. Off. On. Off. On. The staircase remains in darkness. The further he climbs the darker it grows. His legs shake, but steadily he makes his way, the cries become louder the closer he gets.

Something hits him in the face as he reaches the top and steps onto the landing. Daryl swipes out with his hand, batting it away. It hits him again. Clutching the object he pulls. A snap frees it from the beaded chain that suspends it from the ceiling. Even in the dark the shape is recognisable to his touch.

It is a crucifix.

Noises of wood knocking together suggests there are more, dangling in the draught. Another swipe from his hand confirms the thought. At least twenty. All hanging from the ceiling.

He pushes past them. One catches him unaware. It strikes him in the eye sending Daryl reeling with shock. He holds out a hand to steady himself, finding a wall. His hand grows wet. The liquid feels thick. Thicker than water.

A man calls out behind a closed door. His words are muffled, unintelligible. His tone suggests rage.

Roman screams even louder and the door at the end of the corridor pounds against its frame.

Christ, that poor child! thinks Daryl.

He runs to the door as his eyes slowly grow accustomed to the darkness. Something beneath him catches his foot. He stumbles and falls. The carpet is sodden. Liquid splashes his face as he grazes his chin on the rough texture.

He looks back and takes hold of the object he fell over. It is long. Cylindrical. It drips from one end. Bringing it closer his vision becomes clearer. It is wrapped in black cloth. Not cloth. Clothing. He sees the shape of a fist, clenched and holding onto a simple wooden cross. The other end continues to drip liquid as Daryl throws it back onto the floor.

The door bangs again.

And again.

It rattles against its hinges. The wood bows, threatening to break.

Self-preservation takes hold. Daryl jumps to his feet and runs. He pushes past the hanging mobile of crucifixes and takes to the stairs. In his panic he loses his footing. His feet fall away from beneath him and he careers forward, down the steps, landing at the bottom in a heap of bruises and confusion.

A light flickers down the hall. A silhouette stands through the doorway, in the living room. It watches him.

"Daryl?" a voices calls out softy.

The Polish tones are instantly recognised.

It's Aneta!

We've got to get out of here!

The pain from his fall screams almost as loud as the bawling infant. Hallucinations take hold. Colours once more dance in the dark, obscuring his vision.

Focus on the light.

He staggers to his feet and towards Aneta. Shadows dance in the candle light that guides his path. Entering the living room he takes her hand. She is cold.

Trembling.

Terror reflects from her eyes.

"They want Roman," she whimpers. "They want my baby."

Who?

Daryl's words are silenced before they leave his mouth. The crying grows louder. A thumping. Footsteps, large and heavy crash down the stairs. Step by step. Louder and louder.

The sound is in the hallway.

Thump after thump.

His eyes widen as Daryl turns to see the living room door slowly creak open. At the top of the door a set of fingers curl round, gripping the panel. They are a mix of blacks and greens, with long, talon-like tips at the end. They are monstrous.

The claws scratch at the paint, pushing the door open wider.

A figure walks in. Daryl guesses it is scraping eight feet tall. Its body is a palette of similar shades to its claws. Its skin looks rough, but hard, somewhere between the scales of a snake and the shell of an insect. Its knees bend inversely as the muscular legs carry its enormous bulk. The creature's arms are long, out of proportion to its body, at least in human terms. Broad shoulders nearly brush the ceiling, and between them protrudes a prehensile, tentacle-like appendage; a trunk-like neck supporting the flushed face of a screaming new born baby.

"Roman!" Aneta calls out.

Its cries are like waves of pain that course through Daryl's every fibre.

Its screwed up face looks towards Daryl as it drops a dismembered torso from its other hand. The body hits the floor, spraying blood across the wall. There is no head, just a neck, hacked and torn. Flesh and skin hang from a brutal tear. A bloodied priest's collar is barely visible amongst the rivers of gore.

Daryl steps backwards. His senses sharpen. The dim light of the room brightens through his dilated pupils. It reveals secrets. Limbs. Torn. Chewed. Squeezed into black rubbish sacks.

Fragments of fabric, frayed and pulled, weave around the body parts. A postman's bag. A police officer's vest. A social worker's suit jacket. The badge still pinned to the lapel displays the smiling photograph of a Miss June Palmer.

How long has this been going on?

Daryl already knows the answer. His sleepless nights are a testament to the arrival of this horror.

He looks towards Aneta for help, but her gaze is fixed on the demon in the doorway.

Is that a smile?

As the creature approaches, he has nowhere to run. The exit is behind this lumbering beast. Through it. He is trapped. Helpless.

Two doors down, Margaret Woods wakes from her sleep. The seagulls are loud tonight. She shudders at their sound, disturbed at the way, when she's really tired, they sound like the blood curdling screams of the dying.

NIGHT PATROL
PAUL M. FEENEY

The police car slipped through the thick fog, like a great white shark silently prowling the depths of the ocean. Its headlights pushed out before it, barely penetrating more than a few feet into the dense vapour.

Inside, their faces lit in sickly shades of green and yellow from the console lights, were Police Constable Alison Durant and Police Sergeant Michelle Preston. Durant drove, hunched close to the steering wheel as she peered out at the mist-shrouded road; going only as fast as she dared, which amounted to little more than a crawl.

Preston wrote a few final words in her notebook then flicked it closed with a decisive snap. "Thank fuck that's *that* shit up to date. Now I'm ready if it all kicks off tonight..." She looked out the passenger window and shook her head. "Mind you, we'll not see much in this even if it does."

Durant glanced at her sergeant for a brief moment.

"Do you think it will, Sarge? Kick off I mean." Her voice was quiet, slightly tense. Though she was a few months out of her two year probation period, she still occasionally experienced that mild apprehension that came in anticipation of a job being called, and having to up her concentration driving in this weather wasn't helping. She wondered if it would ever fade and made a mental note to ask Preston.

"Well, you never know. Weather like this tends to bring out the burglars, muggers and such. Concealment, you know? Plus, I've got that niggle, a bit of tension...police intuition, I guess." Preston fiddled with a piece of equipment on her stab vest, then turned and smiled at Durant. "But don't worry, that doesn't always mean anything."

At least that answered Durant's unvoiced question.

She turned the vehicle down a side street to her right. The thick mist swirled and parted as they passed through, more like liquid than vapour. Fuzzy pinpricks of orange street-light hung disembodied above. Buildings, parked cars and other street fixtures loomed in barely identifiable shadows; the rare pedestrian appearing suddenly like a phantom and disappearing just as quick, swallowed up by fog and distance.

Outside, all was hushed, muted. Inside, the only sounds were the soft hush from the vehicle's environmental controls, the occasional bleep from the radios, and the low rumble of the engine; something Durant felt more than heard.

Even the occasional broadcast from the police radio seemed detached, dispassionate; dispatches from a distant universe. It erupted into loud life now, the panel light illuminating in tandem; causing Durant's pulse to briefly spike and eliciting a tut from Preston. Her sergeant moved to turn the volume dial down, then paused as she registered what was being said.

"Control to all patrols in the Hillington area, be aware of a group or groups of people wandering about possibly threatening or alarming others. We've had three separate calls from concerned members of the public, though they haven't given much detail beyond feeling intimidated and alarmed. We'll try to get more information. In the meantime, keep your eyes peeled and question any likely looking gangs."

Preston picked up the radio handset from its magnetic holder on the dashboard and called in to acknowledge the message. After replacing it, she turned to Durant with a lopsided smile. "I fucking love it when the civvies try to tell us how to do our job. Glorified receptionists, most of them. As if we'd pass by a bunch of likely suspects and *not* speak to them."

Durant was in no mood to indulge her sergeant. The call – coming so soon after her own thoughts had run along the same lines – had set her heart thumping, adrenaline seeping into her system. She felt blood pulse through her wrist, as though someone were tapping impatiently at the skin there. "I hope it's nothing, though. Probably just a few civvies getting jumpy in the weather, don't you think?" Though her words were casual, her voice was pensive and tight, and Durant did not feel the reassurance they intended. She wasn't even sure *who* she was trying to reassure. Her fingers tightened over the top of the steering wheel.

"Well, it's not the kind of weather for public demonstrations or riots, I wouldn't have thought – as if we'd get anything like that around here anyway – and Hillington isn't exactly known for its gang violence. More than likely just a group or two of kids wandering about, putting the shitters up the more sensitive locals for a laugh. Though who'd be out on a night like this, I don't fucking know. Relax, Ali…I'm sure it'll be a quiet night. Nothing we won't be able to deal with." Preston gave Durant a big grin and a wink as she adjusted the passenger seat controls and settled back.

Durant guided the police car around another bend and slowed at a junction which appeared, as if conjured, out of the mist. After checking as best she could that the way was clear, she pulled out onto the main road turning right; all the while a quiet mantra of *please no traffic, please no traffic* repeating in her head.

Preston's relaxed manner was helping calm her own nerves a little and the truth was, Durant wasn't normally as jittery as this. She put it down to the letter she had received that morning, its contents playing on her mind.

They drove all the way down to the main street roundabout without seeing any other vehicles on the road. Choosing a direction at random, Durant manoeuvred the heavy car around the wide central island and exited down one of the smaller side roads.

The fog didn't seem to be dissipating; if anything, it appeared thicker in this part of town. There also didn't seem to be any pedestrians in this area, at least none Durant could see, and it all added to that sense of unreality, isolation and dislocation. If she were of a fanciful mind, she could imagine she and Preston were the only two people left on the planet; or perhaps had somehow been shunted into another dimension without realising it.

She experienced a little shiver at the idea, then put it out of her mind; it was the kind of thing her ex-boyfriend had been fascinated by, a near obsessive interest in all things science fiction and horror. Though she had tried to take an interest in his passions – an effort that wasn't reciprocated by him in the slightest – she remained ignorant of how anyone could find that sort of thing remotely entertaining.

Of course, thoughts of the recent split led to thoughts of the letter and she wasn't ready to deal with that just yet, so to divert her mind from that path, she asked Preston; "Have you ever been involved in a riot situation, Sarge?"

Preston turned slowly to regard her partner; the motion lethargic, like someone moving through thick, clear liquid. Her brow creased in thought. "A riot? Hmmm... I'd have to say no. A few hairy incidents at letting out time, with boozed up punters and the like. But an actual riot…no, can't say I've had that pleasure."

"Oh…" Durant was about to say something else when Preston interrupted her.

"Mind you, I have been told a few *stories* about riots…"

She paused and Durant glanced sideways at her. "And?"

Preston turned away, but not before Durant caught the whisper of a smile on her sergeant's face; her superior was clearly enjoying the mild teasing.

"This was back when I was in the forces – and it's always possible it was already second- or third-hand info when I got told so bear with me if I seem light on details – but…basically, the one I really remember is one of those stories people tell each other when it's late on stag duty to keep each other awake or there's a quiet moment and you want to scare the new recruits."

Durant snorted. "You mean like you're doing now?"

"Ha. Well…maybe just a little. Anyway, it's a story that's always stuck with me, was on my mind for a long time after I heard it.

"This happened in Northern Ireland, back at the height of 'The Troubles', as they were called, late seventies or early eighties, when tensions were very high, loads of horrible shit going on every other day. We…I say 'we', I mean the army; I wasn't over there then, it was just before my time. We were reasonably safe within the barrack compounds. It was only really when you went out on patrol that you had to worry; that you had to keep yourself sharp and alert. The local coppers…they had a *really* shit time of it; having to check under cars in the morning for bombs, watching what they said in pubs, all that crap." She looked at Durant. "You're pretty young, eh? Probably don't really remember much of that, but it was a fucked up time, that's for sure.

"Anyway, what happened was, there was a funeral for some fellow or other…IRA terrorist. As per normal, we would have had – we *did* have – patrols in the area. Not too close to the crowds, not with a heavy paramilitary presence among the mourners, but definitely visible on the outskirts…but *waaay* on the outskirts, if you know what I mean. These funerals tended to play host to a lot of people; a lot of upset and *angry* people, and it wouldn't have taken much to set them off. Well…it *didn't* take much…"

Durant squeezed her fingers tight and moved her hands back and forth over the steering wheel; the leather gave a stuttering squeak. She guided the police car around the empty – as far as she could tell in the thick fog – streets, waiting for Preston to continue her story. There was a tight knot in Durant's belly; a twisting of her guts that always arose when she had something to worry over. Though why Preston's tale should make her feel this way, she could not say.

"One of our patrols took a couple of wrong turnings through the housing estate near the graveyard. Two young squaddies in a jeep; two green lads who should never have been on together, but you know how these things go when resources are thin. The mourners must have numbered in their hundreds by this point – maybe even near a thousand – and once the coffin was in the ground, the mood shifted. You see, the guy whose funeral it was had been killed in a joint army/police operation, and the more volatile people in the crowd were getting a bit riled up, getting vocal against the forces. Understandable, I suppose. Don't get me wrong, the dead guy was a scumbag; he'd been caught in a raid on a house where he and a few others had been making bombs, planning to blow up a school. A fucking *school!* Instead of coming quiet, he grabbed a gun and frankly, he got what he deserved.

"Anyway, these two soldiers got a bit muddled driving around the area and came out of a side street right into the middle of the funeral crowd. And I guess they panicked and froze. Before they could think to reverse back up the street, the crowd had got behind them; completely surrounded them. They should have put the foot down and drove through but – I guess – they were too frightened to think; maybe thought they'd just get a beating before being let go. Maybe they didn't realise the seriousness of the situation and didn't want to hurt civilians. Who knows? I think their lack of experience in the forces and in the country probably played a part. So they got surrounded and the crowd started pushing the car, screaming and shouting at them, egged on by the paramilitaries in the crowd. I imagine there was a lot of coercion there, too, a lot of threats."

Durant's heart thrummed, an aching fast-paced pulse. Being possessed of a vivid imagination since childhood, she could clearly imagine the scenario Preston was describing. In her mind, she saw the vehicle as it exited the dark mouth of the alley; saw it jerk to a halt as the driver realised his path was blocked by scores of angry and gesticulating people; saw the sweating white panic and fear on the faces of the two young soldiers (and in her imagination, they looked no older than teenage boys), their eyes wide; watched as they scrambled around the suddenly too small interior of the car, seeking futilely for a way out; saw the swirling crowd corral the vehicle, moving as one massive entity to cut off any escape; saw dozens of arms reaching out to push against the vehicle, rocking it back and forth. She could imagine the shouts and yells of the crowd, as their frenzy and anger grew and grew, while shadowy figures slunk amongst them, whispering and encouraging; giving instructions of violence and hate, promising pain and retribution should anyone disobey. Her stomach clenched again, lazy waves of discomfort and Durant was almost tempted to tell Preston to stop. She knew this tale would haunt her thoughts for weeks to come.

Her voice, however, decided to betray her, asking in a quiet, wavering tone; "What happened to them?" Dreading an outcome she was almost certain she could predict.

Pursing her lips and slouching lower in her seat, Preston stuck her hands inside her stab vest. She no longer wore a mischievous expression; instead, she looked as uneasy as Durant felt. What had started out as a simple tale to put the frighteners on a relatively green police officer had clearly gotten under the skin of Durant's sergeant again; perhaps she was reliving the first time she had heard the story, feeling the same dread and mounting horror, the same nausea-tinged sympathy for the plight of these two unknown soldiers as she had the first time. Feeling the same emotions that Durant was experiencing now.

Preston sighed. "The crowd got to them. It must have happened fast – far too fast for the two lads to fight back; they didn't grab their weapons, there was only a quick, garbled message on the radio...I don't even think they were trying to call for help. Maybe one of them caught the transmit button with a foot. I never heard the recording of the call, but the guy who told me this story did. He said it was the single most horrifying sound he'd ever heard, and he'd seen a lot of action. He was old school, been in a while. He said you could almost taste the terror in their voices...and behind their screams, the dull roar of the crowd. Then there's glass breaking and it all cuts off. It only runs for a few seconds but what he heard chilled him. I could see it in his eyes.

"The crowd smashed the jeep windows and dragged the two lads out. I think they intended initially to just give them a severe kicking, but the paramilitary guys in the crowd started giving orders, and the civilians were just as scared of them as anyone else. They stripped these two soldiers; lads who had done nothing wrong in their lives except maybe a bit of shoplifting before they signed up.

Lads whose only crime was to have been born in a country and join an organisation that these fuckers saw as the enemy..." Preston paused to take a deep breath, closing her eyes. Her voice had been rising in pace and volume, bitter anger palpable beneath the words. She continued in a more controlled tone, though the strain was still there. "They did beat them. They ripped their clothes off, dragged them about and threw them to one another; hitting, kicking and spitting on them. Scratching them, pulling their hair out in clumps. One of the lads was missing an eye when they found them, the other had most of the fingers on one hand broken in multiple places. And once the crowd had finished with them – though I expect they'd had their fill long past the end and only kept going out of fear of the paramilitaries – the members of the IRA in the crowd got the two soldiers onto their knees, had folk hold them upright and put a bullet each into the backs of their heads."

A tense, weighty silence filled the interior of the car following the end of Preston's story. Durant was numb, horrified. Though she was far from innocent of humankind's potential for brutality and violence towards itself – just over two years working in a relatively busy police force in a large town in the north east of England had put paid to any illusions she might have still clung to in that regard – there was something about this particular incident which had particularly unnerved her; which had crept past her normally solid defences and caused her deep unease. It might have been the matter of fact way in which Preston had related it; or maybe she identified all too readily with the two young soldiers, who couldn't have served much more time in the forces as she currently had in the police. Regardless, the story and the images her imagination had generated had burrowed deep into her thoughts and were now playing over and over on the screen of her mind.

She tried to think of something – anything – to say, to send both of them off on a different, and hopefully lighter, topic of conversation; but each half-formed thought that surfaced slowly in her mind was immediately discarded as inappropriate or ludicrous. And all the while, as the silence grew thicker, the mood seemed to become more strained; darker and thick with portent.

It was Preston who broke the spell with a small voice; which nevertheless still managed to startle Durant. "I kind of wish I hadn't told you that, now. Didn't realise it would affect me so much either, after all this time. Hope I haven't depressed you too much."

Durant offered her a tight smile. "Well…it *is* pretty grim. I just can't stop thinking about those two fellows, what they must have gone through. Horrific."

"Aye. I'll tell you something, though…I came to a realisation when I first heard that story."

"Yeah? What was that?"

"Well, I'd always had a thing for zombie films, you know?"

"Can't say that it's my thing, Sarge." Durant nearly told Preston that her ex-boyfriend could have spoken for hours on the subject – though his enjoyment of these and other violent horror films seemed far less wholesome – but bit her tongue on the matter.

"Well, I used to love them. Mainly because they freaked me out, but it was enjoyable in a way. But I never knew why they affected me so much until I associated them with the two lads and what happened. Then it came to me. It's the mob. One zombie on its own is pretty creepy, two or three are, too; but hundreds of them all shambling towards the camera? That was fucking terrifying to me. It wasn't until I realised they represented the mindless mob, the single entity of a crowd, that I understood just *why* they scared me. Haven't watched a zombie film since. Guess that sounds a bit daft, eh?"

Turning the wheel slowly, Durant guided the car to the side of the road. When it was parked, she turned to Preston and spoke quietly and earnestly. "I don't think it's daft at all. It's a horrible thing to have happened. I'm not surprised it put you off them films. It's...I can't stop...*picturing* it; imagining what they must have felt like when...when they were finally held on their knees, knowing they were going to die, that no one was coming to rescue them. It's...*unfathomable* to me how people can act that way towards others, how a group of folk can just go along with the violent orders of a small minority simply because they're scared..."

She stopped, before any more words tumbled from her lips unbidden. She had been on the verge of disclosing everything currently on her mind, without volition; all her half-formed thoughts on the nature of humanity's violent streak; her disgust and complete incomprehension of historic incidents from the earliest atrocities in the Roman Coliseum to the brutal mass murders of millions by the Nazis and the Soviet Union, and all the way up to the current spate of modern terrorist attacks. Sickening images wheeled leisurely through her mind; black and white photos in textbooks of piles of bodies; torture implements ingeniously designed to inflict the most intimate pain on a body; and on a more personal, intimate level, the emotional and mental abuse perpetrated on her by her now ex-boyfriend, culminating in the letter she had received that morning. Though it had no identifying markers attached, though it could have come from any modern printer, she knew it was him; the vicious, spiteful tone, the varied threats of harm and violence, and the oddly pathetic pleading all pointed to her ex. And she knew she had to do something about it; about him. She had a duty, if nothing else. Yet she did not want to disclose this monumentally personal information to anyone she worked with, least of all Preston, whom she barely knew beyond a working relationship. And Durant had to admit to herself that she was deeply embarrassed. She was a police officer who had allowed another person to dominate and control her life, even if just for a short time; and even though they had now separated, he was still affecting her emotional state, still occupying her thoughts. She felt the shame of such a thing becoming common knowledge – the judgemental staring, the whispered rumours and hearsay – would prove to be too much, necessitating a change of work location, or even resignation. It all conspired to cause turmoil in her gut, worms of anxiety coiling uncomfortably.

Trying to divert her thoughts from the path they had cantered down, Durant slipped the vehicle back into gear and pulled out onto the mist-shrouded road.

They drove in silence for a few minutes, each blanketed in their own thoughts, and when the radio burst into sudden loud life, it made both of them jump this time.

"Fuck! I thought I'd turned that down!" Preston sat upright in her seat, like someone jolted from deep sleep.

She quietened as the message came through, slight tension clear beneath the dispatcher's voice.

"...units in Hillington. Make your way to the High Garden area. Just had a report of an elderly man being attacked and apparently assaulted. No descriptions on the assailants, other than there were at least five. Condition of the victim isn't known. Say again..."

Preston turned the volume down. "I don't think we're far from there, let's go."

While Durant turned the car in the direction of High Garden, Preston called in to let control know they were responding; that done, she pressed the button to turn on the flashing blue lights. "I think we'll leave the siren for now, don't want to scare the locals anymore than they already might be..."

Durant nodded. Her stomach churned, the tension from the call adding to her already present discomfort. There was every possibility the incident would be nothing; at most, they might have to deal with a distraught and possibly slightly injured pensioner. But the oppressive weather, the downbeat mood from Preston's story and her own, personal anxieties all conspired to set her nerves jittering.

It was a mounting apprehension that wanted to translate as increased pressure on the acceleration pedal and Durant had to exercise a powerful effort of will to keep the vehicle moving as slowly as they had been.

As they headed towards the area of High Garden, the thick fog reflected the strobe of their blue lights back in fractal patterns that shifted and seethed, casting strange shadows either side of the car. A dull ache began to throb behind Durant's eyes in rhythm with the pulse of the lights.

With only two streets until their destination, the radio burst into sudden life again.

"*All units, all units, another report coming in of an attack, this time in the Oak Crescent estate. Victims are a young male and female couple, serious injuries to both. Informant states he is a friend of the victims but managed to get away before placing the call. He said that it was a gang of people, indeterminate genders and ages, little vague on descriptions, numbering about seven, all dressed in muted greys, hoods up. He's staying out of sight a couple streets over from Oak Crescent, on Stanford Avenue. I repeat…*"

"Should we attend the new call, Sarge?"

Preston bit her lower lip and shook her head. "No. We keep going to the first. We're nearly there anyway, and there's still a potential victim to see to." But Durant could tell her sergeant was troubled, caught between the vagueness of the first call and the apparent seriousness of this fresh one. Preston's eyes darted about, never settling on anything; the fingers of her right hand unconsciously played with the radio clipped to her tactical vest; her boots drummed a skittish, arrhythmic beat in the passenger footwell.

Durant herself felt keenly nervous; acid jostling in her stomach, bile rising to taint the back of her throat. When they pulled into the top end of the long High Garden road, the tension in her nerves seemed to increase, a high pitched screech only she could hear.

She slowed the vehicle even more, scanning through the driver's window though there was little to see in the obscuring mist. Preston was doing the same on her side.

"Maybe put your window down, Ali? See if you can hear anything…"

The thought sent chills squirming up and down Durant's back. For no rational reason, she was utterly reluctant to open the window; was appalled at the idea of allowing the fog in. She had no cause to feel this way, no cause to fear a simple weather condition, but the mere thought of removing the thin glass barrier caused images to flash through her mind; grasping hands reaching in to grab her; pale, sickly faces with dead fish eyes emerging from the mist to leer at her. But rather than indicate her irrational hesitation to Preston, she moved one trembling digit over the button to open the window. It slipped twice before catching and the glass pane slid down with a shudder and low hum.

Chill air seeped in. Durant shivered, and not just from the cold.

With the window down, the rumble of the engine was far louder; yet also curiously flat, as if the mist was absorbing the volume. She took a sniff; the air was cool, clean, but there was a lingering odour similar to that following a heavy lightning strike. The scent of burnt air. The vehicle's tyres thrummed wetly on the road, a vaguely unpleasant squelching sound. Other than that, there were no other noises she could make out. She also noticed that Preston hadn't opened the window on her side.

It took them a minute to traverse the entire length of the road, in which time they saw nothing untoward or out of the ordinary.

Durant turned the vehicle to face back the way they had come and parked up.

Preston shifted around in her seat. "Well that's fucking odd. Unless some helpful neighbour's taken him in or something…but you'd think we'd have been contacted."

"What should we do Sarge? Get out and do an area-search on foot?" The suggestion had come unbidden, automatically; the last thing Durant wanted to do was set foot outside of the car. Her nerves shrieked at the thought; it was bad enough sitting here with the window open and the thick mist swirling only a few feet away. Shifting and twisting even though there was no wind to cause such movement. There was something vaguely nauseous about it, yet it was also hypnotic. On a spur, she decided there was no need for the window to remain open and kept her eyes on it all the way as it slid back up. When it thumped closed, an unexpected yet welcome relief washed through her.

"Nah...I'll give control a shout, see if anything new has come in." Instead of using the vehicle radio, Preston pressed the button on her personal handset. Durant reached out quickly to turn the vehicle radio's volume down to prevent feedback. "Control from Echo fifty-seven patrol, we've arrived at High Garden but can't find any trace of the victim. Have there been any updates?"

She waited.

No reply.

After a few long seconds had ticked by, she picked up the vehicle handset. "Control, this is Echo fifty-seven patrol attending the incident in High Garden. We have arrived on scene and cannot find any trace of the victim. Can you advise if there have been any updates? Please respond."

Again, long moments passed in weighty silence.

Preston spoke in a breathy whisper. "What the *fuck*?"

Durant didn't think the tension in her nerves could

increase any more, but it seemed she could actually feel the tightening of her sinews, an aching twisting of her fibres. She felt a tremor begin deep inside, as if her very bones were rattling. She wasn't sure she trusted her voice to sound steady but she needed to ask. "Why aren't they answering Sarge?"

"I don't know. Maybe it's a dead spot 'round here but the car radio should have a strong enough signal. I've never had a radio blackout on this system before. Unless they're dealing with something serious but we would have heard, for fuck sake!" Her voice rose in anger and frustration on these last words and she threw the handset onto the dashboard of the car where it lay like a small wounded animal.

"What...what should we do, then?"

Preston rubbed her face and sighed. "I don't know. Let's just head back up to the top of the road. I'll try them again."

Grateful for something to do, Durant popped the vehicle in gear and headed slowly back the way they had come.

Halfway up the road, the car radio burst into life with a high pitched squeal that sent white light flashing painfully through Durant's head. Preston yelled and put both hands up to her ears.

"...all units, all units! Multiple incidents...of Hillington...serious assaults and injuries...members of the public. Reports...than one group responsible, with members...least ten in each group. Descriptions...vague, various... All units in Hillington...with locations. Control out."

Even with the inexplicably broken signal, Durant could hear the strain in the dispatcher's voice, the shrill tones of near panic.

Preston grabbed the handset again, spitting into its receiver. "Control, this is Echo fifty-seven patrol! We're still in the vicinity of High Garden. Can you advise on new locations, over?"

And again they waited on a reply that never came.

"Christ almighty, I do not fucking get it! Why are they not *hearing* us?"

Durant had no answer and suspected her sergeant wasn't really expecting one.

"Let's just go...somewhere. *Anywhere*. Maybe we'll see another car."

Glad to have some direction – even something as flimsy as this – Durant pressed down on the accelerator and headed for the end of the road.

Which then failed to appear out of the fog.

She hunched forward over the steering wheel and watched as the street seemed to unfurl endlessly before them. "What the *fuck*...? Where...where's the bloody junction?"

She slowed the vehicle.

"Did we get turned around, maybe? Heading the wrong way?" Beneath Preston's tight voice, Durant could hear a strong note of hysteria threatening to consume her sergeant. She made an effort to sound calm herself.

"No...no, we couldn't have. And even if we had, the street runs into a junction in that direction, too. Either way, we'd have reached another road. This...this is just in-*sane*." At the use of the word, Durant felt her mind actually yaw slowly from its axis as the sheer impossibility of what was happening began to encroach her understanding. Perhaps it was just an illusion created by the climate conditions and the emotional stresses, but a slowly growing buzz in the depths of Durant's mind indicated that her sense of stability was about to slip loose its moorings.

"Maybe...maybe we need to turn around, then. Go back. See if we can get out that way. Quick. Let's go!" That hysterical note was still present, in every clipped word, but Durant did as Preston said anyway. What else was there?

They pushed slowly through the thick, undulating clouds of mist. Again, the road seemed to go on forever, whispers of shadows sliding by on either side. As they passed beyond where Durant expected – was sure – the road should have ended, she felt tremors start to unseat her hands and clamped them down on the wheel. Her heart fluttered erratically like a moth caged in fingers. That heavy sense of dislocation, of unreality, grew in her mind, a black balloon of threatened madness.

Beside her, Preston stared out at the road with wide, terror-filled eyes. Her arms pressed against the interior of the car, as though bracing against impact. Durant could think of nothing to say so she simply kept driving.

And then the road did end; or rather, it opened up into what seemed to be a circular cul de sac that hadn't been at either end of the road before, the undulating fog moving back to reveal the pavement curling away either side. It was so unexpected that Durant stamped her foot on the brake pedal in surprise. The car lurched to a stop in the centre of the clearing and though they hadn't been travelling all that fast, she was still thrown painfully against the tightening seatbelt. She was dimly aware of Preston's grunt; whether shock or injury, though, she couldn't say. Her foot slipped on the accelerator and the engine cut out.

The silence that followed was heavier than she would have expected, like the aftermath of a violent crash or explosion. She sat there, her hands hooked limply on the steering wheel, feeling dazed as if she had a concussion. The headlights of the vehicle pushed out weakly in front of them and the strobing blue from the emergency lights that were still on bounced back from the wall of mist.

Durant turned to Preston to see she looked as confused and disoriented as Durant felt. In an effort to dispel the sluggish cloud which seemed to have descended on her, she shook her head and placed her hand on the ignition key, intending to turn the engine back on. Before she could, swirling movement from outside made her pause.

At first she thought it was still more fluctuations in the weird mist, eddies and lazy flurries from whatever strange currents were moving within it. But it was more than that. As she watched, figures emerged from the fog, a solid wall of people who seemed to have stepped forward of the mist's threshold as one; or perhaps the cloud had moved back just enough to reveal them. The thought curled through Durant's mind in lazy horror.

She turned the engine on and threw the car into reverse; but when she glanced into the rear view mirror, she saw that the ring of people was complete. The road they had come in from was blocked; they were surrounded.

In the dull light, the figures appeared in shades of grey; and other than the way they all held completely, eerily still, there was no other uniformity to them. All different heights, ages, shapes and, as far as Durant could tell, genders. She wondered in a distant way what had brought them all together and – the thought arriving and departing like an assassin in the dark – what they wanted; what they were going to do. A low mewling sound reminded her of Preston. Her sergeant was lethargically clawing at the interior of the car, as if trying to escape somehow; or perhaps she was testing the solidity of the vehicle, its potential for protection.

Preston's story came back to her, flashes of an angry mob pulling the two soldiers from their car, her mind embellishing the images with more violence – bodies torn to pieces, limbs ripped off and thrown about, blood spattering through the air and on the ground – and she stared out at the silent, unmoving crowd and waited, her guts running with ice water, her blood like dust in her veins.

She sat there, feeling utterly alone in the universe – her foot testing the accelerator, one hand resting on the handbrake, one on the steering wheel – and hoped they'd make their move soon.

CUT TO THE CORE
REBECCA S. LAZARO

"You fucking bitch!" Ellie raged and threw her mobile phone across her bedroom. It bounced off the ridged radiator under the window and skimmed across her deep green carpet, settling under the chest of drawers that spewed out her gothic clothing.

The seventeen year old pummelled her pillow and screamed at the top of her lungs. She kicked out her skinny white legs at the air, and shook her head fiercely, growling to vent her fury, her long black hair whipping in rats tails across her tear-soaked face. Rin had pushed her to her limit this time. She couldn't stand it. The arguments, the insults; they tore each other apart when they should be together.

Stomping out of her room in her slash-necked black metal t-shirt and knickers, Ellie rubbed the mascara stinging her eyes and headed determinedly downstairs to her father's spirits cupboard in the upper half of a locked burgundy dresser. She knew where the key was and he hadn't noticed when she'd stolen the odd few shots of rum or vodka over the years; she'd been careful, but this time was different. Ellie didn't care what her father would say; he was away on business anyway. Right now, she needed whiskey, and the whole bottle of Jim Beam went back upstairs with her.

Unscrewing the top, Ellie pressed play on her stereo and her favourite metal band sounded out, screaming and thrashing guitars. Tipping the bottle, she let the sour liqueur sting the back of her throat three or four times before gasping her breath back. Then, she repeated it, twice more, until she choked and spluttered, spitting down herself; she wiped her chin and bellowed like a cow.

Rin had called her crazy. She would show her what crazy was.

Ellie pulled out her stash and lighter, settled on her bed, and packed her bong full of weed. She took a long hit, the dirty water bubbling furiously, and held her breath until it hurt. She did it again, and again, until only ash remained and her head felt thick yet light, her mind swirling and lifting like smoke.

Physically, Ellie felt calmer, her body eased back against the cushions with the effects of the alcohol and weed relaxing her muscles. The loud music from her stereo felt amplified and took her over for nearly a whole minute, crunching through her awareness as if she existed only in every millisecond that angry song continued to play.

After that, creeping thoughts slid in from the edges of her consciousness. Rin had called her unstable. Ellie heard it again and it cut to her core. Her mother had been unstable - she was nothing like her mental mother. The denial came swiftly.

"I'm nothing like her!" Ellie sat up and yelled at the full-length mirror on the back of her door. Her reflection told her she was wrong, she looked exactly like her mother. "You're the crazy one! You're unstable, Rin, you stupid slut!"

Ellie downed another few gulps of whiskey and gasped out her desperation.

"You're worthless... and ugly!" A warped, raspy voice crawled inside her head, her own bitter negativity turning against her. As she clutched the whiskey bottle between her feet, Ellie burst into tears and began rocking back and forth.

"You're pathetic, look at you... blubbing! You think you're the victim, any excuse to get wasted!" The cruel voice echoed in her head, and Ellie crumbled further under the harsh, reflective spotlight of her vanity. She banged her fist against her forehead. She knew it was true, though she wished she was stronger, but this is how Rin made her feel: pathetic, like a complete victim. Rin knew her inside out and, here, alone with her twisting thoughts, Ellie couldn't pretend to be confident.

"Why don't you drink the whole bottle?" the voice said clearly as Ellie tipped up another large shot into her mouth. *"You might choke on your vomit!"*

Ellie pulled the bottle away from her dribbling lips and frowned through her tears. She had a morbid image of doing just that: her nose and throat filled with sicky, alcoholic fluid, unable to breathe. She didn't know where that thought had come from. She glared at the bottle of Jim Beam worryingly.

"If that doesn't work, you could hang yourself out of the

window..." the voice said seductively.

Ellie looked over at her window, actually considering how she might do it. How did people hang themselves? Knot sheets together? Tie them to the radiator? No, that was how to escape from a prison, wasn't it? Rapunzel used her hair, didn't she? Ellie tried to shake sense into her stoned head. She could thread together twine from her sewing basket until they made a rainbow-coloured noose - that could do it.

"You should get in your dad's car and drive it over the bridge!" the voice enthused.

However, Ellie didn't contemplate it this time, she sat feeling shocked at such a suggestion. She would never disrespect her father by taking out his Jaguar – even if she had a licence! Never mind destroying it! Taking her life was one thing, but writing off her father's beloved vehicle was something she would never dream of.

The idea of doing any of those things scared her, choking on her vomit terrified her, and she pushed the bottle away. She reached for her bong instead and stuffed it full of the green grass, before lighting and pulling hard through the mouthpiece. It blew her head through, and Ellie blissfully heard only the music again, blaring through her speakers. She put down the bong and climbed unsteadily off her bed. She wanted the music to stay in her head, no more thoughts - those were not her thoughts.

Realising the warped voice had said *"your dad"* – Ellie knew she would never refer to her father like that, something must have possessed her, like a demon! Ellie repelled, and shrunk into herself - she must be losing her mind.

Slowly plugging in her headphones to her stereo, her

eyes casting swaying glances across her bedroom, Ellie returned to sit cross-legged on her floor. She felt uneasy, as if something was watching her, hovering over her skin. She wore no bra under her black t-shirt, she felt vulnerable, and all she could do was tighten herself in a ball and wrap her headphones around her ears, listening to her favourite band through her stereo, close and personal, so she could think of nothing else.

Just as she felt enmeshed with her music again, Ellie thought she heard the vocalist yell, *"You can't get rid of me that easily!"* But it didn't sound like part of the lyrics to the song she knew so well. Suddenly, she felt the headphones yank backwards off her head. Ellie turned in surprise and wondered if the lead had caught somewhere between her and the stereo, but the path was unobstructed. The headphones lay behind her, emanating tinny screeching, so she picked them up and, with shaking, nervous hands, fixed them back over her ears.

Within seconds, the volume shot up to an unbearable blast through her skull, and Ellie screwed up her face and screamed as she tore the headphones away. She spun around, clambering to her hands and knees, tripping with bewilderment, and drunken uncertainty. Something was in her head, a real demon, and it was playing games with her. She was going fucking crazy, she knew it.

"I'm still here, you dumb skank!" it retorted with spite.

Ellie freaked and retreated back against the radiator, her teeth chattering with fear as her eyes darted around the room. She couldn't understand whose voice she was hearing if it was not her own. She needed to phone someone for help - she needed Rin.

Slithering sideways across her green carpet, she

scanned the floor for her mobile with blurred vision. It was under the chest of drawers where she had launched it earlier and it lay just out of reach towards the back. Ellie slid her thin arm through the gap and tapped it further away, but with one full stretch from her elbow, scraping the skin at her shoulder, she grabbed it and pulled it out.

Just as Ellie began dialling with jittery fingers, the phone leapt out of her grasp and fell on the floor. Ellie stared in shock, had she dropped it?

"No one can help you now! It's just you and me!"

Moaning with dread, Ellie threw herself across her floor, but her foot tangled with the headphones and it tugged the lead out of the stereo. Raging metal music flooded the bedroom, louder than she had ever dared to play it before, so loud it frightened her. She reached up onto her bed, disoriented, found the bottle of whiskey, and dragged it down onto the carpet with her. She put it to her lips and glugged, three, four, five times, she caught her breath, vomited into her mouth, swallowed it, and glugged again, three more times, until her eyeballs ached, until her veins rushed with fire, until her brain felt like it was oozing out of her ears. She just wanted that awful voice to disappear; she had to pass out soon, she had to.

"You retard! You think I'm going to let you escape now?"

The demon laughed, somehow louder than the pounding music, and the sound terrorised Ellie's soul. She screamed at the top of her lungs as the bottle shot up out of her grip, hovered threateningly over her head, then slammed down against the radiator beside her, smashing into large chunks and spiny splinters. Ellie stared down at the mess, at the wasted whiskey seeping into the carpet with growing horror, recalling watching *Poltergeist* years back.

"Pick it up, Ellie."

Scared out of her wits, Ellie's brain did what it was told by the dark force that had her cornered. It was easier than fighting something she had no power to control, and in her intoxicated state, and with no frame of reference for how to battle evil, Ellie would make a futile warrior. She sunk with resignation like the pathetic victim she had accepted she was. Whilst the deafening roar of the metal band crashed through her room, Ellie ran her fingers across the translucent, shining slivers, and with glazed, faraway eyes, selected a devastating shard, the sharpest and pointiest of them all, as if she were choosing the finest diamond ring to bond her forever with the devil.

"Open... your... skin..." the creeping voice said slowly, persuasively.

Ellie took the shard in her shaking right hand, balanced her left elbow on her knee, and pressed the end down into the flesh of her forearm. She didn't feel any pain, she was experiencing a rush of adrenalin as she saw blood trickling down in thick, bright red streaks that dropped and splashed on her naked thighs. Ellie watched her skin peel apart as easily as a ripe grape as she made the slender gap longer and longer.

"Again... deeper..." the dark voice said, sounding aroused, hungry, or thirsty.

Looking down at her thigh already stained with blood, Ellie honed in on the fleshy inside and knew she could dig in deeper there. She pushed her knees wide and stared between them. With the red, sticky glass slipping against her palm, Ellie pressed harder and felt an eruption, a release of pressure, from within; it looked, to her stoned mind, like a red rose in bloom. The soft tissue prised open willingly, the network of her flesh underneath visible as fatty pebbles. She peered inside, fascinated, but her eyes spiralled out of focus.

Her gaze drifted down inside her t-shirt, hanging open at her chest, the small triangular mounds of her breasts like pale pyramids, untainted by age and strangers. She saw the black, slash-neck tugged gently down until one peachy nipple poked out. Almost as if on autopilot, Ellie raised the glass and sliced slowly and carefully across the skin over her heart, tearing the flesh inside. Blood spurted out over her small breast, covering it in a curtain of warm, liquid energy. She tilted the end of the shard into the wound, and twisted it, scooping out the quivering pulp from within. A tangible thrill shot through Ellie at being able to see, close up, what the inside of her body looked like, and she cut out a congealing flap, hanging over the edge of her wound, like a man overboard, desperately fleeing for the lifeboats. Ellie felt like a God for a split second.

"You think you're important..." the voice spoke from beyond her being. *"Your life is worth nothing, you are no one! Nothing you do matters to anyone! No one cares for you, no one will save you... you might as well end it all now!"*

Dropping the shard of glass, Ellie crawled on her hands and knees towards her chest of drawers and drunkenly swiped her arm over the painted black surface before collapsing onto the floor. Her bottles and cans of toiletries fell on the carpet next to her, and squinting hard to focus, whilst her loosely looping mind collected some ideas, Ellie grabbed an aerosol can of deodorant, and hauled herself up to an unsteady kneeling position as if she were a propped puppet on the end of strings. She lifted the can with two hands and fiddled with the nozzle with every one of her fingers and thumbs until it pointed at her face.

Co-ordinating which of her fingers to press proved another tricky job, but soon, Ellie found that if she held the can with one hand and pressed the nozzle with the other, she could shoot a jet of freezing hot gas onto her skin. Honing in on one area, Ellie held the spray an inch away from her cheek, as still as she could, and held her breath from inhaling the cloud of white particles that bounced off her skin. She didn't stop until it was nearly empty. Ellie threw the can down, fanned the cloud away, and retrieved her breath, only then did she feel the heat spreading across her face. She didn't want to look at the burn in the mirror, so she didn't know that the skin of her cheek had bubbled into red pustules, reacting to the chemicals. She didn't know why she had done it, just as she didn't know why she was reaching for the bottle of nail varnish remover.

Ellie unscrewed the lid and tipped the whole bottle down her gullet. She swallowed it even as it stung the back of her throat, worse than the whiskey, and fumes escaped from her nostrils as if she were a baby dragon, not yet mature enough to breathe fire. Ellie coughed, retched, and vomited down herself, she didn't attempt to catch it, just let it cascade down her front in a luminous pink waterfall. It splashed into the wound on her breast, and Ellie gazed at the mild stinging sensation, her head nodding as her mouth leaked the steaming fluid melting her insides.

Falling to her elbows, Ellie's head swung from the mixture of poisons she'd ingested swirling havoc through her system. She saw the wound on her forearm displaying its contents, open, almost vaginal, oval, and dark inside. She didn't know why she'd done that, what had compelled her to, what was happening to her. At the same time, her other hand somehow located and dragged a bobby pin from the mess on the floor, and she brought it to her lips, bit off the tiny round plastic protector between her teeth, and aimed the sharp, thin metal end at the wound.

"This is what you deserve..." The voice sounded a deranged sort of calm. *"You deserve to suffer."*

Helpless to stop it, Ellie felt her hand being guided by an unseen force. The tip of the pin dug into the wound, piercing through the flesh under her skin, springing forth fresh trickles of blood. She watched her fingers drive it deeper and deeper until the whole pin had buried between the layers of fat and muscle. Ellie stared at it, then gave a shriek of horror, her eyes welling in shock at having done that to herself. She would never have thought of doing such a thing, Ellie's remnants of consciousness realised; it must be the demon, making her do it. The pressure on her hand from elsewhere, it was touching her, moving her! Ellie thought again that she must be going mad, to hear such an otherworldly voice in her head in the first place, now to imagine her body manipulated by it.

But here it came again, that strange pressure on her wound, something was squeezing it, closing the gap around the pin inside. Ellie felt a searing spasm as her wound clutched around the foreign object, and then, a dull twang, a fuzzy numbness, and her arm flopped down, swinging at the elbow. Something had snapped or severed, Ellie's fear resumed as she tried to lift her arm but couldn't.

"All's fair in love and war!" the voice said, in a taunting,

spiteful tone. Ellie felt a grip seize on top of her head, and a scalpful of pain followed as her hair was pulled from its roots. She raised her good arm to hold it down, but whatever had it, held it fast and no amount of grasping and tugging at her hair could release it from the demon's torturous vengeance.

"What do you want from me?" Ellie screamed. "What do you mean love and war?"

"For all the pain you gave me, for all the times you made me hurt myself, this is what you get for being a nasty, selfish, cruel, unstable, crazy bitch of a girlfriend!"

Her eyes goggling out of her head, Ellie felt a low-down tremble in her stomach, the volatile concoction threatened to climb up her throat like a condemned soul escaping from the fiery pit of hell.

"RIN?" Ellie shouted over the music, still blaring.

Ellie couldn't believe the voice she was hearing was her girlfriend. They had argued on the phone less than an hour ago, how could she be here, in the room?

"Is it you?"

"Yes, it's me, 'the stupid slut'!" The voice now formed Rin's recognisable whine. *"I slit my throat because of you, because of the way you spoke to me, how low you made me feel!"* Rin spat passionately from the ether. *"So I came to find you, and I'm going to make you suffer like I have, but worse, much, much worse!"*

"You've already fucked me up!" Ellie shouted, feeling the throb in her cheek become a wicked agony. "Just leave me alone!"

"I told you, you're stuck with me!" Rin's voice drifted around Ellie's neck. *"There's one more thing you have to do for me..."*

The bloody shard of glass Ellie had discarded earlier now manifested back into her hand and Ellie found herself seizing it tightly without intending to. Her hand felt as if it belonged to a five year old clutching a course paintbrush, with a well-meaning teacher gripping over hers, guiding and showing her how to move it firmly and gently. But this grasp was neither gentle nor patient - the ghost of Rin didn't care about scratching Ellie's groin as she dug the glass shard under the fabric of her knickers. The black material split and peeled away from her thigh, exposing her trimmed pubis and sending Ellie into jolting shrieks of fear.

"What are you doing?" Ellie cried, desperately trying to stop the glass dipping downwards again towards her private area.

"Cut... it... offffff!" Rin growled, and pressed heavily down on Ellie's hand until the glass tip made contact with her skin, poking her outer labia.

"What do you mean?" Ellie shrieked.

"You'll never fuck anyone else, no one will have you, not like this!"

"Like what?" Ellie gasped as the glass edged further down her sensitive slit. She felt every excruciating scrape as she watched - now her senses had come rushing back to her - she was feeling this with every heartbeat, though none of her other injuries were leaving her breathless as was the anticipation of what Rin was about to make her do.

Before her eyes, the precious skin of her inner labia felt tugged out from its cosy nest, and Ellie fell back against her radiator in awe, her feeble arm rolling idly by her side, unable to push or pull away whatever had her by her most delicate parts.

"*CUT IT OFF!!*" Rin's voice grated through Ellie's psyche, drowning out even the racketing noise around them from the stereo.

"No, no, no, please, no!" Ellie cried, but felt her hand hopelessly compelled towards the centre. Within an inch from the bulging skin around her clitoris, Ellie saw her hand shaking with her willing resistance, but still it defied her and urged inwards. The incision began at the lower end, and as Ellie screamed and screamed, she watched the glass in her hand hack slowly upwards, deep into the nerves, and as blood squirted in high arcs, it serrated clean through her tender bud.

Ellie felt her head go limp, and she slumped back against the radiator. Her hand fell open, the glass stuck to her palm with red gel, and her eyes rolled back in her head. The last thing Ellie saw, before she blacked out, was Rin's ghostly apparition hovering over her, grinning in that hideous way she did when she was being cruel.

"*I'll see you on the other side, bitch...*" Rin taunted. "*We'll be together forever.*"

THE GLEN
NATHAN ROBINSON

He dug the shallow grave whilst his daughter gathered wild flowers and danced halfway up the hill, humming a made up tune. That was the only music he listened to nowadays. It was nonsense. But it was beautiful nonsense. A concoction of her own imagination and recycled cartoon theme tunes that she remembered from before. The bright May sunshine betrayed his mood, but he smiled when he could. For her. He had to. He had to live for something. They both did.

"Daddy, watch me cartwheel."

That would do. It was plenty deep.

He stabbed the shovel into the mound of soil he'd taken from the earth and pulled back the worn leather work glove. Loose soil fell from behind his watch, a dirty ring of sweat marked off his exertions.

He removed his gloves and tucked them into his back pocket.

Quarter to eleven and he'd already dug a grave. It had been a strange morning; stranger than most, but not the strangest by far. He remembered the city with a shiver, glad he'd left it behind. He preferred the country. He did now anyways. He'd always lived in the city, but they'd all become places of poison. It was safer in the sticks, quieter, which is what he needed. Not for the peace, but to increase his chance of being alerted in case something should sneak up on them in the night.

He looked at the grave, then at his daughter cart wheeling without caution.

All it would take was for her to break her neck. An arm could give way and she'd slip and separate her vertebrae. It would be over and I could end it. It would be done. Neither of them would have to suffer anymore. He was done with winning this lost life.

He chided himself for wishing his daughter's life away. She was his future, his only light.

He'd found a gun; a pistol, tucked into a dead soldier's holster. He'd taken it though he'd never had the courage to fire it in case it alerted the world around to their presence. He kept it in his bedside drawer at night and the glovebox whenever they went out. Although dangers probably still existed (they'd seen no other trace of life in months), he didn't like to keep the gun on him. It was as if admitting he was scared, that he had something to fear. Some bad things can't be killed with bullets.

"Darling come down here. Don't play too close to the trees."

She tumbled and rolled, steadying herself she looked up at him, pushing her long, overgrown mop of hair from her face. It needed a cut. She looked wild, not unkempt in anyway. But free and a little bit dangerous, such is the way people had to be nowadays.

"Why not, daddy?"

"You know why, just come back here. I'm done. We're ready."

"Okay daddy." She got to her feet and pelted down the hill through the long grass, carefree and happy as always. This was all a game for her. His brave face had kept the charade up. This was normality for her, she was used to this. For him it was hell. But he made it heaven for her.

We're playing a game. We're hiding. Want to play?

She came and stood by the grave, next to him and took his dirty fingers in her dainty hand.

"I'm thirsty daddy."

"You're thirsty? I've been digging all morning."

"Can I have a drink?"

He ruffled her mop of hair and looked back to the red pickup parked on the other side of the fence, behind the mossy kissing gate that led into the glen.

We start out as dreams and end up as memories, he mused.

"I've some water in the truck. Let's go get Charlie."

He handed his daughter a bottle of mineral water from the open, polythene wrapped pack of sixteen (eight missing) sat in the rear cab and then walked around the back of the truck.

Following him, she held the bottle out for him, "Can you open it for me please. My fingers aren't strong enough."

"They will be one day," he said, taking the bottle back from her.

"Yep. Then I can beat you at arm wrestling."

"You already do."

"That's just you pretending. I want to beat you for real," she grinned.

"Drop and give me ten."

His daughter fell to the ground and knocked out ten push ups right there in the dirt with a rampant eagerness. When she'd finished she jumped back up and he passed her the opened bottle.

She knocked it back, pushing her delicate throat to the sun, glugging the bottle dry. He watched her muscles pull the water down inside, emptying it all with the efficiency of a hungry pump. It was true, she was thirsty.

"That better?" he asked, slipping his gloves back on.

"Much better."

"Good. I'll fetch Charlie," he said, opening the back of the truck and reaching for the blood stained bed sheet, "you can carry that fuel can for me."

He didn't drop her in, but placed her down gently at the side of the mound and jumped into the five foot deep grave. Then with a crack of his back, he reached back up and grabbed the sheet and lifted her in. She felt lighter, as if the lost life of a being weighed more than just a soul. He knew that wasn't the reason. He should have covered her in another sheet to quell his daughter's curiosity, the dark stains raised questions.

Crinkling his nose at the smell, he placed her gently on the flat dark soil. This wasn't the first he'd dug, but still, he kept his graves neat, out of habit perhaps or maybe because he had time to spare nowadays. He encouraged a sense of pride in disposing the bodies of those that he knew. Strangers, who happened to clutter his neighbourhood, were wheel barrowed into a pile on waste ground at the edge of town and burnt in a pyre. It still paid to be efficient despite the luxury of time.

In his mind he had weighed up the scenarios of leaving the bodies out and about the surrounding areas and the stench and disease they'd create against disposing of them, which of course meant getting up close and personal with the faces of the dead.

It took a strong stomach and a few days, but soon the embers died and the grim stench of barbequed flesh dissipated to the wind. In the long run, he figured he'd made the right choice, even if it cost him a few nights of lost sleep from the warped faces and rictus grins that plagued his thoughts whenever he closed his eyes.

The dead were dead and they were staying that way. He just didn't like what came before.

He climbed out the grave, making a mental note to sanitise his hands despite the protection of his gloves. Over time, he found it all too easy to lose his antiseptic nature and had to remind himself that cleanliness was still important, even more so given the way of the world.

It had taken him a few days to decide on a suitable burial spot. Three days in the rising heat of May had been his limit. Three days of hiding his tears and his bubbling madness and he still had the garage floor to scrub free of gore. He'd even considered starting afresh in a new house. There had been more blood than he expected, but thankfully he kept it all out of sight behind a locked door. Her dreams had been saved, but the emerging smell was kept at bay with open windows and air freshener. It could have been much worse. It could have been mid-August.

His daughter looked down upon the bloodied sheet,

with curiosity and part disgust.

"What's going to happen to her? She's going to heaven?" she asked earnestly.

"Yeah, doggy heaven if you like. She's playing with all her doggy brothers and sisters."

His daughter twisted the end of her nose as she considered his answer, squinting at the sun. She stared at it, closed her eyes and held her hands together.

"Dear God, please look after Charlie as we can't any more. She was a good dog and I'm sorry that she died. I don't know why she died. Daddy says she had an accident. And baby Jesus, could you tell Santa Claus that I would like some roller skates for my birthday. I'm six in September, so you've got plenty of time."

He smiled. She had an oblivious, innocent humour unlike anyone he had ever met and it always brought him joy. He added another mental note about the roller skates. He'd have to keep an eye out for them in her size. Purple if possible, her favourite colour.

"That was beautiful sweetie."

She smiled once then returned her hands to her side. "Do you believe in God, daddy?"

"I don't think so. Not now. Not after what happened."

"What will happen to you if you don't believe in God?"

"The same if you do believe in him I should think."

"What happens to your body? Does Jesus take it? That's what they told us in assembly."

He smiled at her innocent face, ruffled her hair and pulled her head to his hip, trying to make the situation less weird than it needed to be.

"No, you stay exactly where you're buried. Forever."

"Does it hurt? Death I mean."

"Death doesn't hurt, but dying does as I'm to understand."

"Was Charlie hurt?"

"A little, but I helped her." He shivered inwardly at the memory, and the hope he wished for that Charlie's final whimpers wouldn't wake his daughter. He'd made enough noise already.

"What do you do in your grave? Won't you get bored?"

"No you're not there anymore. It's just your body. Like an empty jug." He gestured to the grave. "That's not Charlie in there. Charlie is in our hearts and in the stars. Her body is having a dreamless sleep in a quiet grave. Eternal rest from now until forever, so she'll never wake up."

"Can we have ravioli for dinner?"

And that was that, his explanation of death to his daughter was replaced by hunger as easily as day turns to night and rain falls from grey skies.

"You not want something cold, like a sandwich? We made bread, remember?"

"I just fancy some ravioli. I know you don't like using the tins, it's just what I want right now."

"Of course you can. How can I turn you down?"

"Are we going to bury Charlie?"

And back to death.

"Yes, but we're going to have a fire first. To keep her warm."

"Won't she burn?"

"Yes, but she won't feel a thing, remember? It'll help

her get to the stars."

"Oh," she nodded, as if agreeing on his faux science.

"Listen, we'll need some wood, to help the fire get going. Would you go and fetch me a few sticks?"

"Sure daddy."

"But stay to the edge. Don't go past the tree line. If you see anyone, I want you to run back to me."

"Okay daddy."

He felt it important that she have freedom in her childhood. Other parents would bunker away and board up the windows, but he wasn't like that. Sure he was careful, but that's no childhood. Youth was sunshine and running aimlessly, sweet food and laughter. He wanted her to have that. He wanted her to have memories of this beautiful world. Well, whatever was left of it and what joy he could salvage from the wreckage humanity had left behind. He didn't want the landscape of her childhood to be four walls and a roof, cowering and being scared of whatever lurked outside. That was no existence. They'd done that for a few weeks, but after a while, whatever madness was happening outside, stopped.

No more fires, shouts or screams. The shooting stopped as did the buzz of helicopters overhead. Nobody ever tried to get into the house (that he knew of), and he was thankful for that as his family was unscathed and disease free.

The streets were morgue quiet and as still as picture. He brought his family down from hiding upstairs (they had a small balcony filled with plants, and a water butt to harvest rainwater from the guttering. It had saved them after the mains electric and water was turned off. It had gotten them through a few bad weeks.)

Breaking through the barricade, they found a world empty, the living gone, the sick dead and rotting in the streets having run out of things to eat. They'd seen so much from their little vista on the balcony, venturing out only at night. But up close, the world was pretty much ash.

They recovered supplies, and prepared for the worst. But no one came. It was the three of them and Charlie. But they made do with what was left of the world.

A generator, a cleanup of the neighbourhood (bodies and litter), and soon they had the house back the way it should be.

Life goes on, no matter what.

Someone once told him that today is the first day of the rest of your life.

That mantra was bullshit.

How are you supposed to forget who you are? If you're a terrible person, you take that with you to your grave. Sure you can be less of an arsehole, but you can't change what you've done. Folk remember. You can't forget your scars.

Today is the day you start lying to the new people you meet about all the wrong you've done, would be a more apt proverb.

He'd not had a drink for three years and despite what had happened to world, that hadn't changed. Keeping it straight, he needed to keep it together for her. Some dark part of him had patiently wished her gone. Not dead in any particular way, he hadn't fantasised about killing his daughter, nor would he start. Just gone, vanished one day without a trace. Reset his responsibilities back to zero.

Only then would he give up. All his reasons would be gone and he could get his oblivion over and done with, using the proper methods. Out and about, he'd seen a bottle of *Evan Williams* that had looked appetising. It was okay to give up after everyone else had.

He looked to the sun, bathing in its glow. They had a good few hours left. They could go shopping. Or what passed for it nowadays. Uninterrupted shoplifting.

"Is mummy coming back?" his daughter called back as she galloped for the tree line.

It took him a moment to find his voice. He swallowed. "No. Not tonight sweets."

"Is she still at grandma's?"

"Yeah, she'll be gone awhile."

He looked back to his truck, then back to his daughter. He had hoped that she'd stop asking questions, that she'd get bored and suddenly find a hobby. But she was smart and she'd soon click on that something was amiss with the world around her. As much as he wanted to be honest with her, he couldn't deal with her questions and tears. It wouldn't be likely that she'd forget her mother anytime soon.

When he'd taken her shopping last week and she'd remarked *"It's very quiet today daddy,"* as if she'd just started to notice the world had gone to shit.

Her mother was a constant and another matter entirely.

The glen was one of her favourite places, North of the town and far away from the bedlam and chaos of any of the cities. It would be natural to come here. She would have liked it here. They'd enjoyed walks with Charlie, through the glen and down by the river. It was calm and quiet, and all you'd need to clear a cluttered mind.

Everywhere was calm and quiet now, but at least this

place had looked as it always had. It had kept its integrity, though the grass was long and there were no birds tweeting in the trees. He suspected most of them were in the cities as there was plenty of food on the streets. A protein free-for-all.

The world had changed and there wasn't much he could do about it, except live with it. Watching the world eat itself was frightening. Soon no one was left, and somehow they made it through unscathed. His family was intact and there was nobody to bother them. The sickness had burnt itself out.

Their self imposed quarantine had worked.

Until three days ago.

He looked back to the truck.

Explaining the death of their dog was easy enough to a five year old, but to say to that same five year old that he had, in fact, bludgeoned her mother to death with a hammer after he had found her with the still yelping dog's entrails in her mouth. How do you do that? What would he gain from telling the truth? Nothing.

Seeing his wife the way she was made him understand how the world had gone to shit with ease. The flu like symptoms (*it's just a sniffle, get me some Beechams*, she'd said, FLW), the lethargy that would bring family members closer as they tried to help, then the sudden, maddening hunger that would tear them apart. He guessed, after the world had eaten itself, they all starved.

Living was hard, dying was easy.

Murder was easy, living with it was hard.

It wasn't murder. It wasn't murder. It wasn't murder.

He'd released her from the disease. That was his final reasoning.

Well the hammer had, turning her brain off in a single sweep. Yet, he hadn't stopped. He carried on, a maddening fury over taking him as he smashed her face into pieces. He didn't want to look at her anymore. Afterwards, the chunks of brain were so small, they puddled into the chips he taken out of the concrete floor.

Any recollection of the haphazard clean up hadn't gelled to his mind. Some magical part of his brain he was indebted to had somehow blocked out that memory, for the time being at least. He daren't sleep for what terrors his dreams might bring.

He fetched his wife's body, wrapped in a blue tarp as he couldn't find a sheet big enough to contain the gore and lowered her into the grave as he had Charlie, laying her beside her beloved dog. He poured the petrol into the grave, savouring the old familiar smell of the fumes as they stung his eyes and took the gruesome stench away.

This was life now.

His daughter was rushing back with a bundle of sticks in her little white arms and a smile beaming.

As much joy as she brought him, as many smiles as she conjured up from his weary soul, he knew one day it would all end for both of them. It might be her first, in which case he'd end it straight after, that was easy, his only final comfort. He hadn't been born to watch his child die. But it was something he would have to accept.

The flipside was even worse.

The scenario was evident that he might go first, by accident or even the sickness returning.

A chill shudder electrified his body. The thought of turning on her in this empty world filled him with a cold, hollow dread. To be her end was perhaps the most chilling thing he could imagine, and he wouldn't even be around in his mind (he assumed) to see the betrayal pool in her eyes.

Her terror would be endless without him.

He thought about that bottle of bourbon and returning to his old wrecked self one final time. He could get her some juice. Hide the taste of whatever concoction he gave her. She'd be sure to suffer painlessly then.

Murder was easy. And he wouldn't have to live with it for long. A short life of joy would be better than dragging it out and it ending in a moment of teeth and terror.

Most likely his teeth.

He didn't want to fail her in that way. It could be on his terms, he could make it fair.

A cough tickled his throat, creeping up the confines of his oesophagus as if he'd swallowed a spider and now it was revealing itself with a deliberate, meandering entrance.

It was only her and him now. Nobody else. Nothing else. Them alone.

He always liked coming back to the glen. It helped him think.

THE VILE GLIB OF GIDEON WICKE
LILY CHILDS

A coin. That's all it was, bent and barely recognisable but I knelt and plucked it from the mud, hoping for an old guinea. Even from that first caress, the tarnished piece resonated in my palm as though spat from the gullet of an electric eel, still carrying the current. I held onto it for maybe longer than I should but something stopped me from dropping the coin into my bag of riverside treasures and I decided to call an end to the day's scavenging. The wind had turned. It spewed out a violent belch of cold air which hit me straight in the face, peppering my skin with salt and dirty sand. The tide would be turning soon too. I'd left an oxtail stew simmering on the stove and Betsy, my faithful retriever would be needing a walk, a wee and my pitiful affection. Poor girl; she wasn't long for the world.

I trudged along the exposed riverbed toward the steps

built into the harbour wall, sleet pelting at my back in fine shards. The ladder-like stairs were in desperate need of repair and I counted my blessings, feeling the rusted metal give slightly with every step up. The worst was at the top and the handrail, minus its fittings, banged against the stone in dull discordance. But I made it.

Darkness fell quickly on the short walk home and it wasn't until I reached my front gate that I realised I'd been clutching the old coin the entire journey. I turned it over, once. . . twice. Only the sound of Betsy baying behind the door of our small cottage shook off the odd sensation that the monetary piece was trying to tell me something. I wasn't sure I wanted to hear its message.

Betsy died that night. She'd messed herself and lay shivering in her own filth in front of the stove. She cried when I entered the room and *I* cried when old Doc Deemus gave her a great big shot of death two hours later.

"You want me to take her, Joe?"

I shook my head. He'd waive the fee, I knew it, but that wasn't the issue.

"I'm fine, Doc. Thanks. I'd like to say goodbye to her properly and. . ."

I'd stopped talking but what went through my head was that I'd bury her in the garden under the apple tree where she used to lie in the summer, chugging with the heat, that great tongue of hers lolling sideways out of her mouth.

Deemus nodded; he dispensed death and witnessed grief every day but the long craters etched into his kindly face declared he had never come to terms with that hardest side of his profession. He left quietly.

Come midnight, Betsy – wrapped in her favourite blanket – lay safe in the cold ground and I had come back inside to the acrid smell of burnt oxtail stew. I no longer wanted it anyway. I found a bottle of stout left over from the previous lonely Christmas and poured it into a teacup, sipping at it before it had a chance to settle, not caring what it would do to my frazzled gut. I piled all the candles I owned into a shrine at the end of the table; the wax would stain the wood permanently but I didn't care for aesthetics. And whilst my doors and small windows let in little air, they were being sorely tested by the winter storm cursing the skies outside which sent shrill banshees to whistle and wail through invisible cracks. The candle flames rose and fell in a fiery dance until, there – I saw it, its dull surface catching the light. Had I placed the coin on the table? I couldn't remember, but here it was, its shape undulating in the shadows. I imagined tall, skin-and-bone forms twisting this way and that, coiling skeletal fingers around the coin which had now made its way into my hand without my having picked it up. I stared at it, felt its cold throb, caught sight of a number 3, or was it an 8, and there I remained until I awoke the following dawn with a crick in my neck and a perfectly polished Charles II shilling in my pocket.

Despite the warped shape, I reckoned the coin would still earn me a few hundred quid – enough to feed me and Betsy. . . ah, just me then – for a few months. Even as the plan played out in my head it was wiped away. I'd never sell the shilling. I'd carry it to the grave. And deep in the core of me, I knew that journey wouldn't be long for me now either. It wouldn't be long at all.

She stood at the top of St. Mrythin's Mount, a stalagmite of a thing at the edge of town that used to haunt my dreams when I was a boy. I don't know when I grew out of the nightmares, but seeing my aunt up there this morning brought the memories back with a punch, a punch that doubled me up on the street. No-one stopped to ask after my health; judging me a tramp, drunk already at this time of day. By the time I dragged myself upright, bile raging at my teeth, I realised it couldn't possibly be Aunt Gert for she was already old when I was young, and here I am kicking eighty-three. When I stared up at the summit of the great earthy wart, she was no longer there.

My belly hurt; it hurt more and more these days. Betsy used to lay her head there, her wet eyes saying, "You really need to get that seen to, old man." She was right. My clothes were hanging off me and I was shitting blood. Too late now. Maybe I'd better go see Doc Deemus. Ask if he'd got a syringe full of death to stick in me too.

So that's what I did.

He tried to talk me out of it; told me about the Hippocratic Oath which compelled him to keep his clients alive, but his soul revealed the truth despite his obligations.

"Take this, my friend," he said finally. "Don't eat. Don't drink. Let it hit your stomach and go lie down."

I took the bottle of filthy liquid from his hands. I didn't want to know what was in it.

"Thank you."

Deemus couldn't keep the kind smile up any longer. I swear I saw his eyes water and I realised that even though we weren't friends exactly, we'd known each other our entire adult lives and a mutual respect had developed between us. I reached out to him and he stared down at my hand before shaking it firmly, with gentle understanding.

"Goodbye Joe. I'll collect you in the morning."

I left the back-room of the good doctor's house and wandered off to my cottage, St. Mrythin's Mount gloating in the distance. I thought, when I reached the front door for the last ever time that I saw my aunt again, turning the corner of my tiny road. Madness. Whoever it was, they were of no importance now. Snow was falling and I had a bed to make of it, out in the garden beneath an apple tree.

The thin piece of land, once an orchard, stretched between windowless factories, their walls black with hundred-year old smog. Once I'd gone, my little cottage would be pulled down in the blink of an eye. The corporation had already tried to evict me on various grounds, shifting from a pretention of concern for my welfare through to open threats of compulsory purchase, but I'd thwarted all attempts to kick me out of my family's home. It wasn't much, but it was mine, and now there would be no-one to pass it on to. That ghost of an aunt would have no claim, because she didn't exist.

I figured it would be a painful demise, so I gathered all the bedding I could find, spread it over Betsy's grave and returned to lock the house up for the final time. I had left everything 'just so', as my old Ma used to say; I didn't want people casting judgement even though I wouldn't be around to witness their condemnation. The bottle, its ingredients moving in murky promise, waited for me to collect it from the otherwise empty mantelpiece. It took a moment before I could bring myself to pick it up. My hand shook as I reached for the vial and as I pulled it towards me it knocked something to the ground. The shilling. I'd have bet its value it was still in my pocket, but it glinted there upon the floor, twinkled, urging me to pick it up and carry it along with me on my journey to the end. My knees cracked as I went down and I actually chuckled as I drew the old king's profile to my line of vision.

"I'll take you with me Charlie," I said. "Ain't long since you've seen the light of day and now you want to go back into hiding, eh? Did a fair bit of that in your lifetime too, I gather." His Royal Highness did not respond. Maybe Deemus would be able to prise the coin out of my stiff fist, sell it on to cover the debts – monetary and otherwise – I owed his good self. I grasped it, slipped the bottle of poison into the pocket of my only good jacket and went outside to die.

Cold, so cold. It's snowing in my ears and on my tongue and I can hear the moles scritching and scratching, digging through Betsy's corpse in a race to find mine. And the rats! They're everywhere, falling from the factory roofs and crawling all over my blankets, waiting – just waiting – to eat me all up. Their claws hurt and their eyes shine like pale rubies. I try talking to them but they laugh like rats always do, and go on with their business of pissing and fornicating on my sheets, on my skin, as everything inside me starts to close down. I never knew it would be like this; I expected some dull agony but this is raw and sharp, hack, hack, hacking with multiple needles and knives.

I can't see anymore.

Can't move.

But a shadow falls over me, and when her voice says, "You're coming with me," I realise there is no end, not now, not ever, and against my will I rise from my inert body and follow Aunt Gert into the dark.

Colours; there were colours, little dashes and flickers wherever I dared to look – but only until I blinked, when the pale shades moved or disappeared like floaters in a rheumy eye.

My old town spread out in front of me, the mount up on the right, bare, covered in raw brown earth not grass. Over to the west, the tidal Ouse seemed wider somehow. Even from this distance I could make out the waves lapping greedily at the shore, threatening the harbour walls. And all along those walls, shadows of men and women swaying in the strong breeze.

"Might be you'll find yourself a doxie down there, old man."

I turned to Gert, the whine of her voice thick like treacle in my ear. In her place stood the ugliest man I'd ever had the misfortune to encounter.

"Who the hell are you?"

My words were simple, much better articulated in my head than formed on my tongue.

"Gideon Wicke," the man said. "Your guide. Though whether through Hell, Heaven or Purgatory makes no difference – it's all the same. Just different colours."

He sneered at me, the end of his nose almost touching his top lip. A smile, I presumed.

"Where's my aunt?"

"So many questions! She's long gone. Her pathetic life snuffed out years ago when you were just a snivelling kid – surprised you don't remember. Dragged her down here myself; kicking and screaming, she was."

His eyes juddered in their sockets as he spoke, as though not real but an automaton. I didn't understand him.

"But I saw her. She brought me here."

"Did she? A woman that looked exactly the same as when you last saw her, what – seventy-odd years ago, when you went to her for help and she just. . ."

Threw me off the mount.

That nightmare. Always the same. Me climbing to the top of St. Mrythin to get away from my uncle. Finding her there instead and running towards those open arms only for her to push, not save me. Me falling backwards as she turned her back and walked through a door into the summit of the mount. That was when I would wake up sweating and scared, confused by her rejection – every time.

Wicke surveyed me with satisfaction, reading my dreams, my memories. Something glimmered in his hand as he turned it over and over. My coin.

"Hey, that's mine."

"Just watch."

It revolved and it flipped and with every moment the glint grew brighter, mesmerising until hot tears rose and spilled from in my eyes, stinging my face. I slipped out of the trance, the despicable truth triggered in my heart.

"She *knew*. I thought she would protect me from him. Stop him from doing it, but all the time. . . she knew."

Wicke slapped the shilling into my palm.

"You've got it. That's one thing off your list, now let's get down to the river. There's someone I want you to meet."

I couldn't speak but followed him blindly, assessing my aunt Gert's deception, allowing me – a child, and who knows how many others – to be mauled by her dirty old man. I was glad she was dead, glad I finally understood the dream but angry… *furious* I didn't get to kill her myself.

"Hang on though," I said. "She brought me here."

"Don't be so bloody naive."

His form shimmered, briefly rising in height. His face shifted, revealing Gert as I remembered her, before bloating into a visage ravaged by sickness, her breath a stinking sewer of death. I fell back, shielding my mouth with my arm. I didn't want to suck her in. When I looked again, Gideon Wicke had regained his appearance, or at least the image he'd first presented to me and I wondered how many identities he actually had. Wicke had tricked me, taken my soul when it should have been plucked instead by God to deal with as He saw fit. And God knows I just wanted to sleep. I was mad with the injustice of it, yet my fury was countered with irrational gratitude. I let it lie, I needed to know what Wicke would do next.

We neared the river. My eyes must have failed me before. Where I'd seen water, all that tickled the harbour walls now were weedy fronds, slick with spume. They lay across the riverbed, undulating with a semblance of life – whipping rodent tails, gaping mouths of bottom-feeders and the scavenging of crows. Or so it appeared. Where had all the water gone?

"We no longer need it down here," said Wicke in his unnerving way of answering questions I hadn't voiced. "You've no skin to keep moist, no blood to run through the canals of your flesh. This Ouse is the bodily river of your memories, that's all."

And so it was. I thought I saw Betsy raking through sand by the lighthouse, Ma picking pebbles by the shore. I wept for them and ran. I wanted to feel their love, share the warmth of our reunion. But even as I sped on legs that could barely crawl before my death, I gained no distance. The old ladies shimmered in the dull light of an interminable dusk, never really there. Wicke sniggered at my shoulder.

"You'll learn."

Vapid wraiths moved around us, layer upon layer of them, passing through one another. The air throbbed with dull moans, of aches, of knowing there would be no recovery, of the loss of hope.

"Are we destined to remain sick forever?"

The weight of despair in this dreadful place was tangible, despite the wandering spirits' translucence. It leaned in on me, puncturing my lungs, heavy on my chest as though it could snap my ribs with opaque density.

"Sick? You misunderstand. This is your paradise, your golden apple. You simply need to find it."

I turned to question his contradiction. He was gone.

Loneliness let me wander those strange drains for immeasurable time, travelling the gurgling passageways where mists fell and rose like the breath of slumbering goliaths. If heaven had a doorway there, I had to find it by myself. Yet when I looked down at my arthritic feet, they were clean; they'd gone nowhere. The journey was wishful thinking.

Death, I had always presumed, should naturally sever one's senses. Logic dictates that as we rot and turn to dust, to be consumed by earth-travelling creatures, by maggots and the like, we feel nothing, know nothing. This river I imagined I walked beside, stank. I smelled its sulphur with my every impossible breath, tasted its crystalline salt on my tongue – dry as it was. Wicke had shown me an empty riverbed yet whilst I saw it, confirmed it with my own dead eyes, I could *hear* rushing torrents that were simply not there. I resolved to touch the hidden water, plunge my hands into it to make it true but as fast or as slow as I walked, still I gained no ground and could not approach. I stamped my foot; petulant, child-like.

"Try turning your back."

I did turn, to seek out the owner of the voice, for it was gentle and soothing. Words I could not distinguish continued to flow around me in a lilting lullaby. Their meaning was unintelligible yet I drew a strange comfort from the very sensation of them, unlike that of the vile glib of Gideon Wicke.

I *had* turned a half-circle but found myself staring at the riverbed once more as though I had not moved at all. In confusion, I sought out the soft speaker again, desiring her vocal embrace but there was no-one present aside from shadows. I tried taking a step towards the river. This time, the vista grew closer. I took another step, and another until I was almost running on dead legs, the stranger's song resonating in my ears. I imagined I felt her mouth there too, lingering in lament.

When I reached it, the shore was soft but solid beneath my feet, as it is after the tide has been out for hours and you can walk the river's edges before the water surges back in. That's when you have to take your chances. That's when the best treasures reveal themselves.

"Don't they just," Wicke appeared at my side once more. "Except what treasures does a soul need in a place like this?"

Glimmering silver, the muddy jewels I'd fleetingly

spotted peeking from the sand before Wicke's interruption sank away, leaving me no opportunity to grab them. What was the point anyway? Wicke was right about that. He stood before me now, blocking the riverbed from view.

"If *I* were dead," he said, his sneer so smug. "Which, of course I might be, I would reconsider what brought me here, my life's journey." The long coat he wore dropped away as he spread his arms and threw back his head for theatrical effect. His shirt billowed in a sudden gust. It fell from his skin in tatters as though unstitched, unmade by invisible hands. He strained, the spindly chest bowing, the ribs almost bursting from his torso.

"Come, come," he said, eyes rolling back into their sockets. He wiggled his extended fingers, beckoning. A small cry, I could not determine whether it was of agony or pleasure, left his lips as upon his bare chest a blackened web began to form. Tinged with red, the lines spread out and up, a design being etched into his body with a tattooist's skill. I thought of the faded green scribble on my own left arm and couldn't even remember what it said.

Wicke could barely stand now; his moans grew louder as the drawing continued relentlessly up and over his shoulders, down the wasted biceps and onwards towards the wrists, perilously tracing the veins beneath Wicke's skin. His palms were held out; I couldn't imagine the pain as they filled with tiny lines, right to the last dot on the third finger of each hand.

"See?" he said, twisting his head to indicate the river.

I stood back. The tattoo was a perfect replica of the Ouse behind him. The Ouse of my history. A corporeal facsimile. As I watched, small blooms of colour began to rise in patches along its length and a map of the city trembled into view. Ignoring Wicke's shudders, I approached him and squinted at the scene. In a forested area to the west of the city was a near-exact rendering of the former Ash Hill Hospital, where I was born.

"Breach!" Wicke shouted.

I never knew that. My mother must have been petrified; perhaps it explains why she had no more children. I almost killed us both.

I reached out to trace the streets. They rippled beneath my touch causing tiny electric shocks which resulted in spasms and cries from the tormented Wicke.

Our family house in Beggar's Row stood out, made larger by the drawing to distinguish it from the others on the road, others that had been replaced by concrete blocks twenty years ago. Here was Cleaver's Bridge where I kissed Harriet for the first time and where I drank myself stupid after she was killed in an accident the week before our wedding. The bridge throbbed on Gideon's skin. I wanted to knock it down.

"Do it then," he said with a grunt. "Will it."

I had no hammer, my hands were weak… *Will it.* All at once, I understood. I stared at the image then squeezed my eyes shut, the bridge still clear but displaying in negative behind the veil of my thin eyelids. I visualised myself raging at the structure, screaming at it, throwing all my weight at the mighty stones. I became a wrecking ball. By the time I opened my eyes, the bridge had been reduced to a pile of rubble. I ducked below Wicke's outstretched arms to look at the actual river, and there Cleaver's Bridge had fallen too.

"Do you get it now?" Wicke spat at me.

I did.

I travelled the Ouse from that moment on, systematically destroying the mistakes and losses of my past and renovating the landscape of my soul.

Wicke had no patience.

"Take your blasted time, why don't you?"

With every action I took, my strength, my confidence grew. My fear of Gideon Wicke – tour guide through death's abyss, or whatever he was – melted away. But still he stood there, as if suspended.

"Just finish what you've started."

He said I had just one more thing to do, but I couldn't fathom it. I had revoked and restored, demolished and rebuilt. The life I'd left behind was brighter, better. Even the shore on which I stood was no longer a turgid grey but a deep rust, reflecting billions of sand crystals; behind me, the grass once more verdant, and lush. "*It's all the same. Just different colours,*" Wicke had said when I arrived. Now he hung his head, weary. It struck me how much he'd sacrificed to help me find my way. In turn, I had sucked his strength dry. But I felt no guilt, no shame. Instead I forgave him for bringing me to this terrible place. And therein, I found my answer.

It was a small plot, beneath a yew tree. Spotting it etched inside the crook of Wicke's arm I quickly walked away from his exhausted near-corpse to find the place they'd buried me, beside Ma. I briefly questioned how long I'd been wandering down here with Wicke because it seemed to be both moments *and* years. But it didn't matter, it didn't matter at all.

Deemus must have found my instructions; he would have dealt with the burial quickly and quietly, God bless the man. There would have been no funeral. I knelt down to the small headstone. Ma's name had begun to wear away but mine was sharp, clearly etched into the granite.

Joseph Willoughby, 1904 – 1988
Sadly missed

Faded plastic flowers drooped over a broken yellow pot. I'd bought them in memory of Ma too many years ago, and never went back because it hurt too much. I drew the pot away. A fat worm slithered and pulsed, quickly burying its head in the soil until the only truly living thing I'd seen down here – Wicke didn't count – had disappeared from sight.

I smiled, stroked Ma's name; *Emily May*.

"I'm sorry Ma," I said. "But I'm here now."

As I forgave myself, the world around me took on a different hue; a lighter, bluer shade where the air smelt fresh and a hint of warmth blew against my cheek in a mild breeze. The grass over my grave filled with a bed of daisies that burst into life; red-stained, white dart-like petals that waved up at the new sky, faces sunny.

I looked down at my feet and they were dim, fading like the rest of me. It wouldn't be long now, for good.

Gideon Wicke was sitting on a bench when I found him again. He was smaller, wiry – no longer an illusion.

"You said you wanted me to meet someone?"

He didn't reply, but waited until the obvious hit me.

"Ah. I see."

That someone was me.

"So you've got all your answers now," he finally said. "You'd best be off. No need to thank me."

He rose to his feet, an old man with a bad back, a stoop, a fatty liver and a rattling chest full of death. I thanked him anyway.

Behind me the earth growled. The wart that was St. Mrythin's Mount opened its doors and there stood the saint, older than the Christian title bestowed on her in a fruitless attempt to bind her ancient power to the church. She was as old as the land itself, and she was as beautiful as she was terrifying. She wore a gossamer gown of green that danced around her in tendrils. On every ribbon I saw the faces of loved ones, of hated ones, of those I'd forgotten and those who were vaguely familiar, who I'd passed in the street every day without offering a greeting. I bowed my head to Mrythin's glory and asked if I might enter. Her reply was that lilting lullaby I'd heard earlier, those thousand words sung in harmony – just as when she'd guided me to turn my back on life's stupidity. Her voice was a symphony of bells and the shattering of glass.

"Look up, old man," she said.

At her feet lay Betsy, smiling and panting, her tongue lolling in an imagined summer heat. Ma stood to Mrythin's left, her white hair pinned upon her head, errant strands making a halo around her dear face. To the saint's right – my Harriet, come to fetch me.

Mrythin held out her hand.

"You may come in," she said. "But it will cost you a shilling."

I dug in my pocket for treasure, and handed it over. A shilling was all I had left to give.

RED MASK
LINDSEY GODDARD

Billy didn't know where he was. That happened sometimes when he got nervous. For thirty-two excruciating ticks of the clock, he couldn't recall what he was doing or how he had come to be in this room. An old painting had been propped against the wall near his feet. He breathed deep, smelling flowers and formaldehyde. He remembered now. He was in Zollner Funeral Home. He had removed the painting to look through the peephole.

Thin, white dust rimmed the opening. He blew it away and pressed his face to the wall. The hole on the other side was small, the size of a nailhead, but it provided a perfect view of the two men in the next room, dressed in shiny suits and silk ties. *Dressed even nicer than usual. It must have been one fancy funeral today.*

Dusk faded into night outside the window, and lamplight washed over the room, dim and yellow. Both men remained standing, ignoring the leather loveseat and the desk with plush suede-lined chairs. Their voices were muffled, but Billy could hear them with his ear smashed against the wall and his hands cupped around it. He alternated positions - watching them, then listening, then watching, then listening…

"We can't keep him," Mr. Zollner said. He walked over to his brother, who was also named Mr. Zollner, and leaned in closer. "I caught him hugging the corpses. Do you hear me? Clutching them and crying like they were his own dearly departed loved ones. The kid is unhinged."

"He wasn't hurting anyone, though, was he?" the other man said. "The dead don't know the difference."

The first Mr. Zollner rolled his eyes. "I knew you would do this. I knew you would defend him! Let's get rid of him and hire someone else. *Please.* Someone who can do the job without constant supervision. Someone who doesn't require room and board."

It confused Billy having two bosses named Mr. Zollner, so he thought of them as Boss One and Boss Two. Sometimes Billy mixed up their faces and couldn't figure out who was who, and then he'd remember: Boss Two had hair like dead grass and made Billy feel stupid. Boss One had darker hair, and he was nice. His soft eyes put Billy at ease.

With one eye closed and the other pressed to the hole, he saw Boss One sigh and look away from his brother. "It's not that easy," he said.

"But it *is* that easy," Boss Two said. He turned and began to pace the floor. The lamplight cast deep shadows around his eyes, and Billy shivered. He felt nervous just looking at the man's spiked blonde hair and cold blue eyes. Boss Two hadn't liked Billy from the moment he'd laid eyes on him. That's how Billy could tell the brothers apart when their faces blurred together in his mind. The brain damage hadn't stolen his intuition. *Just everything else*, he thought.

He pulled away from the wall and rubbed his eye, grimacing. It felt like sand was scraping around in there. *Only dust from the drywall*, he thought. He glanced at the mirror across the room and considered taking a closer look but decided against it. He didn't like what he saw there, the reflection of a sad man, black hair in need of a trim, one side of his unshaven face slack and dopey-eyed. Dark circles under his eyes made him look ten years older than the twenty he really was. *That's not the Billy I remember*, he thought. Tears filled his irritated eye, so he blinked a few times and returned his attention to the hole.

Boss Two spun on his heels, resumed pacing and said, "Look, I'm not bitter that you own dad's business. I get it. I don't expect to waltz back in and take control after moving away for so long, but, little brother, you've got to listen to me on this one. Get rid of that guy. He gives me the creeps."

Boss One ran a hand through his light brown hair, stopped to scratch the back of his scalp, then shook his head. "I knew Billy, the real Billy, before that bullet entered his brain. Before he lost his family." He fixed his brother with a hard stare. "He was a good boy. He *still is* a good boy. He's just been through Hell."

Boss Two's lips pressed together in a thin line, one eyebrow cocked. "No," he said. "This isn't acceptable. Deceased or not, those were someone else's children he was holding. Hugging their cold naked bodies to his chest." He cast his eyes to the floor, took a long pause and added, "I mean, Jesus… What would Dad say?"

Boss One frowned and looked away. "Dad made it look effortless, didn't he? Running this business, doing it with no complaints like the stress never cost him a wink of sleep." His voice shook a little as he said, "Well, I'm not Dad."

Boss Two stopped and eyed his brother in silence. Something like compassion crossed his features. "I thought you were sleeping better now. Didn't the doctor give you something?"

A heavy sigh. "Yes. And it works. I'm out by eleven every night. I just wish I didn't need the pills. I wish I could handle the stress on my own."

Boss Two said, "Sounds like you need to cut some stress from your life."

Boss One shook his head again. "No." He turned away from his brother and ran a hand through his hair so roughly it looked like he was yanking it out. "He's got nowhere else to go, no income, no home."

"No sanity. No morality. I mean… fondling dead kids…"

Shame burned in Billy's cheeks. *It's not like that*, he thought. He picked at the wall, carving a notch with his fingernail.

"It's innocent," said Boss One, straightening his tie.

Boss Two widened his eyes. "Innocent? Are you serious?"

"He blames himself for everything that happened. And those two, they're young like his niece and nephew were. The sight of them probably just... triggered something. He's not right in the head, but not in the way you're thinkin'."

Billy's heart began to pound. He felt like he'd been here before, watching this same conversation through the peephole. *It's happening again,* he thought as Deja Vu washed over him. It came in a wave, accompanied by nausea and a light-headed dizziness. He clutched a chair for support and tried to brace himself, but he was falling. His cheek scraped the carpet as he landed in a heap. Blackness filled his vision.

Billy heard his sister screaming. He opened his eyes, and he was standing in the living room of his old house, with its paneled walls and dark blue carpet. A figure in a ski mask stood, silent, holding the corpse of a dog. *Billy's* dog. Blood matted the fur, leaking from a gruesome head wound, staining the carpet at the killer's feet black.

Billy's insides felt as shattered as his dog's skull. *God, no. Not Winnie. I'm so sorry, girl. Please, no.* His sister's screams grew more frantic by the second, but instead of alarming him, they only deepened his heartache as he gawked at Winnie's limp body dangling from the intruder's fist by her tail.

The killer dropped the dog and turned to Dee, who stood defenseless in the corner. His dark eyes glistened inside the red ski mask. Billy snapped out of it. *Move your ass*, he thought. *Save your sister.*

His throat was dry, his forehead drenched with sweat. He turned away from Red Mask and sprinted for Dee. She was dialing her phone with trembling fingers and nearly lost hold of it as Billy scooped her into his arms. Dee had been hit by a car at age four and hadn't been able to run since, and all Billy could think was to sling her over his shoulder and do the running for both of them.

"Hey!" she yelled. She beat her knuckles into his back and screamed, "Go back! Get the children! Not me! Put me down. Get the children!" Struggling to reach the front door under the weight of Dee's writhing body, Billy checked to see if the killer was coming for them.

He wasn't. Red Mask just stood there, facing the direction of the long hallway that led to the bedrooms, both of his fists soaked with blood. *Cindy and Jonathan*, Billy thought, and his stomach flipped at the thought of his niece and nephew all alone in their room. *But I'm so close to getting Dee out of here. I can't stop now. I'll get her out and come back for the children.*

He turned the doorknob as Dee sobbed and begged him to put her down. They crossed the threshold, and she yelled for her children, "Cindy! Johnny! Hide, babies, hide!" He cleared the porch steps, set her down in the grass and dashed through the front door in time to see Red Mask disappearing down the hall.

"Billy!" another voice called, much deeper than Dee's.

"Billy, wake up." When he came to, he was on the floor. There was a pillow under his head. Everything appeared sideways, and he realized he was laying on his side.

Boss One stared down at him, wrinkles at the corners of his sky blue eyes. "You okay?" he asked. Billy couldn't find the words, so he nodded. "We were in the next room and we heard a thump. Found you on the floor."

"What were you doing in here anyway?" Boss Two asked.

"Damn it, Ken. Give it a rest," said Boss One.

Boss Two narrowed his eyes and made an indignant noise in his throat. "If he's so innocent, what's he doing lurking around in dad's old office and peeking through holes?"

Billy's heart sank as Boss One looked up and saw the hole in the wall, the blonde-haired man sticking his finger through it and sneering down at Billy. "Looks intentional to me," he said.

Billy sat up, too quickly, and his vision checkered.

"Woah, easy," said Boss One, sliding a warm hand behind Billy's neck to keep him from flopping over. "You don't have to explain right now if you don't want to," he said.

Blood rushed to Billy's face. He didn't look at either of them. "I thought… I thought I might get fired, so I…" He couldn't finish, skin flush. He felt like his head weighed fifty pounds. He didn't know if it was from the seizure or the shame.

"This is too much," said Boss Two. Billy snuck a glance and saw him shake a finger at his brother. "You dated his mother fifteen years ago. He's not even family."

"He is," Boss One said.

"It's him or me, Richie. You don't want to run everything on your own again. There has to be somewhere else he can go." With that, Boss Two turned and left.

Billy sat motionless with the lid of the old shoebox gripped in his fingers. He didn't want any moisture marring the precious contents of his box, so he waited for the tears to subside. When he was able to draw a breath without his bottom lip quivering, he removed the top and set it beside him.

He poked his fingers through the assortment of newspaper clippings and pulled a small article from the pile. Two children smiled up at him from a grainy black and white photo. He read the headline for the millionth time. Red Mask Killer Claims Two Lives & Puts One In Critical Condition.

He clenched his teeth, frowning, as he remembered the fear he'd experienced during his four days on life support. He'd been trapped in that final moment, living it over and over again in his endless dream-like state. Seventeen months now, and even still, Billy replayed it every day.

He was on the bottom step of the porch. He bent over and dropped his wailing sister to the ground as she kicked and screamed. "Billy, get the kids! Get the kids!" He turned around, wiped sweat from his eyes, and cleared the stairs in two bounds.

Billy ran through the front door and nearly went sprawling face-

first into his dead dog as he tripped over a pile of shoes, but the sight of Red Mask turning and heading down the hall spurred him forward with a steady momentum.

Cindy, Johnny. I can't let them down, he thought.

The carpet made a wet slurping noise and splashed over the tops of his bare feet as he ran through the puddle around Winnie. He didn't look at her. He rounded the corner and saw Red Mask approach the closed door at the end of the hall.

No! he thought. Fuck! No! Please, no!

Jonathan screamed and Cindy cried as the intruder burst into their room. Red Mask's dark coat blocked all sight of the children, a black abyss in their doorway, but he heard them whimper and scramble away. Red Mask pulled something from his waistband, raised his hand. Billy pumped his legs so hard they burned, screaming, "No! Don't!"

There were two quick blasts - bam, bam - the sound forever implanted in Billy's mind, even deeper than the bullet that eventually entered his own brain.

He raked a hand through his unkempt hair and rubbed the hard lump of scar tissue at the side of his head. He could still feel the pain, exploding like fireworks inside his skull. Worse than that was the permanent damage it had done to his mind, turning him from a hopeful college candidate into a basket case Boss One employed out of pity.

From the pixelated newsprint photo, the eyes of his niece and nephew stared up at him. *You should have saved us first*, they said. *We were helpless, innocent, and you saved her first. You saved Mommy and left us to die.* He choked back tears. Their tender faces - four and six years old - seemed to question him behind false smiles. *Uncle Billy, why did you let the bad man get us?*

His throat tightened, and he forced himself to swallow. At the core of his sadness was a seething anger, like a bear trap ready to snap. Red Mask had taken eight more lives since killing Johnny and Cindy, and still, he hadn't been caught. He had no methods and no time frame. When Red Mask decided to kill, he killed whatever and whomever he pleased. There was not a shred of justice to be found in the matter.

Billy let go of the clipping. It fluttered back into the box. He put the lid on so he didn't have to worry about his tears hitting the paper, and Billy cried. He had cried every day for months now. Some days it felt like he might never stop.

He couldn't sleep. He sometimes got nervous for no reason - a side effect of the brain damage. "Anxiety," the doctors called it. This was different. He felt it deeper in his gut than usual, and no amount of tossing and turning would quell the voice inside him that whispered, *Something's wrong.*

He sat up in bed and looked out the window at the moonlit lilies and willow branches swaying in the night breeze. His gaze rested on the portion of building parallel to his room. Zollner Funeral Home had been designed in an unusual 'U' shape. The main office and viewing room made up the front, with two long wings on either side. These two wings faced each other with a memorial garden and cobbled walkway in between. Billy's bedroom, hastily built into the business side of Zollner when Boss One had decided to house him, had a window that looked straight across the garden into Boss One's room.

The blinds were always drawn, and Billy wouldn't spy into another man's bedroom anyway, but he found it comforting when Boss One turned out his light at night. Billy had been the last one to bed every evening when he had lived with Dee, first hugging the children goodnight, then watching Dee's bedroom light blink out. Perhaps he needed the comfort, some small semblance of his old life.

After he had moved into Zollner Funeral Home, it had troubled Billy to discover Boss One was plagued with insomnia. Seeing his light flick on and off throughout the night made him nervous. Little things like that always made him nervous now. He couldn't relax until the house was calm.

Boss One had gone to a doctor, though, and for the past few months, the soft yellow light floating across the pebbled-lined garden blinked out by eleven and stayed that way. It helped Billy sleep because he needed to know everyone was calm, comfortable... *safe*. And tonight, he was bothered - deeply bothered - to see Boss One's light still shining. It had stayed on all night, now getting past 1 AM.

If he can't sleep, Billy thought. *It's because he hasn't tried. Why wouldn't he try? I know he would. He would have shut off the light and tried to get some rest by now. Something must be wrong.* He groaned into his pillow. *I won't be able to sleep if I don't go check on him.*

He stumbled over to his light switch, flipped it, and slowly opened the door. The hallway was pure gloom, but soft light from Billy's bedroom sliced the darkness down the middle, casting a dull glow in both directions.

To his right was the door to the embalming room, where bodies were stored until their service and burial. His eyes were drawn to this door every time he passed it. Sometimes he thought he heard them calling - Jonathan and Cindy. He knew his niece and nephew were six feet under at Eternal Peace Cemetery, but knowing they had been in that very room, that their funeral service had been held at Zollner Funeral Home while he was trapped in a coma, sometimes he felt like they weren't really gone - like they were only sleeping at the end of the hall, just like old times.

He took a deep breath and turned in the other direction, his spine rigid with tension. He passed a small office the Zollner brothers had converted into a storage room. It rarely got used, and that's why Billy had gotten the bright idea to use it for eavesdropping earlier that day. He frowned and wished he hadn't done that. The door was closed, lights off, and Billy crept onward.

Moonlight from the beveled glass of the front door illuminated the end of the hall, sending strange patterns across the floor. He inched toward it, passing the main office, the inky blackness of its spacious interior like a dark chasm through its half-open door. And the viewing room, even bigger, its French doorway a yawning mouth full of shadows.

The ceiling fan softly hummed in the hardwood foyer, but nothing else stirred. He moved through the foyer into the other hall, perspiration oozing from his pores despite the house's perpetually cool temperature. The sweat coating his skin became cold and clammy upon reaching the air, but he couldn't make it stop. Couldn't force his heart to slow or his knees to stop quaking.

There was a scraping sound like the grinding of monstrous teeth. He passed a room to his left, its door closed, and a room to his right, filled with ominous shadows that dared him to enter their bottomless pit.

But Billy's eyes were fixed on the hardwood floor outside his boss's room, on the dark fluid leaking from underneath the door into a patch of light cast by thin gaps around the jamb. Billy drew closer and recognized what he was seeing, blood, and what he was hearing, the teeth of a metal saw tearing into something hard.

With trembling hands, Billy pushed open the door and peered inside. The smell washed over him first, the coppery scent of blood. All he could see was red. So much red. Puddles of it reflecting the lamplight, streams of it leaking from where Red Mask kneeled on the floor with his back to Billy, mutilating the corpse of Boss One.

Memories washed over him like acid rain, the familiar, helpless feeling of being sucked into the past...

He was in the hallway at his old house. Dee was outside, hobbling up the porch steps with her bad leg. She screamed into her phone, "87 Corbitt Lane! Hurry!"

Billy ran at full speed, plunging himself down the hall. Red Mask stood just past the threshold of the kids' room, his bulky frame blocking the doorway. He raised the gun.

"No! Don't!" Billy screamed.

Bang. Aim. Bang.

The second blast sent a spray of blood over Red Mask's shoulder. Chunks of pink tissue splattered the door and the floor around his boots. Billy fell to his knees in the hallway. The world seemed to slow down. There was a tightness in his chest. He didn't think he could draw a breath and didn't care. He couldn't run, couldn't be bothered to save his own life. He just knelt there, eyes wide and frozen.

Red Mask approached Billy. He could see past him now, into the bedroom. Cindy was on the floor, her pajamas stained with gore. He couldn't see Jonathan, but a lifeless arm poked out from behind the bed, blood streaming to form a puddle around the upturned palm.

He finally took a breath and burst into tears. He sobbed into his hands, slumped over on the floor, and when Red Mask fired a bullet in an attempt to end his misery, Billy's misery only began.

Weeks later, the hospital would deem Billy "fully recovered", but he wasn't. He would never recover. His sister blamed him for their loss. "Why didn't you get the kids, Billy? Why did you force me outside when they needed us?" She would pace the floor at night, and when Billy would ask if there was anything he could do to help ease her mind, she'd say, "Why did you save me first? Because you couldn't live without me? Well, I don't want to live anymore."

Dee hung herself six months after her children died.

Fresh tears filled his eyes. They had been a small family, and a broken one, but they had loved each other deeply. And Red Mask had taken it all.

As he watched Red Mask kneeled on the floor, sawing into the corpse of the only person left in the world who cared about him, the angry bear trap inside Billy snapped. At first he felt dizzy. Then Dee's voice echoed in his mind: "Get the children! Get the children!"

As if sensing Billy's presence, Red Mask went stiff and slowly turned his head. His eyes glistened like poisonous black oysters inside the red shell of his mask. He was nothing if not a soulless killing machine.

The children! thought Billy. *I have to save them!*

Red Mask stood. He tossed the bloody saw to the ground and pulled a long knife from its sheath, lamplight glinting off the blade in Billy's peripheral vision as he turned to run. He used his long legs, pumping them furiously as he cleared the hall, running past the other rooms on his way to the children.

In the foyer, he turned, passed the main office, the storage room, his room. He skidded to stop when he reached the door at the end of the hall. He flung it open, flipped the lights, and there they were, Cindy and Jonathan, asleep on the metal tables under their white sheets. He pulled the sheets off and scooped them up, their skin cool and leathery against his.

He turned and looked and saw Red Mask closing in on them, walking with his knife held out menacingly.

"We can't get past him," he whispered to the kids. "We'll have to go through the window."

"Uncle Billy, I'm scared," said Johnny.

"Don't let him hurt us," said Cindy.

"I won't," he said. "I'm here for you." He hugged them close. "I have to set you down for just a second." He left them on a table, slammed the door to the room and locked it, then slid open the window. "Come on," he said. He hoisted the children into his arms and helped them escape.

Hours later, they found Billy crying and cuddling two corpses behind the bushes at the back of Zollner Funeral Home. "Cindy and Johnny," he called them, repeatedly, though those were not the names of the deceased. Officers on the scene wore grim expressions, their lips drooping and foreheads wrinkled as they ushered him into the back of a police cruiser.

From inside the car, he overheard a cop say, "The footprints lead away from the murder scene, then back again. Our killer chased Billy here *first*, then went back for the second victim." He shook his head and sighed. "If he had called the police, or alerted the other man in the home, he might have saved that man's life. But instead, this--" he gestured his hands toward the small bodies being hauled away on stretchers.

Billy only clutched himself and muttered, "I saved them." He rocked back and forth and smiled absurdly, mumbling, "I got them out, Dee. I saved them this time."

THE RING OF KARNAK
DANIEL MARC CHANT

Carter Donovan liked to so arrange his life as to encounter as few surprises as possible. For him, change was something to be abhorred rather than embraced. Each day he rose at exactly 7 a. m. Breakfast was at 8 and invariably cornflakes or toast if he was feeling adventurous, which he rarely was. Brunch was at 11, Dinner at 1.30 and Tea at 5.30.

He took a walk in the morning and a walk in the evening. The rest of his time was spent in scholarly studies, which were greatly facilitated by a personal library of over five thousand painstakingly indexed and cross-referenced books.

It was this need for a well-ordered existence that had given him the impetus to move from London to the sleepy village of Fennelcliff where few things ever came out of the blue. The locals were fond of saying that nothing ever happened in Fennelcliff and it was Carter's most earnest wish that it should ever remain so. Which is why he was perplexed one morning to unexpectedly receive a package from the firm of Pickett, Carpenter and Smyth.

"What the hell?" he muttered to himself as he closed his front door on the postman. "I thought I was done with those fellows."

Recently, an uncle of whose existence he had scarcely been aware had passed away and left him a sizable amount of money. Although glad of the windfall (he was after all not a wealthy person and his scholarly endeavours were far from lucrative), he had nevertheless been extremely put out at having to deal with the paperwork and other legal necessities surrounding the bequest.

In his opinion, Messrs. Pickett, Carpenter and Smyth had handled the matter badly and placed too many demands on his time. Once his inheritance was secured, he had hoped never to hear from the firm again.

With his mood soured, Carter took the package to the library and dropped it unceremoniously onto his desk. The grandfather clock that stood between two of his mahogany bookcases struck 10, informing him that it was time for his morning walk. The parcel would have to wait until he came back.

Out in the hallway, he put on his coat, hat and gloves and was on the verge of opening the front door when he hesitated. That damn parcel, as he thought of it, was playing on his mind and he knew it would so long as he remained ignorant of its contents. If he left it alone, his walk would be far from enjoyable.

With ill grace, he removed his outdoor clothing and

The Ring Of Karnak

stormed back to the library. Muttering obscenities as he did so.

"Right then! Let's see what we have, shall we?"

In a moment, he had unwrapped the package. Within he found an object wrapped in crumpled parchment and a terse letter from Messrs. Pickett, Carpenter and Smyth.

Dear Mr. Donovan,

Before your uncle's untimely death, he deposited with us this item which he requested be bequeathed to you in the event of his demise.

Yours sincerely,

Mr. Pickett.

Carter removed the parchment from the object and uncovered a ring etched with unfamiliar symbols. The ring had a silvery lustre with a hint of dullness that suggested an alloy of lead and perhaps tin or silver. It was an ugly thing, possessing none of the grace or beauty one should expect of jewelry, and Carter felt certain it could be neither valuable nor of any scholarly interest.

Quite why his uncle should have left it in the hands of lawyers was beyond him. As far as Carter was concerned, it belonged in the rubbish - and that's where he was going to put it the moment he returned from his walk.

He placed the parchment on the table and saw it had been written upon, evidently in some haste to judge by the scruffiness of the writing.

Carter had trouble deciphering the scrawl but he finally made it out: *Destroy this thing. Be stronger than I.*

The jeweler handed the ring back to Carter. "I really don't know what to tell you," he said. "I'm not sure what metal it's made from, but I'm certain it's none of the precious ones."

"So you wouldn't say it had much value?"

"Not so far as I can tell."

The jeweler spun the ring in his fingers in curiosity as he spoke.

"And you can't tell me when this ring was made or by whom?"

"I'm afraid not, Mr. Donovan. It's like nothing I've ever seen before. If anything it looks like it's probably a relic of some kind and that's not my area of expertise."

"Well, thank you for your time. I appreciate your efforts." So saying, Carter turned to leave. As he reached the door, the jeweler called after him.

"You might try the University. Ask for Professor Mayfield. He's very knowledgeable when it comes to strange artifacts and arcane symbols."

"My dear Mr. Donovan! How wonderful it is to meet you!" Professor Mayfield shook Carter's hand with a vigour that threatened to dislocate his shoulder. "Come in. Please do." The Professor ushered a startled and bewildered Carter into his study. "Do take a seat."

Carter's first inclination when he saw the contents of the study was to turn and leave. The place was out of his worst nightmares. Piles of books littered the floor, between and on top of the books were what appeared to be the contents of a museum. Here was a mummy sarcophagus; there a stuffed dodo. Elsewhere a fanged human skeleton lay beside a wooden fertility idol.

"Do excuse the mess," said Professor Mayfield as he seated himself behind a desk mercifully free of clutter. "My landlady threatened to evict me if I didn't - as she put it - get this rubbish out of her house. I, of course, flatly refused to do anything of the kind. But then her son Russell, who used to be a professional boxer, had a quiet word and persuaded me that perhaps my landlady had a point."

"I see," said Carter, feeling obliged to say something in return. He sat opposite the professor. "This is quite a collection."

"I can't tell you how thrilled I was to hear you were coming to see me." Professor Mayfield leaned forward and placed his elbows on the desk. "This has really made my day."

"It has?"

"I've been an avid follower of your work for years, Mr. Donovan. Your dissertation on the navigational techniques of the Spanish armada was masterful! And your paper on Aztec military engineering left me possibly breathless. It's so rare in this age of specialisation to meet someone with such a wide range of expertise. You, Mr. Donovan, may very well be the Last of the Renaissance Men."

Carter felt himself blush. It had been a long time since he'd received such praise - in fact any praise at all - and he had no idea how to deal with it. The Last of the Renaissance Men indeed! *Perhaps*, he thought, *I'll have that etched on my gravestone when I'm gone.*

"I was flattered," Professor Mayfield went on, "to be told you were seeking my advice. Something about a ring I believe?"

"Yes." Carter fumbled in his pocket and brought out the item in question. He placed it in front of the Professor. "I was hoping you could tell me something about its nature and origins."

"Well, yes. I'll do what I can. Now let me see." The Professor placed a jeweler's glass in his eye and examined the ring. Almost immediately, his face drained of colour. "It can't be!" He threw the ring at Carter whose attempt to catch it failed. "Get it out of here! Get it out!"

Fearing the Professor had lost his sanity and might attack him, Carter hurriedly retrieved the ring from the floor. "What's the matter with you?" He backed towards the door. "It's only a ring!"

"No it isn't! In the name of all that is holy, get rid of the bloody thing! But not here! Heed my words. Take it as far out to sea as you can manage and let the ocean deal with the consequences."

"Don't you think you're being a little melodramatic?"

"Get it out!" Professor Mayfield stood with a suddenness and violence that sent his chair flying. "And until you do you must stay away from me, Donovan! Do you hear? Stay away from me!"

Carter fled from the office. He hastily paced through the University's ancient corridors and cloisters and he didn't stop until he reached his car.

Getting in, he saw his hands were shaking and concluded he was in no fit state to drive. *Now*, he reflected, *would be a good time for a cup of herbal tea.*

But it wasn't herbal tea he needed. No amount of comforting infusion would bring him peace of mind - not while he had a mystery to solve. A sudden air of enthusiasm enveloped him and he forgot about his routines, his schedules and his structure. Questions gnawed at him more strongly than the pull of his routine. What was there about the ring which had caused his uncle to afford it a special status and Professor Mayfield to act in such an unscholarly manner?

As much as it grieved him to do so, he made a rare call on his mobile phone and was swiftly through to Matthew Pickett of Pickett, Carpenter and Smyth.

As usual, the lawyer spoke as if he had a rod in his rectum and a bad smell under his nose. "How may I help you, Mr. Donovan?"

"It's about the package you belatedly sent me. The one with the ring in it."

"Oh yes. That horrid thing. Why your uncle sent such a worthless piece of tat to us for safe-keeping is beyond me."

"When exactly did he send it to you?"

"Well, that's the strange thing. The post mark was dated two days after his death. That's the sort of detail I notice you know."

"And do you have any idea how it came to be in his possession?"

"I have every idea. Your uncle - a long time client of this firm as you well know - posted it to us himself with a request that we pass it on to you."

"How could it be post marked after his death?!"

"The Royal Mail isn't what it used to be. Bizarre he met his end shortly before the ring found its way to us."

"What a coincidence."

"Coincidence? I think not, Mr. Donovan. I'm by no means superstitious, but I am nonetheless convinced you should rid yourself of it at once."

Mr. Pickett abruptly hung up.

Accepting the uncomfortable truth that his own library could offer him no clues to the ring's origins, Carter availed himself of the University's library, where he sat in a secluded corner, searching through ancient volumes and obscure journals. After a few hours, his eyes were sore, his neck was stiff and he was no wiser than before.

The notion that the symbols might after all have no meaning hung over him like a cloud. Perhaps his uncle had treasured it because it had been bequeathed to him too. Perhaps it was merely a family heirloom with no value beyond sentiment.

But then there was the note on the parchment imploring him to destroy the ring. Add to that, Professor Mayfield's outburst and Carter could only conclude there was far more to the ring than met the eye.

The library closed at eight. At five to eight, Carter reluctantly closed the book he'd been browsing through and rubbed at his weary eyes. It was no use. If the answer lay anywhere in the library, he would surely have found it by now.

I should take all the advice I've been given and get rid of the ring. Accursed or not, it's making my life a misery.

As he got up, he saw the librarian approach. She was an elderly lady with a pink cardigan slung over her shoulders. "Mr. Donovan?"

"Yes, yes, I know. It's time for me to go."

The librarian held up a book. "Professor Mayfield sent this with his compliments. He says you're welcome to keep it."

For the second night running, Carter found himself burning the midnight oil in his library. The book was a volume written by Professor Mayfield entitled *Before Paganism – Ancient Religions of the British Isles*. A note on the title page advised that the volume had been privately published in a limited edition of 100 copies.

Carter found it fascinating. Although it covered a subject in which he could rightly claim a fair amount of expertise, it contained much that he had previously been unaware of.

The Professor was clearly a diligent scholar, adept at finding documents and other sources overlooked by better known historians. Much of what he detailed was based on local legends which he had gone to great pains to verify.

Carter worked through the book from the beginning. His need for order would not allow him to skip pages let alone whole chapters. He felt duty-bound to follow the Professor's thread of reasoning in order to judge the soundness of his conclusions.

He was halfway through the book when he turned the page and saw something that made his heart skip a beat. It was a colour photograph of the ring inset with pictures of the twelve symbols engraved upon it.

Plate vii. said the legend at the bottom of the page. *The Ring of Karnak with details of its symbols.*

At last! Now he would have his answers.

He began to read the following page and felt like he was in a movie that had skipped a few frames. Puzzled, he turned back to the page before the colour plate. He again scanned its final sentence, which served to close Chapter 18. "The exact cause of the Druid's death may never be known," he muttered, "but few at the time doubted that devilry had been at work."

Again, Carter turned the page and read on. "- the magistrate, being more than satisfied that the ring of Karnak was no more, declared the matter closed and returned to London with what some might term undignified haste.

"Let us now turn our attention away from Karnak to the nearby hamlet of Little Dentney, famed at one time for its fabulous cheeses."

With a sinking feeling, Carter realised that several pages had been excised from the book. He had no doubt that Professor Mayfield was the culprit, but what could have induced the fellow to mutilate his own work?

"Sacrilege," he murmured. "And madness!"

He eased his chair back, stood up and rubbed his legs to restore circulation to them. Then he rolled his neck, wincing at the cracking sounds thus produced.

The grandfather clock struck five. He'd been up all night, seemingly on a wild goose chase.

"Blast Mayfield!" he spat. "What did he mean by wasting my time like this?"

Carter's bed beckoned like never before. He took a step towards the door and then stopped.

"Of course!" he slapped his forehead. "If I wasn't so tired, I'd have thought of it at once."

Shortly thereafter, he was back at his table, skimming through a small pile of atlases and gazetteers. To his utter disgust, he could find no mention of a village or town called Karnak. Once more, he was in a pit of despair.

Just for the sake of completeness and without any expectation of success, he ploughed again through the books, this time searching for Little Dentney. Running his finger down the index at the back of an old atlas, he spotted an entry for *Great Dentney. Page 137. E18.*

Carter held his breath as he hurriedly turned to the map on page 137 and sought out square E18. As was to be expected, the village of Great Dentney was marked as being there. Almost immediately, his gaze picked out the name of the neighbouring village!

That was it! It had to be. Like many a place in England, the spelling of its name would have changed throughout the centuries, only becoming fixed with the advent of dictionaries and the printing press.

"Right!" Carter exclaimed. "Carnach here I come."

Too weary to contemplate tackling the stairs, he placed his arms on the table, rested his head on his arms and fell into a deep, dreamless sleep.

The drive to Carnach was a pleasant one, taking Carter across gently rolling hills peppered with pleasant villages that seemed to have turned their backs on modernity. For lunch he stopped at a pub beside a tranquil river where he sat in the beer garden and watched a proud mother duck shepherd her brood into the water.

When he arrived at Carnach, he immediately fell in love with its quaint cottages, its Norman church, its village green complete with duck pond and its shops that were all family owned. Nowhere did he see the corporate monstrosities he considered a blight on the British landscape.

As much as he loved his house in Fennelcliff, he began to entertain ideas of selling up and moving to Carnach.

The village pub was named The Green Man. It was built in the Tudor style and had an air of antiquity about it. Carter parked up outside, took his suitcase from the back seat and went in. The handful of drinkers in the bar looked briefly at him with friendly curiosity before returning to their conversations.

Behind the bar, a young lady treated him to a warm smile. Apple cheeked and freckle faced, she was the very picture of health. "What can I get for you, sir?"

"I understand you have a room to rent."

"That we do, sir."

"I'd like to take it, if I may, for a couple of nights."

"That will be our pleasure, sir." The barmaid took a step back and tilted her head. "I hope you don't mind me saying so, sir, but you bear a remarkable resemblance to a gentleman who stayed with us not so very long ago."

"That could be my uncle," said Carter after a moment's thought.

"A lovely man. Very polite and very personable. He weren't here long but he is fondly remembered. If you don't mind, I'll put you in the very room he occupied. I'm sure you'll love it as much as he did." The girl reached under the counter and produced a set of keys. "My name's Hannah. If you need anything, you just ask. I'll see you right."

It was a small room in the attic. The furniture was delightfully rustic and the sloping ceiling, far from being an inconvenience, added to its charm. A small window gave a view of green pastures and brightly sparkling rivers.

"It ain't much I know," Hannah said apologetically, "but you won't find much better in Carnach."

"It's lovely," Carter reassured her. "In fact, it's perfect."

"Oh good. Some folks do love this room, while others hate it. I guess it comes down to what you're used to." Hannah went to the bedside cabinet and opened it. As she bent down, Carter couldn't help but notice how comely and curvaceous she was. "Ah, here it is." Hannah retrieved a bottle of whisky and held it up for Carter to see. "Your uncle bought this from the bar downstairs. Said it was his favourite brand. For some reason he left it behind unopened, so I guess it's yours now."

Hannah put the bottle on the cabinet then pulled down the bed covers and fluffed up the pillows. "Right, I'll leave you to it, sir. Remember, if you want anything, I'll be in the bar or thereabouts."

"There is just one thing before you go," said Carter, dipping his hand into his pocket. "I wonder if you can tell me anything about this ring. I believe it originates from these parts."

"I ain't never seen nothing like that before. Now if you'll excuse me."

Hannah hurried out of the room. Though Carter was sure she was lying, he reflected that at least her reaction to the ring was preferable to Professor Mayfield's.

After unpacking and freshening himself up in the tiny but adequate en suite bathroom, Carter sat on the bed, drinking his late uncle's whisky while holding the ring in the palm of his hand.

The more whisky he drank, the more he felt like he was on the verge of suddenly understanding the ring's strange symbols. After a while, he felt compelled to take from his case his pen and notebook and to scribble whatever thoughts concerning the ring occurred to him. It was, after all, what they did in detective films: make a note of every relevant fact in the hope of seeing some sort of pattern emerge.

Somewhere along the way, drunkenness gave way to sleep and Carter found himself in a dream. When he awoke, it was with a dry mouth, a pounding heart and a feeling of dread. Within moments, his memories of the dream had dispersed like dew on a sunny morning, leaving him with a vague impression of having experienced something quite awful.

It took a second or two for him to become conscious of that which had awoken him: the rattling of his door, as if someone was trying to get in but had not the wit to turn the handle.

The room was in near darkness with just a hint of moonlight spilling through the window. Who was bothering him at this time of night? And why?

Carter's puzzlement turned to fear as the door handle slowly turned. He held his breath and considered pretending to be asleep. Perhaps that would allow him to take the intruder by surprise.

The door stayed closed.

He grabbed the half empty whisky bottle and wondered if he shouldn't scream or make some sort of commotion. It was then that his attention was grabbed by a movement on the floor.

For a moment, it seemed to him that the wooden boards had lost their solidity and were undulating like sheets of rubber. But he quickly realised he was looking at the rug and there was something crawling beneath it.

A snake! he thought. Dreading what might happen

should the serpent emerge, Carter leapt on the carpet, hoping to squash what lay beneath.

He missed the writhing creature, but did enough to scare it off. It slithered from under the rug and speedily retreated through the gap at the bottom of the door. The rattling of the door stopped.

Carter's curiosity got the better of his fear and he scrambled across the floor to peer through the gap. He was just in time to glimpse a tentacle disappearing down the stairs.

As he got to his feet, he looked at the bottle of whisky and was shocked to see how much he had drunk.

Is it any wonder I'm seeing things? he asked himself, undressing so he could return to bed in a decent manner. *I'll be regretting my indulgence in the morning, that's for sure.*

Carter was wrong. He woke up feeling refreshed and with no trace of a hangover. As he attended to his ablutions, he gave little thought to the events of the previous night, dismissing his nocturnal visitor as nothing more than the consequence of drinking beyond his limit.

Once he was dressed and feeling ready to face the world, he decided a walk would be in order. The village of Carnach promised many delights and he was determined to sample a good number of them before lunch. Then he would dedicate the afternoon to researching the ring, which after all was what had brought him to Carnach in the first place.

It was just gone 11 when Carter left the Green Man and headed towards a small row of shops he had seen when he'd arrived in the village. Tucked between a butchers and a bakers, the Speckled Hen Cafeteria offered a full English breakfast with toast and tea at a very reasonable price. Carter decided to make it his first port of call.

The owners of the cafe had gone out of their way to make the place feel rustic, with gingham table cloths on the tables and Constable prints on the wall.

As Carter entered, the only other customers were two burly men sat opposite one another, attacking bacon sandwiches the size of doorstops with great gusto. They both acknowledged Carter with a nod of the head.

Carter had barely sat down before a middle aged lady came out of the back of the cafe with a pad in her hand.

"Good morning," she greeted, sounding like she was genuinely pleased to see him. "Welcome to the Speckled Hen. May I recommend today's special which is egg and kippers?"

"I'm rather in the mood for a full English breakfast."

"Well, you've come to the right place. You'll go a long way before you find an English breakfast half as good as ours."

"With tea, please."

"One toast or two?"

"Just the one."

To pass the time while waiting for his breakfast, Carter delved into Professor Mayfield's *Obscure Pagan Cults of the British Isles* and was soon lost in tales of witchcraft, human sacrifice and bizarre rituals. In what seemed to him like no time at all, his breakfast was laid before him.

Putting down the book, he noticed the pendant around the waitress's neck. It bore a symbol identical to the one on the ring.

"I say," he said. "That's an interesting pendant you

have there."

"Interesting?" The waitress seemed surprised that he should comment on it. "This old thing? I'd throw it away but for the fact that it's been in my family for generations."

"Do you have any idea as to what the symbol means?"

"It's just a few squiggles as far as I can see."

Carter took out the ring. "Look. There's the exact same symbol on this ring. It must mean something."

The waitress's sunny countenance became grim. She leaned towards Carter and whispered, "Get out of here. Now."

"I beg your pardon?"

"I won't tell you again." The waitress emphasised her point by taking Carter's as yet untouched breakfast. "We don't want you in here."

The two burly men got to their feet.

"What is it, Sandy?" the eldest of them asked. "Is this gentleman bothering you?"

"No," she said. "He's just leaving."

"Yes," said Carter, putting both ring and book in his pocket. "I'm sorry for any trouble I've caused."

Outside, Carter felt a belated surge of anger. All he wanted was a little information which he was sure could be supplied by just about anyone in Carnach. If the ring upset them, they ought to tell him why, instead of treating him like a pariah.

"Damn yokels," he muttered, crossing the road and making his way towards the church. "Superstitious rednecks, the lot of them."

The church stood in the middle of a well-tended graveyard filled with mausoleums and stone angels.

Without really knowing why he was doing it, Carter wandered through the rows of gravestones, noting that some were so weathered as to render their epitaphs unreadable. The mausoleums intrigued him, not least because there were so many of them and their walls were engraved with cherubs and Christian symbols. It suggested to him that many of the families in and around Carnach were wealthy.

One mausoleum in particular caught his eye. Shaped like a pyramid and bereft of carvings, it seemed out of place in a Christian graveyard. Carter went over for a closer look and saw a strange symbol carved on its oak door. He took out the ring and immediately found a match for it.

Clearly, he concluded, *the mausoleum, like the ring, is ancient in origin. But what is it doing in a Christian graveyard?*

"Can I help?"

The gruff voice cut into Carter's thoughts. He turned round to find himself facing a priest. "This is a fascinating graveyard you have here, Father. I'm something of a historian and I find places like this to be a great source of information."

"You're the fellow boarding at the Green Man." It was statement rather than a question. "I expect you're not staying in Carnach very long."

"This mausoleum here: is it very old?"

"Older than you can imagine." The priest took a step towards Carter. "Now get out of my graveyard."

"I beg your pardon?"

"The dead are entitled to their peace the same as the rest of us."

Carter's gander was well and truly up. He had a good

mind to tell the priest to go to Hell, along with the rest of Carnach. Marching out of the graveyard, he made himself a promise not to leave the village until he had the answers he'd come for - and God help anybody who got in his way.

For a while, he walked without much care as to where he was headed. It was a good way to let off steam and to think at the same time. By the time he reached the village green, he was a whole lot less inclined towards violence but no less determined to complete his quest.

The village pond beckoned. Carter decided he would sit by it until he had found his equilibrium once more. But it was not to be. On the way to the pond he came across a well. At first sight there was nothing particularly interesting about it, but as Carter drew near he could make out symbols engraved on its side.

He took out the ring and walked around the well. As he'd suspected, the symbols on the well not only matched those on the ring, they were in the same order.

Carter felt certain he'd stumbled upon centre of the ring's mystery. He peered into the well and found himself looking down at pitch darkness. Were the answers he sought somewhere down there?

They must be, he told himself. *But how am I going to get to them?*

Perplexed and frustrated, he returned to the Green Man. Perhaps he'd find someone in the bar who'd talk to him about the well. If not, he would return to the University and plague Professor Mayfield until the fellow revealed to him the contents of the missing pages.

Hannah was behind the bar. She greeted him with a sympathetic smile. "You look like you could use a whisky."

Carter shuddered. "I've had quite enough whisky for now. I don't want any more nightmares."

"Oh, I do hope you didn't have too bad a night."

"No. I just had a strange dream about something creeping into my room. That's what I get for drinking too much of the hard stuff."

As Carter spoke, he was uncomfortably aware that everyone else in the bar had stopped speaking. He looked round and saw he had become the centre of attention.

"It's on the house," said Hannah, breaking the spell. Conversation resumed as she poured a generous measure of Scotch into a tumbler. "This will put hairs on your chest."

The Scotch was golden. It gave off subtle aromas that made him think of campfires, honey and heather. Now that Carter thought of it, a good slug of Scotch was just what he needed. Besides, it would be rude to refuse Hannah's generosity.

"Slainte!" she said, raising a glass of her own in salutation.

One sip told him he was drinking a whisky of exceptional quality.

"Your uncle was a man for his whisky," said Hannah. "He seemed very knowledgeable on the subject. Actually, he knew a lot about a lot of things. You and he must get along like a house on fire."

"Actually, we've never met and we never will. He very recently passed away."

"That's a shame. You'd have liked him."

Carter pulled up a stool and sat down at the bar. Normally not the most loquacious or sociable of men, he found conversing with Hannah both pleasant and therapeutic. The fact that she kept topping up his glass did much to break down his barriers and soon he was chatting to Hannah like she was an old friend. Although he was sure he'd regret it later, he opened up to her in a way he'd never opened up to anyone before.

Eventually, the conversation turned to the reason for his visit to Carnach. Carter told Hannah how the ring had come into his possession and how it had turned his life upside down. He reported his meeting with Professor Mayfield and his eventual discovery of the connection between the ring and Carnach.

By now he had consumed a goodly amount of whisky and the room was gently swaying.

"Have you tried the ring on?" Hannah asked, leaning on the bar so her face was intimately close to his.

Carter drank in her beauty. He felt a strong urge to kiss her. She was, he decided, the most attractive woman he had met in a long time and - unlikely as it might be - she seemed attracted to him.

He giggled. "Try it on? I should think not."

"Not scared are you?"

"Why should I be scared?"

"Because you think that ring is cursed."

"I think no such thing. Here - look." Carter produced the ring from his pocket. Drunk as he was, it took him several attempts to get it on his finger. "There!"

"You're a brave man, Carter Donovan. I doubt there's anyone in this village would do what you just done."

"That's because they're a bunch of superstitious yokels." Carter thought he was whispering when in fact he was speaking loudly enough to be heard by all his fellow drinkers. "I'm a scholar, Hannah. A man of science. I deal in facts, not fancies."

"Oh dear," said Hannah. "I think the drink's gone to your head."

"You're right," said Carter, feeling ashamed. "I shouldn't have used the term *yokels*. That was unforgivably judgmental of me."

"I tell you what. Let's you and me go for a nice walk to help clear your head."

"You know, I think I'd like that. What a fine idea."

When he stepped out of the Green Man, Carter was somewhat surprised to find that night had fallen. Surely he hadn't been in the bar that long, had he? Where had the day gone?

Hannah slipped her arm through his and led him in the direction of the village green. For now at least, all thought of the ring was forgotten as Carter wondered how things might turn out between him and Hannah. Could he persuade her to return with him to Fennelcliff? Or would he have to move to Carnach? How should he go about telling her how he felt about her? When should he do it?

Slow down, he told himself. *Don't go rushing in and making a damn fool of yourself like you usually do. Reel her in gently, Donovan.*

"Tell me, Carter," said Hannah. "If you could give a present to anyone, who would it be and what would you say to them?"

"That's a strange question." Carter scratched his head. "I suppose the someone would have to be my niece, Zara. She turned 16 just last week and it made me realise I've never really gotten to know her. All my fault, of course, for caring more about books than my own flesh and blood."

"So what would you say to her?"

"I don't know. Something along the lines of *I wish I'd known you more.*"

"That's sweet."

"Seems rather prosaic to me."

"You should write to her first thing in the morning. Let her know how you feel."

"Oh no. I couldn't. I wouldn't know what to say."

"You've just said it." They were outside the graveyard now. Letting go of Carter's arm, Hannah took from her pocket a sheet of paper and fountain pen. "Look, I think you'd better write it down so's you don't forget."

Hannah lay the paper on the wall and handed the pen to Carter who spotted at once that it was an antique and worth a considerable sum of money. He rested a hand on the paper and got a small surprise.

"This is parchment," he said. "Just like my uncle sent me with the ring."

"Don't forget what you were going to write."

"I'm afraid I already have."

"It was *I wish I could have given you more.*"

"Was it? I thought it was something else. Oh well, I guess it will do." He hastily scrawled the message on the parchment. "There. That should do it."

Hannah took the parchment and pen from Carter. "There. Come on, let's go have a look at the well. Perhaps we can work out what the symbols mean."

Before Carter knew it, he was standing beside the well with Hannah, shaking his head. "It's no use. I doubt I'll ever divine their meaning."

"Let me tell you what they say. That first symbol

stands for *pasher*. And that one reads *tagoth*."

Carter was amused. "You're making this up, aren't you? Having fun with me."

"Am I? Let's see." Hannah slowly circled the well, pointing at each symbol in turn. *"Pasher tagoth imra… Pasher tagoth imra… Yrgasol."*

As Hannah came full circle to rejoin Carter, he heard a noise that chilled him. It was an obscene slurping, suggestive of some voracious carnivore licking its lips while simultaneously sucking air through its teeth.

"What's that?"

Hannah laughed. "That's Yrgasol."

A tentacle erupted from the well and flopped onto the side with a loud squelch.

Memories of the previous night came back to Carter. That thing in his room -. *Dear God! It was real! And it's here!*

Carter turned to flee and immediately fell flat on his face. The ground beneath him rocked like a boat on a stormy sea.

He tried to stand but could only make it as far as his knees. Behind him, something slobbered.

Dozens of torches came to life, illuminating the crowd of people advancing towards him. Amongst their number he discerned the waitress and burly men from the cafeteria as well as the priest and the people he'd seen in the bar of the Green Man.

"Help me!" Carter pleaded. "Please!"

Hannah knelt beside him. He felt her warm breath on his cheek. "There, there, lover boy. It will soon be over." She took his hand and raised it to her mouth. "Parting is such sweet sorrow."

She wrapped her lips around Carter's finger and eased

it into her mouth sensually. Then she bit down hard.

The pain was intense. Carter instinctively lashed at Hannah, catching her a glancing blow. Blood arced from the stump of his finger.

Laughing, Hannah took his missing member from her mouth and removed the ring. The ring went in her pocket. The finger she discarded like a used cigarette.

"You bitch!" Carter yelled as a tentacle wrapped itself round his neck, shutting off his air supply. He was lifted into the air. Other tentacles sprouted from the well and held him in their obscene, unrelenting grasp.

Hannah and the villagers cheered as Yrgasol pulled her latest acquisition into the depths of the deep, dark well. Several of them were already removing their clothes in preparation for the orgy that followed a human sacrifice to their god.

The priest came up behind Hannah, cupped her breasts and kissed her rosy cheek. "Yrgasol is pleased. Who next do we have lined up for her?"

"A rather tasty morsel if I'm not mistaken, Father." Hannah held up the parchment with Carter's brief but touching message. "She'll be here soon."

THE GIFT
SHAUN HUTSON

Dean Morton prodded the food with his fork for a moment then speared a piece of meat and pushed it into his mouth.

He chewed noisily, the sound filling the small kitchen of the house.

Bill Morton looked edgily at his son and thought about rebuking him for making so much noise as he ate, but then he merely sighed and continued with his own meal. At the other side of the table, Carol Morton took a sip of her water and then sprinkled more salt on her dinner before continuing to eat. The washing up was piled in the sink nearby but it would have to wait until they got back from the hospital. They'd have to leave as soon as they'd finished their meal. They liked to be there at the beginning of visiting hours so they could spend the longest amount of time possible with their daughter Holly.

Carol sniffed and dabbed at her nose with a tissue she

pulled from her jeans. Even the thought of her daughter could provoke this kind of reaction these days it seemed, but she forced back the emotion building within her and continued eating. As she chewed she glanced again at Dean. He and Holly had been born within minutes of each other, nine years ago in the same hospital where Holly had lain for the last ten days. Despite being classed as twins, the two of them had only minimal physical similarities. Both had dull blue eyes and dark hair but Dean had always been a larger child. His features were fuller and he was bordering on chubby if Carol was honest. Holly had always been more petite and slim. Mind you, Carol told herself, if she ate like Dean did then perhaps she too would look bigger. He was perpetually hungry and that was one of the reasons that Carol had piled his plate so high with food this particular dinner time. He'd never been a fussy eater as he was growing up. Quite the contrary, he'd accepted and consumed everything put before him since he'd been a baby. It was something which she thought she should be grateful for, not chastise him for and particularly now. If he was eating for comfort then so be it. God alone knew he and the rest of the family had to seek that particular commodity wherever they could find it at present.

The three of them sat in silence around the small Formica topped table in the corner of the kitchen, the sound of the television filtering in from the living room occasionally to break the stillness.

"There weren't any lights on in Mrs Beecham's house when I got back earlier," Carol said finally, tiring of the silence and also of her own thoughts.

"Perhaps she's gone away for a couple of days," Bill offered. "She's got a sister in Devon hasn't she? Perhaps she went there?"

"Without telling us? She'd never do that," Carol reminded him. "She always gets us to watch the house if she goes away and I go in and water her plants for her, you know that."

"Well nip in when we get back from the hospital then, you've got a spare key," Bill insisted.

"I can go if you like," Dean offered through a mouthful of food.

"That's very kind of you, Dean," Carol told him. "But it depends how late we get back."

"She'll be fine," Bill said. "Perhaps she's just saving electricity."

"I haven't seen her out in the garden for a while either come to think of it," Carol muttered.

"With all due respect, love, I think we've got other things to worry about at the moment," Bill reminded her.

Carol nodded.

"If Holly got a new heart she wouldn't die would she?"

The question hung in the air and both Carol and Bill turned towards Dean who had uttered the words and was now shovelling more food into his mouth.

"I could give her mine," Dean said, smiling. "I'd do that for her you know."

Carol felt tears welling up in her eyes and she looked first at her husband and then at her son with an expression of pure love.

"That's a beautiful thing for you to say, Dean," she said, her voice cracking slightly. "I'm sure that Holly would say the same thing if she heard you."

Bill got to his feet and crossed to the boy, sliding his

arm around his shoulders.

"Mum's right," he echoed. "That's a wonderful thing to say but if you gave her your heart then you'd need one too, wouldn't you." He ruffled his son's hair.

"What's wrong with Holly's heart?" Dean insisted. "Why does she need a new one?"

Carol Morton sucked in a deep breath, looked across at her husband and then decided that she was going to have to find the words to satisfy her son's curiosity.

"The Doctors said that there's a hole in it," she said, quietly. "It's been there since she was born but it's been getting bigger. They can't stop it from happening." Carol swallowed hard and sniffed.

"So that's why she needs a new heart?" Dean murmured.

Carol and Bill nodded.

"Have you been thinking about it then?" Bill asked the boy.

"Sometimes," Dean admitted. "Why can't they do anything to help Holly?"

"Because she needs someone else's heart to replace hers," Bill explained. "They call it a transplant. The doctors would take out Holly's heart and put in a healthy one."

"And then she'd be alright?" Dean beamed.

Bill nodded.

"Why don't they just do that then?" Dean went on.

"Because they have to wait until a heart is available," Bill told him. "And so far there hasn't been one that she can have."

Dean nodded.

The three of them remained silent for a moment then Bill pulled on his jacket, glancing at his watch in the process.

"We'd better go," he said, quietly.

Dean hurried from the table and headed for the kitchen door.

"Where are you going?" Carol called. "We've got to leave for the hospital now."

"I've just got to get something from my room," Dean told her then she heard his feet pounding up the stairs.

"I told you it was bothering him," Carol said, her voice catching. "Just because he doesn't talk about it much, doesn't mean it isn't on his mind."

"I know," Bill admitted, sliding an arm around her shoulder. "But at least he talked about it today, didn't he? The more he knows the more he'll understand. The doctors said that, didn't they?"

"And the more he understands the more it'll worry him."

Bill shook his head.

"He's a good boy," he insisted. "It's nice to know he cares so much about his sister."

They both heard more thudding of footsteps as Dean blundered back downstairs. When he appeared in the kitchen doorway he was holding a plastic shopping bag in one hand.

"I got some presents for Holly," he announced, holding up the bag. "I thought they might cheer her up. I used my pocket money."

It was all Carol could do not to burst into floods of tears. She crossed to her son and hugged him warmly.

Bill too was finding it hard to control his emotions but he took a deep breath, composed himself and fished in his jacket pocket for his car keys.

"Come on," he said, smiling. "We'd better get going so we're there for the beginning of visiting time."

The three of them trooped out of the house and towards the waiting car, Dean proudly holding the shopping bag and its contents. He slipped into the back seat and put on his seat belt.

The drive was completed in relative silence. It wasn't more than half an hour from their house to the hospital and the roads were relatively clear. Dean contented himself with gazing out of the side window at the houses they passed, his eyes finally widening in anticipation as they reached the hospital itself. Bill found a parking space as close as he could and they hauled themselves out of the car and began the walk towards the main entrance of the imposing building. As they made their way through the reception area, Bill and Carol spotted other regular visitors and nodded or waved accordingly. Some of the staff even offered greetings or waved good naturedly and those signs of recognition, though welcome, only served to remind them of how long they'd been coming to the hospital to see their sick daughter. Familiarity hadn't bred contempt but just deep and aching sorrow. And if they were honest there was no sign of that sorrow coming to an end.

They rode the lift to the third floor and made their way to the ward where their daughter lay.

Before they approached her bed they composed themselves as they normally did, not wanting to show the pain they felt and certainly not wanting any stray tears to fall. Holly had enough to worry about without them burdening her further. As they approached the bed they could see that she was sleeping or at least that she had her eyes closed. Did she, Carol wondered now as she had done so many times before, actually realize the enormity of her condition? Did she understand how close to death she actually was? Could a nine year old girl contemplate matters as grave as that and still retain her sanity? Carol pushed the thoughts to one side as best she could and leaned forward, touching her daughter's hand gently.

Holly opened her eyes immediately, saw who her visitors were and smiled.

They pulled up plastic chairs and sat around her the way they always did.

Dean sat swinging his legs back and forth still clutching the shopping bag to his chest.

When the usual small talk had run dry and there were no more other ways to ask Holly how she was feeling, if there'd been any changes or if anyone new had come into or gone out of the ward, Carol nodded towards Dean and squeezed Holly's hand a little more tightly.

"Dean's brought you something," she said as Bill poured more water into the plastic beaker that stood on Holly's nightstand.

Holly tried to sit up but couldn't and she coughed gently.

"Are you alright?" Carol asked.

Holly nodded and looked at her brother who was now standing next to her, one hand inside the bag.

"I got you these," he said, pulling out a small box that had been lovingly albeit clumsily gift wrapped with what looked like faded Christmas paper.

"Where did you get that?" Carol wanted to know, glancing at the paper.

"I found it in your wardrobe," Dean announced. "I was looking for the scissors."

"You unwrap it for me," Holly said.

Dean did as he was asked; pulling the paper free to expose a small box of chocolates which he laid gently on Holly's bed. She smiled at him.

"There's more," he said, proudly and produced another small package.

As Holly looked on with delight he ripped open that too and revealed a set of coloured pencils.

"I thought you could do some drawing," he beamed. "You like that don't you?"

"I feel like it's my birthday," Holly said.

"They're like early Christmas presents," Dean told her. "But this one is the best one." He took another parcel from the bag and pushed it towards her. "I hope you like it."

Holly accepted the box, infected now by her brother's excitement.

Carol was reaching for the parcel, preparing to unwrap it when Holly shook her head.

"I can do it, mum," she said.

Dean was rocking back and forth now, his own excitement reaching fever pitch. He looked from the parcel to Holly's face, waiting to see her expression when she unveiled the gift. She pulled away the last piece of paper and gazed at what she'd revealed. It was a large biscuit tin that had been painted blue using Dean's water colours. The top had been sealed with sellotape and Holly began picking at the clear material with her thin fingers, eager to peel it away and remove the lid.

"You have been busy, Dean," said Bill as he watched his daughter continuing to pull the tape away. "It must have taken you ages to wrap that."

Dean beamed up at his father and then looked expectantly at Holly as she tore the last of the clear tape free and began to lift the lid of the tin.

She pulled it free with a small grunt.

Both Bill and Carol leaned forward to inspect the contents of the tin and as they did they recoiled from the foul stench that rose from within. Only Dean stood there smiling broadly as his sister looked down into the tin, her eyes widening until it seemed they would burst from their sockets. She tried to push the tin away but her hands were shaking so violently she couldn't seem to muster any strength. Carol took one look inside the tin and turned away retching. Bill also felt his stomach somersault as he fixed his gaze on the contents of the tin.

It was a human heart.

Lying in a puddle of partly congealed blood it lay there like some dark crimson offering, trickles of red fluid still dribbling from the roughly cut veins and arteries.

Dean was still smiling.

"It belonged to Mrs Beecham," he said, puzzled by the reactions of his family. "She was old. She didn't need it like Holly does."

Bill opened his mouth to say something but no words would come forth.

"She always said she'd like to help Holly," Dean went on. "And now she can. Holly can have her heart. I cut it out this afternoon. I thought it would help."

Holly began to scream.

"What's wrong?" Dean asked, the smile fading from his face. "Don't you like your presents?"

The screaming continued.

THE FATHER
RICH HAWKINS

The town on the coast was the end of the line for many travellers, coloured in rust and rain, mired between the sea and the sodden hills where the roads were worn and black. Cort slowed the car to a crawl as he passed the remains of a small church, glancing at the lop-sided spire above crumbling walls and the bowed roof that was succumbing to rot. Dark innards of fungi blossoms and empty pews were glimpsed past the shattered stained glass. No congregation to serve but forgotten shades and shadows. The graveyard was overgrown, headstones strangled by creeping vines and weeds. A place where wild things capered. The gates were wrapped in iron chains as thick as a man's wrist.

He drove into the town, which seemed like a displaced echo or an idiot's dream. Something out of time in the dark country. Drizzle pattered against the windscreen. He switched on the wipers and winced at their squeal upon the wet glass.

The car passed squat houses upon the cold streets. A man with a crooked leg hobbled along the pavement. A young woman pushed a pram while she spoke on her mobile phone, her red painted mouth moving like the folds of a carnivorous plant. An old, overweight woman in a plastic raincoat stared at the sky through misted spectacles.

The town breathed an asthmatic drawl around him.

His car was one of the few on the roads. He drove down a street lined with B&B's and shabby hostels, their bleached facades fading into the downpour. A pub with windows lit dirty yellow. Below a neon sign flickering in the soft rain, the shapes of tall men wreathed in cigarette smoke huddled in the doorway like conspirators making malignant plans.

Ahead of him was the sea, deep blue and immense, leading to the dark, flat horizon that rose to merge with the sky. He wasn't far now. His hands gripped the steering wheel with bloodless fingers. He parked the car by the promenade, got out and lit a cigarette, and when he inhaled the smoke it was like nectar in his lungs. Then he turned towards the water and looked out to the ships and little boats breaking through froth and surf, silhouetted against the mist that was forming upon the sea. He closed his eyes for a moment, and the world seemed empty. He wished for a silent Earth devoid of terrible machinations and murder.

There weren't many people along the seafront, apart from a few pensioners all hunched and meandering, muttering in pairs and day-trip groups. They pottered upon the promenade pathways in a dazed fugue, their bones frail with age and arthritis, clutching portions of chips in gnarled hands. Bad hair and flaking scalps. Dentures within pained grimaces. Dodgy hips, dried skin and liver spots. A white haired woman skulked in a wheelchair, a tartan blanket draped over her legs as she stared at the sea with a longing that broke Cort's heart.

All of them fading into the quiet desolation. Cort was adamant that would not be him one day. He would make sure. A promise to himself.

He took a walk along the sea wall, passing a stone memorial to those taken by the deep water in the long ago. It was gnawed and scratched by the feral wind, and scattered around its base were scraps of trash. He finished the cigarette, killed it underneath one foot and lit another. Gulls and terns cried overhead, gliding on air currents. The sea let out a pained shriek that made him turn sharply and expect to see a dying creature spill onto the shingle beach.

He walked past shuttered arcades and closed up gift shops. Faded pictures of ice cream and hot dogs. No trade in the middle of winter. A fat man stood behind the raised counter in a mobile fish and chip van, perfectly still and staring at nothing. There were no customers.

Ahead of him, a gang of youths in hooded jackets, cheap tracksuits and trainers lurked around a metal bench. Hands in pockets and furtive glances. Jackal-like giggling past curled lips that sucked on roll ups. A bottle of cheap cider was passed around. The tallest of them, a lad on the cusp of adulthood with a wispy beard and acne, stared at Cort but didn't rise from the bench. Cort took the stone steps down to the beach, watching his feet on the steep decline. He kept walking, keeping the sea wall between himself and the youths. He heard them laughing. One of them shouted something but it was lost to the wind.

One foot after the other, crunching upon the shingle. Rolling clouds overhead. He moved down the beach in incremental steps until he was sure he had left the youths behind, and slowed to a crawling pace. The waves advanced then retreated, and it would always be this way. Ebb and flow. They left behind glistening pebbles and detritus.

Further down the beach he found a blubbery white-grey thing washed up and rotting. It had small teeth and scraggly patches of fur, and a rope of slippery intestine hung from its ravaged body. A seal, attacked by something nasty out in the water; or it had died and been scavenged by other marine life. Maybe both. Small crabs scurried around the corpse, picking at it with pincers and claws, pushing morsels of meat into their chewing mouths. Cort didn't linger for long, because the stink of necrosis made his eyes water.

He climbed the scarred hills to the cliff tops and stood before barren fields and giant electricity pylons wreathed in mist. The cliffs were the colour of iron and slag. His aching bones were older than his years, and the inside of his head spun with exertion, so he sat on a bench and looked out over the sea. The beach he'd walked from was set in a curved bay. The seafront was grey, but there were dashes of colour: a bright purple coat; a yellow kite rising into the sky from the hands of a thin silhouette; something red and round bobbed on the water where the shallows began to deepen. Up on the cliff tops the wind was stronger, pulling at his clothes, his skin, stinging his eyes. He took a miniature bottle of Jim Beam from his pocket, unscrewed the cap and took a swig. Burn in his mouth, in his throat, into his sternum.

He finished the bottle in less than a minute, and when he was finished his face was flushed with warmth. He placed the empty bottle on the bench then took a tattered, discoloured blue teddy bear from his jacket pocket. It was about the size of a kitten. One of its eyes had been lost a long time ago. The left ear crumpled by a small mouth of infant teeth. Its fur was matted with the grease and dirt from a little boy's hands.

Cort pulled the bear to his face and inhaled the scent left behind by his boy, closing his eyes as he breathed in deeply, shoulders trembling. His chest hitched with shuddering breaths and hot tears ran either side of his mouth to dampen the bear's fur. The bear was a part of his boy, the only part he had left. All that remained.

Cort took the bear with him to the edge of the cliff. His last friend. His final witness. He looked down on black rocks sharpened by waves. It would be quick, at least, a small comfort for a mourning father. And even if the fall didn't kill him, the water would smash him against the rocks until he was shattered and broken.

He swallowed. Took one last look around as the rain fell harder. This beautiful, filthy, dying world, part dream and nightmare.

He moved one foot over the edge and hesitated, the skin of his face hot and loose as he lowered his face to observe the hundred feet drop. His heart pounded and he felt sick. Bile frothed in his throat, mixed with the taste of metal and whiskey. The sharp wind tested him, sizing him up and stealing his breath. The sea roared. Gravity pulled at him with pinching fingers. He thought he could hear children's voices but it was either his imagination or carried by the wind from far away.

All he had to do was lean forward. As simple as falling down. The sea was in his head and in his lungs. The call of the ocean and its siren song.

The wind raged. The rain was constant and there was no sun. The cruciform shapes of gulls swooped through the mist.

Cort hesitated at the threshold, drenched and half-blinded by the torrent. One little step, that was all. Nothing but falling. He squeezed his eyes shut and counted to ten, but pulled out at the last second. Then he put his hands together, clutching the bear as he gritted his teeth and prayed to a god he despised to give him the strength to fall. This had to be done. This was his end game. The final chapter of his story. The light would go out and he would be glad.

The wind wailed.

He opened his eyes, crying at his own weakness. He unclasped his hands and scratched at his face until the skin was tender.

There was a little girl down on the beach. Looked about ten years old. She was alone, facing the sea, like an image taken from an old photograph. She was wearing a white dress. Cort looked up and down the beach but couldn't see an adult nearby. No sign of her parents on the stretches of empty shingle. Even the promenade was empty.

Maybe she had lost her parents, he thought.

He staggered down the hillside, losing sight of her in the rain. When he got to the beach the girl was gone. He looked around, but there was no sign of her. The possibility that she had walked into the sea made his stomach cold. He trudged back and forth along a stretch of the water's edge, scanning the wet shingle.

A small noise, like an inhalation of soft breath, made him look up. And he saw the girl standing about forty yards down the beach, her back to him, a small form in white. He opened his mouth but his voice failed him, and the girl was already walking away by the time he realised he should follow, so he went after her and called out, but she didn't respond as she moved towards the dark cliffs.

Cort quickened his pace to a slow jog, but she remained the same distance ahead of him. The mist was moving inland. He suddenly felt exhausted and dazed. She became a shade in the mist. He followed silently in her wake, up the hillside, where he lost sight of her.

The mist cleared and she was gone. The rain stopped. He thought he heard a child's voice on the wind. His first thought was that she'd done what he could not and jumped into the sea.

There was no body on the rocks or in the water.

He turned in a circle, searching for her, but he was alone, like he had been for a long time.

Dripping rainwater, Cort returned to his car parked on the promenade. He felt heavy and weighed down, but empty. Used up. He unlocked the car and was about to climb in when he noticed a small, round object on the roof. And after he picked it up he stared at it in the palm of his hand. It was a fossil – an ammonite, if he remembered correctly. The shell was rippled with grooves. This had once been a living creature, back when everything here was the ocean and the water teemed with sleek predators. But who left it there? And why?

Cort looked in each direction, scanning the deserted walkways and the shadows in the rain. The sea pushed against the shore, insistent as ever.

He put the fossil in his pocket and drove away.

Cort found a backstreet café in the town centre and sat in a dark corner drinking sweet tea and staring at the hardened sugar in the bowl while a radio spat football results and weather reports. He had nothing to go home for. The surface of the table was sticky against the underside of his arms. Above him the lighting strips winked upon a stained ceiling. The woman serving behind the counter was wearing too much make-up and her hair was pulled back in a severe ponytail. She picked at her fingernails as she glanced at Cort with the glimmer of a smile. Maybe she had noticed the discoloured band of skin on his finger where his wedding ring used to be. He ignored her and watched the walls glisten with grease.

Apart from Cort, the only other people at the tables were a few lone men clad in dark coats, hunched over plates of fried food and copies of *The Sun*. A family was gathered across the other side of the room: two parents and a little boy with a gap-toothed smile who looked about six years old. He was walking a Spider-Man action figure back and forth over the table, pretending to shoot webs from its wrists.

Cort didn't realise he was staring at the boy until the mother glared at him. He looked at her, his face flushed with heat, trying to smile, but the shape of his mouth felt all wrong, and he turned away. The woman said something to her husband, and in the corner of his eye he saw them look his way. The husband was thick-armed and apelike, scowling and bearded. Cort pretended to read the newspaper left behind by the table's previous occupant, until they looked away. He glazed over an article about the country's prolonged period of bad weather. There were a few mentions of climate change and melting icecaps.

He finished his tea and left without looking back.

With night approaching he decided to stay in the town for a while, to gather the courage to kill himself. He rented a room at a small B&B on a quiet street. It was owned by Mary, an old Irish lady with small hands and excessive skin. She smelled of lavender soap and Deep Heat. Dark hairs bristled above her mouth. The knitted cardigan over her shoulders gave the suggestion of a shroud covering a terribly thin corpse. She was polite but aloof, and she took Cort's money without any questions about why he was visiting the coast. The building was Victorian, cold and austere. On the walls, paintings by obscure artists depicted visions of the Circles of Hell and damnation, purgatory and salvation. Gods and monsters. People writhing in lakes of fire. At the top of the stairs before his room, a watercolour of a wide carnivorous mouth greeted him, quickening his heart.

His room was four walls of grey and a thin carpet. He watched a documentary about lion prides on the Serengeti. Afterwards he lay on the lumpy bed and sobbed in the dark, listening to the man in the next room masturbating noisily.

He needed a drink, a proper drink, so he found a pub in the next street. Some warmth, some light, some comfort. He bought two double whiskeys from the tattooed man behind the bar and slumped in a corner booth away from the other loners and reprobates.

He drank, savouring the whiskey in his gullet while he held the fossil in his hand and ran his finger over the striations and shallow folds in the stone. It smelled of earth and damp. Time passed in a dazed fug, and he drank until the room was blurry at the edges and people's faces were indistinct and easier to look at. The rasping voices at the bar rose and fell in volume then reached a crescendo that filled his head until it faded into soft murmurs and coughs. Figures clutching pints of lager hobbled past him. He ordered more whiskey and listened to the jukebox pump out the Human League's greatest hits as darkness fell outside. The rain tapped at the windows. The girl from the beach would not leave his thoughts even though he tried to push her away with Wild Grouse and Eighties' synth-pop.

At some point there were younger voices in the room, a threat of violence in their cackling and shouting. Cort looked up from his drink towards the bar and watched the pack of youths he had seen at the promenade. He tried to count their number but they seemed to melt into one another, like a hive of insects. The older patrons retreated silently from the bar and into the corners of the room, where they kept their eyes downcast.

Cort felt his bladder tighten. He staggered to the toilet, skirting around the laughing pack, and when he walked through the doorway the smell of urinal cakes and old piss stains hit him like a wet slap. The floor was sticky and the walls sweated. In one of the cubicles, through the opening between the door and the frame, two young men were snorting lines of ketamine from the top of the cistern. The marker pen graffiti on the walls was mainly sexual organs and crude insults. A phone number for a good blowjob.

They looked up at Cort and wiped their noses, brazen and grinning, almost wolfish. Cort stood at a urinal and felt their gazes upon his back. He couldn't urinate. A stifled laugh from the cubicle. A bead of sweat ran down his forehead. His cock drooped. Footsteps behind him.

"You alright, mate?" one of the young men slurred as he stood at the urinal to Cort's left. He sniffed, ran his wrist under his nose, spat into where he was pissing.

"Fine, thanks." Cort recognised him from the pack out in the bar. He seemed to be the leader of the group, all sinew and hustle in a white tracksuit. His hair was slick with grease and he stank of chemicals and old sweat.

The other man stood in the urinal on Cort's right, so that they flanked him. He unzipped his trousers and placed one hand against the wall as he pissed. Darker skin, twitching jaw, wide shoulders.

There was a casual drawl in White Tracksuit's voice. "I know you, don't I?"

Cort looked at him. "I don't think so. I'm not from around here."

The man grinned. His face was too dry. "You were at the beach yesterday, weren't you?"

"Uh, yeah."

"What were you doing?"

215

Cort hesitated. "Just taking a walk."

The man to Cort's right grunted like an animal.

White Tracksuit finished and put himself away. "You sure that was all you were doing?"

"Yeah. Why do you ask?"

White Tracksuit turned his body to face Cort. "I'm just a concerned citizen, that's all. A lot of perverts and weirdoes out there. We get 'em in town. They're drawn to the coast, for some reason."

"So what's that got to do with me?" said Cort. He buttoned his trousers up and went to move, but the other man put a hand on his shoulder, and he froze.

White Tracksuit said, "We get a lot of kiddy-fiddlers out here. They like to come to the coast and see the sea. Watch the children play on the beach. We caught one a few months ago. Sorted him out. They're old men, usually. How old are you, mate?"

Cort didn't break eye contact with the man. Blood pulsed at his temples. "Thirty-six. Not that it's any of your business."

White Tracksuit grinned to show missing teeth. "Oh, I think you'll find it is my fucking business. It's my business to know what perverts are lurking around my fucking town. You understand?"

The man behind Cort snorted. "He understands, Freddy. He understands alright."

Anger flared in Cort's chest. "Are you accusing me of being a paedophile? This is fucking ridiculous."

Freddy didn't answer. His eyes gleamed.

"Just leave me alone," Cort said. "I haven't done anything wrong."

Freddy raised his hand and placed it to Cort's cheek;

he flinched and backed into the other man, who nudged him back towards Freddy. Cort's arms were shaking and terribly heavy.

"Not yet, you haven't," Freddy said.

"Fuck off."

Freddy laughed. "Don't get touchy, mate. You really want to watch your mouth." There was a flash of silver as he put a penknife to Cort's throat.

Cort looked into his awful, shining face.

"Maybe we should teach you a lesson in manners." Freddy slid the blade gently across Cort's skin, but not deep enough to draw blood. Not quite. Part of Cort wished for the blade to go deeper, to puncture his throat, severe his carotid artery, so he'd bleed out on the dirty floor. So he grabbed Freddy's wrist and held the knife in place.

"Go on, fucking do it. Please."

A sliver of confusion passed over Freddy's face. He snatched his arm back and the knife with it. He puffed out his chest. "You really want it that badly?"

Cort found himself grinning. Maybe it was the whiskey, but he doubted it. He nodded, wiped his mouth.

Freddy said nothing.

The other man's hand gripped Cort's shoulder even tighter, and without thinking he shrugged it off and elbowed the man in the face. The man staggered back against the wall, clutching his nose, a muffled sound in his throat. Cort turned back to Freddy, who still had the knife raised towards him, eyes wide and mouth gaping. He'd never seen this before. He hadn't even contemplated it.

Cort took the knife and pushed him against the urinals. He raised the knife to Freddy's left eye. His other hand was on the younger man's throat. Freddy looked like a little boy, lost and frightened, unable to comprehend the situation.

Cort sneered into Freddy's face. "You coward. Didn't even have the balls to cut a stranger."

"I'm sorry," Freddy said, fishy breath steaming from his mouth. "We were just fucking about. Havin' a laugh. You know what I mean."

"Very funny," Cort said as he lowered the knife. "This is how you cut a stranger."

Freddy gasped as the blade slipped into his left thigh. It went in easy, without resistance. Cort placed his hand over Freddy's mouth. A wave of revulsion passed through him at the man's warm breath on his palm.

"We're all dust," Cort whispered. "And we remain." He didn't know what he meant by those words, but they sounded right. He withdrew the knife and took his hand from Freddy's mouth. Freddy was covered in sweat. His mouth moved, but there no words. The other man was slumped on the floor with two hands stemming his bleeding nose.

Cort pocketed the knife, walked out to his table and downed the last of the whiskey. He left the pub and walked into the storm.

He left his car at the pub and headed back to the B&B, slouching against the rain as he stumbled between rows of black buildings. A car drifted past, spraying water. The streetlights were dim and tired. He was sure he was being followed, but he didn't look back, and kept walking.

In his room he lay on his bed and stared at the ceiling. His vision swam. Bile in his chest. He didn't care about what had happened in the pub toilets, because the men had started it. They had seen him as a victim. He hated violence, but he was apathetic towards any pain he'd caused to the men. It was a strange feeling. It was probably the drink, and he hoped he wouldn't be overcome by guilt when he sobered up.

He passed out with the blue bear in his hand.

Cort was woken by a scream that might have been from a gull or a small child. He had dreamt of eels and fluthers of jellyfish struggling in the deep sea. The eels tearing at the jellyfish with razor mouths; and the jellyfish wrapping thin, stinging tendrils around the eels until they were conjoined in death.

He was sure that someone had stood by the foot of his bed. He could smell saltwater. On his bedside table, alongside the fossil, was a rabbit skull. He thought he was imagining the skull, until he picked it up. Smooth and bleached by age, egg shell-thin. It had been cleaned with care and love, a delicate treasure in his hand.

Someone had left it there for him, just like the fossil. A present or warning, or maybe a threat. He felt the urge to take the knife and finish what he started on his wrists last year, when Beth had left him and gone to live in Spain with her ex-pat parents. But in the end he realised he didn't want to take his life in a dingy B&B. If he was going to finish it all he would do it with the wind at his face and the roar of the sea in his head.

The sea was a long way down from where he was standing. Black rocks and surf. He stepped towards the edge of the cliff, ready to let go of everything, but then stopped when he heard a wet sniffle behind him. He turned around.

Freddy was back.

"You," Cort said.

Anger in Freddy's face, and violence in his eyes. "No one gets the better of me."

Cort opened his mouth, but despite his bad leg Freddie was upon him before he could say a word and grabbed him by the back of the neck and punched him in the stomach. Cort staggered, winded, the air knocked from him, and looked up just as Freddy hit him again.

Cort fell down.

Freddy stood over him, panting and sniffling. "I'm gonna teach you a lesson. No one fucks with me." He pummelled Cort with kicks to his ribs, legs, shoulders, back and neck, swearing and spitting, making animal-like sounds.

The world became blinding pain.

Then Freddy screamed.

When Cort peered from between his hands, there were small feet around his prone body. Children's feet, bare or clad in old shoes, scurrying to the sound of whispered voices.

Freddy screamed again, and then was silent. Cort looked up, flinching. His skin ached and throbbed all over. Freddy was gone. He was alone again.

The children were gone, too.

He got to his feet and looked over the edge of the cliff. Freddy was down there, crumpled and smashed; he opened his mouth to cry out until the sea gathered him up and shredded him upon the rocks.

Cort hunched over and vomited over the cliff's edge, and when he was done he turned to leave but was confronted by the children. He gasped.

Such gaunt and pale things, who reached out to him with their frail hands.

The sea raged and waves smashed against the shore. The storm was rising, full of swagger and muscle. Cort ran back to his car then drove back to the B&B, struggling to absorb what had happened on the cliff top. He locked himself in his room and sat on the bed, terrified he would be arrested for murder. Someone must have seen him on the cliffs. When Freddy's remains were found, the police would make the connection if they heard about what happened in the pub yesterday. So he just sat there and waited for the knock at the door.

But he hadn't killed Freddy; the children had killed Freddy. Why? How many had there been? Seven, eight, nine? One of them was the blonde girl he had seen before. Were they responsible for the fossil and the rabbit skull?

He had to leave the town. Yes, that was the best thing to do. He lit a cigarette, hoping the nicotine would calm him. His pockets were empty when he checked them and found that the blue bear was gone. He had lost his boy's favourite toy.

Cort went into the bathroom and splashed cold water

on his face. He looked into the mirror, wincing at the dark blotches under his eyes and the weak shape of his mouth.

Just visible through the doorway's reflection, the children were sitting on the bed, their heads bowed. One of them, the blonde girl, looked up and smiled at Cort. His heart almost stopped and he slammed the door shut and put his back against it, his hands planted against the cheap wood.

The children made no sound on the other side of the door. He waited, breathing hard, and minutes later, after composing himself to some degree, he opened the door, but the room was empty.

The blue bear was a damp bedraggled shape on the bed.

Cort picked up the bear and held it against his chest. Rain hammered the window. The building moaned in the wind. He felt a terrible weightlessness, as if the building was about to be plucked from its foundations and snatched into the sky.

He went to the window and looked out. The drains were full and the roads were starting to flood. His insides loosened.

The children were standing in the middle of the road, staring up at him. They were slouched and forlorn under the black sky. Thunder boomed over the town, and it was unlike anything he had ever heard. People were out on the street, staring at the clouds.

Lightning streaked the sky in glowing daggers.

The sky was falling.

Cort went outside, the blue bear in one hand. People were panicking, running down the road as torrential rain battered the street. The floodwater was ankle-deep already.

The children led him up the street. He followed without complaint. They pushed through ranks of screaming people fleeing inland, fear and shock on their faces. Traffic jams filled the roads. The world was collapsing. He kept hold of the bear and knew he would never let go.

The children glanced back to make sure he was still with them. They smiled at him, and he smiled back. They walked past the abandoned promenade to the shore. The beach was lost to the sea. The water was rising, encroaching on the land.

The children linked hands and Cort joined them. The blonde girl held his right hand while a little boy with freckles and a limp took his left. They looked up at him with large, expectant eyes. They told him who they were and he listened.

Emma Portroy, 1978, drowned by the rising tide while looking for shellfish.

Seth Underhill, 1958, swept out to sea by a freak wave.

Gladys Briggs, 1926, fell from a cliff top on to the rocks.

Johnny and Sam Blake, 2007, drowned after their dinghy overturned in the deep water.

Michael Short, 1895, drowned by his uncle in the shallows.

Catherine March, 2002, fell over the side of her father's yacht and drowned.

The children gathered around his legs, held onto him with their small, damp hands.

Out to sea, a giant wave a mile high filled the sky.

Cort closed his eyes. The children called him father.

ORANGES ARE ORANGE
STUART PARK

It's fifteen steps, I've counted them many times before, although it used to be seventeen when I was younger. Papa could do it in thirteen as he had longer legs than me. I know Papa would have been angry as the jackdaws had made another nest.

One step already, but I never count the first one. I wonder how many steps until the end?

I remember the jackdaws. One day there was lots of smoke in the fire room. Uncle Edward and Papa took me to the roof and said jackdaws had built a nest in the chimney, they showed me a pile of sticks and feathers and baby birds. Everything from the roof looked foggy like in the fire room.

Uncle Edward was worried about the smoke and

about the big picture above the fire. Papa said the picture was of Grandma and Grandpa. He told me it said Lord and Lady Fawley on the gold bit of the frame.

He told me that he killed Grandma when he was a baby, but I'm sure he didn't mean to. Papa told me Grandpa hurt himself four times, that's when he was sent away so he couldn't hurt himself anymore; that made Papa sad. It would have been sad if Papa was hurt and sent away.

Mama said this was Grandma and Grandpa's house, this was why we lived in it with Uncle Edward and Auntie Carol. I liked Auntie Carol, she gave me hugs like Mama. There used to be more people in the house but they all went away; now Mama and Papa do all the work.

Mama liked to see outside so she kept the windows very clean. She was cleaning them all the time. Papa said we had the cleanest windows in England. Once I picked up a spade and Mama said *what are you doing with that Jackie?* I said I was helping her clean them. She shook her head, it made me laugh.

The house was next to a river with grass all around. It has sixty-eight rooms. I've counted them many times before with my friends.

Dr Olden used to visit our house and play chess with Papa. He walked funny and had these big old glasses on. He used to laugh all the time; that made me laugh too. Dr Olden said that Papa had only beaten him once before at chess, Papa didn't say anything about that. I used to sit and watch them move their armies across the board. Dr Olden would say *now I'm advancing on your father* and *now I'm capturing his men*. They talked about war a lot. Papa said it was wrong to call the war *great*. Dr Olden said *look at this Jack* and showed me a big cut on his leg, he said there was metal inside from the war.

Papa and Dr Olden worked at the same job. Once Papa was *struck* I didn't see Dr Olden ever again. Shame. He brought me toys that I kept losing. I later found them in the basement, but can't remember putting them there. Must have been mother.

Dr Olden said *Jack you're growing up too quickly*. He said I might be as old as him one day, somehow I don't think so. I need to know big words like Dr Olden does to get old.

One morning I woke and could feel an itching on my hands and arms, it wasn't very nice. I always wake up on my back, but go to sleep on my left side. I looked down and saw two spiders on my right arm, one on my left arm and another six on my blanket. There were more on my floor, but too many to count. I screamed.

After the third scream, Mama and Papa rushed in and saw me in bed with spiders on my arms and my blanket and my floor. They dragged me out of bed and took me outside. I had to take my clothes off so Mama could check for more crawlers. It was cold, but Mama made me. She hit me on the head as I had four more spiders in my hair. Mama squashed them with a stone until they were flat. I took the stone from Mama and threw it at a tree. Father took my bed outside and burnt it, he said there was a nest inside. I remember I was eight. I cried because I liked my bed, it kept me safe. The spiders made Papa burn my bed so I don't like them anymore.

I told Uncle Edward and Auntie Carol and my friends

about the spiders and the nest in my bed. Papa said, *Jack we've heard all this before.* He told me to be quiet.

Papa would sometimes not sleep and walk around at night, other times he would wake up and scream and scream and scream. I wonder if he and Mama had spiders in their bed. Maybe I should burn it.

I talked to each spider I found and called them all mean, then I would show them to Mama.

Father used to say I talked too much, he said the only time I didn't talk was when I was asleep. I'm not so sure. I used to talk then as well, but I didn't say that. He used to ask me who I was talking to, I said Ruth and Frank and Mary. He told me to be quiet so I talked quieter, then Papa said I was being rude. He beat me and put me in the cupboard at the end of the hallway. That was fine but Mary said father was a mean man.

I found all the cupboards in the house, there were thirty-two. I liked to sit in them and play with my friends. That way Papa couldn't hear me. Mama used to call *where are you Jackie?* But I used to play hide and seek with her, Mama used to shout and get angry. Frank said it was funny.

I went to school sometimes when I was ten, I liked it at school, there were more children to talk to. I had even more friends than I did at home. But I didn't like Royce, he wasn't very nice to me, he used to push me. Once he pushed me over and I ripped my clothes. That made the other children laugh. I didn't like that, it made me cry and I ran away. When I got home from school, father beat me for ripping my clothes. I told Frank and Ruth about Royce, we all said he was a nasty boy.

I sat next to a boy called Robert, I liked Robert. It was eight steps from the classroom door to my seat. I told him about Mary and Ruth, Robert put his hands over his ears, that made me laugh. I then told him about Frank and he snapped two of my pencils and said rude things, but that was fine as now I had four pencils. Robert was sent to the headmaster, then so was I. Mr Baker said I talked too much. Funny, that's what Papa says.

Mama and Papa came to my school once. Mr Baker told me to write my name, then read it to them. He gave me a new pencil and said I could keep it, I like Mr Baker. I wrote my name, Mama and Papa and Mr Baker watched me. After I read it out loud I had to wait on my own, so I talked to Ruth.

One day at school we all played hide and seek, I was good at that game. I knew the best cupboards and best places to hide, just like at home. No one found me and when Frank left I got lonely. I thought it was best to give myself up so we could play again. When I came out it was night time and everyone had gone. A man with a mop found me. Mother was waiting with Mr Baker, she cried and beat me. When I got home father beat me as well. I think I won the hide and seek.

I never went back to school but Mama taught me just like I was at school. I showed her I could count things. I tipped out Mama's pins, there were 352 in pot one, 512 in pot two and 489 in pot three, she said, *well done Jackie*. I missed my friends from school and drew pictures of them with my pencil from Mr Baker. But I liked my drawings of Frank, Ruth and Mary the best.

Uncle Edward and Papa shouted at each other lots about Grandpa's house and all the things inside. Each time this happened Mama and Auntie Carol took me into the kitchen. Mama put her hands over my ears but I could still hear the rude words. Mama told me to be quiet and not go in the fire room.

One time father came into the kitchen after shouting with Uncle Edward. I showed him the picture I drew of Mary. He ripped my picture and broke my pencil from Mr Baker. He then beat me. Mama shouted, he then beat Mama. I ran to a cupboard and cried with Mary.

After Uncle Edward died we went to a church. Auntie Carol cried lots so I gave her a hug. She said, *I'll miss you Jackie* and that she was sorry she wouldn't be there for my twelfth birthday. I never saw Auntie Carol again, that made me sad.

One day I helped Papa carry some boxes out to another man's car. He was a smiley fat man and said he liked my Papa. I told the man about Ruth and Frank and Mary, he asked if he could meet them; that made me laugh. Papa told me to be quiet and not be so rude. I didn't say rude words, like Papa does. The fat man said he would be back for more boxes and handed Papa some green and brown paper, Papa was smiley too.

Father said there was something new that could help me with all my talking and my friends, he called it a Low Bow. He seemed very happy with it and what it would do. He needed to talk with some doctor friends first.

Papa made a bed on the kitchen table, he said if I lay on it he wouldn't beat me. I'd never laid on the kitchen table before. Father told me to lie very still and not talk.

He put a strap around my head and said *this will make you sleep Jack*. There was a loud buzzing and a pain in my head three times.

But I wasn't asleep.

I didn't move or talk just like Papa said. Mary talked to me but I didn't talk back, she knew what father had said so she told me a story of a little boy who went to visit his friend and played by the river. I listened to Mary and could feel how warm the sun was in her story.

Papa had a long needle, like one of Mama's knitting needles. He put the needle in the corner of my eye, I was brave like Papa asked. He hit the long needle with a hammer and I heard a crunch behind my eye. Papa pushed the needle in further and Mary told me about the two friends playing leap frog. I played that at school once. I missed school. There was lots of wiggling with the needle, going this way and that. Father pulled it out and said, *right, next one*. He then did the same thing with my other eye. First was the hammer and the crunching, then the wiggling. Father said a rude word, I saw he only had half the needle in his hand. He looked around and said another rude word, then walked out. I didn't know if I could move or talk yet, but I couldn't close one eye. Papa had gone so I touched around my eye with my hand; I could feel the needle. I heard Papa come back so I laid still again. He gripped the needle and pulled with a tool he'd found. Mary had stopped talking. I guessed she had finished her story. Papa said I should sleep, but I didn't feel tired. He put a smaller needle in my arm.

I must have been asleep as I was in my bed and not on the kitchen table. When I woke Papa asked how I was. I guessed I could talk now. I said I was tired, which I was.

He gave me some water and told me to sleep more, which I did. He made me stay in bed for two days, Mama brought me my dinner and gave me hugs. Everything was quiet.

I asked Papa where my friends had gone, he said I didn't need them anymore as I had Mama and Papa. Maybe they went away because they didn't like me anymore. Maybe I wasn't very nice. I tried to remember if I was horrible to them and made them go away. I was sad that my friends had gone.

There was only me with Mama and Papa. After Mary and Ruth and Frank had gone I asked Mama for a brother or sister. I knew how these things worked. I knew Mama and Papa made me when Papa got back from the Great War. I asked Mama but she just cried, I was beaten for that.

Papa took me to a church and showed me a stone. He asked me if I remembered when Uncle Edward died, of course I remembered, we saw lots of people, but most were sad. Father told me I had a brother who was younger than me, but he died when he was only a baby, his name was James. Since then mother could not make any more babies, that's why she cried.

When I got home I ran to Mama and gave her a big hug, I kissed her tummy and said I was sorry. I thanked her for my baby brother but wanted him to be alive and not dead. She said I would see him in heaven, but I didn't want to go to heaven, I wanted my friends back.

I got very lonely. I would find the cupboards where I had the best talks with Mary; that was in the hallway. I would remember the stories she told me about the slippery fish and the big bus. Frank used to make me laugh. His funniest joke was told in the cupboard in Mama and Papa's bedroom. Ruth taught me songs and we would sing together about Mama's mashed potato that tasted all milky. And about the fluffy dogs that licked my face and chased the stick I threw.

I would sit for days, waiting for my friends to return. I watched the sun rise, then the blue sky turn to a black sky. The moon and the stars were not my friends, they would not talk to me, even if I shouted at them. Father beat me for shouting at the moon. The sun would rise again, then the moon, then the sun. I didn't even notice Mama cleaning my windows.

Mama made me help with some cleaning. She showed me how many times to wipe a plate until it was dry and how to make sure each hanging picture was straight. There were 142 pictures, she told me to count them, but I had no one to count them with.

Mama got sick. She stayed in bed and coughed all the time. I could hear her at night when I was trying to sleep. In the day I would sit on Mama and Papa's bed and talk to Mama. She didn't say much but that was alright, I talked for both of us.

One day Mama stopped coughing, Papa said she died, just like Uncle Edward. Papa said I couldn't hug Mama anymore. I was sad as I liked Mama's hugs. I did give her one last hug when Papa wasn't looking. I cried and wanted to tell Ruth but she wasn't there. That made me cry even more.

We went to the church again like when Uncle Edward died. I saw lots of people and got lots of hugs from everyone. I told them my friends had gone and asked if they would come back, they said they didn't know. Papa said they put Mama in the ground, he showed me the stone with her name on. I gave the stone a kiss.

I cried lots after Mama died. I saw Papa cry once but I didn't tell him. Papa told me that spiders drink from your eyes when you're asleep. The more you cry, the more spiders will come and drink. Since then I don't cry.

Sometimes I do cry, but I don't show Papa.

Since Mama was gone I didn't have any more birthdays. My last one with Mama was eighteen. I had that many candles and that many hugs. I asked father if it was my birthday again but he didn't know. It was 392 days since my last hug with Mama. Papa told me to clean like Mama used to and count the number of steps I took. I counted but I didn't want to clean on my own.

Papa made me help him in the garden, I would tell him how many bees I'd seen. He showed me how to dig and put seeds in the ground. I now know where potatoes come from, but you have to dig to find them. Papa said there was going to be another big war with more fighting like last time. I liked the worms and the beetles. I would put them in my pockets when Papa wasn't looking. Once he saw me and beat me. When it was time to go inside I would find a cupboard to sit in and talk to them. I would tell them about the bees and about Frank and Ruth and Mama and Mary, but they didn't talk back.

Papa said there were worms in his shoes. I ran before I was beat, but I don't remember putting them there.

Papa sat by the fire and didn't talk. I talked to him but he told me to be quiet. I asked him for a special drink but he didn't let me. One time I gave Papa a hug and knocked over his special drink. He beat me so I ran away and hid. He shouted for me to come back, but I didn't want to. That made me cry, but I cried really quiet so Papa and the spiders didn't hear. I miss Mama.

Every night I would sneak down the stairs and watch Papa sleeping in his chair. I would talk to him, but only real quiet. He would snore which made me laugh. One time I laughed too loudly, Papa woke up and saw me laughing. He came over and hit me so I pushed him hard, I know Frank would have told me too. Papa fell over by the fire and hit his head. He started shaking and reached for me. I think he was sorry so I gave him a hug. When he stopped shaking I lifted him in his chair. I hugged him all night. When I woke up Papa didn't move but he was awake as his eyes were open. The next day Papa was still in his chair, I called him a lazy man but he didn't beat me. After two days he started to smell bad and still didn't talk. I liked Papa in his chair, I could give him hugs and he didn't tell me to be quiet.

When I found a spider I would stab it with one of mother's needles, right through the middle. I then pinned it to the wall or a picture frame. I would sit and count each one of the legs until they stopped moving, then it was like Mama and Papa and Uncle Edward and baby James.

I wanted Mama and Papa to be together like before. I remembered the church and the stone where Mama was. It was 3,572 steps to the stone. When I got Mama I wondered if I'd find potatoes like Papa showed me. I put Mama in the other chair by the fire looking at Papa. I was glad we were together like before. I locked all the doors and hid the keys so no one could take Mama and Papa away from me again.

I was still lonely even with Mama and Papa with me, they didn't talk like before. I was sad, I must have done something wrong. I remembered my friends but they didn't come back. I sat in my cupboards and cried but some of them were a bit small for me now. I wanted the spiders to find me so I could stab them.

Sometimes with the big spiders, I stabbed them with a needle and put the needle in my arm like Papa did with the Low Bow. I laughed at the spiders as they couldn't move on me and drink from my eyes.

I was the only one talking in the house. I moved all the mirrors into the fire room, there were lots in the basement. Sometimes I was in three mirrors, other times in eight mirrors, then I was in all mirrors. It looked like I had more friends, like in school or at church. But I was still lonely, I needed some friends that would talk to me.

In the attic I found Papa's doctor bag, inside was the needle that made me sleep. I watched him and remembered what he did.

I went to the school to find some children to be my friends, the school looked the same as when I went. I said to Jean I was Jackie and asked if she would be my friend, she said *yes*. I made her sleep. It was 2,833 steps back home.

I talked to Jean, she was my friend. She said she wanted her Mama so I said we could talk to my Mama. When I showed her my Mama and Papa she cried and ran, but she couldn't leave. She didn't stop crying so I put her in the cupboard in the hallway.

I thought Jean would be lonely so I got some worms and beetles from the garden and put them in the cupboard for her to talk to. Jean kept saying, *please Jackie, please* all night and cried. I told her spiders would drink from her eyes if she kept crying. Then after four nights Jean stopped crying, but she also stopped talking. That made me sad. I put her in the fire room with Mama and Papa.

I got William from school, he was also my friend. He didn't like my Mama and Papa and Jean and cried the same as Jean did. I put him in the cupboard in Mama and Papa's room. At night I sat in the cupboard with William so he wasn't so lonely. He missed his Mama and Papa like I did, but didn't talk too much. The next night I sat in the cupboard with William and showed him some of the spiders I pinned to my arm. That made him cry more.

William cried and didn't talk even when I hugged him so I got Howard. When William did stop crying I sat him next to Jean.

Howard was my friend, he liked the spiders on the walls and pinned some to his arms like me. He drank Papa's special drink, that made me laugh, but Papa didn't beat him. I told Howard about the spiders in my bed and he laughed. We talked to Jean and William, Howard dressed them in some of Mama's clothes and Papa's hats.

The next day I couldn't find Howard. I guessed he was playing hide and seek with me. I searched everywhere, even in my special places, but couldn't find him. I asked Jean and William but they didn't know where he was. He was better than me at this game.

I sat in a cupboard and listened for Howard, he must

have been very quiet. I wished really hard for Ruth to come back so I could stroke the soft fluffy dog she talked about. I remembered the smell of Mary's slippery fish as it wriggled out of my hands. I could still taste the sweet apple that Frank gave me. All these things made me smile and sad at the same time.

I then wondered if anyone else looks through my eyes and hears the sounds in my ears. Or was it only me?

There was a knock on the front door. It was like Dr Olden's knock, but it wasn't Dr Olden, it was Howard. I told him he was good at hide and seek and asked if he wanted to play again. He said he was sorry, then some men came in, I counted seven. They saw Mama and Papa and the children from school. One man went over to Jean and started to cry. The man shouted, *Jack, what have you done?* The men tried to grab me and beat me so I ran away. I ran up the stairs and saw Harry lying on the floor.

I had forgotten about Harry.

I ran up more stairs and more again until I was outside. When there was nowhere to run the men grabbed me and lifted me high in the air. As they carried me I counted the steps they took to the edge, it was fourteen, not fifteen like mine or thirteen like Papa's. Papa would have been angry, the jackdaws had made another nest.

Maybe I can tell him, as I will soon be like Papa and Jean and William and Mama and Uncle Edward and baby James.

I have no friends anymore and I'm so lonely.

I'm ready to go to heaven.

DRIP
DANI BROWN

Drip. Drip. Drip.

Cold and wet. Ceaseless. Rhythmical. Predictable. Maddening. Drip. Drip. Fucking drip. Seemingly never-ending.

Usually never landing in the same place twice, but every now and then, with no clear pattern, it will. Drip. Usually no more than one drop at once, but sometimes not. Fucking drip drip. Then fucking drip. Drip. Drip. Drip. Continuous dripping. Drip. Drip. Drip. Drip. Drip. Drip drip drip, there goes a triple. Followed by drip drip. Then back to drip. Drip. Drip. Drip.

You try to count how many times but can't think of the numbers. Drip. You don't even know what is dripping on you. It is probably water but it's impossible to know for certain. Drip.

You can't escape. You've already tried that once since waking. Drip. You worked yourself into a panic and took ages to calm. The ceaseless dripping was no help. You don't know how long ago that was. It seems like an eternity ago but was probably no longer than five minutes. Drip. Fucking drip.

Drowning is an option. If you don't lose your mind first and gouge out your eyes to shove in your nostrils. Then you'll attempt to swallow your tongue. Drip. There it goes again.

Now you can feel it on your trousers. You don't know if it was always dripping on your trousers or if this is a new thing. Drip. Drip. Drip. Hello mister drip, how are you today? Would you like to purchase some fucking long distance service? Call friends and family abroad for cheap, cheap goddamn cheap. Drip. Fucking drip.

One thing you know for sure is that whatever the liquid is, it is cold. Frigid, in fact. If it didn't land with such a splash and break apart on impact, you might even call it ice instead of liquid. Ice would have broken your skin by now and you'd feel the warm beads of blood droplets escaping your skin. Drip. Killing you slowly. But at least you would have a better idea of what is landing on you.

Your nipples are raised so high in hard coldness that they're probably cutting the fabric of your clothing. But you can't tell because your body is slightly numb and cut off from you. Except for the feeling of being trapped in a walk-in freezer with the temperature set so low you might as well be drowning in a circle cut in ice for fishing in the frozen far north. Maybe you are trapped in a large freezer that is bobbing up and down in an ice fishing hole? But you don't feel any movement. You would if that were the case.

Drip, drip fucking drip. A triple goddamn whammy.

Each droplet hitting the same place, one after another with hardly a break. Whatever this liquid is, it feels like it is leaving a giant crater where it lands without ever breaking the skin with only one drip. You don't dare think of what three landing in the same exact place have done to your appearance. Drip. You're probably a map of pseudo pock-marks trying to masquerade as the real thing.

Drip. You open your eyes. You're surrounded by darkness so deep it seems like it has swallowed you whole and left you with only the continuous onslaught of fucking drip. Drip. You can't escape. You've already tried. You lost more than one fingernail in the process. You think. You can't really tell for sure.

Taunted. Hazed. Dazed. And harassed. You can't remember a time before the drippings.

Tired. You want to go to sleep but drip, drip fucking drip keeps you from your slumber.

Whatever is containing you is too small to squirm away from the drip drip. There's hardly any room to twist and turn. And especially no room to do these things with thinking very specifically about where each part of your body is before moving another part.

Drip. That was a forehead drip. Some liquid splashed into your eyes. It didn't burn but was uncomfortable and more annoying than other droplets. Drip.

You try to raise your hands to wipe the liquid away but they're greeted by something hard on both sides. You get a bit further when you lift your arms directly up before your knuckles meet something smooth blocking their path. You bend your arms at the elbow and follow the curves of your body up – vaguely noting the strange feeling of whatever it is you're wearing, something frilly with lots of lace and very wet. Drip. Both elbows brush against something hard when they reach your neck. Drip. One hand can go on if you scoot over.

You should know this box well by now. It has kept you locked up for as long as you can remember. But your body's automatic reflexes forget that.

You slide over with surprising ease (and some drips) until one side of your body is shoved against a hard, smooth surface. You're curious to examine it further to see if you can discover its secrets (obviously you haven't been trying hard enough) but first you would like to wipe your face and examine your attire. It doesn't give you much space but enough to trace your hand up your body to wipe your eyes without bashing your elbows again.

Your skin is smooth. Not a crater for your fingers to fall in and become trapped. Your nose feels flatter than you remember. You wished you had a light and a mirror, that way you could see yourself (and the box).

Drip. The liquid lands in your open mouth, just a slit small enough for the tip of your tongue to fit through if it so desired. It has a taste reminiscent of the mud-pies you made as a young child but with added copper. In a way you enjoy it for the memories but you'd like to shut your mouth because droplets occasionally falling in there is a tease to your thirst and throat which feels like it is as dry as sandpaper.

Your jaw is painful and stiff. Closing it is an exercise in will. But finally, it snaps shut banging your teeth together. There's a cramp in it now, like something is swelling and knitting together. The pain brings tears to your eyes. With your hand still on your face you wipe them.

It might be a good idea to open your mouth – even slightly to relieve some of the pressure. And you can suck the tears from your fingers. It probably isn't enough liquid to take away the dryness but every little helps.

You have just discovered it is more painful for freshly knit bones to come apart. Automatically you cry out. The pain was so rapid when you opened your mouth to scream that you saw stars dance in front of your watery eyes. At the same time your brain registered an echo in the scream. Your eardrums felt like disowning you.

The scream continued bouncing off the walls, the floor and the ceiling of the tight enclosed space that you found yourself in, shaking with the echo for what felt like at least a minute. It could have been longer or shorter. You couldn't tell. You couldn't do anything, not even rub your hand against the side of your prison while the sound bounced around.

Drip. This one landed on the tip of your nose. Hand still on your face, you wipe it away. It's annoying, the constant dripping, but at least the liquid doesn't burn.

You push away from the wall with your arm and leg. You really want to see if you're wearing your watch. You can't feel it around your wrist but you're so used to wearing it you don't feel it any longer. If your watch is there then you can at least monitor how much time is passing. Unfortunately it isn't one of those watches that also keep you informed of the date.

The wall is smooth where your hand pushed against it but your foot was met with difficulty. For the first time, the box has demonstrated that it can break. In the enclosed space you didn't hear a crack exactly but something like putting your foot through soft wood.

There's definitely a hole where your foot kicked.

It wasn't as loud as a dry stick breaking in two. It didn't feel like it either. Dry wood, even if it has been weakened, puts up a resistance. Fresh green wood bounces back and is difficult to break. Your shoe felt like it simply went through and was met with something soft. But not too soft.

You could very well be wood because the faint scent of pine and polish penetrates the atmosphere cutting through the smell of dirt and decay. You'll contemplate it later, after you see if you are wearing your trusty watch. Once you view your watch, you'll keep an eye on the time and then make another escape attempt.

Armpit shoved against the other wall, it'll prove impossible if you suddenly desire moving your other arm. Let's hope you don't. You raise your hand following the same movements you did to wipe your eyes. You raise your wrist gradually from over your eyes – you don't fancy bashing it against the ceiling, that action could damage your watch. You don't want to do that. You've had that watch for years, it is your oldest and dearest friend.

Drip. This one landed in your hair line, right where your forehead and hair connect. You have to ignore it in favour of your watch (moving your other hand up that far would require once again kicking off the walls, you don't currently want to find out if the other wall is as compromised as the first). It tickles as it isn't absorbed by the hair or skin. It didn't break apart on impact either (some of them don't but drips of this variety are a rarity). It follows your hair parting, sending tingles and tickles through your scalp until it rolls off.

You adjust your wrist so it's within your sight. The

glow of it is so bright in your dark confined place that it threatens to blind you. It burns. Drip. Drip. A pain and an annoyance that threatens to drive you mad at once. You shut your eyes. Drip. You'll have to open one very slowly so you can inspect your watch.

Drip. Better get it done and over with. It needs to be the eye over the watch. Cautiously you begin the task of lifting the lid. It is easier to think about than to actually do; the other keeps threatening to lift its lid too on its own accord despite your protests.

You were careful enough and managed to open only one of them a sliver. You get burned again. Immediately you shut that eye back down. Drip drip. The liquid lands on your cheek just below it.

You pause what you think is a few seconds, but could be as little as one or as much as half a minute, and make another slow attempt. Your eye is beginning to adjust to the brightness but you still need to shut it rather rapidly.

Third attempt lucky. The second try didn't hurt that bad. But you're going to wait until you count five drips. Now that you are welcoming them, they don't seem to come. You wait in the lonely dark – the enclosed space seems to stretch for miles yet won't let you move.

Perhaps somewhere there's a drip that you can't feel or hear. Dripping in the dark above your head or below your feet. Maybe even landing on your toes but your shoes won't allow you the feel of the necessary splash.

Drip. Finally. On the tip of your nose. Now you have to wait for the next one. But will a little peek hurt you? If you keep your eyes closed too long you will have to once again get used to the brightness and repeat the entire process. Drip. Drip. Only two more to go though. You decide three is enough.

Very cautiously you open your eye. It doesn't burn but the light from the glow in the darkness is very bright. You can't make out the face of the watch, instead it is a blurry circle of sorts floating in the dark.

You decide to open your other eye. It might help with the focusing. Slowly you begin to lift the lid. Drip. There's that fourth drip. It landed with a splash in your eyebrow but your eye wasn't open enough to take in any of the liquid. You continue opening your eye, hoping the watch will be easier to see.

Both eyes fully open, the light of the watch starts to dim in your head but it is still like gazing at the reflection of the summer sun. You never thought glow in the dark could be so luminous. It isn't LED, but simple glow in the dark.

Drip. There's the fifth drip landing in your hair. If you waited this long you would have probably had to start the eye opening process all over again.

The glow dims more. You wonder when it last saw light. When the watch was new the light of the day would keep it charged up until the next morning. That's why you never replaced it with one of those fancy LED watches. Your trusty old watch was exactly that. It never failed you. You never even had to replace the batteries.

Drip. Drip. Drip. All three land on the top of your head but not in the same place. The glow dims to a circle now. Soon you will be able to see the hands staring back at you. You want to close your eyes and relax but doing that will result in having to go through the entire eye opening process all over again. You keep them open feeling the drips as you wait for the glow to dim enough to see the time.

After what seems like an hour to you and your body which cannot move, the hands come into focus. Slowly at first as the circle fades. Two lines glare at you but they're a bit blurry. They'll come into focus, eventually.

Drip drip fucking drip. There it goes with the triple. Hopefully none will land in your eyes because you need to wait with them open. You don't want to have to repeat the entire tediously annoying process. As if thinking about it caused it to happen, two drips at once, both in your eyes. You close them against the sting.

Wallowing in frustration you feel something small and slimy and gross move onto your leg. You didn't feel it on your ankle. Your socks must be staying up for once by some miracle granted to you by the Gods. You kick trying to move it. Your toes and knee bash against the ceiling. A sound like breaking wet wood vibrates on the air. Something falls on your foot. Whatever it is rather annoyingly finds its way up your trouser leg and comes to a rest on your sock. You can feel the weight of it.

Whatever the slimy gross thing is, it now finds itself on your calf. It tickles. You don't like the feel of it but you can't kick to escape from it. Perhaps you can crush it beneath the weight of your leg.

Whatever is on your ankle has splinters that penetrate your sock and prick your skin. You don't want them to fall beneath your leg. They'd penetrate your skin when you try to crush whatever is squirming on your lower leg. You need to kick them away but very gently and without encouraging the slimy gross thing to find a place where it can't be crushed.

You lift your leg about an inch off the floor very

slowly. The thing sliming its way up your calf halts. It feels like some of it drops off. Then you feel slight suction where it still is. And what you think of its full length is back on you moving up, trying to get into the crevice on the back of your knee like it read your mind.

Another slimy gross thing joins its friend. You don't know how it got there considering the one inch or there about elevation of your leg. Something else falls on top of your foot threatening to slam it to the floor. You resist. The stuff falls off your leg but gets caught in your clothing. You gently kick being careful not to hit your foot on the ceiling, walls or floor. Kicking doesn't do much good. If only you could sit up, fingers feeling in the dark, you'd be able to pull out the splinters.

Frustration makes you want to scream but you restrain yourself by biting your cheeks. This wasn't such a good move either. In fact, it was probably worse than the brain-scrambling echoes of a scream bouncing off every surface at once. Probably.

The skin of your cheeks has broken away beneath your grinding teeth, all of which feel much sharper than the chiselled remains of what you remember. There's no blood; you have that to be grateful for. But instead, there's a bitter sticky substance – possibly pus. It is worse than blood. In comparison, the taste of blood would be a welcomed treat.

Drip drip drip. Three tickling drops all at once all landing in the very nearly same place on the tip of your nose. With your hand still over your eye, it isn't that difficult to move it and wipe the droplets away somewhat relieving the tickle.

You stop biting your cheeks. It does nothing to stop

the deluge of pus in your mouth. Rather stiffly you turn your neck with your leg still elevated. You try to spit. The side of your face lands in a puddle.

You trace the outside of your face with your hand. Quickly you let it run along the outside of your saturated and odd clothing. When it is on your hip, you allow it to sneak over to the floor being careful not to hit the wall. The floor is very wet. It seems that you are lying in liquid. That is rather worrisome. You need to find a way out of here but first you must rid your mouth of the awful sticky vomit-inducing substance.

You turn your head, knowing it would be difficult to turn your entire body. Your neck gives out a creak of protest but does as it is told.

None of the liquid you are in seeps into your mouth. That is unfortunate. If it was it might rid your mouth of the sticky bitter substance.

You spit, or at least try to. Your attempt was unsuccessful. You can't produce the saliva required to rid your mouth of such filth. All that happened was the bitter tasting probable pus spread further in your mouth towards your throat and oozed between your teeth and out of your lips.

You let your exceptionally long tongue (even longer than you remember) slip out of your lips to lap up the liquid on the floor. The tip just about reaches the liquid's surface. A cool mineral taste reaches up to embrace it. You bring it inside your mouth – a droplet of the liquid on it. One droplet isn't enough to rid your mouth of the bitter taste. You repeat the action. Two droplets isn't enough.

Assumed pus leaks out of your lips and oozes down the side of your face until it mixes with the puddle on the floor. You can hear it and feel a slight splash as it hits the liquid.

Drip. It falls into your ear surprising you. You jolt upwards. Your body bangs against the ceiling then the floor with a splash. You bite your tongue, releasing more of the bitter thick sticky substance into your mouth. You try to spit it out. Again, this isn't met with success.

You can feel the drop travelling through your ear canal. It both itches and tickles but either way, it isn't very comfortable. You wish you could stop it just by thinking about it but you can't. You have to try your best to ignore it. The spreading bitterness in your mouth should help in that regard.

You need to drink some of that liquid from the floor. That'll sort out the probable pus in your mouth. But you might need to swallow some of it down with the liquid. It could choke you it is so thick. Or it could result in vomiting. That would definitely choke you. You have nowhere to turn around and violent heaves will throw you against all sides of the enclosed space.

Drip. This time it hits the side of your ear but doesn't go in. It follows your cheek bone. You have a choice – continue with your head to the side and risk more liquid travelling to meet your eardrum or try to turn all the way over in that dark confined space. Then the water can taunt your neck and have nowhere to enter you. But turning over could result in being stuck with your sides shoved against the ceiling and floor. It is worth the risk, you decide. Once on your front you'll be able to let all the probable pus ooze out of your mouth too.

Your neck is almost over already. Any further turning until your body catches up will result in it being snapped.

The best course of action would be to turn the way you're already facing.

You shove your shoulder underneath yourself and point the other one at the ceiling. It's a tight squeeze. Already you can feel pins and needles in the arm under you. In this enclosed space, you don't know if you'll be able to get rid of them.

You need to turn your hips now. They're wider than your shoulders but not by much, a minor deformity. The prospect worries you. But the sooner you do it the sooner you'll be on your front and therefore able to rid your arm of pins and needles. You turn your lower body. As expected, the space is too narrow for your hips. You squeeze them in anyways. It is worth the risk.

You're stuck. Drip drip into your ear. You can't do anything about it. Due to the proximity of your ear to the ceiling, the drops follow further into your ear canal before breaking apart. That's three drips in your ear, is that worthy of an infection?

But you think you're just narrow enough to not be stuck for long. You swivel and squirm. The skin stretching over your hip bones feels thin and dry. There should be a layer of rather thick fat to protect them too but isn't. Or at least it doesn't feel like there is. No worries, that can work to your advantage. You twist, turn and squirm, freeing your hips with more ease than anticipated propelling the rest of you face down.

You land with a small splash on a surface that although solid, feels like it could collapse at any moment. The liquid dripping from the top isn't helping. It is probably breaking down whatever the floor is made of (you assume the same material as the walls and ceiling, which broke away with too much ease). If the floor breaks, you don't know how far you'll have to fall before reaching a solid surface to land on. You push the thought to the back of your mind, it serves no purpose thinking about it.

The liquid you are lying in has a slight chill. You don't like being face down in it. You could drown if you carelessly fall asleep.

You open your mouth and let the probable pus seep out. It should disperse in the liquid on the floor, then you can have a drink. It is infuriately slow moving. You try to encourage its departure with your tongue but this only spreads the bitterness in your mouth. You have to be patient. There is nothing you can do except wait for it to exit and then disperse.

Drip. It isn't as annoying when it lands on your neck or the back of your head. You must have been flinching slightly when it landed on your face for fear of the drips getting in your eyes.

Something above you moves. The movement wasn't in your box but above it. You try calling out, but you've lost your voice. All that escapes your mouth, other than probable pus, is a dry croak. You try again. Drip.

More slimy gross things find their way onto your legs. You kick, confident that even if it doesn't rid your legs of whatever is crawling on you, you'll be heard.

Something with many legs scuttles over your hand. You can feel its movement when it climbs onto your face. You shut your mouth. Probable pus builds up below your sealed lips. But you don't want that thing to enter your body. You can feel it below your chin.

You slam your chin down hard on the scuttling thing. You feel a crush and something warm on your skin.

You've killed it. Immediately you open your mouth and allow the probable pus to continue its slow exit.

You don't like the feel of the scuttling thing's guts on your chin but it is preferable to its living form entering your body via your mouth. You rub your chin on the floor in an attempt to remove as much of the creature's guts as possible.

Drip. These drips are getting easier to ignore. Drip. Drip. You have more important things to worry about.

Most of the guts come off. It still feels and tastes like most of the probable pus is still inside your mouth. Your legs feel like they are being pulled under by slimy gross squiggly things. That isn't very pleasant.

You kick with more violence than you did last time. It does nothing to displace the increasing number of things squirming up your legs but it does impact upon the ceiling, which seems to cave in just above your legs. The new-found lowered ceiling does nothing to discourage the slimies. The material isn't heavy or uncomfortable but you don't like the thought of it breaking away. You don't know what is above it.

Trapped and thinking about what to do next, you hear more movement above. You wonder if there's enough space to peek at your watch so you can time the movement. Surely whatever is up there heard the cave-in?

Probable pus is still coming out but you make another attempt to say something or even scream. A small sound, slightly above a croak comes out. Encouraged, you try clearing your throat even though that means the bitter taste will spread down your oesophagus.

You pause. You think you can hear voices. You can't make out what they are saying no matter how hard you strain your clogged ears.

Slowly and cautiously, you move your hand with the watch on it until it is in front of your eyes. You start to open the lids. And then shut them immediately. They're not burning but something on your lower body is. On your upper thigh, you feel an intense penetrating heat.

Drip drip drip drip. The drips are all around you with threats to drown. The increase is being caused by the movement above. You hope it is a rescuer. If it isn't then the rest of the ceiling will either cave in or the drippings will become a rain and your lungs will full with the liquid (that is probably water but you can't be certain).

Something scorches your back. Then there's a painful scraping numbed only by the saturated fabric of your probably eccentric clothing. The burning spreads to your legs and then your upper back.

Through your clogged ears you hear the rapid intake of breath.

"Quick, turn down the light," a voice above you calls out.

The burning subsides. You can feel the weight of the caved in ceiling being lifted off your legs piece by piece. Unfortunately the little squirming gross slimies aren't being taken away.

You feel air above you. A slight breeze lifts your hair. It would feel nice and refreshing if it weren't for your saturated clothing that clings to your body.

You open your eyes. You can see the faint outline of your hand in front of you. You can see the outline of your trusty old watch and even see the hands.

You try to stand up. A hand on your bottom pushes you back down but not hard.

"Easy partner."

Your mouth is still leaking probable pus. You can see it now. It is the weird beige colour of pus. Or, at least, you think it is. The light is pretty dim to the point that it barely exists at all. But how it burns.

You can feel a hand on your hip, pulling you up slowly and stabilising you. You're on your hands and knees.

"Slowly now."

Obediently, you gently push up from your hands. You are on your knees. You can see above your broken confines.

In a pine box in a shallow grave, probably in a church yard. You see other graves dotted about in a vague resemblance of a pattern. To imperfect eyes, it probably looked like perfection but you know better.

You're offered a hand, which you gladly accept.

RENEWAL
WILLIAM MEIKLE

After five funerals in two days, George Sanderson needed a drink—he needed a lot of drinks. The temptation to buy a couple of bottles of Scotch and hole-up until they were as empty as he felt was almost too strong to resist.

But the lads deserve better. They deserve better from me.

Dan Cunningham's burial was the worst of the lot—the Scotsman had been the closest thing George had to a best friend and he hadn't been looking forward to seeing what was left of his pal get put in the ground. But he went—he'd let Dan down once too often to do it again one last time.

The send off had been just down the road in Bromley—George didn't stay for the wake—he didn't know anyone there, and he felt like he was being stared at, as if his uniform—worn out of respect—was causing more grief than it needed to. He felt like the Grim Reaper, constantly reminding them all how Dan had died.

The uniform wasn't doing him that much good either—it felt too tight, too stifling, and the wounds at his belly, not yet fully healed, itched and chafed like they had a hundred black flies burrowing and feasting in them.

As the mourners started to drift away from the graveside, George had had enough. He took Dan's wife by the hand, told her that her husband had been a good man—he left out the bit about Dan pissing himself and screaming, and he didn't tell her about the very end—he hadn't told anyone about the very end—then made his excuses.

He got more stares on the train platform—and if any of the young sods had so much as looked at him the wrong way, he might well have decked them. But he got home to Lewisham without killing anybody and changed into his civvies. Dan's dog tags fell out of his jacket and onto the floor—he'd meant to give them to the wife, but had forgotten, having been in too much of a rush to get away. He tucked them away in his wallet so that he wouldn't forget to send them on.

Five minutes later he was on another train, heading into town, making for the center, to be among people, to feel alive—although he wasn't sure he'd ever feel fully alive again.

He got off the train at London Bridge and had a pint in The George, letting the old building remind him that people came and went in this town, but pubs endured. Then after a couple there, he wandered up to Borough Market, had a pie, and a few more beers—a lot more beers—in the Market Porter. Watching the city work around him did much to ground him back to reality, but as he crossed London Bridge heading north a car backfired and all too quickly he was back there, in the sand, with the blood and the shit and the screaming. He almost ran into the first bar he spotted, and started in on the rum—doubles, straight up, three of them before he stopped shaking.

Things got a bit hazy after that for a while—normally he'd have wended his way west, heading for the bright lights of Leicester Square and Piccadilly. But as night fell he was sat in a bar he didn't remember entering, one he didn't recognize—and from the décor and clientele, he knew he wasn't anywhere near any bright lights. It was an old style working man's pub—dockers at a guess—battered wooden tables and chairs, leather seats around the walls which were split and patched with duct tape, and the smoking ban didn't seem to be in effect. He had a large glass of rum and a half of beer on the table, with no memory of ordering either. He was at a window table, and when he looked up it was to see the river flowing darkly outside. Off to his right there were indeed some bright lights, and he was surprised to recognize the new developments at Canary Wharf. Somehow he'd come east instead of west, and was now some way out along the riverside—unknown territory.

And when he looked back, it was to see that he was no longer alone. An elderly woman had joined him across the table.

"You look like you need some company, dearie," she said.

If she'd been younger he might have taken her for a

prostitute, but she reminded him of his old Auntie Maggie, and he was too tired to argue in any case—he merely nodded, and took a smoke when she offered one. It was a Camel, an old favorite he hadn't tasted in many years but whose first puff brought memories—blood and shit and bombs again. He closed his eyes, swallowed some rum, and tried to let it wash everything away—for a while at least. He almost jumped out of his seat when the old lady took his hand.

"Don't worry, dearie," she said. "Surely it can't be that bad?"

That's all she had to say to get George started. Despite a usual reticence, and no wish at all to speak about it, he found it all tumbling out—the tour, the sand, the friends—and the flies, the shit, the bombs and the screaming. The Camel tasted of burnt ash in his mouth, and his wounds itched. He scratched idly at his belly, too much, feeling dampness there as he opened a scab, and not caring, the story pouring out of him in a gush while hot tears ran down his cheeks. The only bit he didn't tell her was about the end—it made his wounds throb just thinking about it.

The old lady never let go of his hand.

"You don't know it yet, son," she said when he finished, wrung out and spent, "but you've come to the right place."

"There is no right place—not any more," George said. He finished off the rum, but before he could turn to order another, the old lady put a fresh glass in his hand.

"What if I told you that you could see them all again?" she said softly.

"I'd say you were talking shite," he replied. "Pardon

my French. But if this is some spiritualist table knocking pish, you can take it elsewhere lady. I'm not buying. Not tonight—not ever."

"Dan said you'd say that," she said quietly.

George started again at that—*Did I tell her any of their names?* It had all come out in such a rush that he couldn't be sure, but her next words stopped any rejoinder he had before he could speak.

"The sigil won't be a problem—you already have the markings of the flesh. Dan said that your token will be his dog tags—they're in your wallet—where you put them before leaving the house earlier."

George's night had taken a lurch to the side, and he felt disconnected—not just because of the booze, although that wasn't helping.

"Will you come?" the old lady said. "It's just round the corner—we'll have a chat and a wee drink, I'll make you some supper—a big lad like you needs to eat when he's drinking—and I'll tell you why you came here—and what you need to know."

She was as good as her word—he'd expected to be led to a house but was instead shown into a modern warehouse conversion—six flats in a space that had once contained work for scores of men in a tall slim red brick building on a newly refurbished quayside.

"I'm the concierge," she said, rather grandly, as if it was a title rather than a job description. She was in number one, just inside the hallway door, and although the conversion was new, stepping into her room was like stepping back forty years or more in time. The wallpaper was nearly as plush as the thick pile carpet and the curtains were hideous—yellow, red and orange flowers each the size of dinner plates. The sofa was the bulk of a small car, and the TV set was a boxy cube some three feet on a side, currently showing only dancing static.

She showed him to the couch and he sat gingerly near the front edge, afraid to relax into it lest it swallow him whole.

The dancing static on the TV turned to a hiss, then a drone, and bagpipes started up—a tune George knew well—one that Dan played for them, over and over. The last time he'd heard it had been as it wafted across the sand on a cold desert night—the night before the pipes had fallen silent forever.

Yet here they were again, and he even recognized the style, the small, but distinctive flourishes that could only have come from one piper.

"Dan?" he started, and didn't get any further—he was still befuddled with the booze and the grief, and having this room shoved in his face wasn't helping his equilibrium. He sat back, almost fell, into the sofa, keeping his eyes on the ceiling and not the dancing static and that helped, a bit. The glass of rum the woman brought him helped some more, so by the time she sat beside him and started to talk he was almost ready to listen.

"You'll have questions?" she said.

"I will have questions," George agreed. "Many of them. Here's an easy one to start with. What the fuck is going on here?"

She smiled, and for the first time he saw the deep sadness in her; something in her eyes that told him she had suffered—still suffered.

"It is an outlandish story, I'm afraid," she replied. "More rum? Or another smoke?"

George said yes to both, although he hadn't had a cigarette in several years before tonight. Now seemed to be as good a time as any to revisit old habits. Two minutes later, he cradled another glass of rum and puffed, more contentedly than he might have wished, on a Camel as she started. He quickly gave up worrying whether it made any sense and let her talk. Sense could wait. What he needed now was something to take his mind off the dancing static, and the drone of distant pipes.

"There are houses like this all over the world," she started. Her accent and her slightly stilted English brought to mind old movies; Universal horrors where little old ladies said things like "Beware the moon," and "You have been cursed." George had to force himself to pay attention; a large part of him wanted to neck down the rum as fast as he could and head for more.

"Most people only know of them from whispered stories over campfires; tall tales told to scare the unwary," she went on. It was beginning to sound more and more like a pre-prepared speech. "But some of us, those who suffer…some of us know better. We are drawn to the places, the loci if you like, where what ails us can be eased. Yes, dead is dead, as it was and always will be. But there are other worlds than these, other possibilities. And if we have the will, the fortitude, we can peer into another life, where the dead are not gone, where we can see that they thrive and go on. And as we watch, we can, sometimes, gain enough peace for ourselves that we too can thrive, and go on.

"You will want to know more than why. You will want to know how. I cannot tell you that. None of us has ever known, only that place is important, and the sigil and token are needed. You have a sigil already, I believe—your flesh is marked—and you have the token in your wallet. You will also want to know about Dan, and the pipes, and the why and how of that too. And again, I cannot tell you. You were drawn here. What you see is what you see, and what you take from it is what you take from it. Only the Dreaming God knows."

George scarcely heard a word of it—all he could hear were the pipes, and all he could feel was the longing. He felt the drone tug at his heart, and a great tiredness washed over him. Unwanted tears ran down both cheeks.

"Please, missus—just tell me what's going on?"

"I'm trying to," she said softly, "as well as I am able. But sometimes it is best if you see for yourself. You'll have number three—for tonight at least, and then we'll see how it goes. Sometimes one night is all it takes."

"All it takes for what?"

But she didn't answer, and when she took his hand again he rose meekly, and let himself be led upstairs, where there was a soft bed waiting.

Darkness called to him and he dove into it gladly.

He woke in the early hours of the morning, hung-over and disoriented, not really knowing where he was until he saw the bare brick walls and the exposed plumbing of the warehouse conversion. Snatches of the old woman's conversation came back to him, fragments that didn't make much sense—nonsense about sigils and tokens and something about being drawn to this place, this house. What with that, and the memory of pipes playing out of an untuned TV set, it all took on the blur and fever of a drunken dream—and it wasn't as if he hadn't had plenty of them in recent months.

He tasted smoke in his mouth and throat, felt sour booze roil in his belly as he struggled to roll out of the too high, too soft bed he'd fallen into. At least he didn't have to go looking for his trousers and shoes, for he still had them on. He had taken his jacket off though, and found it at his feet on the floor when he stood. He bent to lift it, intending to sneak out without having to face the embarrassment of apologizing for getting plastered in a strange house. As he lifted the jacket something tinkled—metal on wood—Dan's dog tags falling out of his wallet. George picked them up. Light flickered in the corner as a TV set woke up—white dancing static, and a hissing that became a drone that became the skirl of bagpipes, distant, but definitely getting closer.

George stepped toward the TV, then stopped—something shimmered in the air between him and the set—it seemed to be a jet-black tear in the fabric of space, no bigger than a sliver of fingernail. Initially he thought he had a hair near his eye and tried to brush it away before he realized he was looking at something several yards away, hanging in space at eye level.

He moved closer, but looking at it straight on hurt his eyes—they struggled to focus, never quite managing it, so that the only way he could really see the thing was by turning side on so that it was just on the edge of his peripheral vision.

It appeared to be spinning slowly in a clockwise direction. As he watched, it quivered like a struck tuning fork and changed shape, settling into a new configuration, becoming a black, somewhat oily in appearance droplet little more than an inch across at the thickest point. It hung there, its very impossibility taunting him to go over and look for the trick strings that had to be holding it in place.

It swelled, and now looked like an egg more than anything else—a black, oily egg from some creature whose nature could only be guessed at. As George stepped forward a rainbow aura thickened around it, casting the whole room in dancing washes of soft colors as it continued to spin and the aurora danced in time to the skirl of the pipes.

Dan's dog tags hummed, hot in George's hand as he moved closer.

The egg quivered and pulsed. And now it seemed larger still. The chamber started to throb, like a heartbeat. The egg pulsed in time. A song started up, somewhere far below—a voice George knew as well as his own—Dan's voice, impossibly, singing and playing at the same time, but it was most definitely him—George had heard the song a hundred times.

He sleeps and he dreams in the deep, in the dark.

The pulsing egg kept time with the song, like a three dimensional metronome.

And now it was more than obvious—it was most definitely growing. The dog tags sent a new flash of heat, like a searing burn in his palm and the drone of the pipes deepened, became a rapid thumping; the room shook and trembled. The vibration rattled his teeth and set his guts roiling again.

The aura around the egg wavered and trembled—and now there were two eggs hung in the air at eye level, side by side, just touching, each as black as the other, twin bubbles only held in check by the dancing rainbow colors. The walls and floor throbbed like a heartbeat. The singing started up again, making the room rock and quake in an almost operatic wall of sound. The eggs pulsed in synchronized agreement and calved.

Four eggs hung in a tight group, all now pulsing in time with the still rising noise. Colors danced and flowed across the sheer black surface; blues and greens and shimmering silvers that filled the room with washes of color. The song got louder. The eggs throbbed, beating time like a giant drum. Soon there were eight, then sixteen.

George's head pounded with the rhythm, and nausea rose as his stomach turned last night's booze over. He started to back away, back toward the bed, hoping for some respite.

Thirty-two now, and the chamber shimmered with a dancing aurora of shimmering lights that pulsed and beat in time with the song as the eggs calved again, and again, everything careening along in a big happy dance. Dan's voice rose in a bellow bringing the song to a final climax.

Where he lies, where he lies, where he lies, where he lies.

The Dreaming God is singing where he lies.

As the last drone of the pipes faded, the last echo of

Dan's voice going with it, the eggs popped with soft bursts of color that left yellow blobs behind George's eyelids as he sat there in the suddenly quiet dark.

"Dan?" he said softly.

"How are you doing, ya big shite?" the Scotsman's voice said in his ear, as clear as day.

The next thing George knew he was standing out in the hallway, looking back into the empty room, with dampness at his belly where the wounds had seeped again and a hot burn in his palm where the dog tags sat. He was breathing so heavily he felt light-headed, almost dizzy, and he couldn't seem to get his legs to move. He almost leapt in the air when a hand touched his shoulder.

It was the old lady—the concierge. She had a dressing-gown three sizes too big for her wrapped tight around her small frame.

"Come downstairs," she said. "We'll have a coffee and a smoke and a wee chat—see what's what."

George wasn't listening.

"I heard him—clear as day," he said.

"And you'll probably see him too, soon enough—if that's what you want?"

George started to pull away, heading for the stairs.

"You don't understand," he said. "This isn't right."

"Right and wrong don't come into it—not here," she replied. "There's only the dreams of the Sleeping God, and what we can understand of them."

"Don't give me any more of that pish," George said. "What have you got me into here?"

"You got yourself into this, dearie," she said—and suddenly her smile didn't look so pleasant. "Perhaps you shouldn't have lied to me—to yourself—in the first place."

For the first time, George started to think there might be more to this than he thought.

"What do you mean?"

"Dan told me about the end—about the six of you in the hole—how you lay there on the ground as they died."

"That's not true," George said—but his wounds—still not healed, still not life threatening—throbbed hotly, and Dan's dog tags burned in his hand in reaction to the lie. Inside the room, the drone of bagpipes started up again, and the static danced in time on the TV screen. George felt the tug of old friendships, old allegiances.

"Yes, you were drawn here," the old woman said. "And now it's time to make a proper ending—Dan needs it—they need it—you need it. Go on."

The sound of the pipes got louder still. Dan's voice rose in accompanying song.

He sleeps in the deep, with the fish far below.

He sleeps in the deep, in the dark.

George's legs started to move him—not toward the stairs, but back into the room.

Four black eggs hung at eye level between him and the TV set.

"What are these bloody things?" he said.

"The dreams of the Sleeping God—impossible possibilities or possible impossibilities? Who knows? Who cares? They are what you have brought with you, and what has brought you. They are why you are here, and if you don't face them now, you never will."

George's legs knew the truth of that, even if the rest

of him didn't. He kept walking forward, through the doorway and into the room. Dan's voice welcomed him.

Where he lies, where he lies, where he lies, where he lies.

He heard bullets, distant cracks, and tasted burnt ash. His belly wounds throbbed, went damp when he scratched them, and the dog tags got hot, almost unbearably so in his left hand.

The four eggs became eight, then sixteen, calving faster and faster, the color and the dance filling the room.

"Just stay down, you fucking idiot," somebody— Jimmy Gordon, he remembered—shouted. The wounds throbbed again—the bomb had caught them all unawares and George had taken the brunt of the shrapnel before the others dragged him into the relative shelter of the stable block. Then it was all gunfire and screaming, sand and pish and blood and shite—and George, on the ground—crying, his belly wet with wounds.

The Dreaming God is singing where he lies.

Two hundred and fifty six black eggs danced above him, the pipes skirled, Dan sang, and George wept, for times lost.

"I'm sorry, mates," he said. "I'm so bloody sorry I'm not with you."

The pipes went quiet to a soft drone and the eggs burst with soft pops—more distant gunfire, but getting further away now.

"Don't talk pish, ya big soft shite," Dan said in his ear. "We're all here now—that's all that matters."

The pipes started up again, as did the singing and George sang along, just like the old days. He turned back to look at the doorway, one last time, to see the old lady shut the door softly, shutting him in. Then there was nothing but the pipes and the song and the dance in the color.

The Sleeping God is dreaming where he lies.

ELEVEN
MATT SHAW

Eleven years old.

Tight little skirt. Grey. See-through white shirt with a white lace bra beneath, not that there was much to fill it. White cotton pop-socks up to her scrawny knees. Cotton underneath the skirt too? The man licked his lips. A tie tied loosely around her neck with the top button of the shirt undone. Mouse-blonde hair down to her shoulders. He wished it had been fashioned into pig-tails as opposed to hanging freely - as he'd requested in the chatroom. Fringe down her forehead, just above her eyes and covering her eyebrows. A smile.

That smile. The smile from the photo.

Pretty as a picture.

"You came," he smiled.

"You invited me," she walked in; school bag slung over her left shoulder.

Eleven years old with the confidence of a young woman.

The man watched her as she walked down the hallway towards his living room, his eyes fixed upon her tight rear-end for longer than necessarily decent. Another lick of his lips and a quick glance outside of his apartment - down either end of the corridor. No one out and about. No witnesses to his little visitor. He closed the door.

With a quick check of his breath, a little blow and sniff into the cup of his hand, he followed in her small footsteps.

"What did you tell your mum and dad?" he asked, closing the living room door behind him.

She took the bag from over her shoulder and dropped it to the floor before sitting down on his leather sofa. He leaned back on the door, happy to watch her a moment longer - really take in the sight. She wasn't the first invited here but - most of the time - they never showed up, nor did he find them in the chatroom again to enquire as to why they disappeared.

"I told them I was going to a friend's house," she smiled.

Eleven years old and already quite the seductress; something in those hazel eyes.

Naughty. Rebellious.

The man smiled at her. "Good girl."

She had told her parents, similar in age to the man standing before her, that she was going to a friend's house. They often let her go out by herself - to this particular friend at least - because she only lived around the corner from them. They gave her a time to be home and - to date - she had never let them down.

The man broadened his smile. Yellow, tainted teeth. Stained by nicotine and years of neglect.

"Well," he said, "you're prettier in the flesh."

He wiped the sweat from his forehead and nervously approached. In his mind he was already picturing all that he would do to her; the places he would touch her, the little whimpers she would make as he gave her feelings no one would have yet had to chance to give her. He sat down next to her, keeping his distance despite being on top of her in his mind - grinding against her, feeling how tight she is.

How wet she is.

"Thank you," she smiled.

Eleven years old and not a care in the world.

"Can I get you a drink?" he asked.

"Yes, please."

"Wait right there."

He stood up and walked from living room to kitchen, the next door down the hallway on the right. The kitchen was filthy, a room left to fester whilst he surfed the chatrooms looking for people to talk to.

Friends to talk to.

Friends to *groom*.

He moved some of the dirty plates from worktop to sink and ran the hot water to give them a soak. Something in the back of his mind told him that - soon enough - he'd have what he really wanted and would then be free to tidy up.

Reaching up to the top cupboard, he pulled out the only bottle of squash that he had.

"Blackcurrant okay?" he called out.

Eleven years old and light-footed.

"Don't you have anything stronger?"

Her voice startled him. An old man's heart quickened in pace. She was standing in the kitchen doorway, casually leaning against the frame. He hadn't even heard her get up from the leather sofa and walk down the corridor. He noticed she'd undone her tie completely. It was hanging there, around the back of her neck, stretching down the front of her shirt. No longer a tie but a tool with which to bind her should she be agreeable to the idea. His mind played out the scenario quick as a flash - her lying on her front with her hands tied behind her back, skirt hitched up, him kissing her buttocks through the cotton of her white panties.

"What did you have in mind?" he asked.

"Got any wine?"

Eleven years old and already knows what she wants from life.

The man raised an eyebrow and looked at her, "Wine?"

She folded her arms and - behind her fringe - raised an eyebrow back, "Is that a problem?"

The man smiled as though scared of making the girl uncomfortable or not giving her what she wanted. He shook his balding head from side to side, "Not at all, here..."

Opening the fridge revealed shelves of leftover food - none of it salad based. Tucked in the side of the door was a half-pint of semi-skinned milk and a bottle of white wine - already opened; not from an evening with company but rather a lonely evening sat in front of a monitor. A few glasses of wine helped him to concentrate and pluck up the courage to talk to the youngsters how he planned.

Questions aimed at both sexes. At that age, they were all tight. At that age, he thought, they all had that innocent quality he liked.

He pulled the wine from the fridge and removed the lid before taking two glasses from the draining board. Washing up long since done and left to dry; an owner too lazy to bother putting it away.

"Say when," he told his new friend.

They both watched as the wine reached the top of the glass. He stopped before she said to do so.

"You sure you can handle that?" he asked.

She smiled from the doorway, "I'm a big girl."

Eleven years old. A false confidence already deeply rooted there. She wasn't a big girl. She was petit, almost stick thin. Just the way he liked them.

"Help yourself," he told her as he poured his own glass, also to the top.

The young girl walked into the room and reached for her glass, passing him in the process. Being close to him, he took the opportunity to breathe in her scent. A body spray of sorts, no doubt endorsed by some celebrity singer that girls of that age idolised. He watched as she moved the glass to her lips and took a sip. Full lips so kissable. His mind - deep in the gutter - imagining them wrapped around him.

Her face contorted when the sharp tang of grape engulfed her taste buds. The man tried to hide his smile.

Eleven years old and acting oh so grown up.

"Did you want to go back in the other room?" he asked. "It's more comfortable."

"Sure."

He led the way, wishing it were the other way round and that he was behind, watching her.

Be patient. You'll see all you want soon enough.

The man sat on the edge of the sofa - the same spot he had perched upon earlier when seated next to her. She sat next to him, a little gap between the two, glass still in hand. She took another sip aware that - although she didn't like the taste - she wasn't allowed it at home so she would make the most of it.

He was looking at the bag, a glimmer of hope in his eyes.

"Did you bring it?" he asked.

She followed his gaze to the bag and knew instantly what he was talking about. She set the glass down on the coffee table situated in front of the sofa and reached for her bag. Undoing the leather buckle-strap on the front she flung it open and reached in. He watched intently, the previous glimmer of hope now making his body tingle. He smiled when she withdrew a lilac leotard; her swimming costume.

"That's great," he praised her.

They had communicated online for a few days now and - within hours of talking - he had asked her if she had any pictures of her in a bathing suit. It had been a conversation that came about when she complained that she sometimes felt fat. He told her that he needed to see such a photo so he could get a good idea of what her body looked like without the baggy clothes she was pictured wearing in photos uploaded to her profile.

"I'd love for you to wear it for me sometime," he said, a glint in his eye that gave him away - not as an old man but as a sexual predator. In his mind, he recalled the picture she sent him and how she looked in the costume. More specifically he was picturing the way the tight material of the costume clung to her body - allowing him to imagine her naked - and the way the front clung to her slit leaving little to the imagination. He didn't want her to wear it for him sometime. He wanted her to wear it now and - when she was in it standing before him - he'd compliment her again and then he would ask if he could cuddle her. From there it would move on to suggestions no eleven year old should be witness to. He didn't push her, though. He knew better than that. If she was to wear it, it would be because she believed it to be her choice.

"Maybe," she said.

Eleven-year-old girl slowly coming to her senses.

She looked around the room, temporarily ignoring his leering eyes and the way they slowly undressed her.

"They've gone to stay with my ex-wife," he told her.

"Oh."

He was talking about the imaginary puppies, a lie he had planted early in their online conversation. She had spoken about pets, one of the early questions being whether she had any. She answered that she had a hamster but wanted a dog and that's where his puppies came in. He had a new litter, so young they had yet to open their eyes. Cute little things that fit in the palm of your hand. Of course, she was interested in seeing them when he offered. A conversation that ended with an offer to come round sometime to play with them. Again, it was never forced upon her. It was always her choice. It was her choice to send the picture. It was her choice to meet him a few nights on the trot to continue chatting with him, once she'd finished with her homework, it was her choice to pluck up the courage to lie to her mum and dad to sneak out to see him. Always her choice.

Or so she thought.

"I like your uniform," he said - changing the subject before she asked too many questions that would cause his lie to unravel.

"I hate it."

"Why? You look great in it! Very classy. Although I'll be honest, I do wish you wore your hair in pig-tails like we discussed. That would have made it much smarter," he said. "Can I show you?"

She hesitated a moment, "Sure, I guess."

The man reached forward and took two handfuls of hair from off her shoulder. With a tight grip, he held it away from her slightly to give the impression of having them tied there.

"Very cute," he said, nodding towards a mirror on the far side of the room.

With her hair still gripped by his strong hands, she slowly twisted her head so she could see. Her eyes weren't fixed upon what he was doing to her hair, but the look on his face instead.

An eleven-year-old girl oblivious to the understanding of lust.

In his mind, he was behind her. She was bent over the settee, facing away from him. Her hair - still in his hands. Her screams muffled by the sofa's cushions.

She pulled away from him.

He quickly changed the subject so as to keep the conversation flowing, "Are your friends being nice to you now?" he asked, hiding the lust and replacing it with an insincere smile.

"What do you mean?"

There was a look of panic on her face that he couldn't quite gauge. "You said they were calling you fat and ugly? Remember?"

The conversation had only been a couple of nights ago. It was strange that he would have to remind her of it, especially as she had remembered to pack the costume.

"They're still doing it," she said coyly.

"Kids can be cruel, but I mean what I said; you're not fat." He paused a moment before he started to take it to the next level, "Do you still feel fat?"

"Sometimes."

"That's a pity. I guess it knocks your confidence? You know - if you wanted to - you could be a model."

She laughed, "No I couldn't."

"Of course you could. You're a pretty little thing. You have a nice frame, you have a good height and a nice smile and you have a good head on your shoulders. You're smart, not like other girls of your age. In fact, when I first saw your pictures, I could have sworn an agent would have already picked you up for catalogue work!"

"No they haven't."

"Have you ever sent them any pictures? There's a lot of money involved. Imagine the stuff you could buy. Or holidays for your mum and dad, like when they took you to the beach. You'd like that, wouldn't you? To be able to treat your mum and dad?"

"I guess."

"Here, look…" He jumped up and disappeared from the room. Before she had a chance to do anything, he came back again with a Polaroid camera clutched in his sweaty hands. "Look what I have." He raised the camera, "Here, smile."

Before she could react, he aimed the camera and took a picture. The camera's flash illuminated the room and a couple of seconds later, a photograph slid out of the front. He pulled it away from the camera and waved it in the air a couple of times to speed up the drying process. And then, with a smile, he handed it to the girl.

"See. Pretty little thing."

She looked at the picture and blushed. She looked like a rabbit caught in the headlights.

"You know why your friends call you names?"

She shrugged.

An eleven-year-old girl embarrassed.

"It's because they're jealous."

"Why would they be jealous?"

"Because they know you're pretty and they're plain. I was thinking..." he paused a moment before continuing, "No... No... Forget I said anything."

"What is it?" she asked.

"It's stupid. Forget it."

"Please, tell me."

"Well - okay. I was thinking - would you let me take some more pictures of you? I know some people who work for catalogues and I could probably get you an agent."

"Really?"

An eleven-year-old girl easily led.

"Yes. I mean - if you want to do that." He laughed. "Can you imagine the look on your friends' faces? They'll be so jealous. And no one could call you names then." He took a moment to give her time to think things through.

She smiled at the thought of her friends being envious. "What do you say?"

"Okay."

"Okay?"

"Okay!" she exclaimed suddenly confident, suddenly sure of herself.

He beamed again, those stained canines. "Sit up with your back straight," he told her.

She did as he instructed and he started to snap a couple of photos. For each one, he told her something different.

"Smile." Click.

"Look to the left." Click.

"Look to the right." Click.

Each photo spat from the front of the camera, one at a time.

"You're a natural," he said, taking another photo.

He didn't see the pictures as they came out of the camera. He was focused on the pictures that he could have been taking. A young girl with her shirt unbuttoned. A young girl sucking sweetly on a lollipop. A young girl sucking on her index finger whilst staring seductively to the camera. A young girl twiddling with her hair. A young girl with her skirt hitched up, teasing at the panties beneath. A young girl pulling said panties to one side, a reveal of a near-hairless pubic mound.

He lowered the camera, "What about holidays with your mum and dad? Did you like the idea of them?"

"Yes," she said.

Eleven-year-old girl carried away in the moment. The promise of all things shiny and new.

"Catalogues fly their models to nice locations," the man said. "If they think you have what they are looking for - and I know they will love you - this will be easy."

"What do you mean?"

"We take just a couple with you in the swimming costume - maybe get you wet in the shower to make it look as though you've come running out of the sea or something... And we can send them. I know they will go crazy for them and before you know it you'll be flown all over the world with your mum and dad."

"Really?"

"Would I lie to you?"

He had given her wine - not that she drunk it - and he had paid her compliments. But, more importantly than that, he hadn't tried to tell her what she should or shouldn't do and she liked that. It made her feel grown-up.

"Okay."

"You want to do it?"

She nodded.

He tried to contain his excitement - both on his face and between his legs, hidden beneath grey trousers.

"You're going to be a star!" he said. "Why don't you go through to the bathroom and get changed and then, when you're ready, jump in the shower in your costume and give me a shout. Okay?"

"Really?"

"Yes. It's fine. I'll wait here until you're ready for me." He started looking at the pictures he'd already taken, paying her little attention, as though what she were about to do was no big deal to him.

Without another word, she took a hold of the costume - and her bag - and disappeared into the bathroom down the hallway, directed by him calling out when to turn left.

The bathroom door closed and he instantly started picturing her in there, slowly peeling off her clothes until she were standing in the nude. A tight body without a blemish. No ugly sign of ageing. No sagging. No wrinkle. Small breasts starting to form. Few hairs getting in the way of a perfect, untouched vagina. A tight little butt with pert cheeks. One hand on the camera, one hand moving down his body - down his chest to his crotch. A gentle squeeze.

Hard.

He knew his work here was nearly done. She would soon be dressed in the costume he longed to see her in. She'd soon be standing there with water cascading down her. Her skin so perfect and wet. The tightness of the leotard accentuating her figure, pulling into her crack. A shower of water to go with the shower of compliments.

He'd take the photos of her, he'd say how good she is. He'd say they were done and that she could get dressed now. He'd hand her a towel and invite her to take off the costume to dry herself. Slowly peeling the wet fabric away from the skin that it clung so tightly too. But first - before that - he'd give her a big hug at a job well done. By the time he was done, she'd feel so confident and they'd have had so much of a laugh together that it wouldn't seem odd to her. Why would it be? They'd be friends by then. Proper friends - not just because they had met online. Not just chat buddies. They'd be something more because he was helping her do something great with her life. Something that would help her family.

An eleven-year-old girl. Somebody's daughter.

After the hug, he'd hand her the towel and then he would ask her if he could kiss her. The moment of truth. Would he have made such an impression on the young girl that she would say 'yes' - an answer brought about by the fact this man was so cool? Offering her things previously forbidden - photoshoots and alcohol… Or would she still be this timid little mouse in which case a kiss would not be granted but - instead - taken by force.

Hand still on crotch as he waited for her to call him through, he didn't care which outcome came about now. By the end of the day he would be inside of her and she would be bleeding over him; a hymen ripped from where he'd push through it. On the one hand, it would be nice to hear her say 'yes' and progress things as friends. A thought of him lying upon his back as she painfully eased herself down upon his shaft. But on the other - screams could sometimes be good too.

The bathroom door opened and she stood there - down the hallway - in the lilac costume.

"See - you don't look fat! You look amazing!" he said, sensing she was nervous. "Are you ready?"

She nodded.

He walked towards her - smiling all the way - with the camera by his side. As he got near, he nodded. "Go back into the bathroom." He was pleased to see her follow his instruction with no argument. "Stand by the shower," he said, "and then look back at the camera."

She stood at the shower, he directed her to look as though she were stepping in, and looked back to the camera. She was smiling - albeit a nervous looking smile - but was soon told to stop. It was better if she didn't smile for this type of shot. At least, that's what he told her.

Click.

The picture printed out and dropped to the floor.

"Bend over slightly, as though you're in mid-move."

She did as she was told and another picture was taken; this picture was put on the side carefully.

"That's good."

"Yeah?" she looked for reassurance.

"Trust me, you're a natural." He lowered the camera. "Okay - get in the shower and turn it on. I want you to look as though you're washing your body with imaginary soap…" In his mind he was already picturing her with a hand between her legs, pressing her inner thigh. Another hand on one of her small breasts. A hopeful wish that the water took a while to warm and made her nipples stand to attention for him just as he was - unseen by her - standing to attention for her.

She stepped into the shower and turned the water on. A slight delay before it cascaded from the shower-head, raining down upon her. He started taking pictures of her when her hands started touching her body - pressing the imaginary bar of soap against herself.

"That is excellent," he said turning his body slightly to hide his true reaction.

An elderly man's wish that it was his hand pressing against her wet skin. His hand, his touch… His tongue…

He took more pictures until there were no more available to take. He set the camera down on the side of the sink and smiled at the girl.

"We're done."

He walked over to the shower and leaned in, soaking his arm in the process, to turn the pouring water off. It slowed and then trickled to a stop. She stood there, shivering from where the water had yet to warm up. Her nipples - as he wished - raised beneath the costume.

"You looked great! My friends at the catalogue will love you. I reckon you'll be working with them in no time."

"Really?" she seemed unsure of herself - no doubt feeling exposed, standing there - shivering - in nothing but a soaking leotard.

"I promise." He patted her on her arm, a move that was supposed to offer reassurance. "I'll get you a towel," he said.

He turned away and she stepped from the shower cubicle, dripping droplets of water onto the tiled floor next to her bag. He pulled the towel from a handrail and turned back to the girl. His eyes went wide and he dropped the towel as the sharp blade pierced his chest with force. He gasped and pulled himself away from the blade.

An eleven-year-old girl standing there, smiling.

Her bag was open. A smile on her face. A kitchen knife in her hand.

The elderly man clutched his chest as blood pumped out and - without a word - he dropped to his knees. He opened his mouth, a want to form a sentence, and blood trickled out. He coughed and some more claret splattered down his chin and onto the floor, mixing with the puddles of water from having the shower on without closing the cubicle door.

"I know what you are," the girl told him. There was no fear in her eyes. There was no emotion in her monotone voice. She was completely calm. She bent over and put the knife back in the school bag, from where she'd taken it when he turned his back. She stepped forward and snatched the towel from his hand and - with both bag and towel in hand - she walked from the room.

The man tried to get up but instead fell forward, stopping himself from face planting with a hand to the floor - keeping one pressed to his chest. He could feel himself getting colder as the blood seeped from between his fingers and continued leaking from his mouth - choking him in the process. He tried again to call out but nothing came, merely a splutter. He rolled onto his side as a numbness started to spread through his limbs.

In the living room the girl peeled away her wet costume. Letting it drop to the floor, she stepped out of it - naked and wet. A smile on her face as she imagined him bleeding out in the next room, picturing the look on his face if only he could see her now. She patted herself dry with the towel and started to put her school uniform on once more, fishing it from the bag she'd stored it in to keep it dry and free from splatter.

Less than five minutes and she was dressed and out of the door with the same bag over her shoulder - containing nothing but a wet costume, a damp towel and a bloodied blade. Whistling a tune, she skipped merrily down the stairs towards the apartment complex's entrance. Out of the door and across the road - she continued - to where a car was parked.

Eleven-year-old girl being picked up by a loving mum and dad.

"How did it go, sweetie?" her father asked, looking at her via the rear-view mirror.

"It's done," she said sweetly, putting the bag down in the foot well before sitting back and fastening her seat-belt.

"We're proud of you, honey," her father continued. "And your sister would be too."

Her mother didn't say anything. She was sitting in the front of the car clutching a photograph; a family at a beach - a mother, a father, a girl in a lilac swimming costume and a second, slightly older girl. A tear rolled from the mother's cheek and splashed the photograph. It didn't go unnoticed by the father of the girl. He leaned over and gave his wife's leg a squeeze. She looked up at him and he smiled.

"It's done," he said. "Your daughter did well."

His wife - the girl's mother - smiled back at him. She turned to her daughter in the back of the car.

"Thank you," she said.

"When can we do it again?" the girl asked as she casually flicked through the photographs the old man snapped of her. She had collected them from around his apartment, making sure as to leave none of them behind. Not just because they were evidence but mainly because she thought she looked good in them.

For a dirty old pervert, he sure did manage to capture her good side.

Eleven-year-old girl. Someone's daughter. Someone's sister. No one's victim.

MUTANT
BUILDING 101
DUNCAN P. BRADSHAW

The whitewall tyre came to a convenient halt touching a thick, painted white line underlining the word 'STOP'. As one bored soldier trudged towards the driver window, hurriedly scanning down a list of names on a clipboard, his fellow entrance guardian sauntered over to the passenger door and rapped his chapped knuckles on the window.

Accompanied by a squeaking, the glass barrier slowly inched down into the thick metal door, the soldier rested his arms on the sill, tipped his tin helmet back and drawled, "Say, you ain't one o' those Reds are ya boy?"

The child looked up into the fat ruddy face inches away, he recoiled from the stench of stale sweat and cigarettes. Breathing through his mouth he replied, "No sir, we're good honest Americans. My papa works here, helping build stuff to keep those pesky Ruskies away."

"Good on ya boy. Say, what cha got there?"

Small hands held up a see-through plastic box with a green lid, breathing holes had been bored through the top, plastic shavings stood up from the drilled edges like ornamental trees. "This here is Sidney sir, he's my pet snake," the kid answered matter of factly, holding the container deep into the personal space of the inquisitive guard.

A chubby hand plucked the helmet off his head, the other rubbed a sheet of sweat from his brow. A milk snake, wrapped in bands of red, yellow and black looked from its transparent cage and flicked its tongue out lazily at the new spectator, losing interest quickly, it coiled up into a multi coloured length of flex and went to sleep.

"Say, I'm not so sure you should be bringing pets into this here top secret military base. Hey Bert…"

Having finished checking the drivers credentials and ticking the name off the list, Bert looked over to his chum, "Can it Randy, this here is Doctor Schmidt and his young 'un Timmy, they could have Castro and Krushchev getting to second base in the back and we'd have to smile and pass them a wet towel."

Randy replaced his helmet, spitefully flicked the plastic box invoking a dead eyed stare from the snake, and headed over to the thoroughly unimposing barrier of a metal pole clutching a circular 'STOP' sign, which he lifted by pushing down on one end.

As the soldiers saluted, the DeSoto Fireflite growled like an irked alsation and drove towards a large concrete hanger sitting like a squatting dwarf at the end of a blacktop road. "Gee dad, I sure love *bring-your-child-to-work* day," swooned Timmy.

Dr Schmidt nodded curtly and swung the car round to reverse into the parking bay emblazoned with his name. "Don't touch anything," he warned.

Timmy nodded with the enthusiasm of a puppy working as a tennis ball chewing tester. "You betcha papa, I won't touch a thing, isn't that right Sidney?" The snake sulked, thoroughly unimpressed within the Perspex box.

The thin door clicked back into the frame, and another nameless square jawed soldier saluted whilst simultaneously pulling his M14 tight in to his cliff face of a chest. "Doctor Schmidt, this way please," shouted a scrawny bespectacled man, his bleached white lab coat betrayed no sign of ever having entered the real world.

"Sanderson, what have you got for me?" Schmidt asked, leaving Timmy floundering in his wake. The boy watched on, as his father walked off with the funny man and looked around at the assorted items in the corridor. Cork noticeboards with bizarre messages pinned to them, announcing cash for 'a good time', hung over a table with overflowing ashtrays and discarded coffee cups, elliptical brown lip stains were stamped on the rims.

The soldier guarding the door resumed his duties and added another dredged coffee mug to the burgeoning collection. He cast Timmy a wary gaze. "Wotcha looking at kid?" he demanded, the question was answered with a French shrug and the guard got back to staring at a patch of missing paint on the wall, which bore a striking resemblance to Jayne Mansfield.

Timmy idly kicked the first in a line of metal barrels which ran down the opposing wall of the hallway, a dull clank told him that it was full. Noticing a strange symbol on a sticker plastered to the side of the casks, he placed

Sidney's home on top of the barrels, and began tracing a line around what looked like a black three bladed propeller, stamped onto a yellow background.

He made sure to make the appropriate plane sounds whilst doing so.

"So are you telling me that it's a complete failure Sanderson? But how can that be? We had enough Uranium from the last batch to make the whole east coast glow in the dark," Doctor Schmidt said angrily, his assistant shrunk from him like a scalded child, hugging himself with his bone-thin arms.

"I. . . I...I don't know what to say Doctor Sch-"

A hand shot up causing the intended words to dribble into nothingness. "It's okay Sanderson, I'm not blaming you. Just we promised the President we'd have a new lead on this by winter, and we're running out of time."

Sanderson relaxed a little and shoved his glasses back up the bridge of his nose, "Perhaps we got the mix wrong? We can't be far off, the last test we did showed us we were close. So close."

"Well we can't waste time standing here. Bring the data with you, we'll head over to the offices and go over it, it's got to be something simple. You men. Start disposing of the waste from the last test would you? Put it down in the cellar with the rest," Schmidt commanded.

A shoal of soldiers with sack trucks burst into life and buzzed past the scientists and into the corridor whence they came.

Doctor Schmidt wrestled with bulky ring-binders and reams of printed wide carriage paper. Commanding the agility of an arthritic sumo wrestler, he barged his way back into the hallway where Timmy was learning the finer points of three card stud from Chad the hanger guard.

"Come on Timmy, follow me, hope you got your filing fingers on, cos plans have changed," Doctor Schmidt panted out, his words caused the kid to huff and do an air-kick in frustration.

As the Doctor reached the door, Timmy called out, "Papa, where's Sidney? I left him right there on those big metal barrels and they're all gone now."

His father sighed disapprovingly, "I told you to leave him at home didn't I? Come on. Hey Chad, would you mind going to waste storage and bringing my son's snake over to the offices? There's a good fellow."

The torchlight slashed through the deserted basement, Chad grumbled to himself about the absurdity of a highly trained killing machine being asked to locate and return a kid's pet snake, "Goddamn waste of taxpayer's dollars if you ask me," he whinged aloud.

The rod of light ran over the tops of barrels and came to rest on the rectangular plastic box, Sidney was staring off into space, lost in a daydream about hunting mice in the overgrown field where he had been snakenapped. He rued the day the snivelling child had grabbed hold of him and ran all the way home, clutching him tightly in his sweaty wart ridged hands.

His insides were still trying to settle back into their original shape.

Chad picked up the box and turned to leave, as he did so, he felt the hair stand up on the back of his hand, it was like a fair maiden stroking him suggestively. He brought his hand up to his face and squealed as his brain confirmed the unwanted diagnosis of an arachnid playmate.

The container incarcerating the snake crashed to the floor as Chad emitted notes usually reserved for a falsetto. He brushed the spider off and spun around, his mind convincing him that a multitude of arachno-babies were now burrowing into his flesh and setting up home in dank folds of his body. The butt of his rifle smacked into a barrel with a loud CLANG, followed by a trickling and slurping sound.

Looking down, Chad shone the torch onto the floor, a pool of luminous green liquid was being discharged onto the ground, creating a slow, but steadily moving wave of sludge. In its wake was the snake box, mumbling to himself again, "I don't git paid nuff for this," he turned around and made his way back to the doorway.

As his hand wrapped around the cold metal door handle, he heard a tearing and shrieking sound from behind him, as if a labour of unclipped moles were burrowing out of an orang-utans love sack. The sound died with a gurgling and slapping sound, accentuated by metal hitting concrete, annoyed that he would probably need a bigger mop and bucket, Chad turned around and looked into the gloom.

The pool of green goo was still visible on the floor, it looked like it had stopped moving, which was a relief, but there were areas which appeared to be obstructed. "For Pete's sake…" He clicked the torch back into life and scanned the darkness, beginning at the base of Lake Greencrap, which bubbled and protested at the light. As the beam rolled up, he froze and emitted another squeal which did not match his butch physique.

A beam of fat red light bathed him from head to toe,

in the amount of time it took for Chad's wife to say "No," to his generous offer to see 'The Sound Of Music' on Broadway, he was reduced to a pile of fine carbon and bone. The light desisted and the room went back to a gentle green glow.

Timmy's paper clip sorting adventure came to an abrupt climax as the emergency klaxon wailed into life like a grizzly newborn baby. The metal poles which they were affixed to, shuddered with the reverberations, people walked out of their offices and hangers in a daze, as if woken from a pleasant dream.

Doctor Schmidt, Sanderson and Timmy stood on the path which ran from the main base to the offices, which lived on the perimeter, not cool enough to hang out with their far more foreboding building brethren. The child held his hands to his face, shielding his eyes like a visor and scanned the distance, a crackle of automatic gunfire broke up the moaning sound of the alarm. The trio shared nervous glances before jogging back to where they had just come from.

As they approached they saw a semi-circle of khaki smothered soldiers, rifles pulled into their shoulders, loosing off rounds into a darkened doorway. "Sergeant, what are you doing? There are explosives in there, one stray bullet and we'll all go up," Doctor Schmidt shouted over the barrage of noise.

The makeshift firing squad stopped, looked at the civilian and reloaded with barely checked contempt. A Sergeant, brandishing his Colt 45, held up a hand to his men. His teeth relented their bear trap grip on his cigar, rolling the end around in his fingers, the Sergeant grunted,

"Sir, there's something in that there hanger, two of my men went in and aside from a bright red light, nothing has come out again, now if you don't mind, let us get back to our indiscriminate fire, it ain't hurting anyone."

The gruff Sergeant turned from Doctor Schmidt and allowed his teeth to resume cigar chomping duties, "Men, on the count of three, open fire into the building again. Ivansson, good shooting son, you've only got a few unbroken window panes to go. Ready, One…"

A series of metallic clanks and thuds rang out as the soldiers readied for another volley. From the guts of the hanger, a strange high pitched squeal worked its way down the labyrinthian corridors.

"…two…"

The squeal built up to a crescendo, the narrow hallways and side rooms added to the harmonics and created a wave of alien noise, Ivansson fell to his knees, clutching his ears with his hands, trying to keep the sound from boiling his brain.

"…thr-"

Before the Sergeant could finish his brief countdown, a large hairy leg crashed through the outer wall which had been perforated by the initial assault, masonry and shards of glass were ejected from the impact site.

Another leg burst through the wall, the soldiers, their get up and go, gone, staggered back from the strange sight, only the Sergeant defiantly stood his ground. As he raised the pistol and aimed at the middle point between both legs, a large reptilian head, wrapped in neat bands of red, yellow and black emerged from the gloom. Its long, smooth forked tongue flicked the air. A pair of large black orbs, passing themselves off as eyes, looked unblinkingly at the world beyond its birthing chamber.

"What in tarnation are you? Men, get ready to fire, this here thing is an illegal on our base, f-"

Before the Sergeant could complete what turned out to be his last order, the snake eyes shot out a beam of superhot red light, the one expended bullet was vapourised as it left the pistol muzzle, its elemental parts mixed with the skeletal and powdered remains of the man. The cigar, still aflame at one end, sat atop the ashen heap, acting as a budget entry eternal flame.

More masonry cracked and fell to the floor as the creature pulled its way into the warm morning air. The head was part of a long thick neck which formed the body of the beast, the tail waved behind it. It was transported on eight legs, each ending in a sort of thin, pointy fingernail, which made a clacking sound as they struck the ground and scuttled into the vast expanse of concrete which sat next to the hangar.

It stood around eight foot tall, the shadow of the building masked its bizarre form. One of the soldiers found a reserve of courage and attempted to rally the wavering men, "Come on fella's, there's nothing to him, we can take him."

The snake head swung this way and that, taking in the sights surrounding him, spindly legs carried the creature into the sunlight. As the first ray of sun stroked the beast's head, its mouth opened with a mix of pain and pleasure. The legs quickened and the monster stood in its entirety beneath the warm disc of light from above.

"Ha, look at him, he's scared, eight of us, one of him, let's get him boys," the soldier shouted again. Sufficiently geed up, they all formed a line and aimed at the abomination. A cracking and ticking sound rumbled through the ground. As the sun shone on the monster, it bowed its head, its body and legs started to shake as if electricity coursed through its corrupted veins.

With a massive screech, the snakes head arched backwards, the creature started to expand like a virulent strain in a petri dish. All the while, there was the sound of bones being stretched, cracked and then fused together. Skin tore and then slurped back together again, tendons snapped and clicked, still the screeching rose highest of all.

The soldiers stood slack jawed and looked at the beast growing in size, it was as if it had knocked back a container or twelve of industrial strength Miracle-Gro, their trigger fingers forgot any sense of self-preservation.

At once the base fell silent, the klaxon stopped bleating, the potshots from sentries abated and the screeching ended. The giant snake head looked down from the sky onto the toy soldiers scattered around its feet, each leg was now half the size of the hangar it had scuttled out from, the body ran to around two thirds the length of the building too.

The giant forked tongue flapped in the air, tasting the dust and pheromones, it grew disinterested and discharged another burst of red light from its eyes, wiping out the canteen in one shot. A ripple of gunfire rang around the base as those not stupefied with fear sought to fight back. Each shot that hit the scaly hide bounced off, doing no harm. Even the bullets which connected with the creatures gangly legs fared no better, ricocheting off the steel like bone within.

"Sidney?" Timmy asked tamely, his pet which now formed one half of a giant mutated monster ambled lazily around the facility, spearing some, disintegrating many and flicking the odd human into the electric fence. It seemed to like hearing them snap, crackle and pop.

"What are we going to do Doctor? WHAT ARE WE GOING TO DO?" screamed Sanderson, clawing at his own face with stubby fingers, the nails long since chewed off and spat onto the ground. Behind him a woman screamed and fainted.

Doctor Schmidt struck the assistant across the face with a mighty slap, "Pull yourself together man, this is nothing more than science, you hear me? SCIENCE. All we have to do is go and see where this happened, I can then formulate a plan from there, come on, it must've been in the basement where Timmy's snake was taken, let's go."

Frank lay in his foxhole, making sure the *thing* hadn't seen him, he squeezed off a few more ineffectual rounds. "Hey Red," he bellowed.

Two foxholes down, Red was in the process of reloading, "What's that Frank?"

"What the hell do we call this thing Red? I mean, that monster we had down in New Mexico, half-scorpion and half-tornado, that was easy, Scornado. Man, that was one cool name, tough sonnavabitch, but you weren't going to forget him in a hurry, but this one?"

The pair ducked back in their crappy ditches as a chubby red beam took out the two foxholes in-between them, thin wisps of smoke rose from piles of freshly created ash. Red rolled onto his front and shot off a few rounds, "Dunno, half snake and half spider, so...Snider?"

Frank joined him in the mini salvo, the bullets pinged

off the creature, who had turned his attention from them and was firing wild shots at fleeing Huey's, "Yeah, erm, a Spake? Spiderake? Snader?"

The mangled remains of a helicopter slammed into the ground, a survivor crawled from the burning wreckage only to be stabbed through the head by the unnamed creature's foreleg.

Red pushed another mag into his M14, "Well, I guess the best we have for now is we call him Spike, but can't say I'm too happy about it. Sounds more like a beatnik vampire than a terrifying monster, remember Sharkadillo? Heck, that was a good name. Look Frank, the tanks are finally here."

Within the dingy basement, muffled explosions and pained screeches were still audible.

"Look papa, over there, all that green gunk, there's Sidney's box and all. Aww shucks." The kid deflated seeing his handiwork having gone to waste, Doctor Schmidt patted him on the head roughly.

With a test tube in one hand and a spoon from a coffee mug, Sanderson knelt down by the vibrant liquid and scooped some into the glass tube, it fizzed and bubbled. "Strange…" he remarked.

Doctor Schmidt shone the torch through the vial, as the light hit the goo, it erupted like a baleful volcano, shooting lumps of coagulated green goo into the air. Sanderson dropped the test tube instinctively.

"Interesting," the good Doctor concluded thoughtfully.

He spun and looked at the two of them, "The enemy of my enemy is my friend…" he mused rhetorically.

Pulling out a folded IRS envelope from his jacket, he licked the end of a pencil he had retrieved from his breast pocket, making hasty scribbling sounds, he scrawled in a frenzy.

Mere seconds later he slipped the pencil back into his pocket, folded the envelope and passed it to his son. "Timmy, I want you and Sanderson here to go into town and bring me these items, okay?" He looked up at the assistant and passed him a Mervyn's keyring with two brass keys. "Take my car, don't be long, we need the Snakider up there to still be in the vicinity if this is to work."

The DeSoto Fireflite shot through the now unmanned checkpoint a half hour later, Timmy sat in the front seat, peering into the footwell behind him at the goods they had procured in town. Sanderson skidded around burnt out tank husks, one driver hung out of the turret, his upper body reduced to a smoking skeleton whilst his legs and midriff remained all fleshy and dewy.

Another chunky beam lanced through the last of the guard towers which up until that morning had stood proudly on each corner of the sprawling estate. One of the guards who had not been reduced to cremation output, screamed as he fell to the floor. His death curdle ceased as the structure fell on top of him and pushed the life, and his lungs, from his broken body.

The Snakider tip-tapped around the concrete ground, the metal things which had made a lot of noise and fired bigger things at him, had stopped working around ten minutes ago. He had made some sport of a couple of them, deciding to hold back on the lazer eyes and instead try and tip them onto their backs. Two tanks were in such a state, their tracks churned aimlessly in the air, the occupants lying in piles of bone and dust as they had fled from the upheaval.

Sanderson yanked the wheel violently, as a red beam lashed out at them, he careened into a stern looking officer who was hiding in the midst of a verdant prickly bush. The impact sent the cowardly man flying through the air, the Snakider flicked out its tongue like a whip and severed the man in two.

Parking abruptly, the assistant grabbed armfuls of stuff from the back of the car. Timmy did likewise and the duo dashed back into the hangar and made their way to the basement.

Doctor Schmidt stood in the doorway to the goo room, with a trolley and an expectant grin.

"Did you get it all?" he asked excitedly.

Sanderson, flushed with exertion nodded limply, "Most of it Doctor, though I'm not sure what you intend to do with it all."

The words were met with a smile laden with self-importance, "Sanderson, I intend to use science to defeat this monster. It was created from this liquid, we shall use the same thing which spawned it to create something which will destroy it. Tell me Sanderson, what is the natural enemy of a snake?"

The assistant puffed his cheeks out at the sudden general knowledge quiz question, "Erm…I guess it would be a-"

Doctor Schmidt held up a cage with a miffed set of eyes looking out. "That's right Sanderson, a mongoose, and tell me Timmy, what likes to eat spiders?"

Timmy looked up into his father's eyes and chewed

the inside of his mouth. "Well papa, Old Yeller back home eats those spiders we get on the porch."

He was met with a disappointing shake of the head, "Son, you know the answer, I gave you the list to get this all didn't I?" He walked across to a tall cage covered with a thick cloth, picked it up and held it out to Timmy, "Son, an *eagle* eats spiders."

Sanderson coughed awkwardly, "Oh Doctor...I meant to say, the pet shop in town was all out of eagles, sir."

"But, I was explicit in my list, mongoose, eagle, nine inch nails, a shotgun, duct tape and a Twinky," the Doctor replied forcefully. "So if you didn't get an eagle, what mighty bird of prey did you get me?"

The assistant sagged and refused to hold his boss' stare, "I'm sorry Doctor Schmidt, it was all they had."

"POLLY WANT A CRACKER," chirped out from the cage interior, Schmidt pulled the cloth off slowly, revealing a brightly coloured parrot. With a shake of the head, he looked at Sanderson with a stare that spoke of bottomless and crushing dismay.

"But...but...I wanted an eagle, y'know, symbol of America, what better animal could we splice with a mongoose than the majestic eagle. Something that would really look good on the résumé, the President would gladly sign our grant cheque for-"

"POLLY WANT A CRACKER."

Doctor Schmidt hit the cage.

"Shut it," he shouted.

"SHUT IT," replied the parrot.

"This could go on a while, fine, a parrot will do. Now I must get all of this stuff just so..." Doctor Schmidt crouched down and rifled through the items.

Sanderson regained some of his poise. "Doctor, I get the mongoose and parrot, which is a sentence I never thought I'd utter until this morning, but the rest of the stuff? What's that for?"

The Doctor was a whirlwind of activity. "Of course Sanderson, I forget that you are not the intellectual titan that I am. Well, if you haven't noticed, the Snakider-"

"Is that the best name you could come up with Doctor? I was thinking Spike or-"

Doctor Schmidt threw a look at Sanderson that hinted what myriad of injuries would befall him if he interrupted again, "As I was saying, the *Snakider* has got lazer beams in his eyes, not too sure how that happened, so I figured I'd beef up our little creation a bit. These nails should mean that it has talons of pure iron, the shotgun a devastating ranged weapon infused with the radiation slurry."

Sanderson coughed nervously, "And the duct tape and Twinky Doctor?"

Schmidt ripped off the Twinky wrapper with his teeth, "I'm hungry, and my tail pipe is on the verge of falling off, so need to fix it later on."

The assistant looked at him blankly.

"What? You were going to town anyway, may as well get me a few things whilst you were there. Right, everything is loaded onto the trolley as needed, now comes the real work," Doctor Schmidt had put both cages on the bottom of the trolley, scattered a handful of nails through the wire bars and rested the gun on top of the lot. He coughed impatiently.

Sanderson shrugged his shoulders, as if asked the

answer to an obvious question.

"Sanderson, do you honestly think I'm going to go in there? We're like scientific implements, I am a Geiger counter, precise, exacting, you are more of a spatula, now push the trolley in there and rupture a radiation drum over it. There's a good fellow."

Sanderson sighed and began the short journey into the basement.

"Oh, and Sanderson," Doctor Schmidt piped up, the assistant looked across in the hope that it was a big joke and all was forgiven.

"Yes Doctor?"

"Two things really. One, I wouldn't get any on you, you'll probably die. Two, I wouldn't be in there too long when it happens, as the creature will likely see you as a threat, and...well...see point one. Good luck." With the words of encouragement spoken, Doctor Schmidt pulled the doors to, and peered through one of the windows nervously.

The Snakider lanced another fleeing scientist with its pointy leg and flicked the still mewling body in the air, trying to catch him in its mouth. The bleeding man smacked against the giant snout and went into freefall, landing on the concrete with a splat and a crunch.

Looking around at the wanton destruction, there were next to no buildings or vehicles left which hadn't felt the wrath of the mutated creature. Smoking ruins of A-4 Skyhawks were littered around the area, their strafing runs brought to an abrupt conclusion as the red lazer beam blasted them from the sky.

Deciding that the grass looked greener on the other

side of the fence, the Snakider thought it was time to branch out, leave the nest and make something of itself in the real world. It skittered over to the entrance where a painted STOP sign tried to make it stay within the confines of the base.

As the first of its legs crossed the line, seemingly in uproar at the failure to heed the sign, a CAW-CAW made the Snakider look back. A brightly coloured ferret the size of a Cadillac scurried from the hangar entrance and stood still, letting the embrace of the sunlight wrap its feathered furry body in its warmth.

The beaked face reared towards the heavens, rows of razor sharp teeth glinted from within the maw, the beast, fused with the light grew like Sea Monkeys on amphetamine. As it reached its full size, it unfurled gigantic wings of such magnificent colour and hue. A showy flick of its wings resulted in rows of five feet long metal spikes flash out from the ridges of bone. It swished its tail round as if disgruntled by a swarm of flies.

The wings flapped, slowly at first, each swish displaced vast amounts of air, the beast rose effortlessly into the air, to celebrate its ascension to the sky, it opened its beak and let out an ear shattering, "POLLY WANTS A CRACKER."

Frank dusted off the remains of the tank crew which had coated him in a fine film of ash.

"Red. Hey Red," he shouted.

Red dragged the sheet of metal off the top of his foxhole, the panel had come loose as the last Huey had tried, unsuccessfully, to evacuate the top brass to the secret bunker in the next county.

"What do ya want Frank?" he hollered back.

"Have you seen this new one? What the heck do we call this? It ain't like nuthin' I've ever seen, is that a muskrat?"

Peering over the jagged charred piece of helicopter door, Red looked upon the creature that took to the air, "Jeepers, I think it's a mongoose. My god. They've done it. Those bastards have really done it."

Coughing out lungfuls of tank commander, Frank shouted back, "So, is it a Mongrot? A Paroose? I must say, these folk ain't helping us out are they?"

"And why use a parrot? Surely they shoulda used an eagle or even a kittyhawk. I dunno, just something a bit grander, it's like they're not even trying anymore," Red replied.

The Mongarrot flapped its way over to the two men hunkered in the ground, its tail swung between its legs, the wind from the wings blew the fur to one side, revealing a large chasm in the end. "Say, Red, that tail, does that look like the business end of a shotgun to you?"

A loud BOOM signalled the end of the pair as radioactive buck shot was discharged at them at high velocity. Strands of bright green goo laced over Frank's face, as he patted it, the viscous fluid ate through his skin, his screams marginally drowned out the sound of his skull fizzing away to nothing until his vocal chords melted and his entire body dissolved in on itself.

"SHUT IT," the Mongarrot cawed and turned languidly towards the Snakider who now had its full undivided attention.

"Doctor, did your creation just kill those men?" Sanderson

asked sheepishly, the reply was a withering stare, and the three of them maintained their vigil from the hangar in an awkward silence.

The Snakider clip-clopped across the concrete towards the Mongarrot, as it closed the distance, it let off a beam which caught the flying creature on the shoulder. Letting out an agonised "CAW," the winged monster climbed into the air swiftly. At the apex of its ascent, the Mongarrot banked sharply, tucked its huge wings into its body and corkscrewed towards the Snakider.

As the blur of red and orange swooped in, the Snakider stood idle, trying to work out what the hell was going on. The answer came swiftly. As the winged beastie came in low, it flicked its wings out, metal lances caught the light and twinkled. The Snakider realised what was happening too late, and tried to duck. One of the wing tips raked down a side of the scaly body, rending flesh and sending broken sheets of scale whizzing through the air.

Doctor Schmidt, Sanderson and Timmy covered their ears as the wounded beast let out a shriek, a Frisbee of razor sharp scale thunked into the wall above them. They each swallowed down their fear and sunk back to their watching positions.

Green blood jetted from the wound, splashing against the bone dry ground. It hissed and popped as it sloshed against the concrete, chewing chunks from the surface. The Mongarrot pulled up from its attack run and landed on the top of the hangar roof, looking down like a harlequin gargoyle.

"HA HA," it cawed down at the injured mutant.

The Snakider reeled from the strike, turned towards its mocking assailant and let fly another lazer beam which missed its nemesis but struck the supporting beam beneath the braying Mongarrot. A ball clenching squeal of bending metal was the opening bar to the next movement as the roof gave in to both the weight of the creature resting on top and the blast which has shorn it in two.

With a puff of dust and debris, the Mongarrot landed in amongst the wreckage of the hangar roof, the three humans had scurried from beneath its boughs moments before and were now cowering behind Doctor Schmidt's car.

With a shriek, the Snakider scuttled over to the ruined building, letting off frenzied bursts of deadly red lazer as it went. These slammed into the ground and the surrounding pile of destroyed building, one misplaced shot went on to shave Vostok 2, where Gherman Titov was having a snooze in low orbit.

As the Snakider arrived at the collapsed hangar, its front legs jabbed into the pile of rubble, amongst the sound of bone scraping stone, CAWs of pain rang out. The dust cloud settled and the Mongarrot was visible, laying on its back amongst the remnants of the building, its wings pinned down with huge chunks of roof.

Sensing victory, the Snakider ceased its stabbing and walked over the loose pile of hangar offal, the two mutant faces were a few feet apart. The Snakider's forked tongue rolled out slowly and licked the Mongarrot's face, a strange texture of fur and feathers.

Black pools of nothingness looked down onto the trapped creature, to heighten the effect and drag out the inevitable, the Snakider gradually ignited its eye lazer beams, so that they took on the same colour as two bowls of blood.

Before the Snakider had a chance to fire, the Mongarrot's tail silently wormed its way through a blown out doorframe. With one lightning quick jab, the tip slammed into the side of the Snakider's scaly head, as it realised its time was nigh, the radioactive shotgun tail fired at point blank range, sending huge gobbets of green blood, fused white bone and scales over the remains of the stricken hangar.

The Snakider slumped to one side, pumping out thick green goo over bent steel girders, its legs clicked against each other, trying to rebel against the notion that it was dead. With an almighty effort, the Mongarrot heaved itself free from its shallow grave.

Shaking the dust off with several mighty flaps of its wings, it took a moment and preened itself.

Satisfied, the mutant clamped its jaw around the body of the Snakider, which still shuddered in the embrace of death. Beating its wings like it was trying to drag the earth towards the moon, it took to the sky. With the wilting body of the monster flapping in its mouth, they ascended into the bright morning blue sky.

"Well done Doctor Schmidt, that was quite something," Sanderson said, extending a hand to his boss.

Schmidt took the proffered hand and shook it firmly, "That it was Sanderson. That it was. Mighty close too. By the way, I didn't mean to hold onto the door handle quite so tightly earlier, was just an autonomic response, sure you understand."

The building atmosphere was broken by the desecrated body of the Snakider landing onto the spiked belly of the hangar with a loud crunch and splat. From above, the trio looked on as the Mongarrot soared majestically in the sky, it looped this way and that, diving and then pulling up with a feat of jaw dropping aerial acrobatic skill.

"Good choice with the parrot too Sanderson, gives it the personal touch, the President will like that, especially if we can teach him some pithy remarks when he crushes the commies," Doctor Schmidt clapped a paternal hand on his assistants shoulder.

"He really is quite a wonder...what's that in his mouth?" Sanderson asked, pointing at the blob in the sky, looming larger with every passing second, "Is that?"

The Mongarrot flew in low over the base, as it did so, it released the crushed fuselage of a DC8 onto the boundary fence, it did an inverted loop and fired a blast from its radiation tail shotgun into the smouldering wreckage before peeling away into the air again.

Doctor Schmidt pounded his fist into his hand, "Dammit. Okay Timmy, Sanderson, I want you two to go back into town and get me the following; A jackal, an owl or similar winged predator, seriously Sanderson, you have to think *big* this time okay? I'll also need some TNT, a nailgun, some turtle wax and heck, go on and get us some Marlboro Red, I get the feeling it's going to be a long day."

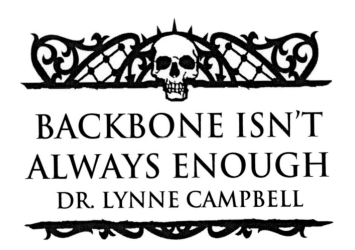

BACKBONE ISN'T ALWAYS ENOUGH
DR. LYNNE CAMPBELL

Once again, as I stared back at my reflection in the mirror, I could plainly see the deterioration of my condition beginning yet again. I knew it was time for the very painful, but temporary, cure. A pain that I would have to endure repeatedly, as necessary, to control this affliction.

I washed my drying skin. Damn, it was peeling once more. I knew peeling skin was the least of my concerns, but nonetheless I found it itchy and uncomfortable, and still do.

Dressing in my best tweed jacket, with brown slacks, and white shirt, all tailored to fit me perfectly whenever I was well, I examined my now slightly sagging attire with dismay. Oh, to be well at all times; what must that be like? Still, I was thankful for what could be done to return me to my original state of being, and so tossing aside my self pity in exchange for determination I put on my hat, and my beige trench coat, and ventured out into the cool Fall evening air.

A light rain soothed my itchy face, white fogging up my tinted glasses. I hoped my wig would stay in place. I knew there is no shame in being bald, but I could admit I felt more comfortable wearing my wig. The dark brown curls also matched my moustache and beard. They weren't real either, of course, thanks to my condition; but they had become somewhat real to me.

I stepped lightly as I walked through suburbia, knowing that too much pressure on my limbs could mean an easy break or worse. My bones were getting old. There was no denying it. They felt old. The delicate nature of the human body angered me so at times. At others, I marvelled at its beauty and complexity. I never used to complain. Back when I was young, I had nothing to complain about. I was the Alpha male. My arms and legs were strong and muscular. I was agile and I stood straight, with excellent posture. I did a lot of running back then. I was so very fast too. There were not many who would dare compete with me. Then came the inevitable changes of time. Time takes away our most precious possessions or renders them nearly useless. I never felt the same again, even with the temporary cure I had found. It just wasn't the same, but for now, it would have to do. I still held hope that during my lifetime, things would change yet again. I awaited the day when all would return to normal. Patience was something I had no choice but to learn I'm afraid. It would be worth it though. Someday, if I survived long enough, I would run again as I once did. Little did I know how precious that gift was when I had it. To be free again. To not have a care in the world. Sweet bliss it was.

I scanned the many houses before me. How in the world would I find the right one? I had to remind myself, like the last time, that instinct would guide me. There were good people out there. I knew that. I kept walking, leaning heavily on the cane in my right hand. My left side always got bad faster than the right side did. I had no idea why. Ignoring the feeling of embarrassment that was creeping up on me, I carried on. I passed three more houses then stopped dead in my tracks. Yes, number 999. This was the place. I had been silly to think I may not find it. It was the stress. Soon, I would be feeling much better, at least for a while.

I walked up to the front door in the dim light of dusk, and rang the bell. I heard movement inside, and then the door was opened by a pretty lady in a blue dress. Her smile was so kind and welcoming that I couldn't help but try to smile back. Some people said I always looked like I was smiling, so really it didn't matter that I just couldn't get my mouth to cooperate.

"Hello," the red haired beauty greeted me. "May I help you?" Her grammar was delightfully perfect.

"Yes, please," I replied. "I have an unusual request, and ask that you please forgive me, but I'm not feeling very well. I've been walking around in these old bones for far too long. I feel as though I may drop."

Her expression turned to one of true concern. "Then you must come in and rest awhile good Sir," she said, opening the door for me.

"Thank you so very kindly dear lady," I responded, stepping slowly inside. As I said, there are good people in the world.

She led me to the front room and then to a large, plush chair. She even offered her arm to assist me to sit. I kindly accepted her help, then leaned back into the chair to catch my breath.

"I'll get you some water," she told me. "Frank?" she called down the hallway. "We have a guest dear."

I heard a gentle male voice answer with, "Alright my dear. I'll be right out."

My hostess told me her name was Angela, and that she'd be right back with my water. I thanked her for her kindness. Angela smiled and then walked off to the kitchen we had passed on our way in.

A moment later, a man in his mid-40's, wearing a grey track suit, approached the front room with a very friendly, "Well, hello there!" He was a wonderfully tall fellow and in good shape. He certainly looked much younger than his years.

"Good evening Sir," I replied. "My name is Bo."

"Nice to meet you Bo. I'm Frank." He reached out to shake my hand, and I complied.

Frank took a seat in a reclining chair, across from me. He was a handsome man with dirty blonde hair, with natural waves, and the rugged good looks of those who spend much of their time in nature.

"Are you a friend of Angela's, Bo?" he asked me politely.

"No Frank. I stopped at your door to ask for a bit of help. I wasn't feeling too well you see. I was telling Angela I've been walking around on these old bones for far too long."

Frank now had the same look of sincere concern on his face that Angela had earlier.

"Oh my," he said. "Is Angela getting you some water? Perhaps you need to hydrate. Many good people fall prey to dehydration at times. It can make one feel quite ill."

I nodded my head in agreement. "Yes it can Frank. It certainly can; and yes thank you, she was kind enough to offer me a glass of water," I replied.

"I bet that will do the trick Bo," Frank said. "However, if you're hungry please do let us know. We've just had dinner and there's plenty of pot roast and vegetables left if you'd like us to make up a plate for you."

I was speechless for a moment. The warmth and generosity I felt from these people, toward me, a complete stranger, was overwhelming. It made things so beautiful and so much harder at the same time.

"Thank you so much Frank," I managed to say. "I will let you know. I appreciate it more than I can say."

Frank smiled. "Not at all friend. The world is a much better place when we're all good to each other."

Once again, I found myself nodding in agreement.

Just then, Angela returned with a glass of water and, bless her soul, a 'bendie' straw. I had such struggles with glasses. It was like she somehow knew.

"Here you are dear," she said, handing me the tall, cool glass with a smile. "I put some ice in it and a slice of lemon, so I thought you may like a straw. I hope that's alright."

I looked up into her pretty green eyes. "It's lovely," I said. "Thank you."

Angela sat on a love seat, next to Frank's chair. I took

a long sip of the cold water. It felt so good. I was a bit parched.

"My name is Bo," I told Angela. "It's a pleasure meeting you and your husband. You're both very nice people. I don't see a lot of that these days."

Angela nodded this time, taking Frank's hand. "I know just what you mean Bo. It's not like it was when I was very young. Those were the good days," she said.

I put my glass of water down on a coaster that was sitting on the end table to my right. Then I looked at them both and said, "Angela, Frank, there is something I must confess."

"Confess?" Frank asked. "Oh now Bo, life can't be that bad can it?"

"I'm afraid it is Frank," I replied.

Angela and Frank both looked concerned again. Other people would have brushed me off, or they would have feared me or thought me mad. Not Angela and Frank though. They really wanted to know what was wrong.

"Go ahead Bo," Angela said. "My mom always used to say 'Nothing ever seems as bad once you tell someone'. What is it?"

Goodness, it was getting more difficult by the second.

"I have a. . . condition, you see. This condition of mine, it tortures me. It's my arms and my legs. These old bones, they're just not working right anymore. It's only going to get worse, I'm afraid. As this is the case, I need to seek out a cure. . . it's only temporary mind you, but it lasts a whole year. It's painful beyond belief, but it works, and while I honestly despise it, I have to keep it up until..." I paused.

"Until what Bo?" Frank asked, with sad eyes.

I looked over at Angela who was already in tears.

"Until the day comes when things will be restored to the way they were before."

"Until the world and the sciences evolve so that there's a permanent cure," said Frank.

"A cure without such pain," Angela added.

I bowed my head for a moment. I felt terrible. They gave me time to gather myself.

"Not evolve," I replied. "Until it devolves."

Angela and Frank looked at each other, then back at me.

"I'm sorry Bo. I'm not sure what you mean," Angela said gently.

I took a deep breath.

"When the world devolves, and it will because humankind never learns from its mistakes, my arms and legs will be healthy and strong, as they were in my youth. I won't need a cure. It will just happen naturally. Then, I won't have to do this anymore."

Frank spoke up then. I could tell by the look on his face that he thought me to be a bit senile, but he was still so respectful. "Well, then you must do what you must do until then," he said, with empathy and not condescension.

"What do you need to do Bo? If you don't mind me asking, of course," Angela added.

I did my very best to explain it to them. The years of suffering, what it was like before my condition, what I needed to ensure a temporary cure, and how and why it really would all be well and joyful again one day. They were speechless. Of course they were, poor things. It was a lot to take in. At one point I was more concerned than usual and asked if they were alright. Angela was crying while Frank held her in his arms. "Let me do it then. Let me help you," he said, kissing his wife on the cheek, then standing up.

Angela slumped down into the love seat. I was almost certain she was in shock.

"My wife is strong, tall, and in good shape, but I'm taller, a little more fit because I'm a runner, and I'm in very good shape," Frank said.

"Yes. Yes you are Frank. Thank you," I answered.

"Let's just get it done quickly Bo please. For Angela's sake, and mine," he asked of me.

"Of course," I replied, standing up, letting the old arms and legs with their old hands and feet drop away from my body, rising to my true height, slipping out of my clothes. I shook my head and my hat, wig, and fake facial hair fell to the floor, along with my tinted glasses. I let the skin peel away, and slithered out of it as well. The itching was gone.

Then, speaking in my true voice I hissed, "Most people don't understand why a snake would want to walk around like a human, but you and Angela do. Evolution took the arms and legs we once so proudly donned and used with both stealth and with great speed, and only devolution can bring them back. Until then, this is the only way I can feel that freedom, and once again be a little closer to what I really am."

With that, I wrapped my body in coils around Frank, but only to stop his breathing; I was careful not to break any bones. Once he had expired, I quickly bit off his arms and legs with my razor sharp teeth. I needed to attach them to my body while they were still fresh, so his flesh would fuse with mine, the way flesh will if you do it just right. They would last me another year, until I had to venture out again, in search of replacements. For now, I just wanted to run home in the cool rain and night air, and in a few minutes, I would.

AND THE LIGHT IS HIS GARMENT
JASPER BARK

This cockroach took a lot longer to die than all the others had. He admired it for that. They shared a kindred spirit. He worked hard to prolong its torment as a fitting tribute to the insect's indomitable will. Its last remaining leg continued to kick defiantly as he peeled off more of its chitonous shell. This was how he knew it was still alive. He always left one leg attached to his victims so he would know they were dead when their leg stopped twitching.

This one's innards were all bared now. There was little left of it except for a tiny piece of outer shell, a sticky yellow interior and that leg, still kicking with determination. He knew exactly how the poor creature felt. They had tried to kill his spirit. Leaving him down here in this dark, dank place. A pathetic attempt to force him to bow before their contemptible delusions. It hadn't worked.

Like the cockroach he was still kicking in defiance. It was the only being with whom he had felt a connection in a very long time.

Soon though there would be nothing of the tiny urge to live left in the creature. Just a collection of dead limbs, fragile wings and brittle antennae. If the miracle of life had ever animated its form he would have crushed all trace of it, stolen whatever divine spark had briefly illuminated it, as though it had never existed.

Looking around his cell, at the huge piles of dismembered cockroaches and the dour resignation etched into his face, it was hard to believe that any divine spark had ever existed.

"I was there at the first fitting you know," said the over dressed courtier. The minor courtiers and even the guards accompanying them looked suitably impressed at this disclosure. "My but they were a sight to behold. No two people who saw the garments could agree on what they looked like. What their style, their colour or even the material was, but every one of us was over awed by them. We all knew they were the finest clothes any human being had ever worn. That was the genius of their construction you see."

The guard who was leading them to the dungeon stopped to unlock a heavy iron gate which was worn with rust. The courtier's party followed him down rough hewn stone steps which curved into a dangerous spiral. A single torch lit their way and they barely saw the carpet of algae at their feet. The courtier continued his lecture.

"They were cut from the raw cloth of our whole kingdom's imagination. Never had an artist, working in any medium, pulled off such a magnificent sleight of hand. Those two tailors had woven the very fabric of our country's faith into that outfit. Our faith in miracles.

"For there, before us all, was truly a miracle. Our beloved Emperor dressed in royal robes of office that were made from nothing but our belief in him and all he stood for. Never had an empire been so inspired and so united by a royal project. The possibilities contained in that parade were infinite. If we as subjects could dress our ruler in nothing but imagination, we could achieve anything. Everything was permissible, nothing was true. We could have re-imagined the world in the likeness of our dreams. We could have relieved mankind from all the ills that ever afflicted it."

The courtiers and guards stopped once again in the tiny, cramped space at the very bottom of the steps, waiting for the head guard to slide all ten bolts on the door before them. They had passed every floor in the dungeon and now entered a narrow corridor deep in its bowels. While the guard extinguished the torch and the minor courtiers lit their candles, the overdressed courtier took the opportunity to bring his lecture to its stern conclusion.

"This was alchemy gentlemen not couture. It was a spell that could have brought about the remaking of the universe. There was nothing our Emperor could not have brought us to believe or inspired us to do at the climax of that most famous parade.

"That is why folk all over the empire still argue about his miraculous new clothes. Why some factions claim that he was dressed in military splendour to lead us to unending victory against the enemies of the Empire. While other factions argue that he wore the simplest of garments to illustrate to us that the true wealth of the Empire lies in the faith of its people not the possessions it accrues or the nations it conquers. And yet another seditious faction of malcontents claim the Emperor wore nothing at all and was naked as the day he was born.

"This is the growing band of dangerous revolutionaries who accused those two divinely inspired tailors of being swindlers and con men. Who have helped to plunge us into this state of crisis, where our Empire is riven with internecine struggle, weakened from within while our enemies mount on every border."

They stopped before a thick wooden door at the end of the narrow corridor. The overdressed courtier raised his candle and the guard pulled back the grill. "One, lone dissenter is responsible for this shameful fall from grace. A single insignificant wretch who broke the tailor's spell with his contemptible ignorance. Who sowed the seeds of doubt and created the division from which we all suffer when he was nothing more than a lowly child. In that one cataclysmic moment he became the most hated creature in the whole empire." The courtiers all jostled forward desperate to catch a glimpse of the infamous prisoner.

"Believers and unbelievers alike know that we lost something precious when we lost that vision of our Emperor. That is why we all loathe him, irrespective of our principles and beliefs. Because he robbed us of something sacred and he must be punished for it.

"Not that we haven't given him ample opportunity to repent. To see the error of his destructive act. To come back into the fold and to help heal the rifts that afflict us.

All in vain though, for he still refuses to admit the truth of what he saw. One word from him and we could flatten the opposition to the throne. They would no longer have a leg to stand on. We could rebuild our unity and return to a time of former innocence and achievement. The empire would be great once more. Even still he continues to defy us, to cleave to his petty reductionist view of what he saw. He refuses to admit the Emperor was clothed. There can be no more reprieves. He must die."

The over dressed courtier turned and looked at the prisoner. It was many years since he'd been an obstinate young boy shouting in the street, but not as many as his appearance suggested. He had finished dismembering the cockroach and as a consequence looked back at the courtier with even more spite than usual. The dim light of the candle flame burned his eyes and made him blink.

The over dressed courtier turned away. "Disappointment," he muttered to no-one in particular. "That's all I feel when I look upon him. One somehow hopes that someone capable of such destruction would appear ... less disappointing."

"Will you be wanting to say a few words to the prisoner m'lord?" the guard asked, as the other courtiers crowded around the door craning their necks.

"No, no," the over dressed courtier waved him away, "I don't think I could find the words to express what I truly want to say, and I'm sure he wouldn't understand me if I could."

Two days later his daily bowl of slops arrived early. It

wasn't anywhere near as rancid as usual and even had cooked meat and vegetables floating in it. That was when he knew they were going to kill him.

The noise of the guards unlocking his cell door startled him. The sound of a key turning in a lock was something he hadn't heard in a decade. He didn't recognise what it was until the door opened.

They had to pad the shackles that they brought because his wrists and ankles were too emaciated to keep them on. His eyes began to ache as they adjusted to the light, like muscles that had almost atrophied through lack of use. He felt as though he was remembering how to use them all over again.

The pure hatred hit him like a blow in the face as he stepped into the courtyard where the gallows were erected. Every bellowing angry face that he saw seethed with enmity. Each curse and rotten piece of fruit, every stone they hurled at him renewed his vigour. His stooped back straightened, he pushed his fallen chest out and soaked up their loathing.

Nothing could have prepared the crowd for what happened next. The rope was around the condemned man's neck, the sentence had been passed and the hangman pulled the lever to open the trap door.

The doors didn't open and the man didn't drop.

The crowd was gripped by a growing feeling of inexplicable hope. Something in the pit of their guts told them the dream they thought lost was returning. Every eye but the condemned man's turned to the apparition that appeared above the scaffold.

No-one saw the exact same vision. One woman, filled with piety, saw an angel, arrayed in vestments of blinding light. A homeless urchin saw the perfect mother he had always dreamed of, whose smile could chase away all his misfortune. A learned scholar of the occult saw a prime being of the celestial sphere descending to the material plane with the knowledge of man's ascension.

When the vision spoke, it spoke in as many voices as there were people to hear it, but everyone heard the same words, or at least the same meaning. "This life is not yours to take," it told them.

"There are greater powers at work here and higher aspirations to fulfill." The apparition bent gracefully down and offered a hand to the condemned man as the whole crowd caught their breath. "Come, your time of suffering is over. Take my hand and step up into perfection. Open yourself to redemption and dream for us all."

The condemned man stared straight ahead over the heads of the crowd without moving. A guard came and nudged him, pointing to the apparition. "Don't you see it?"

For the first time in over a decade he looked up to the sky.

He saw nothing but an empty clear blue expanse.

"See what?" he said with a sneer.

The vision melted from the crowd's view. The trapdoors opened at the condemned man's feet. He would have let out a bitter laugh of triumph, but the rope tightened round his throat and snapped his neck.

For a second everyone froze, unable to accept what they had just seen. Then, with limbs made heavy by dejection, they slunk out of the courtyard. None of them caring to speak, or even catch another's eye.

They knew more had been lost that day than the life

of the man whose body swung at the end of a rope.

"In Great Eternity every particular form gives forth
or emanates
Its own peculiar light, and the form is Divine Vision,
And the light is His garment."

William Blake
Jerusalem, 1804 - 1820

TERRY IN THE BED BY THE WINDOW
LAURA MAURO

"Fair warning," the senior nurse tells Dolores, concluding her handover of the ward to the night staff. "Mr Westwater's bloods aren't looking good, and his blood pressure's been dropping steadily since this morning. Don't be too surprised if he pops his clogs before your shift's up."

"Again?" Toyin kisses her teeth. Dolores is fascinated by her accent: two-fifths Nigerian, the rest pure Bow bells Cockney. "He's been dying on and off for two months now. Trust me, that man isn't going anywhere tonight."

Dolores' mouth creases into a tiny smile. Terence Westwater has occupied the bed by the window since he arrived in February. In those two months, he has not spoken a single word. This doesn't trouble Dolores – nonverbal patients are not unusual on Sycamore Ward.

No, what's frustrating about Terence Westwater is that nobody knows anything about him.

Terence Westwater – 'Terry', as the staff have dubbed him – is what the Americans would call a 'John Doe'. Nobody knows how old Terry is. Nobody knows anything much about him. Entirely nonverbal and barely mobile, he was found sitting in the atrium over at Guy's Hospital, alone and confused, with only a brown leather wallet and a dogeared paperback titled 'Greek Myths and Legends' tucked into the inside pocket of his jacket. Inside the wallet was a receipt from a Happy Shopper in Eastbourne, a Murray Mint wrapper and a membership card for a now-defunct library in Southwark bearing the name 'Terence F. Westwater'. Nobody is certain that this is his real name, and police investigations haven't turned up anything remotely helpful so far.

"Seriously," Toyin says, brow furrowed. She flips through the latest batch of blood results. "Look at these. Remember the last time he was dying? Beginning of March? These look healthy in comparison."

"His Hb is 7," Patricia – the senior nurse – replies. Her uniform is crumpled. Wild strands of hair have come loose from the tight bun atop her head, sticking out like copper wires. Dolores knows she would have arrived for her shift looking immaculate, but she is one of only two qualified nurses caring for eighteen elderly patients, and her ragged appearance speaks volumes.

"Right, and last time it was 5. If he didn't die then, he's not dying now. Take my word for it." Toyin grabs a stack of green patient files. The cardboard is frayed at the edges, filled to the brim with papers and dividers. Most of their patients are frequent visitors; at their age, the body begins to shut down, system by system. There's an observable domino effect: chronic kidney disease begets cardiovascular disease. Perhaps they'll have a stroke. The resulting immobility will cause pressure ulcers; catheterisation increases the risk of urinary tract infection. Care of the elderly, Dolores thinks, is a never-ending firefight. Defeat is inevitable. The geriatricians and nurses are merely there to keep the blaze in check for as long as they can.

"He's tough as old boots," Toyin says. Her grin is impish, her dark eyes alight with impudence. Dolores knows Toyin is fond of Terry; she can talk at him as long as she wants and he never interrupts, just listens, gazing at her with eyes the colour of old denim. "Terry Westwater is going to outlive all of us."

"Maybe he will," Patricia says, watching Toyin go. Her mascara is flaking, a peppering of black in the concavities beneath her eyes. "I can't make any sense of him. He circles the drain for a few days, then perks right back up again. Almost overnight, it seems." She shakes her head. "Well. Hope it's a quiet night for you, Dolores. You've only got two HCAs on, and Doctor Matthews went for dinner two hours ago, so Christ only knows where he might be. Oh, and good luck with Mr Flannery."

Dolores frowns. "Is he deteriorating too?"

"No, no, he's hale and hearty. It's just that he needs repeat bloods, and he won't let anyone with a hint of a tan near him with a needle." Patricia gives Dolores a pointed look, indicating the dark olive of her Filipina skin. Mr Flannery is ninety two years old and thinks the black nurses are trying to eat him. He also thinks Dolores is Chinese, which is about as good as she's likely to get from him. "Always fun and games on Sycamore Ward, eh? See you tomorrow, Dolores."

The night shift on Sycamore Ward, once relatives have gone home, is reasonably quiet. The patients mostly sleep through the night, occasionally calling for assistance if they need to use the commode. It gives Dolores time to deal with the mountains of paperwork the day staff are too busy to attend to.

From her seat at the nurses' station the unlit corridors look almost endless. Some nurses find the darkness and isolation creepy, but to Dolores it's peaceful. As if the rest of the world has ceased to exist, if only for a while. The ward makes strange music at night; the rhythmic hiss of laboured breathing, beeping heart monitors so monotonous they fade into white noise after a time. The healthcare assistants murmuring in the office, just low enough that she can't hear what they're saying. You can actually converse with patients at night, if they're not sleeping. You can ask them how they're feeling and have the time to listen to their answers. You can crack jokes and give comfort. You have the luxury of time.

Somewhere on the ward, somebody is crying.

Dolores gets up. Her chair creaks; she winces at the sudden sound. The old linoleum is always sticky beneath her trainers, though the cleaners buff the floor at least once a fortnight. Sycamore Ward looks perpetually shabby; the faded yellow walls – probably once intended to evoke sunshine and warmth - are the hue of nicotine-stained teeth.

The crying is coming from bay three. A couple of the patients have their curtains drawn for privacy; paper-thin cloth hangs ghostly from the rail, fluttering as she moves past. To her left, Mr Chen is dozing with his mouth open. Spittle glimmers in the ditch of his chin. Dolores tilts her head, listening for the sound.

At the far end of the bay is a window. Terry Westwater's bed is beside it, half-obscured by the drawn curtain around Mr Azzopardi's bed. And inside that curtain, growing fainter as she approaches, comes a series of low, choking sobs. It's the sound of one who has cried out all of their sorrow and is left only with the dregs rattling around inside of them.

Sometimes, in the still, quiet hours after midnight, a profound loneliness sets in. Patients have abundant time to lie awake and alone in a strange bed, the smell of disinfectant barely enough to mask the pervasive undertone of decay, and their thoughts turn to death: the inevitability of it, the way it lurks at the foot of every bed. Sometimes, all Dolores can do is hold hands and whisper reassurances she does not really believe. Those nights are especially difficult.

"Mr Azzopardi?" Dolores pauses outside the curtain, fingers brushing the fabric. Inside, there is only the wet rattle of breath, the slight creak of plastic as someone shifts in the bedside chair. "It's Dolores. May I come in?" There is no answer to the contrary, so she slips through the gap in the curtain, sidling past the bedside table. "Mr…"

From the chair beside the bed, Terry Westwater's startlingly sharp blue eyes stare up at her.

Dolores' heart lurches. She swallows down the

exclamation before it emerges from her mouth. Her instinct is to call for Toyin – or, even more absurd, to grab her phone and take a photograph. In the two months he has been here, Terry Westwater has never once left his bed. He does not talk, or move, or communicate at all. He's spoon-fed, sponge-bathed, utterly dependent on nurse care. He is - as Patricia would say, always out of patient earshot - one step above a vegetable.

And yet here he is, sitting at Mr Azzopardi's bedside – sitting *upright* - looking expectantly at Dolores as though he knows exactly why she's here. Was it him crying? His eyes are wet, but they often are. Perhaps he heard Mr Azzopardi crying and came to offer comfort. Dolores isn't certain that level of comprehension is even within Terry's capabilities. If someone had asked her only ten minutes ago, she might have answered with a kind but emphatic: "No, probably not."

"Hello Terry," she says, the barest quiver evident in her voice. "How long have you been up and about?"

No answer. Terry's gaze falls from Dolores to Mr Azzopardi, settling on the other's man's face with placid interest. Terry's bony hands are folded in his lap, shoulders thin and hunched, listing gently but definitely to the left; it's as though there is nothing beneath those blue-striped pyjamas but a hollow wire frame, and inside that a clockwork heart tick-stuttering its way towards the inevitable.

She turns to Mr Azzopardi. His eyes are closed, his lips slightly parted. He might be asleep, she thinks, but something in Terry's gaze – in his presence – makes her uneasy. Like he knows something she doesn't. "Are you all right, Mr Azzopardi?" she asks, placing a tentative hand on his shoulder. "I heard you crying. Mr Azzopardi? Francis?" Gently, she shakes him. He's slack, pliable; his skin is the clammy consistency of clay.

Her stomach drops. She fumbles for the crash call button with her free hand, pressing it over and over. She can hear the shrill corresponding beep from the nurse's station and, a heartbeat later, the thunder of Toyin's feet as she heads into the bay. Dolores pries open Mr Azzopardi's mouth with a finger, checking his airway for obstruction. The warmth of his breath is conspicuously absent against her skin.

Toyin's reassuring bulk materialises at Dolores' side. "Mr Azzopardi," she says, loud and authoritative, as though she can simply talk him back to consciousness. "Francis, can you hear me?" Her vast hands are a whirlwind of efficiency; she checks his pulse, shakes her head, threads her fingers together and begins chest compressions. The violence of her motion is faintly alarming, but Dolores understands it is necessary. Better a few broken ribs than a dead patient. "Where the hell is Doctor Matthews?" Toyin mutters, looking up at Dolores for the first time since bursting through the curtain.

It is then that she notices Terry.

"Jesus." And then, still pumping away at Mr Azzopardi's chest: "He needs to go."

"I don't think he can," Dolores says. Terry is looking at the water jug on the bedside cabinet, blinking with an almost bovine calm. "I'm not even sure how he got here."

"Oh, Terry, Terry," Toyin says, with no small amount of frustration. She's a little breathless; her great dark hands are a surrogate heart, but they can't keep beating forever. "You couldn't have picked a worse time, darling, honest to god. Where is Doctor Matthews? What is he being paid for, to sit on his backside watching YouTube?"

"I can go…"

"I need you here," Toyin says. She pauses briefly, reaching out to check Mr Azzopardi's pulse. "Still nothing," she says. "Take over, Dolores, I'm going to…"

At that moment, a red-faced Doctor Matthews bursts through the curtain, accompanied by Doctor Mehta, the junior registrar, pushing the resuscitation trolley. "What's he doing here?" he demands, pointing a fat finger at Terry. "Nurse Ayinde, resume compressions. Nurse Ocampo, take this patient back to his bed."

She knows better than to argue with a doctor. "Come on, Terry," she says, affecting a bright tone despite the increasingly hopeless scene unfolding behind her: Toyin breathlessly counting compressions and the wet, invasive sounds of intubation. She holds out a hand to him, expecting nothing, but his hand slowly rises from his lap, an almost automatic motion. His skin is dry, loose; it feels as though it might slough straight off the bone if she pulls too hard. "Back to bed now," she says, closing her fingers gently around Terry's arthritic knuckles. She isn't certain he'll be able to stand without assistance, let alone walk, but after a moment he rises, the dream-slow motion of a sleepwalker. She parts the curtain and they walk, step by ponderous step, back to the bed. As they move, Dolores observes the slow certainty of Terry's motion, the way his limbs hold him perfectly upright – still tilted to the left, the lopsided keel of a long-beached ship – she is scarcely able to believe that this man has not left his bed in two months.

Francis Azzopardi is declared dead at 3.25am. The decision is made to call his family first thing in the morning. His death is entirely unexpected; Mr Azzopardi was initially admitted for a bout of pneumonia but had been improving in leaps and bounds. There'd been talk of discharging him in the next few days.

From her seat at the nurse's station Dolores can see Terry, lying awake and silent. Occasionally, he turns his head, staring at the now-empty bed beside him as though he is completely aware of what transpired tonight. Beneath the jittery dregs of adrenaline lies a deep, uneasy guilt, heavy as grease in her gut. Dolores and her colleagues have all assumed that Terry has no real comprehension of the world around him, that his aphasia and persistent lack of response are absolutely indicative of a silence inside his skull. But he knew, somehow, before anyone else did, that Mr Azzopardi was dying.

"I hate surprises," Toyin says, perching on the edge of the desk. Her eyes are heavy-lidded, her shoulders slack. She rubs at her face with one dry palm.

"I think Terry knew," Dolores says.

"I don't know what to think," Toyin replies. Across the ward, the pale pre-dawn light turns the walls the dull yellow of ancient bones. "I didn't even know he could walk. Did you think, in all the time we've been taking care of him – did you *once* think that he was really listening? Because Dolores, let me tell you, I talk to Terry all the time and I swear, it's exactly like talking to an empty bed."

"Maybe he just isn't interested in hearing you go on about last night's *Hollyoaks*."

Toyin smiles. "Doctor Mehta told me this isn't the first

337

time Terry has gone wandering. He told me that Venetia – you know Venetia, the little fat one with the cornrows? – well, she said she found Terry wandering over in bay one the night Mr Bakshi died. Just walking around, like he was taking in the scenery. Weird, isn't it? Makes you wonder if he's got a sixth sense or something."

Dolores picks out a poorly photocopied Adverse Incident form, scanning the page for the 'Unexpected Death' tick box. They were supposed to have gone paperless months ago. Nothing ever works the way it ought to in the NHS, she thinks, a little ruefully. "What was Mr Bakshi in for?"

"I'm not sure. Cancer, I think? I was never really involved in his treatment. Anyway, the point is, Terry needs another neuropsychological assessment. They must have missed something the first time around."

She thinks of Terry's eyes, the utter clarity in the way he'd looked at her – *go on then, help him* – and the way he rose to his feet at the touch of her hand. He understood everything. She's certain of it.

"Maybe we all missed it," Dolores says.

She stays on past the end of her shift to review the night's events with Patricia and the day shift team. In the light of day, Terry Westwater looks the same as he ever has: crepe-paper skin draped over sharp bones. His hands rest one atop the other on his abdomen, skin pulled tight across the knuckles, giving the illusion of an almost youthful smoothness. He stares dully out of the window. His bed boasts a view of the Thames that even nearby hotels would envy, but the bleached skeleton of the London Eye revolving slowly against the sky might as well be a brick wall for all the attention he pays to it. He looks the same as he ever has, but something is different. She can't qualify this; it's a vague, insubstantial feeling, an instinct, almost, but she *knows*, as sure as she knows that Mr Chen's renal cancer will never get better, that Terry Westwater has changed on some imperceptible level.

Mr Azzopardi's test results and vital signs were all indicative of a man almost fully recovered. His sudden, almost instantaneous decline is baffling. Doctor Matthews is at a loss as to how to explain it to the Adverse Incident panel. A post-mortem is being performed, a tox screen run. His family are in turns distraught and furious, and it is only Patricia's dogged professionalism that has kept Dolores from having to face their questioning in person. Nobody is blaming her. That, at least, is a relief.

At 9am Dolores washes her face in the on-call bathroom. Her cheeks are flushed; pink apples in the round, dark moon of her face. She loosens her tight ponytail. Her scalp aches from the pressure, throbbing faintly as her hair settles over her shoulders. She squeezes a little cocoa butter into the hollow of one palm, rubs it methodically into her hands; fingers first, then thumb, sweeping over the knuckles and down, blue veins bulging over ridged metacarpals like a road map in bas relief. Even in her civilian clothes she feels bound to the hospital, as though she gave a part of herself away when she signed her contract. Her life outside the hospital is a work in progress: she has a few friends, a circle of fellow Filipino migrants, helping one another negotiate culture shock and language barriers. She'd like to meet others, though. Maybe a boyfriend, if she's lucky enough, although it's difficult with the hours she works. But she's still young. She's got time.

She passes Patricia on the way out. "Hey, here's a bit of good news," Patricia says. "Mr Westwater's blood pressure has stabilised. I'm sending some bloods off. With any luck they'll have improved too. There's life in the old dog yet." She shakes her head, but her pink-painted mouth is upturned. "He's a proper mystery, isn't he?"

Dolores looks over into bay three, past the vacant bed. Terry's face is turned towards the nurse's station, cheek pressed against his pillow, sparse hair cloud-wispy against his skull. His body looks crumpled, as if someone cut his strings and left him where he fell. His hands are limp at his sides, swollen phalanges curled into ineffectual claws. In the immediate aftermath of Mr Azzopardi's death she had wondered about those hands, but now she's almost certain that they could not grip a pillow, couldn't hold it down hard enough to end a man's life. As she stares, his eyes flicker open, and for a second she is certain he is looking right at her, pale eyes sharp and focused. A shudder runs the length of her spine. For the life of her, she cannot explain why.

That night – barely rested from her last shift, feeling as crumpled as her uniform looks – Dolores seeks out Doctor Mehta. He is sitting in the on-call room, scanning yesterday's copy of *South London Press*. He's wearing blue theatre scrubs, suggesting some kind of body fluid-related disaster.

"Doctor Mehta," Dolores says. "Do you have a minute?"

"Hello, Dolores," he says. It's only Doctor Matthews who insists on calling all the nurses by their surnames. Mehta is far more relaxed, a prematurely balding and somewhat eccentric little man with a paunch as round and tight as a football tucked up his shirt. "Sit down, if you like. Although if it's about Francis Azzopardi, I'm afraid the post-mortem hasn't been reported on yet."

"Actually, I wanted to ask you about Mr Bakshi."

"Mr Bakshi?" Doctor Mehta lowers his newspaper. A gold wedding band bisects his left ring finger, cutting tight into the flesh. "He died about a month ago. Nice man. Huge family, always brought far too much food. What did you want to know about him?"

She feels foolish. She tucks her hands behind her back, tugging at her own fingers just to have something to do. *It's just curiosity*, she tells herself, though the nervous lump in her throat makes the lie plain. *It doesn't mean anything.*

"How was he doing, the night he died?" Dolores asks. "Did you think he was declining?"

"Well, honestly, no." Doctor Mehta's forehead furrows as he thinks back, casting his eyes up to the ceiling. "He'd been brought in for dehydration – he had throat cancer, you see, and although we'd recently put in an oesophageal stent he'd been finding it difficult to swallow. He was weak to begin with, and his U&E's were initially pretty poor, but he picked up fairly quickly. We were all set to discharge him, actually."

Dolores' mouth tightens. Her fingers ache from wringing them. "Venetia said she saw Terence Westwater wandering in the bay that night."

Doctor Mehta's dark little eyes light up. In his sudden enthusiasm he almost leaps out of his seat, turning fully so his entire body is facing Dolores. His scrub top strains against his big round belly. "I read a story on the Internet once about a cat in an old people's home that correctly predicted the deaths of about 50 patients. It would curl up next to them and go to sleep, and the next day that person would be dead. I'm not saying that Mr Westwater is like the Death Cat, but…" he shrugs, perhaps a little embarrassed by his decidedly unscientific outburst. "Well, all kinds of funny things happen in the world, don't they?"

When she gets back to the nurse's station she finds Toyin taking inventory in the stock cupboard. A little further down, a HCA is doing the rounds with the dinner trolley. Mr Flannery is sitting bolt upright in his bed, shovelling gloopy orange pasta bake into his open mouth. The motion of his arms is robotic, a drumming monkey wielding a plastic spoon. Terry Westwater's tray sits on his meal table, untouched. He is staring at it with listless disinterest. *Someone ought to feed him*, she thinks, before realising that this is an experiment of sorts: they are waiting to see if Terry will feed himself.

Dolores takes a seat. The chair whines beneath her. Under the lip of the desk is a stack of Doctor Mehta's papers. Quietly, she slides them towards her, lifting the first two pages with the tip of her fingernail. They are the discharge papers for a Mr Gabriel Reyes, who is currently resident in bay four. He is being scheduled for release at nine AM tomorrow, pending final consultant review.

"Toyin," Dolores calls. "Are we overseeing bay four tonight?"

Toyin leans out of the stock cupboard, arms full of

urine test pots. "We're on three, four and five," she says. "Kamali's team are on one, two and isolation. Why? Is anything wrong?"

"Oh, no," Dolores says, affecting as casual a smile as she can. "Just making sure I've got my paperwork straight, that's all."

———————————————————

She waits.

Midnight arrives unseen and unannounced. The strange, ambient calm of the night shift settles in like snowfall, coating the entire ward in a layer of muffled sound and slow, languid movement. The sound of Nat King Cole bleeds out of Mr Chen's headphones, just audible above the murmured chorus of snoring and respirator masks. A strip light flickers overhead. Toyin's trainers squeak as she walks, performing endless, restless rounds. There will be no more surprises on her watch.

At one-thirty AM, Toyin goes for a nap, leaving Dolores in sole charge of three bays. Without Toyin's perpetual motion in her peripheral vision Dolores' world is reduced to a desk, the stack of papers upon it, and the bay just beyond.

Just after two AM, she notices a stirring in the distant part of her vision. Something is moving in bay three. Her instinct is to look up, but she resists. She continues filling in forms, handwriting becoming increasingly scrawled as the night wears on. Her left hand is smudged with black ink from her burst biro, a Rorschach blot without form. Bare feet pass by, tacky on the linoleum, the lethargic shuffle of the living dead. The breath is static in her lungs as she waits, pen poised, chest aching with the need to exhale.

At last, the footsteps diminish. Dolores peeks up. There is a brief flash of hospital pyjamas as someone disappears into bay four. She exhales as evenly as she can, placing her pen on the desk, placing her feet flat on the ground, drawing each motion out for as long as she's able. She has to time this right: too soon, and she'll prove nothing. Too late…well, she can't allow that to happen.

Her fingers rise to her pocket. The slender outline of the Lorazepam syringe is reassuring and nauseating in equal measure. Questions will be asked, and she's not certain how she's going to explain herself.

From bay four comes the hiss of a curtain being pulled aside. Dolores checks over her shoulder: the HCAs are attending to a patient in the isolation room, Toyin is still napping and Doctor Mehta is nowhere to be seen. She rises very slowly. The chair is almost silent. She moves very carefully, each step almost comically deliberate, a cartoon burglar in the dead of night. Her heartbeat seems to resonate through the entirety of her ribcage. She's half-convinced the rattle of it is audible.

A sudden, muted cry rings out from inside bay four. Before she knows it she's running, barrelling into the bay, arms outstretched, shoving aside the curtains around Mr Reyes' bed. And there, sitting on the bed beside Mr Reyes, is Terry Westwater. His fingers are wrapped tightly around Mr Reyes' wrist; the veins are horribly distended, skin pulled taut over each blue, pulsating cable.

"Terry," Dolores says, voice miraculously calm, refusing to betray her fear. "I know what's happening. What you've been doing. You have to stop, Terry, do you understand?"

Terry's grip tightens. The wild pulsation of his veins increases; it looks as though there is something trapped beneath his skin, something alive and desperate for release. There's a bright, terrified spark in his eyes, an obvious panic. Beside him, Mr Reyes' olive skin is turning sallow, his eyelids drooping. A lone tear rolls down his cheek.

"Please, Terry," she says. "I know you're scared. Nobody wants to die, but we can do this another way. You're hurting Mr Reyes, Terry." She begins a mental countdown, slow, because she doesn't want to have to use the Lorazepam, but he's not moving away, and Mr Reyes' chest is barely moving now. *Seven, six, five.* "Come on," she says, raising a hand, extending her fingers. "Go back to bed, Terry. Let's talk about it in the morning. We'll come up with a treatment plan." *Four, three.* "I'm here to help you. You know that."

Two.

"Please." Eyes fixed on Terry's even as her fingers slide into her pocket, closing around the barrel of the syringe. She flicks off the cap with her thumb. He does not budge. His forehead glimmers with sweat.

One.

Dolores lunges, hating herself as she readies the syringe. She aims for the scant meat of his thigh, and she almost makes it. She is millimetres from driving the needle home when he lets go, grabbing her wrist with his free hand. His fingers are tight against her skin; he's shockingly warm. Dolores has a moment to register surprise – *how can he move so damn fast?* - when the entire world pitches sideways. Suddenly she's on the bed, hands scrabbling for purchase, and she can see everything. All of it, playing inside of her head with the clarity and focus of an HD movie. Terry's life. Terry's *lives:* hundreds of years, through war and peace and the smog-thick streets of the Industrial Revolution; she can feel the sun burning the back of her neck as she surveys the bright red jackets and white pith helmets of the Boer War. A wife, somewhere along the way, pale blonde braid and ruddy, smiling cheeks. Her heart bursts with joy at the weight of a child in her arms; it's so real, so vivid that for a moment she forgets this is Terry's life she's living, all one hundred and fifty plus years of it condensed into sixty long seconds.

She wonders if he can see her life too, all twenty-four years of it: *the thick monsoon heat of Valenzuela, sweat dripping down the back of her dress in church; unrelenting drizzle pounding the plane windows as she lands at Heathrow, swallowing down fearful anticipation of this strange new place; lying awake in the early hours, listening to the tinny clatter of passing trains on their way to London Bridge, realising that this is no longer alien but comforting, a soothing certainty.*

Her heartbeat slows. She can't move her legs, feel her toes. She's dimly aware of Mr Reyes' legs trapped beneath her spine, the quiet, distant sound of her own cries. When the pictures cease at last she looks up at Terry, only he's not there anymore. There is a tall, unbent stranger, thick black hair and smooth, unweathered skin. Eyes a bright and beautiful blue.

His grip loosens. She longs for the heat of his skin. For the vibrant colour of his life, played out again and again, a theatre of second chances. Is this his third? His fourth? Her mind is fuzzy. She's no longer sure. She's not sure of anything.

"I'm sorry," he says, voice rough despite his newly-restored larynx. "I really am."

As Dolores lays there, the last dregs of her life draining out into Terry's plump, straight fingers – as he pulls away, pushing through the curtains, a young man in a faded hospital gown, passing through the blissful quiet of the ward – she almost believes him.

THREE SISTERS
SAM STONE

*"They met me in the day of success: and I have
learned by the perfect'st report, they have more in
them than mortal knowledge."*

William Shakespeare, *Macbeth*

"I'm sorry we can't be much help," said Cara. "My sisters
and I all suffer from a rare visual disorder. It may appear
that we can see, but most of our vision is tunnel."

"I'm sorry to hear that," said Inspector Philip Peak.

"It's a form of Glaucoma," said Angela. "It's inherent
in our case. Peripheral vision is something that none of us
has."

"Especially if we are all facing forward," added Elise.

"Yes, I understand." Peak said.

The three sisters lived next door to the victim. They

were similar in looks and, in their own way, were all very beautiful women. Peak couldn't remember the last time he had met women like this. It didn't happen often in his line of work. They were well turned out in smart suits. Hair groomed, faces subtly made up but naturally attractive.

Cara was the most beautiful: her hair was lighter red than the other two and she had one pale white streak running through the front. He had thought she was the eldest of the three and then it came out so casually that they were, in fact, maternal triplets. Of course this meant they weren't identical but Peak could see the similarities even more once he knew. Angela's hair was a few inches shorter than Cara's and Elise's was the darkest red of them all: a pure, dark auburn. If you put them side by side, like a colour chart they demonstrated light, medium and dark, and this extended to their skin tone as well.

They were odd though. Peak noticed that they had a strange way of speaking, as though they were always continuing each other's sentences, and it made him feel slightly unnerved.

At that moment a loud barking noise came from the house of the victim. Peak had already determined that the dog was a Spaniel and that it hadn't stopped barking since the police broke in and found its owner's body. Unfortunately, the dog was so worked up that none of them had been able to get near the corpse to examine it for fear of being bitten.

Cara cringed when she heard the sound.

"We have very acute hearing," said Angela.

"Which makes loud noises most unpleasant for us," Elise continued.

"Constant barking is torture," Cara said.

Peak nodded. "Not long now and the handler will take the animal away. Did your neighbour have any relatives?"

The triplets didn't answer because at that moment the animal rescue van arrived. Peak couldn't help but notice how the three sisters turned their heads in unison, like a reflex, to look out of the window of their lounge as Mark Daniels jumped from the car. They stared at him down the tunnel of their vision, classically beautiful faces completely blank. Peak was reminded of something he had read or seen somewhere. A similar image of three goddess statues floated in his mind, but he couldn't quite form the image, or remember where it came from.

"I had better go and speak to him," Peak said.

At the front door his eyes fell on a clear glass bowl. It was full of strange charms on rings, bracelets and key rings. One of the key rings had a pentagram attached that contained a small clear stone at its heart.

"A blood stone," Cara said. "Superstition has it as being used in a ritual for binding someone to an unbreakable promise."

"We research into the paranormal at the university," Angela said.

"Some people believe very strange things," finished Elise.

"Hey Phil," said Daniels as Peak came out of the house.

"Mark," Peak nodded. "The dog is still inside there."

"Spaniel?" Daniels asked.

"Yeah. Nasty little beggar to be honest."

Peak pulled Daniels closer to the door to be out of earshot from the sisters.

"So what's the situation?" Daniels said.

"Looks like the owner died and the dog has been chowing down on the body. It's fairly ugly in there. According to the neighbours the dog has been barking non-stop for the last few days. That's why they alerted us."

"Okay. Leave it to me," Daniels said.

Daniels went inside and more loud barking ensued. Peak glanced at the sisters. All of them, particularly Cara, appeared to be in a great deal of pain. The women huddled together as though this were the most terrible sound they had ever heard. Then the dog yelped. Cara jumped, Angela and Elise jumped a fraction of a second behind her. Then all three sighed as the dog was silenced.

Daniels came out a few minutes later carrying the animal.

"Had to drug it. Too far gone."

Peak nodded. He knew then that even if there were relatives this dog could not be housed now. There was only one place it was going and that was straight to the vet to be put out of its misery. But of course there were procedures to be followed first, it was never that simple and they would have to find out more about the victim anyway. Whether there were relatives or dependents, that sort of thing.

Peak's forensic team entered the house. He glanced back at the triplets and saw they were watching Mark load the dog into the van. They were all smiling. Peak had never seen such a change in demeanour in a matter of seconds. They appeared to be relieved and, for the first time since he met them, relaxed.

I guess that dog really was annoying, he thought.

Cara turned her head to look at him a fraction of a

second before the other two. It was strange how they did that. As if they received some kind of subliminal message from each other. Peak nodded, Cara gave him a beautiful smile. She had perfect teeth, and her green eyes were slightly brighter than her sisters'. The other women just stared. Then, the three sisters turned and went back into their house.

Peak noted how the victim was the opposite of the young and pretty women she lived next door to. This woman was overweight and in her fifties. She was wearing a bright fuchsia top and three quarter leggings that would have done nothing to flatter her extreme curves. Sports clothing, worn by someone who clearly didn't look after herself, was always something Peak had thought was paradoxical.

She was lying on her front, bare calves facing upwards and this is where the dog had fed from the most. It was as though the bloated flesh had been a tasty morsel. Peak felt sick, but tried to hide it from the forensic doctor and the other police officers. Squeamishness was something that soon got around in the station, and he couldn't bear the thought of being the brunt of all of those dead body jokes. He detached himself from the thought that this had once been a human. The bruised, torn flesh around the calves looked like overripe tomatoes that had burst as they rotted. The dog had worried at her forearm too, biting through the ugly top and ripping into the podgy skin beneath. Peak's eyes travelled upwards. Her face was turned towards him. There was a thick black bruise and a smear of blood on her forehead.

"Looks like she fell and couldn't get up again,"

Doctor Shaw said. "May have knocked herself out. Awful way to go."

Peak agreed. It was a terrible thing to turn into your own dog's dinner. He hoped that she had been dead before the meal started.

They took photos – not that Peak would ever have trouble remembering the details of this one – and Shaw took the temperature of the corpse and checked the flexibility of its limbs and the pooling of the blood in the lowest regions.

"Three days is my guess," Shaw said.

"That fits in with the length of time the dog was barking," Peak said. "Must have driven the neighbours crazy."

Peak went outside. He looked around the back, checking the windows and doors. It was all routine though because this case was going to close for certain with the conclusion that the victim had fallen and died. There was no evidence to say it was any more sinister than that. He found a window open in the downstairs bathroom, but it was so tiny that he couldn't imagine anyone being able to pass through it. Even so, he took some photographs for later reference.

Then he saw the neighbour on the other side waving over the fence at him. She was a black woman in her sixties. Smart, well-turned out. Sophisticated. This was obviously a nice neighbourhood. The kind his wife aspired to. He glanced at the back door of the victim's house. He couldn't imagine the dead woman fitting in here at all.

"Hello," he said.

"Can I make you officers some tea?"

"That's very kind of you, but what I'd really like is to

ask you some questions."

The woman nodded, "Of course, officer. Please come round."

The front door was open when he reached it and the woman waited for him.

"Margaret Beech. Pleased to meet you Inspector Peak. Do come in," she said.

Peak wasn't too surprised that she knew his name already. Anyone that he had spoken to so far could have told her.

Margaret led him into the kitchen. It wasn't dissimilar to the victim's but somehow it had more taste.

"This is a respectable neighbourhood," Margaret said. "Janice wasn't one of us, but I'm sorry about what has happened. No one deserves that."

"Deserves what?" asked Peak.

"I heard one of your men saying that the dog …"

Peak let the sentence hang in the air but didn't confirm Margaret's suspicions.

"Can you tell me a little about her?" he asked instead.

"She was fairly friendly when she moved in. But it became evident almost immediately that she wasn't our sort."

"What do you mean?"

"Well her friends for a start. All that coming and going on motorbikes and the cars arriving at all hours. Then the dog of course. She frequently left it locked in there for hours on end and it barked endlessly."

"I see," said Peak. "Did any of the neighbours complain?"

"Of course we all 'had a word' with her at some time or other. But she never did anything about it. I felt sorry for the sisters the most. The stress really got to Cara in particular. They are such nice girls too. No trouble at all."

"They fit in the neighbourhood well then?" Peak said, but it was a rhetorical question and so Margaret didn't answer.

Peak learned then about the petition, the complaints to the council and how Janice still refused to accept that there was a problem.

"To be fair we don't understand why she even moved here. Perhaps her previous neighbours had the same grievance. Anyway, it suddenly went quiet and so we thought she had finally seen sense. That was until the dog started to bark again."

"Do you know anyone who would harm Janice?" Peak asked. Because a barking dog surely wasn't a good enough reason.

"No," said Margaret. "I really know nothing about her private life."

He returned to Janice's house and began to look again at the mess in the kitchen.

"Could she have been beaten with something?" he asked the coroner.

"Not really. Look here. There was a little bit of grease under her foot. And at this angle it was obvious she skidded and fell, hitting her head on the worktop. Here's the trace of blood." The coroner swabbed the blood, adding the sample on a cotton bud to a long thin tube. He pressed a stopper over the top and added the evidence to his bag. "My report will definitely be saying this was a freak accident."

Peak nodded. It seemed so cut and dried and yet he was concerned that he had missed something that might be noticed later on.

Outside Peak admired the street of perfect houses with perfect gardens. Expensive cars in driveways. The men and women he had seen had looked and acted like respectable professionals. It reminded him of an old horror film he had once seen, *The Stepford Wives*, but was that in itself a bad thing?

"Hello, Inspector."

Peak turned to see Cara standing at the front door of her house. The perfectly painted door was surrounded by an arch with creeping vines. She had changed her clothes. The formal suit was gone and she was now wearing a pure white summer dress. Her red hair cascaded over her shoulders, while a crown of daisies adorned her head. She looked like a bride.

"You will have a very successful career," Cara said.

At that moment the sun came out from behind a cloud and hit Peak in the eyes. He squinted. Then looked back at Cara, only to find Angela standing in her place. She seemed to be wearing the same dress as Cara had worn but the flowers in her hair were dandelions, and not daisies.

"A promotion will come your way," Angela smiled.

Peak rubbed his eyes.

"And you will move successfully into the right neighbourhood," Elise nodded her buttercup-crowned head.

Peak blinked. The girls were playing some kind of trick on him. He didn't know why but he found it strangely arousing. He stepped away from the victim's door and towards the three sisters' house.

"We're done now," said the coroner as he led the trolley carrying the corpse out. Janice was already zipped in a body bag.

Peak felt strange. It was as though he were in some kind of crime movie where the crime had already been solved, but the Inspector didn't realise it.

The promotion letter was on his desk when he returned to his office. *Congratulations, Chief Inspector*, it read. He hadn't been expecting it, had thought any further advancement in his career wouldn't happen now, and so his thoughts turned back to the three sisters. They were weird, beautiful, magical – but could they really know the future?

Peak looked at the letter again. He didn't know how this miracle had occurred. It wasn't through hard work. In fact a lot of his recent cases had solved themselves. Like the one with Janice Bailey that day.

His phone rang beside him.

"Darling, our dream house has come on the market!" his wife's voice was brimming with excitement. "Will you come to see it with me tonight?"

"Yes," said Peak. "I've some news too. I've been promoted."

"This is our lucky day. It's meant to be."

"Where is the house?" he asked.

"That neighbourhood we always admired. It's full of professionals, decent sophisticated people. There's no chain, it's at a ridiculously low price, and it's ours for the taking if we want it …"

Peak hung up on Cassie and smiled. Could it be that this was all luck? Or did the sisters truly deliver on their promise when he visited them a few nights ago. The memory of their door opening, Cara waiting for him in a darkened room, all flashed behind his eyes. Somehow he had forgotten being there until now.

Time to go home.

He reached for his keys. The smile slipped from Peak's face. A pentagram with a red stone in the centre hung from his key chain.

Then Peak remembered it all: particularly slamming Janice's face down on the corner of the work top; smearing cooking grease onto the tiled floor and the bottom of her shoe; letting the dog in.

He was going to get everything he wanted. But ... what price would he have to pay? He remembered agreeing to something more while he lay with Cara, Angela and Elise, while blood flowed from his finger and was smeared onto a clear stone. He had watched the stone turn red. At that moment he would have done anything they wanted.

Fear and guilt worked into his conscious. What if someone learned he had tampered with the evidence, made it appear an accident? *No.* He was sure that he had covered everything. Plus the dog, the cause of all the angst, had helped a lot by contaminating the scene.

He smiled again.

The important thing was that Cassie would be happy. More money, a nice neighbourhood and the baby she really wanted to have. She need never know how this all came about.

Peak left the station and climbed into his car. Yes indeed it was their lucky day – even though luck had little to do with it.

"You make your own luck," Cara had explained. "And we need your help."

A brief spark of guilt ignited in his mind, but as he

placed his key in the ignition his finger touched the blood stone. The guilt dissipated leaving a sense of entitlement in his place. How long had he worked the goddamn awful job? How long had he been overlooked for promotion? He deserved this and Cassie had always deserved better than he had been able to give her.

He glanced in the rear-view mirror. Cara. Angela. Elise. Their faces floated behind him in a fog.

"We may need you again ..." Cara said.

"You may need us ..." Angela's voice followed.

"We will always be here ..." Elise concluded.

Somehow it was comforting to think that this was true.

Peak turned the key in the ignition and his car fired up first time. The future, for the first time in his life, was looking very bright indeed.

EPILOGUE

The darkness held invisible eyes. Their unseen stares crowded in their hundreds within the black, each acutely felt by Officer Ridsdale as she unconsciously scratched her neck; not even stopping when she drew blood.

She did not dare look back. The hospital was nothing more than a memory, as was the doctor that lay on the floor, bleeding out from a biro to his throat.

The invisible eyes had watched her commit the atrocious act and she felt their judgement. She felt them all the time. Not even sleep provided respite from the unknown evil that had followed her ever since she walked into *that* room.

As she stumbled down the darkened street dressed in nothing but a blood soaked hospital gown she heard the words of the doctor, his tone a provocative mix of insincerity and damnation.

"You must have tripped and hurt yourself," his words sounded like the vilest of lies. "The room was empty, unused. Your colleagues found you screaming and bleeding from a head wound, alone except for the cobwebs and peeling walls. Their report certainly doesn't mention anything about these *shelves of books* and *walls of skin* you talk of."

His lies were silenced.

His obstruction overcome.

It was with this same determination that the police officer had escaped from the hospital and now made her way back to Horsfield Manor. A moonless, winter night was long and dark, perfect to stay hidden as she approached the edge of the city and made her way down unmarked paths that lined the surrounding fields.

The manor looked empty as she approached it from the woods to the east. The porch light was the only sign of life, its weak illumination colouring the trees closest to the wood and revealing the silhouette of a policeman in the doorway, standing guard over the crime scene.

The poor fool, she thought as she watched the vapour of his breath rise like smoke in the cold air. *He has no idea what's in there.*

Quietly, Officer Ridsdale crept towards the house, keeping herself away from the edges of the porch light, but all the while her gaze was fixed on the sentry.

It was only when she caught hold of his neck, her other hand covering his mouth, did she notice the lack of resistance he put up. Crumpling in her clutches he collapsed, dropping to the floor with a suppressed moan.

Standing over the felled officer she gasped as blood poured from his empty eye sockets. Two black holes filled his face, weeping scarlet fluid over his pale white skin. At his feet lay a book, leather bound and elegant with the gold calligraphy of an unpronounceable title.

Jesus, the policewoman thought as she looked around for anyone else.

The trees swayed gently against the wind and the air teemed with unseen watchers. Their eyes pushed into her soul.

Opening the door, Officer Ridsdale hit the light switch, revealing the house to be empty. The twisted limbs had been removed and tape marked the positions where the pieces were discovered.

Something darted across the room, just outside of her peripheral vision. It startled her and her skin began to feel like it was crawling across her body; a sensation like the dreadful tickle of spider legs against her bare flesh.

Running to the kitchen, Officer Ridsdale rooted through the drawers until she found a large knife. Holding it out in front of her, she made her way back towards the living room, only stopping to pick up a box of matches that rested by the cooker.

Striking a match she held it below a set of curtains and felt the warmth of the blaze as the fire crept up the fabric. Striking another match she threw it into the sofa, another she hurled into the corner of the room, its flame catching the fibres of the carpet.

As the fire grew around her, she placed her fingers on her neck, digging her nails into a self-inflicted wound. The sharp pain brought a maddening sense of relief. A comforting sting made her clench her teeth as she pushed her fingers deeper into her own flesh.

She felt the eyes grow angry and she smiled.

"Pasher tagoth imra," she called, laughing as she

made her way up the stairs towards the room of strange terrors. "Pasher tagoth imra."

Shadows wildly flickered from the flames as it spread up the steps behind her, covering the hallway in a mass of soot-black ghosts; writhing against the walls, lost within a deranged orgy of pain.

The heavy door stood wide open, revealing a gaping, black hole, impossibly calling her towards it.

"Pasher tagoth imra," she screamed once more, reciting the obsessive chant that had tainted her sleep and clouded her waking thoughts.

Lighting another match she brought her arm back, ready to throw it into the dark abyss before her. A searing pain streaked across her stomach, forcing her to freeze in shock. Looking down, Officer Ridsdale watched as blood poured from her midriff followed by a vomit inducing slop as her intestines followed gravity and spilled to the floor.

Dropping the match at her feet she looked at her other hand. It clenched the kitchen knife that dripped with dark, red blood. *Her blood!*

Falling to her knees the policewoman felt the warmth of the inferno approaching ever closer. The eyes in the air crowded round to watch her die. Officer Ridsdale's vision grew dim as she watched the door at the end of the corridor slam shut by unseen hands.

Entrails stained the plush carpet crimson as they lay strewn across the floor, soaking into the luxury shag pile.

THANK YOU

What is true horror?

This darkest of genres seeks to exploit, your terrors and give birth to new nightmares. But while ghosts, monsters and ancient rites, unwittingly read, can all bring about feelings of fear, these dwellers of the dark are nothing compared to the idea of having your life slowly taken away from you, piece by piece.

Imagine having all those precious memories and experiences you spent your life collecting slowly fade from your mind. Imagine being stripped of your dignity as you are unable to understand the world around you. Imagine being thought of as stupid and incapable by everyone you know, including your loved ones. The partner you protected, loved and worked hard with to build a life together, being forced to care for you, and despite their love, you'd still become a burden.

For those suffering with dementia this is something very real.

On my last birthday I was visiting Longleat House, and I directed a lost man to the toilets. His wife then started talking to me, explaining how he was suffering from

Alzheimer's. She explained how he had some days better than others, but it was so sad to see him decline; to see him go for a walk and get lost, unable to remember where he was going or why.

As we talked she explained that he had taken drugs to help him, and they had worked for a while, but over time their effects become less and less. My ignorance was that Alzheimer's was an incurable disease brought about by old age.

I was moved by the devotion of the man's wife, but I could hear the strain in her voice. I could see the sadness behind her eyes as she talked of the husband he had once been; the one she had now lost.

When I got back home that day I went online and read more about the disease, discovered its causes and the research being developed to halt the process and find a possible cure.

So when I began to compile this anthology I knew exactly what charity I wanted to give the profits from this book to.

Certainly I wasn't alone in wanting to support this charity, many of the writers that I approached either had family members that been affected by Alzheimer's or even worked, caring for those affected. (Every single one of them gave their time and talent, free of charge.)

So of the people involved in this book I'm probably one of the least qualified to talk about the disease and the work that goes into research and care.

I am just a person with a willingness to help.

And by buying this book, so are you.

On behalf of everyone involved in this project, and everyone at Alzheimer's Research UK, I'd like to say thank you.

J R Park
31st March 2016

AFTERWORD
HOWARD GORMAN
(SCREAM MAGAZINE)

"The best movies now are called 'thrillers.' Because if you use the word 'horror,' people's associations are straight-to-video crap."
- Eli Roth

Whilst quite the discomforting note to open with, it's a sad truth that, despite having made some serious headway over the last few years, the independent horror scene continues to fight an uphill struggle to distance itself from its tainted reputation. Regardless of the cornucopia of talent working in the current indie scene, any real gems still struggle to get through the "Hollywood filter" as top-tier production companies have that terribly bad habit of putting foolproof moneymaking commercial claptrap ahead of any kind of creativity and innovation. No one can blame them; it's a business just like any other, but churning out remake after regurgitation after rehash means that for every one sui generis horror blockbuster released audiences have to endure another umpteen offensive flops.

That's not to say there's nothing wrong with milking horror, or indeed any genre cliché, just as long as said cliché's feathers are ruffled up sufficiently to provide audiences with something with at least an inkling of originality - don't even get me started on the *Cabin Fever* remake. Genre festivals are living proof that tips of the hat are always welcome, providing they're done right, with audiences jumping out of their seats in appreciation when self-aware directors proudly wear their inspiration on their sleeves. This phenomenon couldn't be better exemplified than the universally-praised Quentin Tarantino who, quite astutely, doesn't try and hide the essence of the films he's aping; and look where that got him. It's this discerning approach and his acute grasp of movie mechanics, both old and new, that has even the Academy slobbering at his feet, despite the fact that the Oscars tend to play a blind eye to movies painting such horrific and violent portraits, unless of course there's a studio or actor "of interest" involved.

Talking of the Academy, this year marked a bit of a blow when the Austrian entry, *Goodnight Mommy*, got pipped at the post in its road to the Oscars. Even so, the fact the film - non-English language no less - garnered so much international buzz is just another of many recent examples that the horror scene has been picking up some serious pace over the last couple of years or three. I mean, just look at the outstanding line-ups celebrated festivals such as SXSW, Film4 FrightFest or the midnight section at

Sundance have to offer; lest we forget VOD companies' continued enthusiasm when it comes to nabbing the rights for genre fare of a more independent kind - Yes, Netflix, I'm looking at you. All of the above, particularly the latter, ensure all the more horror diamonds in the rough get discovered and reach the wider target audiences they deserve.

Should this trend continue, and there's evidence aplenty to suggest that it will, audiences can expect to see an even more heterogenous and devotedly innovative range of genre films more widely and readily available in the not too distant future.

Why Horror?

The indisputable champion of the indie horror scene is, without a doubt, the closely-knitted horror community. Despite the somewhat disheartening start to the preamble above about just how tough it is to get a break in the business, two things remain constant in the horror industry:

There is one absolute hell of a fan base out there and, more importantly, filmmakers' love for the genre, more often than not, outweighs their desires to make a quick buck. One particular group of people I became acquainted with this year who are certainly in this for the long hard slog is the independent company LuchaGore Productions, founded by Gigi Saul Guerrero, Luke Bramley, Raynor Shima, with support from Gordon Cheng.

After a plethora of highly successful shorts on the festival scene, such as "El Gigante" or "Madre de Dios," their goal is to continue making genre-specific films and break into the feature film industry so I grilled them a little for this afterword to provide some insight into what exactly runs through the minds and bloodstream of an up-and-coming horror production company with designs to make a living in such an overcrowded and competitive industry:

"Horror really brings out people's best reactions! You see them scream, squirm and even cheer when splashes of blood cover the frame. For me, the most rewarding feeling, as an artist, is to be able to create unforgettable reactions out of the audience.

I couldn't be happier being able tell and share visual stories, especially in the horror genre. One thing I believe stands out about our work at LuchaGore Productions is that we have created our own memorable style. It's an incredible feeling knowing our work can be recognized. However, that is because we have stayed together as a family with the same team since the beginning of our journey. If you're an independent filmmaker it's essential to build trust and close relationships with crew you collaborate closely with. I am very lucky to have found the team that makes LuchaGore complete. We all know each other so well that creating stories now comes naturally. And it's always about having fun.

In this genre what's important is to never be afraid of taking risks! Horror fans and the overall indie horror community is so supportive that there will always be an audience for the insanity you create on screen!"

Gigi Saul Guerrero
LuchaGore Productions Co-Founder

"Being in the indie horror industry, I've had the great pleasure of working with such a talented group of people for the last 5 years. Just like many teams out there who brand themselves as horror filmmakers, we at LuchaGore Productions have created our very own brand, giving the audience something unique and different that satisfies the appetite of many hungry viewers. Watching our films is like watching something out of the Marvel universe; you can always tell that you're watching a LuchaGore film. Our splashes of color, dynamic storytelling, and mixing different sub-genres together. That's what brings our films to life!

Being an independent filmmaker means using the resources you have, even if you are very limited to what you can create. There will always be a way to make the impossible seem possible. We are storytellers, and we must not limit ourselves to what we cannot do, and always try to push the envelope to tell a compelling story. This is a collaborative effort amongst a team of talented people. Keeping that trust and letting your crew be as creative to push the story forward is the huge cog piece that will keep the wheel turning. I am very proud of our amazing team and it's what has kept us going through all these years."

Raynor Shima
LuchaGore Productions Co-Founder

"Horror is the one genre that has a devoted fan base that will seek out independent films, and be vocal about their support for them. Eli Roth once said that you don't need high budgets and A-list stars to

make a horror film, you just need talented actors and a solid vision, because the scares are the superstars in horror. Luckily, I'm a huge fan of the genre, so making horror films and connecting with fans is a dream come true for me. Since we do things independently, we are free to create whatever concept we can think of and cater to the fans with what we would consider to be an enjoyable and frightening experience.

What's great about horror is it uses all of the filmmaking departments to tell the story; it truly is a collaborative experience. Everything from the choice of lens and position of the camera, to the decorated set and mise en scène, to the sound design and overall color palette, play a vital role in evoking the proper reaction from the audience. To be able to get together with a team and brainstorm a terrifying vision from nothing and bring it to life on screen is extremely satisfying and challenging; and it's also great fun to get out there and cover everyone in fake blood!"

Luke Bramley
LuchaGore Productions Co-Founder

"To look back and see what we've done in the past 5 years is simply amazing. It's very humbling to see how much we've all grown and how much fun we had making all of our films. And to be honest, you have to have fun in what you're doing. It's important as a human being and as artists. As filmmakers you always want to make something to get a message across and I think we've done that through a few of our films, and that is something we're all proud of. I've always said this, and I'll say it again: horror is the funnest genre to be a part of. You get to have cool special effects, visual effects, blood, gore and those twisted shocking moments! I'm proud to say that LuchaGore films provides all of that then, now, and I hope there's much more to come."

Gordon Cheng
LuchaGore Productions Co-founder

Meddling Producers in Extremis?

Independent filmmakers' frustrations tend to share two common denominators: The first is capital, or lack thereof, which goes hand in hand with the second: the producers, who far too often believe wealth gives them a right to meddle with whatever project they choose to support. Encouragingly, there's a new breed of producers willing to take more shots in the dark; not only when it comes to laying their cash on the line but also in giving directors more creative freedom than is the norm.

Two crowning examples would be Elijah Wood's SpectreVision banner and Jason Blum over at Blumhouse.

The former, founded by Elijah Wood along with two long-time friends and cohorts, Daniel Noah and Josh C. Waller, has a clear focus on unique, high-art, low budget movies, with the trio putting all their faith in filmmakers, no matter what they may or may not have achieved before or the potential target audience for the films they acquire. If that isn't the ultimate production risk then someone please tell me what is.

Commenting on what hallmark traits makes a movie a SpectreVision movie Wood said, *"Our output is relatively diverse if you look at the films individually. It's a funny thing. We have witnessed that it's actually a difficult thing to explain specifically what makes a SpectreVision movie. It's one of those things where you know it when you see it. But I think the easiest way to define it is that we tend to want to do what no one else is doing, especially if it's a horror that's travelling a well-trodden path then that tends to be something we're not interested in. I think a defining characteristic of our company, in terms of a guiding principle on some level, is trying to push the boundary of what one considers a horror film. A Girl Walks Home Alone at Night is a good example of that, where it's clearly got genre elements but one wouldn't necessarily define that as a horror film outright. I think it is important for us to explore genre and horror completely and wholly and to make sure that our films don't all feel like the same thing, but that they certainly fit underneath the banner of what SpectreVision represents."*

When it comes to Blumhouse Productions, a company that's served up Oscar-winning material with the sensational *Whiplash*, the banner's real impetus is its unremitting salvo of horror films produced on freakishly meagre budgets. Blumhouse's budgeting policy abides by a rigorously respected limit of between $3 and $5 million to make sure they never overshoot their mark and always at least recoup on any movies that don't get a theatrical or wide release. Accordingly, come hell or high water, there's no stopping Blumhouse's horror output, keeping the door wide open to helping independent genre filmmakers make their mark. A fine example, not a good film by my own personal standards, but a good illustration of Blumhouse's work ethic, is *The Gallows* from debut directors Travis Cluff and Chris Lofing. After sweating blood and tears to get the project completed on what little funds they were able to acquire from local investors, one of the trailers they cut was spotted by none other than Management 360's Dean Schnider who passed it along to the man with the Midas touch, Mr. Blum. The rest is history and it wasn't long before their debut feature won over a number of big studios with New Line and Warner Bros. acquiring the rights after quite the bidding battle with Lionsgate and Relativity. Of course I had to ask them the million dollar question about just how much freedom Blum gave them after putting his faith in their initiative and their response will play like sweet music to any budding independent filmmaker's ears:

Cluff confirmed that they really couldn't complain when it came to creative control commenting, *"We really didn't expect this because we know the stories that people say and tell us but we feel really grateful that they understood our vision and allowed us the freedom to make it how we wanted to make it."* Whilst Lofing continued, *"And many of the key scenes, and our favourite scenes, from the very original cut of the film remained in the film untouched from the beginning which is awesome."*

Whilst the above examples are all good and well, we mustn't forget the detrimental backlash the all too common meddling producer phenomenon has on the indie scene as it's also one hell of a deterrent with so many directors unwilling to climb into bed with people wanting to change their initial vision. That was precisely the case with S. Craig Zahler when it came to shooting *Bone Tomahawk*, a perfect example of a film that ended up getting made for a lot less money than it was initially hoped and which, although still one of the best films of 2015, has me thinking what might have happened if those earlier bidders hadn't tried to force Zahler's hand. Speaking to the writer/director at last year's edition of the Sitges Film Festival he openly commented on the trials and tribulations he encountered to get his directorial debut off the ground and keep it as faithful to his original idea as possible:

"In terms of the funding, part of the problem was that I wasn't willing to cut it down. We were once in a situation with a company where it got to a point where I said that if they asked me to cut one more page from the script I was going to walk away from the project. So we ended up making it for far less money in a very short period of time (21 days) and our budget was less than 2 million dollars but I was able to shoot what I wanted. My feeling was that everyone came onboard for terrible paydays because of the script, so I didn't want to start by injuring the thing that brought everybody together in the first place. There are many much more commercial versions of this movie but I just wasn't interested in making them."

With those meddling mitts, renowned for vitiating the indie film world, becoming more of a deterrent than a temptation my hope is that filmmakers will remain as relentless as the likes of Zahler as I'm sure the success of *Bone Tomahawk* must have had producers kicking themselves for not having lent a more sympathetic ear to his initial pitch.

Then, once you've shot and edited your film but you don't have a big studio like Blumhouse to usher you in the right direction, how does one go about achieving the next best distribution scenario?

The Impact of VOD et al.

One of the indie scene's biggest disadvantages has always been that particularly sore point known as distribution.

Just like Eli Roth's quote that got this afterword ball rolling, VOD too has had to endure that similar stigma although a few success stories do demonstrate just how lucrative and profitable a springboard it can actually be. Take the original *V/H/S* anthology film for instance. The film earned just $100,000 at the U.S. box office, but it was the limited VOD release's success and serious reapings that twisted the studio's arm to cough up a seven-figure deal for a sequel.

Those theatrical figures alone explain exactly why cinemas just aren't willing to take any kind of risk with indie output, be it horror or any other genre. This is exactly where VOD is gaining ground as it serves as a means to an end for indie filmmakers to find audiences and at least recoup the money they fed into the process and, as the V/H/S seven figure example so perfectly shows, VOD audiences may even be as influential, if not even more so, on distributors' decisions than cinemagoers.

Something else worth taking into account is that, whilst VOD is certainly much more convenient for audiences as it allows us to have horror literally on tap, the physical market for indie horror is anything but a write-off and is actually taking the appropriate measures to counteract VOD's popularity. There is still a gaping niche in the market screaming out for all the latest horror DVDs and Blu-rays but, just taking a look at your Facebook friends' walls or on Twitter, it's blatantly clear that there's an even bigger demand for fancy collectors' editions. A lot of us are willing to pay extortionate amounts, and even more if it means importing from another country, to get out grubby mitts on some absolutely lush steelbook and deluxe releases that distributors are churning out now. If you haven't already, right about now is as good a time as any to go pillage the internet for delicious deluxe versions of films like last year's *The Demolisher* or *Deathgasm*.

Other than the beyond the call of duty editions of films there's also a high demand for hyped films that either come out earlier in other countries or just plain aren't available in certain countries for one reason of another. Take for instance James Cullen Bressack's *Hate Crime*, which was banned by the BBFC in the UK; a ban which the director says was counter-productive in the fact that it just fuelled people's desires to be able to see the film:

"I was kind of shocked about that ban really. I don't personally think that we should really be censoring what people are and aren't allowed to watch. It's completely silly to think that adults can't choose for themselves what they are allowed to watch. I understand if someone personally doesn't want to watch a movie but they should have the option whether or not they want to. It's not like it's a movie where we are seeing actual people being murdered. It's a work of art.

It sold out on Amazon in America in a week after it was banned so I would assume that was people in the UK importing it."

Talking of Cullen Bressack, who went on to shoot *To Jennifer* entirely on an iPhone, that brings me to my next, and final, point...

Technology Balances the Playing Field

The market is certainly inundated with options in terms of what equipment a filmmaker can use but we mustn't get sidetracked by technicalities. It's all about what you can actually do with the tools that you have access to.

A sterling example is Oren Peli's *Paranormal Activity,* which was shot on a camcorder for all of $15,000 and went on to make more than $193 million internationally. The secret to the film's success, and the success of many other low budget projects shot in a similar cinema verité style, boils down to the fact that the filmmakers never shied away from their self-awareness of how limited they were in terms of technology. Even Hollywood blockbusters armed with million dollar budgets, the best actors, and state-of-the-art technology won't guarantee the success of a film. Quality isn't determined by 3D, IMAX, megapixels or anything along those technical lines. It's measured by the effect the narrative and shooting style has on the audience.

At the end of the day, technological advances, particularly in terms of how literally anyone has access to some sort of video recording device, levels the playing field and literally puts any Tom, Dick or Harry in a position to compete with Hollywood's hardest hitters. In a recent interview I conducted with Eli Roth for SCREAM magazine, he couldn't have been more succinct when breaking down the advantages he believes technological advances bring to the table:

"I think one real problem here is that someone can make a great short and put it on YouTube and it gets like 200 viewers but with our Crypt TV we have such a loyal following and we can use data to see who is actually watching it and retarget specific shorts to those people. It can really, really get your short or your series an audience. We also helped market The Green Inferno through Crypt TV and it worked out amazing because, as that was such a specific film, you can't just blast ads on TV and hope people watch. You've really got to narrow it down to finding who is your audience that really cares about this movie. I think that doing stuff that we call original for digital - doing things on your phone - is such a rich and creative space right now that I think the next Freddy, Jason or Slender Man is going to come from that and that's okay! I think it all works as a terrific companion piece to feature films and television. Also, it gives filmmakers a voice. One thing that's fun is that the phone doesn't discriminate because you can be Christopher Nolan or a fifteen-year-old girl in New Jersey. If you make a great short, whether you spend 100 dollars or 100,000 dollars, it doesn't matter. The best idea wins. The phone is the great equalizer."

If what I've brought up here goes to show anything, it's that the gap between Hollywood and the indie scene grows smaller every day. With more producers, festivals and distributors willing to take that ever-important leap of faith and put their trust in a rare new breed of brave and innovative filmmaking, this is a crucial moment for the indie scene as filmmakers get the chance to release their output to a much wider audience.

In signing off, I'd like to thank you, the readers, for purchasing this second volume of 'The Black Room Manuscripts,' and also the authors for giving up a big slice of their time and imagination for such a worthy cause. Despite all the stumbling blocks all independent talent may have to get past, I think you'll agree that the points raised in the last few pages bodes particularly well for the indie horror scene's immediate future..... Thanks for reading and thanks to The Sinister Horror Company for their continuing support of the independent horror industry...

CONTRIBUTORS

Chris Hall lives in Porthcawl, Wales with his incredibly-patient wife and two kids. Aside from his day job working in corporate tax, Chris is also the sole individual behind the website – DLS Reviews – a true labour of love dedicated to providing in-depth reviews of horror, sci-fi and dark fiction. Having been an online reviewer for over 10 years prior to the launch of his website in 2014, DLS Reviews was able to start out with 500+ in-depth reviews already published across its numerous pages. Since then the website has continued to grow, making it an invaluable resource for fans of dark speculative fiction. Aside from spending hours on end reading horror novels and then dissecting them for DLS Reviews, Chris spends the rest of whatever free time he has listening to pummelling Death and Black Metal, enjoying fine whiskies, or reviewing a variety of weird and wonderful products for Amazon.

DLS Reviews can be found at www.dlsreviews.com

Tim Clayton studied Creative English at Bath Spa University and lives in Wrocław, Poland. He rarely suffers from writer's block except when asked to write "About the author" sections of books. In 2014 he published The Spokesman; a novel about death, dirty money and cycling, which is pretty good. In 2016 he followed that up with Full

Blast Wrestling; the inglorious rise and destructive fall of the world's dirtiest wrestling promotion, which is really very good indeed. Find out more at timwroclaw.wix.com/fbw-book

Jack Rollins was born and raised among the twisting cobbled streets and lanes, ruined forts and rolling moors of a medieval market town in Northumberland, England. He claims to have been adopted by Leeds in West Yorkshire, and he spends as much time as possible immersed in the shadowy heart of that city. Writing has always been Jack's addiction, whether warping the briefing for his English class homework, or making his own comic books as a child, he always had a dark tale to tell. Fascinated by all things Victorian, Jack often writes within that era, but also creates contemporary nightmarish visions in horror and dark urban fantasy. He currently lives in Northumberland, with his partner, two sons, and his daughter living a walking distance from his home, which is slowly but surely being overtaken by books...

Jack's published works are as follows:

The Séance: A Gothic Tale of Horror and Misfortune
The Cabinet of Dr Blessing
Dead Shore, in *Undead Legacy*
Anti-Terror, in *Carnage: Extreme Horror*
Home, Sweet Home in *Kill For A Copy*
Ghosts of Christmas Past in *The Dichotomy of Christmas*

Jack can be found online at:
Twitter: @jackrollins9280
Facebook: www.facebook.com/doctorblessing
Website: jackrollinshorror.wordpress.com

Graham Masterton is mainly recognized for his horror novels but he has also been a prolific writer of thrillers, disaster novels and historical epics, as well as one of the world's most influential series of sex instruction books. He became a newspaper reporter at the age of 17 and was appointed editor of *Penthouse* magazine at only 24. His first horror novel *The Manitou* was filmed with Tony Curtis playing the lead. *Walkers* was recently optioned by Jules Stewart for Libertine Films. Last year Graham turned his hand to crime novels and *White Bones*, set in Ireland, was a Kindle phenomenon, selling over 100,000 copies in a month. This has been followed by *Broken Angels*. Graham's horror novels were introduced to Poland in 1989 by his late wife Wiescka and he is now one of the country's most celebrated authors, winning numerous awards. He is now working on new horror and crime novels.

J. R. Park is an author of horror fiction, co-founder of the publishing imprint the Sinister Horror Company and responsible for the tome you currently hold in your hands. His novels Terror Byte, Punch and Upon Waking have all been well received by readers and reviewers, even if the sick bucket hasn't been too far away from their bedsides; and he's had numerous short stories published in collections from various presses. Art house, pulp and exploitation alike inform his inspirations, as well as misheard conversations, partially remembered childhood terrors and cheese before sleep. He currently resides in Bristol, UK. Find out more at JRPark.co.uk and SinisterHorrorCompany.com

Paul M. Feeney lives in the North East of England and

has always been heavily into horror and dark, fantastical stories. Since 2010, he has turned his hand to his own writing and has had some small success. His first published short story, *The Weight Of The Ocean*, was released by Phrenic Press in 2015 as a Kindle only to favourable reviews. To date he has had a few more short stories accepted by small publishers such as April Moon Books and Sirens Call for anthologies both forthcoming and currently available, and had his first novella, *The Last Bus*, released through Crowded Quarantine Publications in a limited signed and numbered paperback run in the middle of 2015. Of the 250 copies of this, only about 20 currently remain. He has also recently completed his second novella, *Kids*, which will be published by Dark Minds Press in the middle of 2016, as part of their new novella series. He continues to turn out short stories at a snail's pace, while planning more novellas and contemplating the dreaded first novel. You can find him on Facebook and Amazon.

Rebecca S. Lazaro loves horror stories and movies, but has never written anything horrible before. *Cut To The Core* is her debut offering in the horror genre and she was suitably disgusted with herself afterwards. Rebecca usually writes about female sexuality and the psychology of dysfunctional relationships, and has self-published her full-length novel 'Unravel', a psychoanalytical lesbian love story between a teacher and her student. Previous published works include articles contributing to various LGBTQ magazines and websites. Rebecca is currently writing her second novel, when she's not strutting around the Cotswolds in her leather jacket. She can be contacted via facebook: https://www.facebook.com/rebeccaslazaro

Horror author **Nathan Robinson** lives in Scunthorpe with his darling five year old twin boys and his patient wife/editor. So far he's had numerous short stories published by www.spinetinglers.co.uk, Rainstorm Press, Knight Watch Press, Pseudopod, The Horror Zine, Static Movement, Splatterpunk Zine and many more. He writes best in the dead of night or travelling at 77mph. He is a regular reviewer for www.snakebitehorror.co.uk, which he loves because he gets free books. He likes free books. His first novel "Starers" was released by Severed Press to rave reviews. This was followed by his short story collection "Devil Let Me Go", and the novellas "Ketchup with Everything" and "Midway."

He is currently working on his next novel, "Caldera" and a sequel to "Starers." Follow news, reviews and the author blues at www.facebook.com/NathanRobinsonWrites or twitter @natthewriter

Lily Childs has an obsession with misunderstood demons and takes unsavoury delight in Victorian underworlds, twisted myths and the necrotic. She writes dark, Gothic horror, crime and ghost stories including the recent *Within Wet Walls* (Ganglion Press) and has contributed tales to anthologies from The Sinister Horror Company, KnightWatch Press, Western Legends Publishing and James Ward Kirk Fiction - with more to come. She lives by the sea in the south of England with her daughter, husband and black cat, Scarlet. Lily has recently completed her first novel, a supernatural asylum chiller. Her warped fairy tale *In Search of Silver Boughs* is due to be released as a chapbook by KnightWatch Press in 2016.

Read a selection of Lily's horror and crime stories in Cabaret of Dread; Volume I. Follow her on Facebook: /lilychildsfeardom, Twitter: @LilyChilds and on her blog, The Feardom at http://lilychildsfeardom.blogspot.co.uk/

Lindsey Goddard has been published over forty times. She loves the dark side of life and exploring it in her work. Recent credits include Horror Hooligans, Dark Moon Digest, Perpetual Motion Machine Publishing, James Ward Kirk Fiction, and Sirens Call Publications. She lives in the suburbs of St. Louis. MO with her husband and three children. For more information, please visit: www.LindseyBethGoddard.com

Daniel Marc Chant is an author of strange fiction. His passion for H. P. Lovecraft & the films of John Carpenter inspired him to produce intense, cinematic stories with a sinister edge. Daniel launched his début, "Burning House," swiftly following with the Lovecraft-inspired "Maldición." His most recent book "Mr. Robespierre" has garnered universal praise. Daniel also created "The Black Room Manuscripts" a charity horror anthology & is a founder of UK independent genre publisher The Sinister Horror Company.
You can find him amongst the nameless ones on twitter @danielmarcchant, at facebook/danielmarcchant or his official website www.danielmarcchant.com.

Born and brought up in Hertfordshire, **Shaun Hutson** now lives and writes in Buckinghamshire where he has lived since 1986. After being expelled from school, he worked at many jobs, including a cinema doorman, a barman, and a shop assistant - all of which he was sacked from - before becoming a professional author in 1983. He has since written over 30 bestselling novels as well as writing for radio, magazines and television. Having made his name as a horror author with bestsellers such as SPAWN, EREBUS, RELICS and DEATHDAY (acquiring the nicknames 'The Godfather of Gore' and 'The Shakespeare of Gore' in the process) he has since produced a number of very dark urban thrillers such as LUCY'S CHILD, STOLEN ANGELS,WHITE GHOST and PURITY. At one time, Shaun Hutson was published under no fewer than six pseudonyms (no, he's not Barbara Cartland), writing everything from Westerns to non-fiction. He continues to work under a pseudonym he will not disclose. Shaun has appeared on and presented a number of TV shows over the years. He has lectured to the Oxford Students Union (the original title of the lecture 'Get a Bloody Job and Stop Living Off My Taxes You Sponging Bastards' was changed at the last minute). He has appeared on stage with heavy-metal rock band Iron Maiden 13 times and received death threats on a number of occasions due to his work! His work is particularly popular in prison libraries. The novel 'Honest, Officer, I've Never Seen These Stereos Before In My Life' will follow shortly.

Find out more, including a short story entitled RED STUFF and an interactive story, SAVAGES at www.ShaunHutson.com

Rich Hawkins hails from deep in the West Country, where a childhood of science fiction and horror films set him on the path to writing his own stories. He credits his love of horror and all things weird to his first viewing of John Carpenter's THE THING when, aged twelve, he crept downstairs late one night to watch it on ITV. He has a few short stories in various anthologies, and has written one novella, BLACK STAR, BLACK SUN. His debut novel THE LAST PLAGUE was nominated for a British Fantasy Award for Best Horror Novel. Its sequel, THE LAST OUTPOST, was released in September 2015.

He currently lives in Salisbury, Wiltshire, with his wife, their daughter and their pet dog Molly. They keep him sane. Mostly.

www.facebook.com/rich.hawkins.98

richwhawkins.blogspot.co.uk

The story *Oranges Are Orange* came from somewhere; that's the first and last thing that can be agreed on. Especially since **Stuart Park** insists he's not an author. The story is the bastard child of knee surgery, Radiohead, Chuck and Your Sinclair mag. All gently bathed in a splash of Zen Buddhism and bleached from the caustic scathing of loss and foreboding. One thing Stuart really wants to know is, when you eat a banana, when does that stop being fruit and start being you? When Stuart stops questioning the demise of fruit he can be found indulging in other activities such as, music production, photography, gardening, running and weird-ass arthouse cinema. The results from some of his projects can be found on his site, http://likebreathing.com/. He has been in the background of the Sinister Horror Company since its inception, and helped out by proofreading titles, including: Terror Byte, Punch, Class Three, Upon Waking, Class

Four, The Exchange, Clandestine Delights, Screams In The Night and Hexagram for J.R. Park and Duncan P. Bradshaw, plus a number of other short stories: Easter Hunt, Mandrill, Incident and Soft Centred. Look out for other works (not) written by Stuart. Since, remember, he's not a writer.

Dani Brown is the author of "My Lovely Wife", "Middle Age Rae of Fucking Sunshine", "Toenails" and "Welcome to New Edge Hill" (all out now from Morbidbooks). She is the author of various short stories. You can find the links of them (and sometimes links to free stories) on her facebook page www.facebook.com/DaniBrownBooks. You can watch as she tweets about editing whatever she is working on and complaining about the trains at @crazycatlady4. Like cows being abducted and first look book covers? No problems as that's covered on Instagram DoomsdayLiverpool. The official Dani website is here: http://danibrownqueenoffilth.weebly.com. When she isn't writing she enjoys knitting and thinking of the finer points of invading Finland with an army of chavs mounted on dingoes. She has an unhealthy obsession with Mayhem's drummer and doesn't trust anyone who claims Velvet Underground as their favourite band. Coffee is responsible for keeping her alive. Please send lots of coffee.

William Meikle is a Scottish writer, now living in Canada, with twenty novels published in the genre press and over 300 short story credits in thirteen countries. He has books available from a variety of publishers including Dark Regions Press, DarkFuse and Dark Renaissance, and his work has appeared in a number of professional anthologies and magazines with recent sales to NATURE Futures, Penumbra and Buzzy Mag among others. He lives in Newfoundland with whales, bald eagles and icebergs for company and when he's not writing he drinks beer, plays guitar, and dreams of fortune and glory.

Matt Shaw is the prolific author of over 100 titles. Known primarily for his work in the extreme horror genre and his infamous Black Cover books, he has also penned supernatural stories, dramas, comedy, books on writing, books on depression, erotica and - if you'd trust him with your children - stories for kids! A frequent face signing his books at conventions across the country, Matt Shaw currently has half of his work being translated in both Korean and German as well as having sold film options to a handful of his books after financing and filming one of his stories himself!
Want to know more?
www.mattshawpublications.co.uk
www.facebook.com/mattshawpublications

Ten to twenty 'in the pen' they told him, with good behaviour, he'd be out in eight. Those were the kind of odds that just didn't stack up. **Duncan P. Bradshaw** unscrewed the fountain pen which had been smuggled to him inside of a sock puppet called 'Puppy'. Chiselling his way through the walls, to freedom, he decided that the only way to keep them off his back was to write about the things *they* had beamed into his head at night. When the men howled and Puppy begged for just one more bedtime story.
Follow his escapades on Facebook at

https://www.facebook.com/duncanpbradshaw
or read about his books on his website at
http://duncanpbradshaw.co.uk.

Dr. Lynne Campbell is an avid writer of both horror fiction stories and novels, as well as non-fiction books on the Paranormal and the Esoteric. In 2015 she published 5 books which are Available on Amazon: Jack Hammer (Horror Fiction), A Course In Demonology For Paranormal Investigators (Non-Fiction), Scary Stuff: 10 Urban Legends to Give You Nightmares (Non-Fiction), I Scry With My Little Eye (Occult Thriller/Fiction), and A Course In Magick for the New Practitioner (Non-Fiction). Dr. Campbell is a Forensic Psychologist, Paranormal Investigator, Demonologist, and Occultist. Visit her Author Page on Facebook and her Paranormal Website at:
Facebook.com/Dr.LynneCampbell
ICUparanormal.yolasite.com

Jasper Bark finds writing author biographies and talking about himself in the third person faintly embarrassing. Telling you that he's an award winning author of five cult novels including the highly acclaimed Way of the Barefoot Zombie and the forthcoming The Final Cut, just sounds like boasting. Then he has to mention that he's written 12 children's books and hundreds of comics and graphic novels and he wants to just curl up. He cringes when he has to reveal that his work has been translated into nine different languages and is used in schools throughout the UK to help improve literacy, or that he was awarded the This Is Horror Award for his recent anthology Dead Air, plus an ERA award, a Preditors and Editors Award and a

BFSA Award nomination. Maybe he's too British, or maybe he just needs a good enema, but he's glad this bio is now over.

Laura Mauro was born in south London and now lives in Essex under extreme duress. Her work has appeared in Black Static, Shadows and Tall Trees, and has been reprinted in Best British Horror 2014. In 2015, her short story 'Ptichka' was nominated for a British Fantasy Award, which she will probably never stop talking about. A mild-mannered laboratory technician by day, she spends most of her spare time collecting cats and tattoos. She tweets at @LauraNMauro

Award winning author **Sam Stone** began her professional writing career in 2007 when her first novel won the Silver Award for Best Novel with *ForeWord Magazine* Book of the Year Awards. Since then she has gone on to write several novels, three novellas and many short stories. She was the first woman in 31 years to win the British Fantasy Society Award for Best Novel. She also won the Award for Best Short Fiction in the same year (2011). Stone loves all genus fiction and enjoys mixing horror (her first passion) with a variety of different genres including science fiction, fantasy and Steampunk. Her works can be found in paperback, audio and e-book. www.sam-stone.com

A translator by day, and budding entertainment journalist by late, late night, **Howard Gorman** has always been fervently committed to championing independent film and music. Aside from his role as Associate Features Editor for SCREAM: The Horror Magazine his writing credits

include Dread Central, Shock Till You Drop, Fresh on the Net, Consequence of Sound and MusicOMH.
Follow Howard on Twitter @HowardGorman

Vincent Hunt is a horror loving graphic designer, illustrator and comic book creator. He is currently working on his critically acclaimed series 'The Red Mask From Mars' and also self published the horror comedy strip collection 'Stalkerville'. When not thinking of a bazillion story concepts a day, he also hosts the small press comic book show 'the Awesome Comics Podcast'. Follow Vince @jesterdiablo and check out his comic book stuff at www.theredmaskfrommars.com or
www.awesomecomics.podbean.com

ACKNOWLEDGEMENTS

I would like to thank Duncan P Bradshaw, Daniel Marc Chant, Vincent Hunt, Stuart Park, Chris Hall, Howard Gorman, Tim Clayton, Dr Lynne Campbell, Lily Childs, Graham Masterton, William Meikle, Sam Stone, Rebecca S Lazaro, Dani Brown, Rich Hawkins, Laura Mauro, Jasper Bark, Nathan Robinson, Paul M Feeney, Jack Rollins, Lindsey Goddard, Shaun Hutson & Matt Shaw.

All of which have given their time and talent to help make this book the great collection it is, and giving us a chance to raise some money for a worthwhile charity.

This book would simply not exist without their enthusiasm and effort.

Also available
The Black Room Manuscripts
Volume One

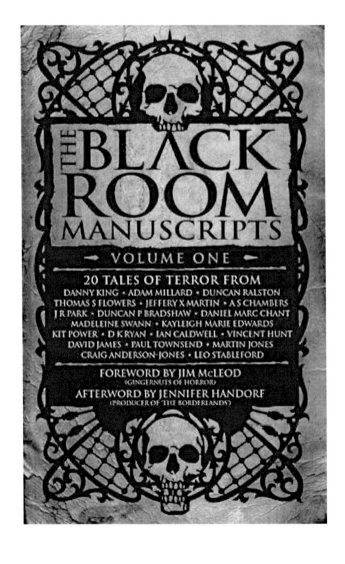

Featuring stories by Danny King, Adam Millard, Duncan Ralston, Thomas S Flowers, Jeffery X Martin, AS Chambers, JR Park, Duncan P Bradshaw, Daniel Marc Chant, Madeleine Swann, Kayleigh Marie Edwards, Kit Power, DK Ryan, Ian Caldwell, Vincent Hunt, David James, Paul Townsend, Martin Jones, Craig Anderson-Jones & Leo Stableford.

A foreword by Jim McLeod (Ginger Nuts Of Horror) and an afterword by Jennifer Handorf (producer of The Borderlands)

All profits from The Black Room Manuscripts Volume One go to Blue Cross UK: a charity helping sick, injured and homeless pets.

"A sumptuous feast of horror in support of animal welfare." – **Guy N Smith**

"The Black Room Manuscripts gives credence to how far horror has come." – **Ginger Nuts Of Horror**

"A quite wonderful anthology. 9/10" – **UK Horror Scene**

"The thing that stood out so much for me in this one was the variety of stories between the covers. Each and every one of them was totally different but equally as scary and creepy. 4.5/5" **Confessions Of A Reviewer**

"Twenty short stories by some of the best up and coming names in the horror genre. 9/10" – **DLS Reviews**

"There is something for everyone. 4/5" – **2 Book Lovers Reviews**

Alzheimer's Research UK — The Power to Defeat Dementia

All profits made from this book will be donated to Alzheimer's Research UK.

In their own words:

'We are the UK's leading research charity aiming to defeat dementia.

We power world class studies that give us the best chance of beating dementia sooner.

Our pioneering work focuses on prevention, treatment and cure.

We are energising a movement across society to support, fund and take part in dementia research.

We aim to empower people across all generations through greater understanding of dementia.

Together we have the power to defeat dementia.'

www.alzheimersresearchuk.org

The Sinister Horror Company is an independent UK publisher of genre fiction founded by Daniel Marc Chant, Duncan P Bradshaw and J R Park. Their mission a simple one – to write, publish and launch innovative and exciting genre fiction by themselves and others

SIGN UP TO THE SINISTER HORROR COMPANY'S NEWSLETTER!

THE SINISTER TIMES

As well as exclusive news and giveaways in the newsletter we'll also send you a FREE eBOOK called "The Offering" featuring three exclusive short stories.

Sign up at **SinisterHorrorCompany.com**

SINISTER HORROR COMPANY

SINISTERHORRORCOMPANY.COM

Lightning Source UK Ltd.
Milton Keynes UK
UKOW02f0859180616

276520UK00001B/40/P